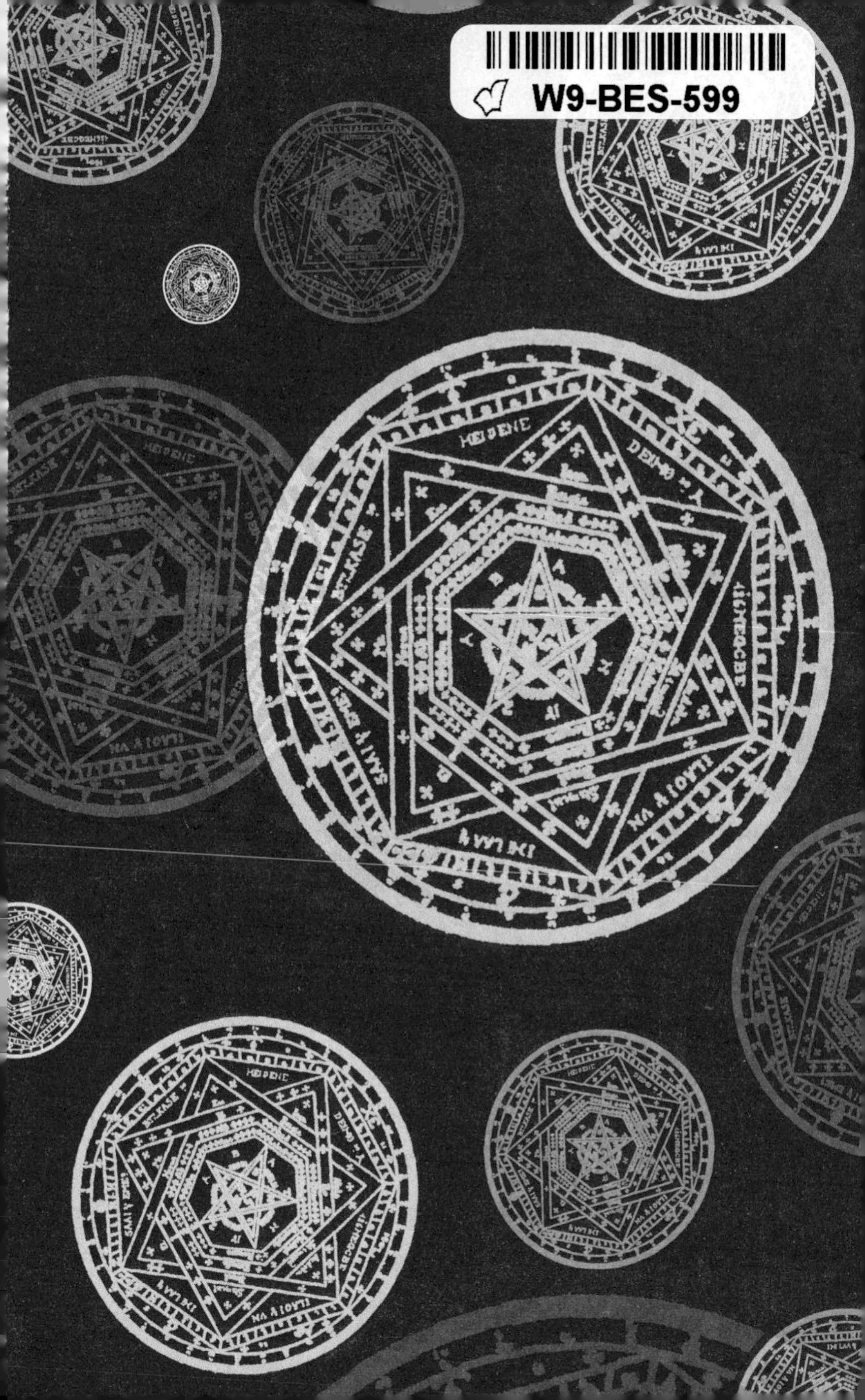

ALSO AVAILABLE FROM 🐢 TOKYOPOP®

MANGA

ACTION

ANGELIC LAYER*
CLAMP SCHOOL DETECTIVES* (April 2003)
DIGIMON (March 2003)
DUKLYON: CLAMP SCHOOL DEFENDERS* (September 2003)
GATEKEEPERS*
GTO*
HARLEM BEAT
INITIAL D*
ISLAND
JING: KING OF BANDITS* (June 2003)
JULINE
LUPIN III*
MONSTERS, INC.
PRIEST
RAVE*
REAL BOUT HIGH SCHOOL*
REBOUND* (April 2003)
SAMURAI DEEPER KYO* (June 2003)
SCRYED*
SHAOLIN SISTERS*
THE SKULL MAN*

FANTASY

CHRONICLES OF THE CURSED SWORD (July 2003)
DEMON DIARY (May 2003)
DRAGON HUNTER (June 2003)
DRAGON KNIGHTS*
KING OF HELL (June 2003)
PLANET LADDER*
RAGNAROK
REBIRTH
SHIRAHIME:TALES OF THE SNOW PRINCESS* (December 2003)
SORCERER HUNTERS
WISH*

CINE-MANGA™

AKIRA*
CARDCAPTORS
KIM POSSIBLE
LIZZIE McGUIRE
POWER RANGERS (May 2003)
SPY KIDS 2

ANIME GUIDES

GUNDAM TECHNICAL MANUALS
COWBOY BEBOP
SAILOR MOON SCOUT GUIDES

ROMANCE

HAPPY MANIA* (April 2003)
I.N.V.U.
LOVE HINA*
KARE KANO*
KODOCHA*
MAN OF MANY FACES* (May 2003)
MARMALADE BOY*
MARS*
PARADISE KISS*
PEACH GIRL
UNDER A GLASS MOON (June 2003)

SCIENCE FICTION

CHOBITS*
CLOVER
COWBOY BEBOP*
COWBOY BEBOP: SHOOTING STAR* (April 2003)
G-GUNDAM*
GUNDAM WING
GUNDAM WING: ENDLESS WALTZ*
GUNDAM: THE LAST OUTPOST*
PARASYTE
REALITY CHECK

MAGICAL GIRLS

CARDCAPTOR SAKURA
CARDCAPTOR SAKURA: MASTER OF THE CLOW*
CORRECTOR YUI
MAGIC KNIGHT RAYEARTH* (August 2003)
MIRACLE GIRLS
SAILOR MOON
SAINT TAIL
TOKYO MEW MEW* (April 2003)

NOVELS

SAILOR MOON
SUSHI SQUAD (Summer 2003)

ART BOOKS

CARDCAPTOR SAKURA*
MAGIC KNIGHT RAYEARTH*

TOKYOPOP KIDS

STRAY SHEEP (September 2003)

VOLUME 1

STORY AND ART BY
WOO

LOS ANGELES • TOKYO

Translator - Lauren Na
English Adaption - Taliesin Jaffe

Retouch - Paul Morrissey
Lettering - Anna Kernbaum
Cover Design - Patrick Hook

Senior Editor - Jake Forbes
Managing Editor - Jill Freshney
Production Coordinator - Antonio DePietro
Production Manager - Jennifer Miller
Art Director - Matt Alford
VP of Production & Manufacturing - Ron Klamert
President & C.O.O. - John Parker
Publisher - Stuart Levy

Email: editor@TOKYOPOP.com
Come visit us online at www.TOKYOPOP.com

A **TOKYOPOP** Manga

TOKYOPOP® is an imprint of Mixx Entertainment, Inc.
5900 Wilshire Blvd. Suite 2000, Los Angeles, CA 90036

ISBN: 1-59182-216-5

First TOKYOPOP® printing: March 2003

10 9 8 7 6 5 4 3 2 1

Printed in Canada

REBIRTH

Vol 1

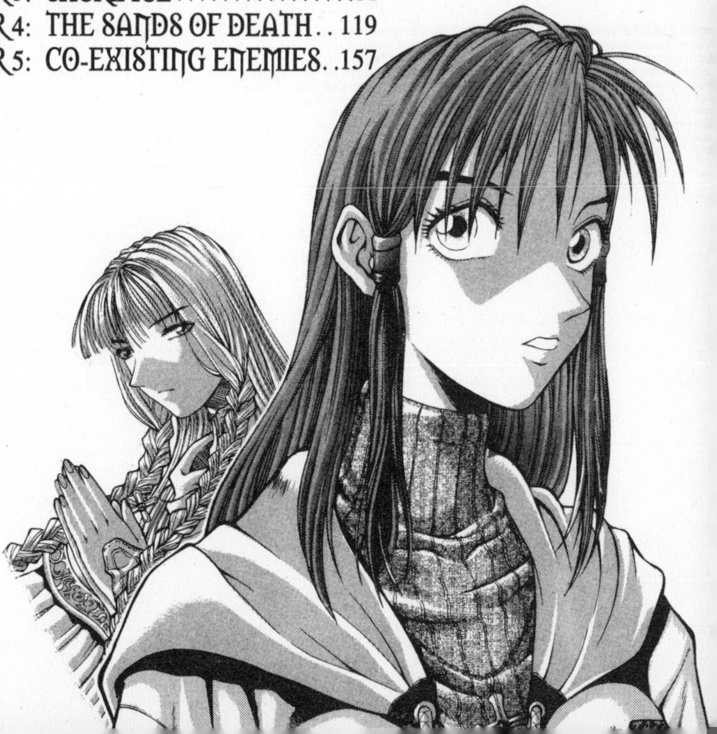

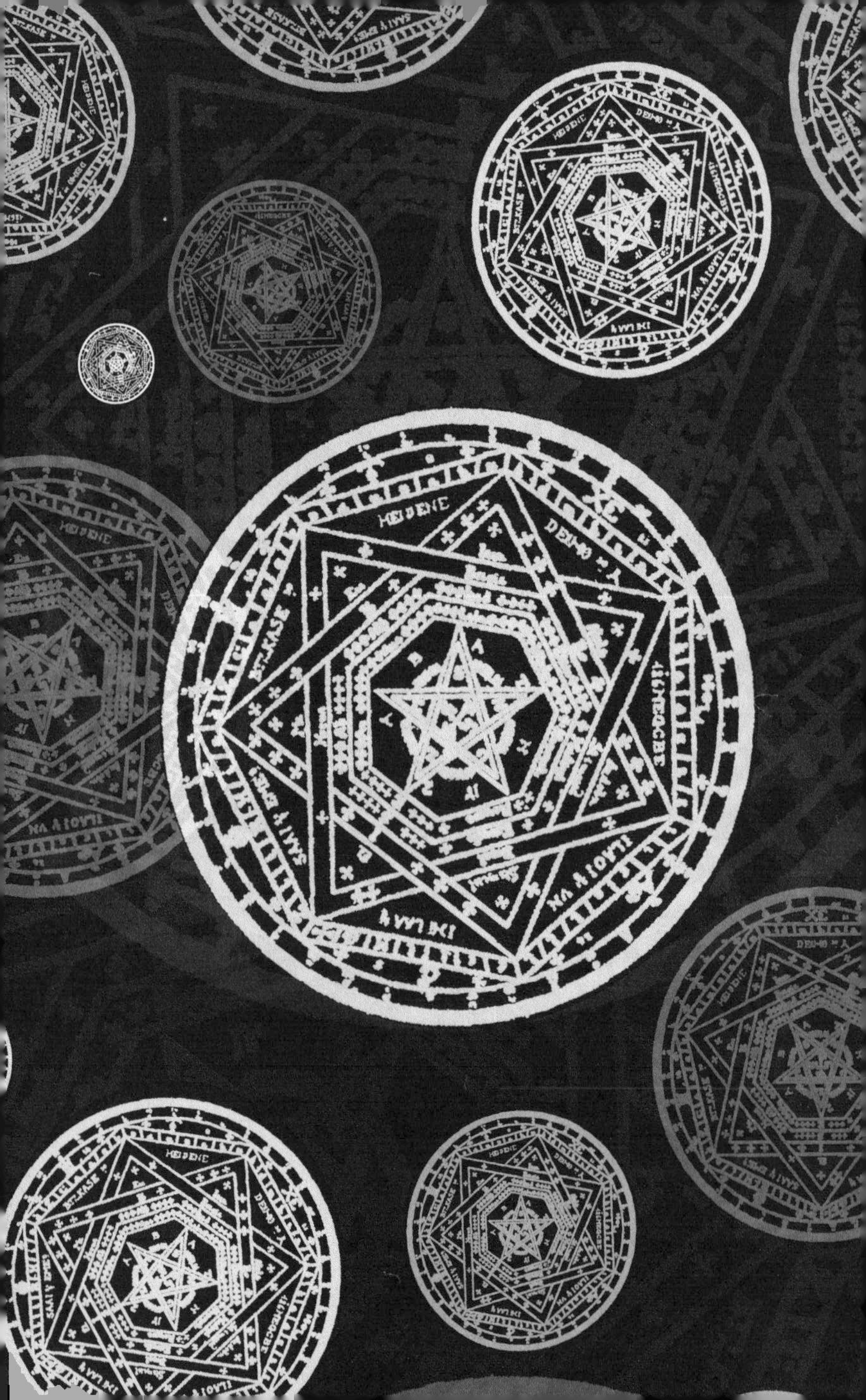

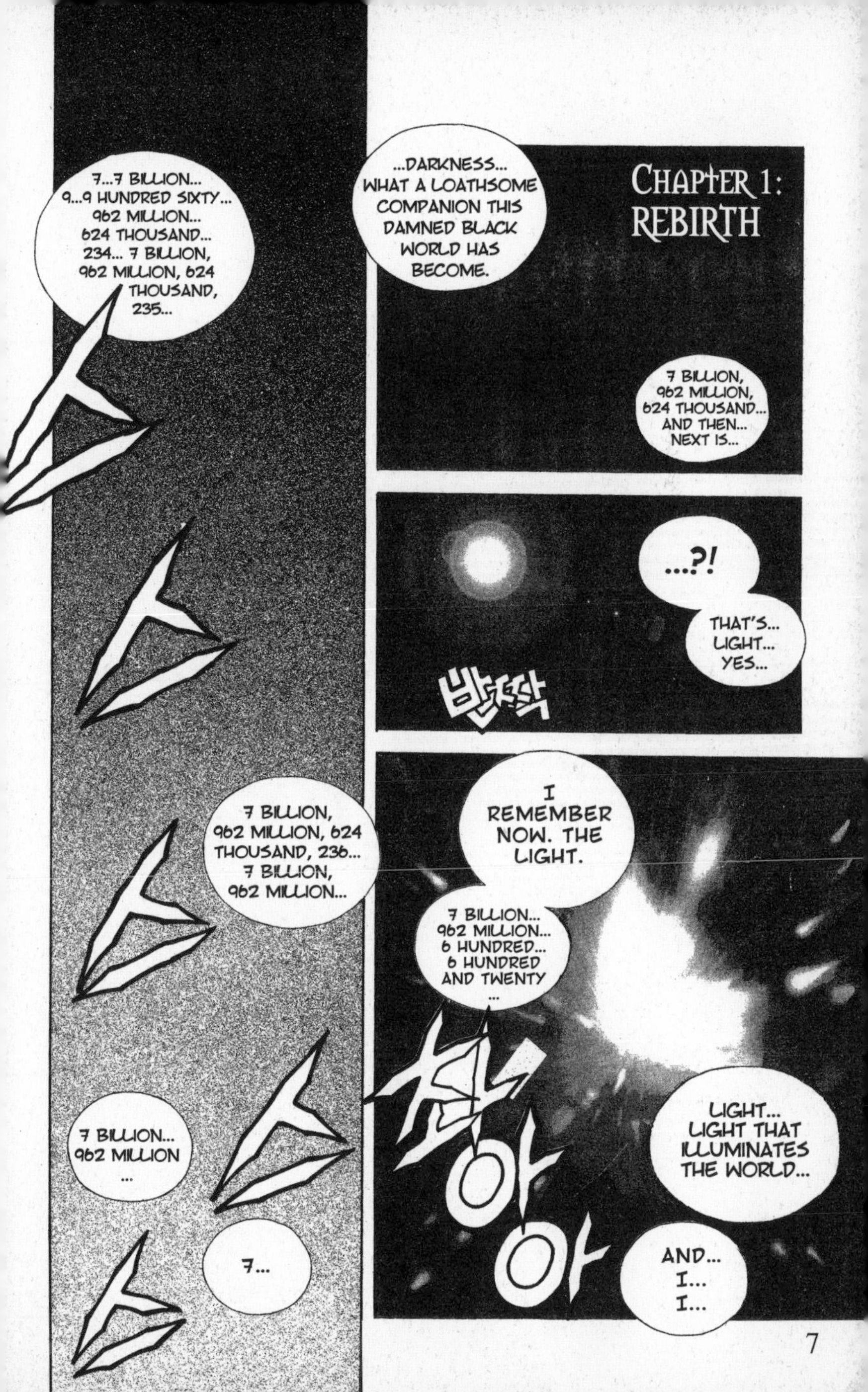

7...7 BILLION... 9...9 HUNDRED SIXTY... 962 MILLION... 624 THOUSAND... 234... 7 BILLION, 962 MILLION, 624 THOUSAND, 235...
7 BILLION, 962 MILLION, 624 THOUSAND, 236... 7 BILLION, 962 MILLION...
7 BILLION... 962 MILLION ...
7...
...DARKNESS... WHAT A LOATHSOME COMPANION THIS DAMNED BLACK WORLD HAS BECOME.
Chapter 1: REBIRTH
7 BILLION, 962 MILLION, 624 THOUSAND... AND THEN... NEXT IS...
반짝
...?!
THAT'S... LIGHT... YES...
I REMEMBER NOW. THE LIGHT.
7 BILLION... 962 MILLION... 6 HUNDRED... 6 HUNDRED AND TWENTY ...
LIGHT... LIGHT THAT ILLUMINATES THE WORLD...
AND... I... I...

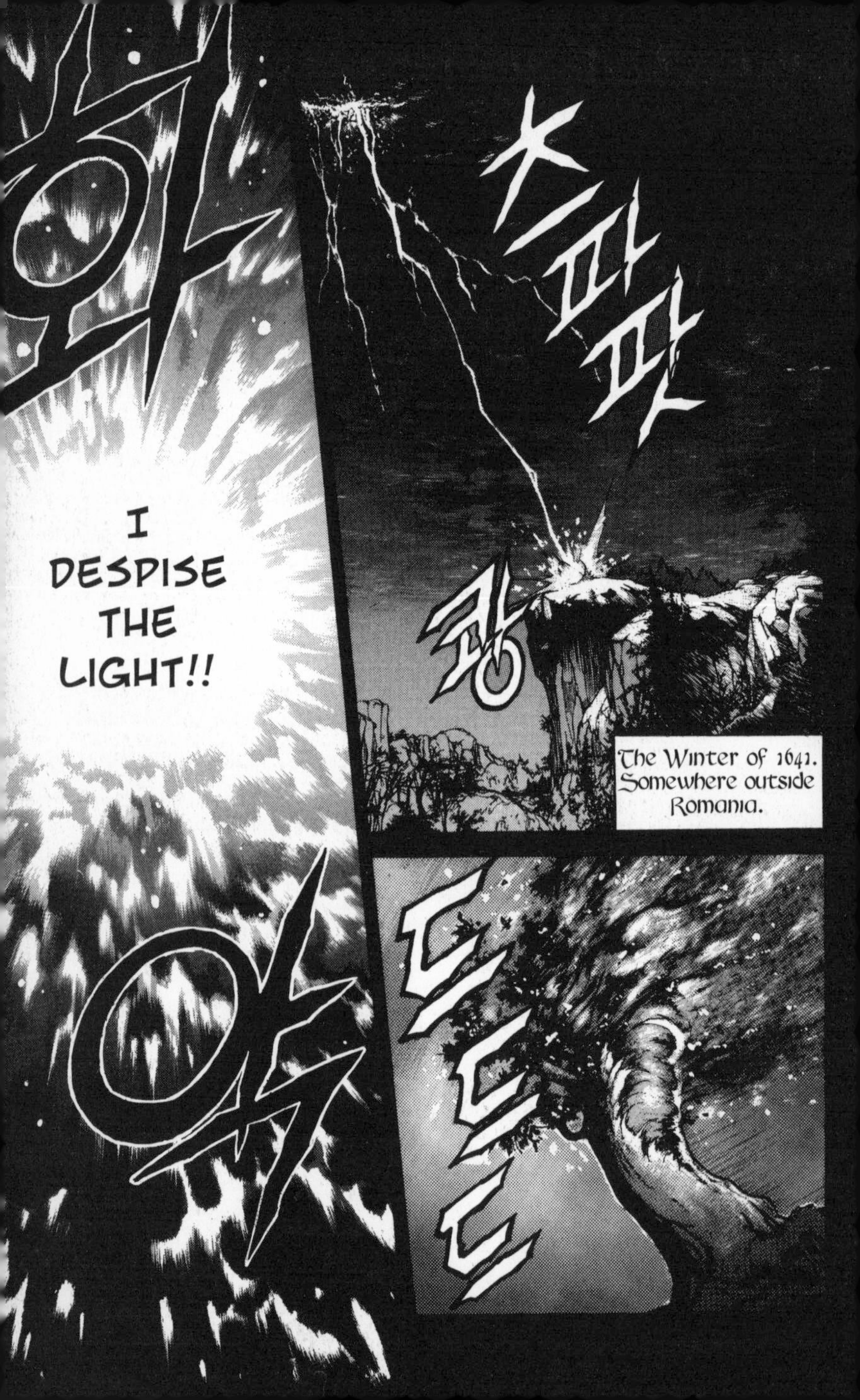
I DESPISE THE LIGHT!!
The Winter of 1641. Somewhere outside Romania.

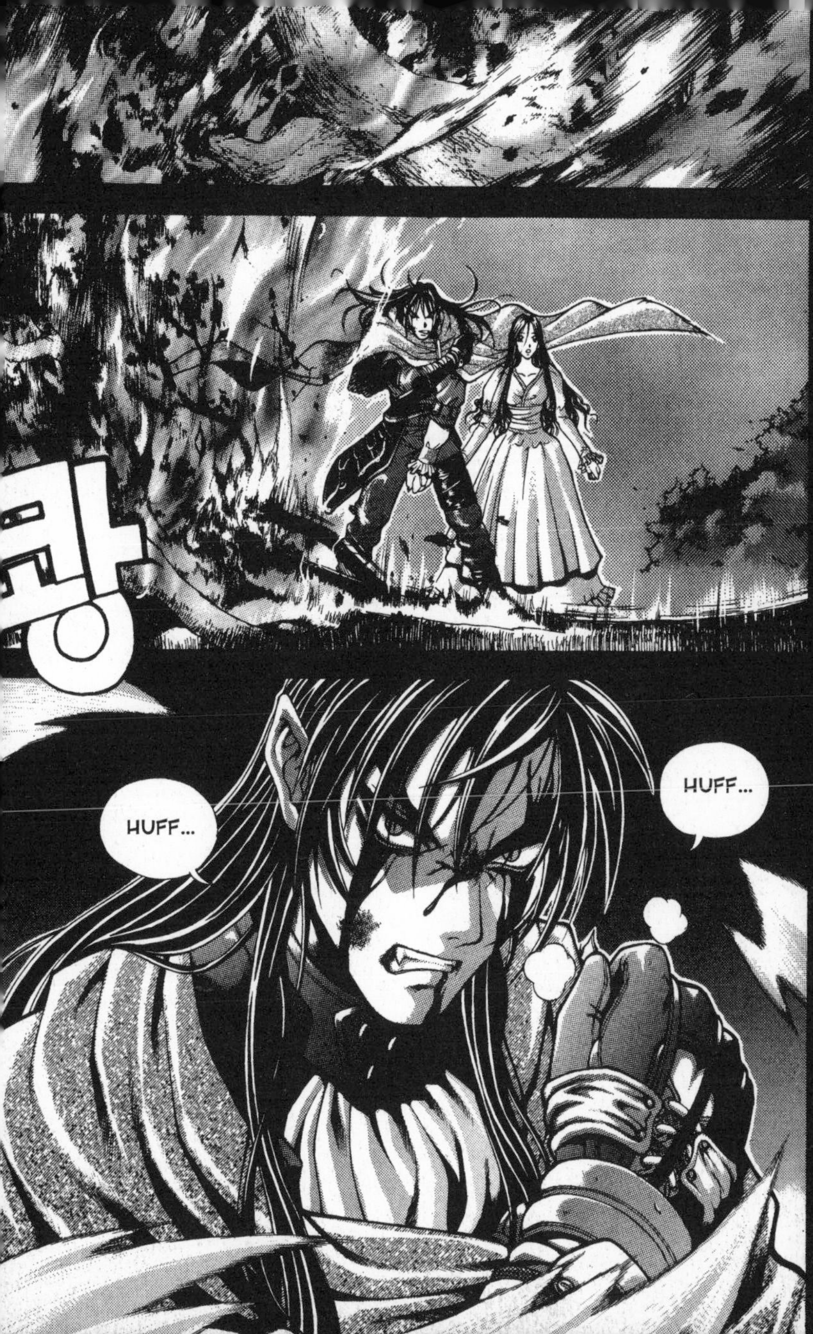
HUFF...
HUFF...

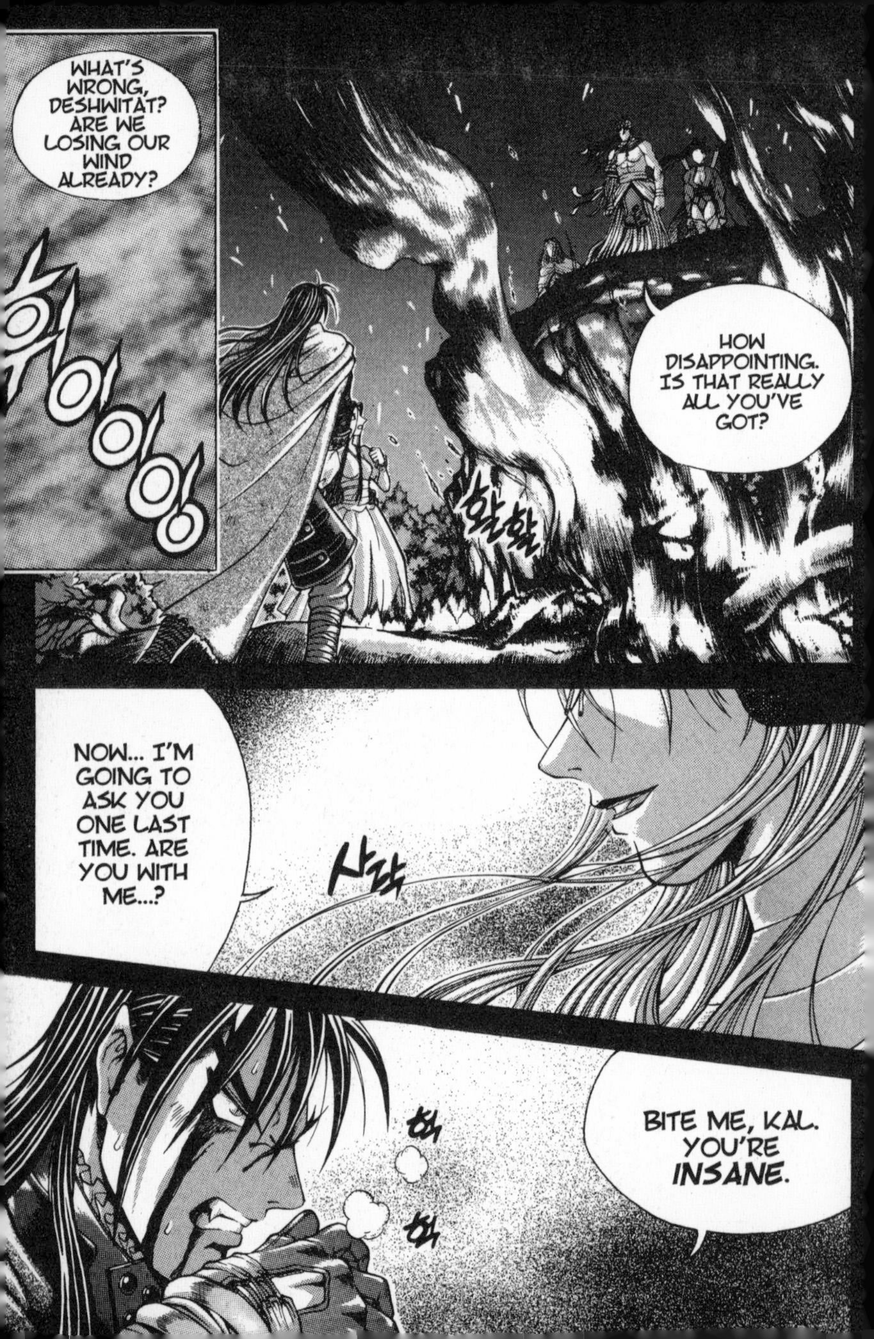
WHAT'S WRONG, DESHWITAT? ARE WE LOSING OUR WIND ALREADY?
HOW DISAPPOINTING. IS THAT REALLY ALL YOU'VE GOT?
활활
NOW... I'M GOING TO ASK YOU ONE LAST TIME. ARE YOU WITH ME...?
하
하
BITE ME, KAL. YOU'RE *INSANE*.

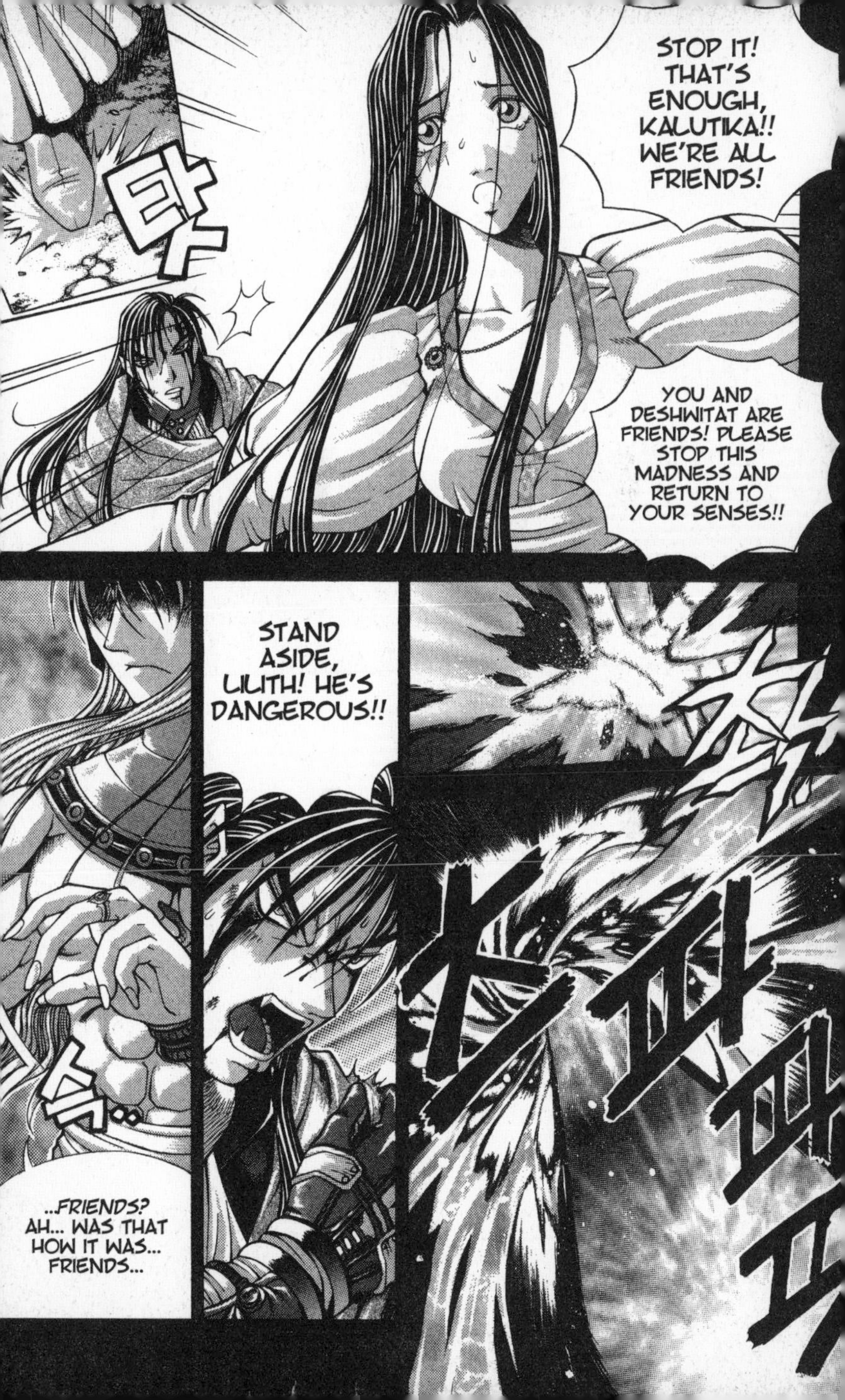
STOP IT! THAT'S ENOUGH, KALUTIKA!! WE'RE ALL FRIENDS!
YOU AND DESHWITAT ARE FRIENDS! PLEASE STOP THIS MADNESS AND RETURN TO YOUR SENSES!!
STAND ASIDE, LILITH! HE'S DANGEROUS!!
...FRIENDS? AH... WAS THAT HOW IT WAS... FRIENDS...

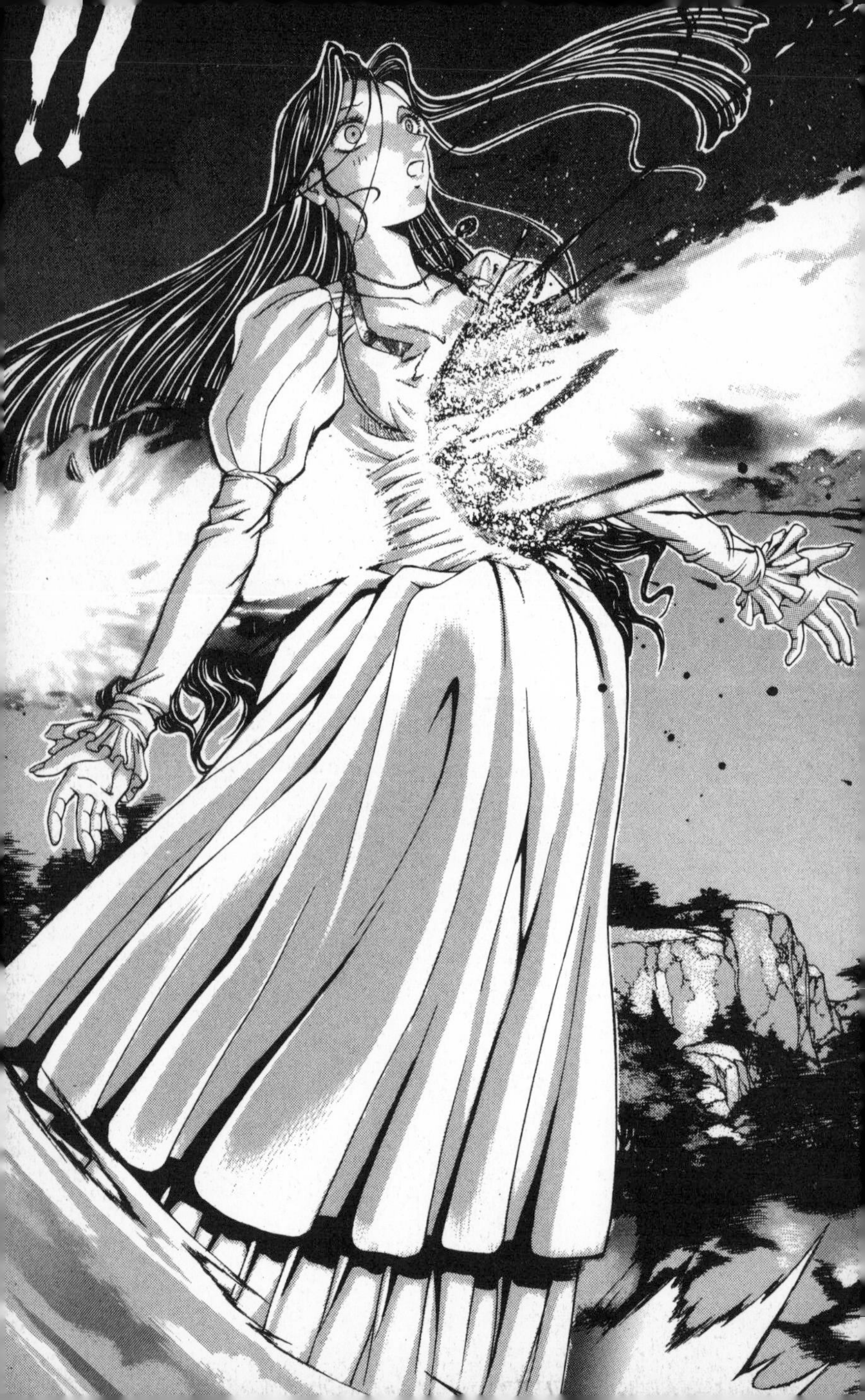
!!

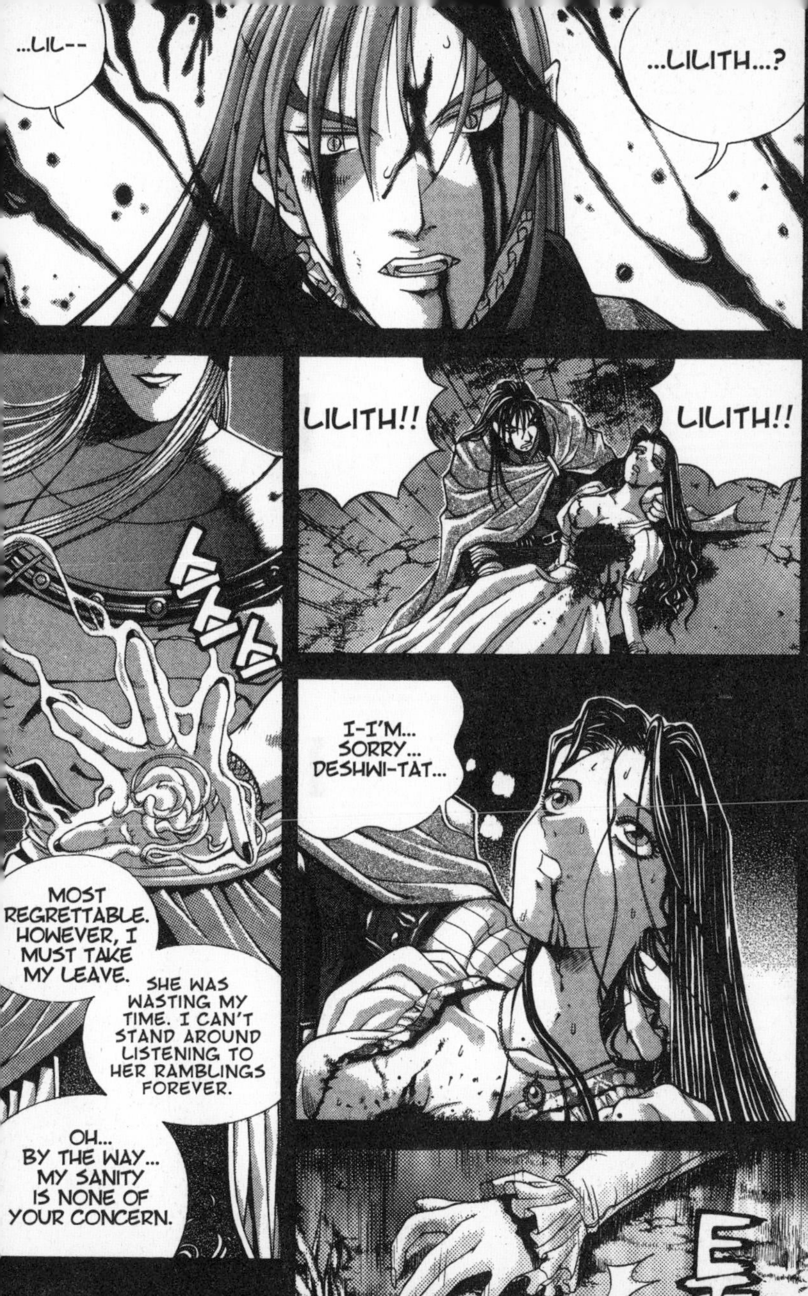
...LIL--
...LILITH...?
MOST REGRETTABLE. HOWEVER, I MUST TAKE MY LEAVE.
SHE WAS WASTING MY TIME. I CAN'T STAND AROUND LISTENING TO HER RAMBLINGS FOREVER.
OH... BY THE WAY... MY SANITY IS NONE OF YOUR CONCERN.
LILITH!!
LILITH!!
I-I'M... SORRY... DESHWI-TAT...

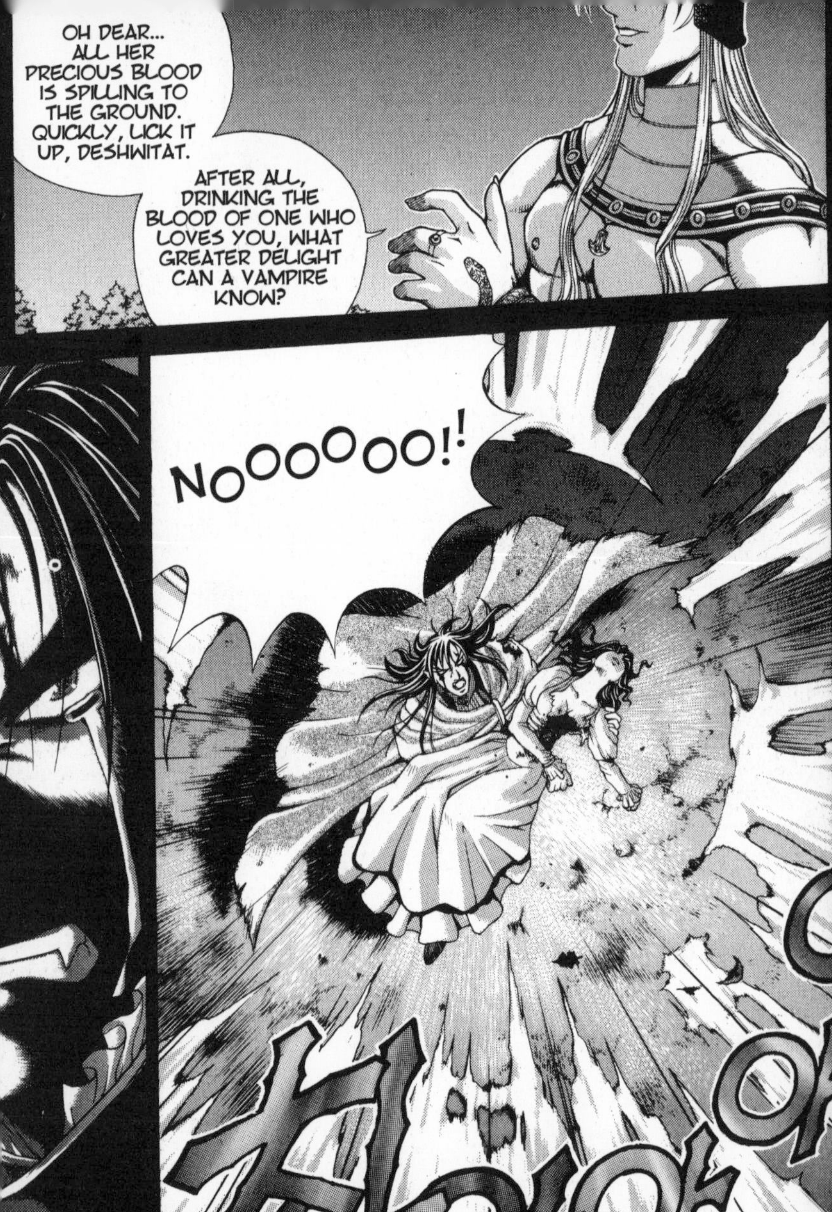
OH DEAR... ALL HER PRECIOUS BLOOD IS SPILLING TO THE GROUND. QUICKLY, LICK IT UP, DESHWITAT.
AFTER ALL, DRINKING THE BLOOD OF ONE WHO LOVES YOU, WHAT GREATER DELIGHT CAN A VAMPIRE KNOW?
NOOOOOO!!

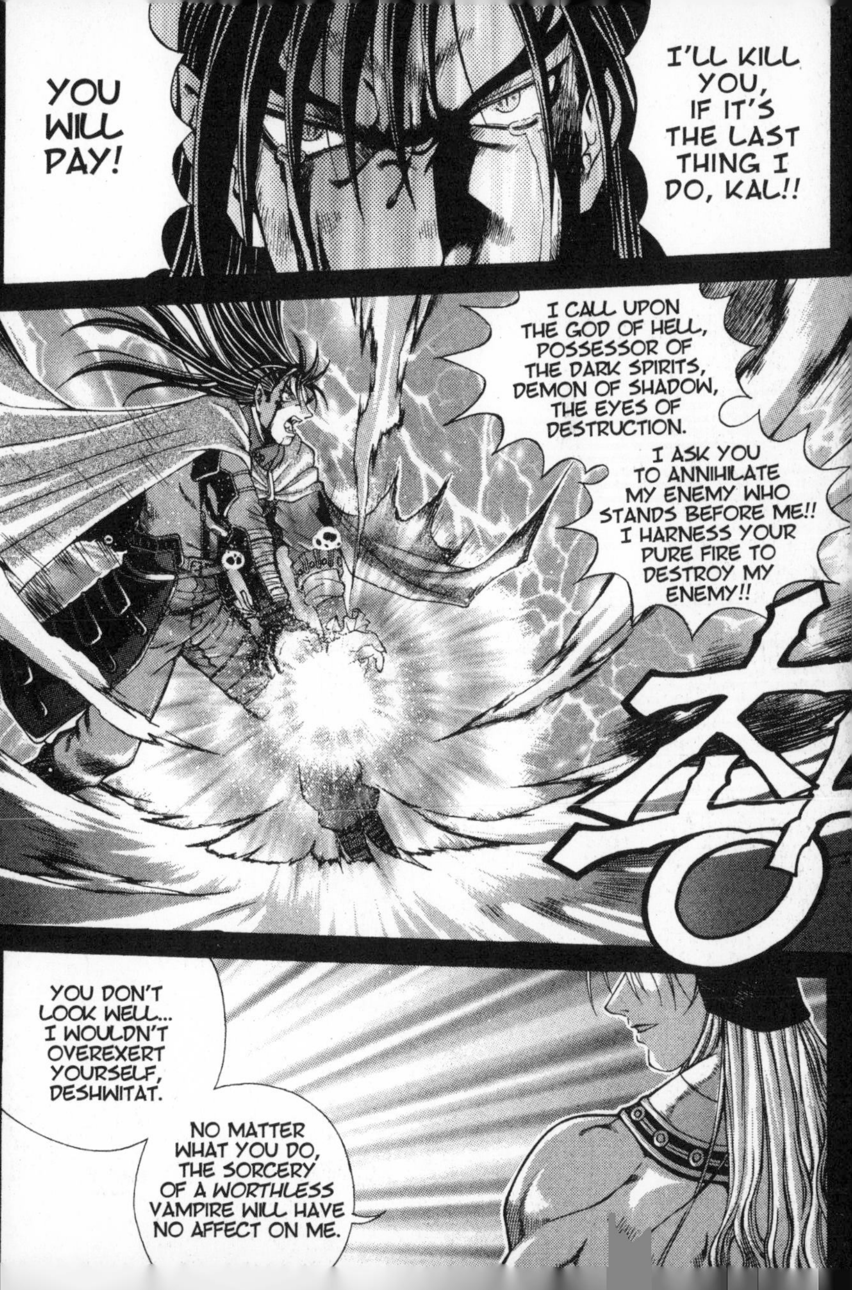
YOU WILL PAY!
I'LL KILL YOU, IF IT'S THE LAST THING I DO, KAL!!
I CALL UPON THE GOD OF HELL, POSSESSOR OF THE DARK SPIRITS, DEMON OF SHADOW, THE EYES OF DESTRUCTION.
I ASK YOU TO ANNIHILATE MY ENEMY WHO STANDS BEFORE ME!! I HARNESS YOUR PURE FIRE TO DESTROY MY ENEMY!!
YOU DON'T LOOK WELL... I WOULDN'T OVEREXERT YOURSELF, DESHWITAT.
NO MATTER WHAT YOU DO, THE SORCERY OF A WORTHLESS VAMPIRE WILL HAVE NO AFFECT ON ME.

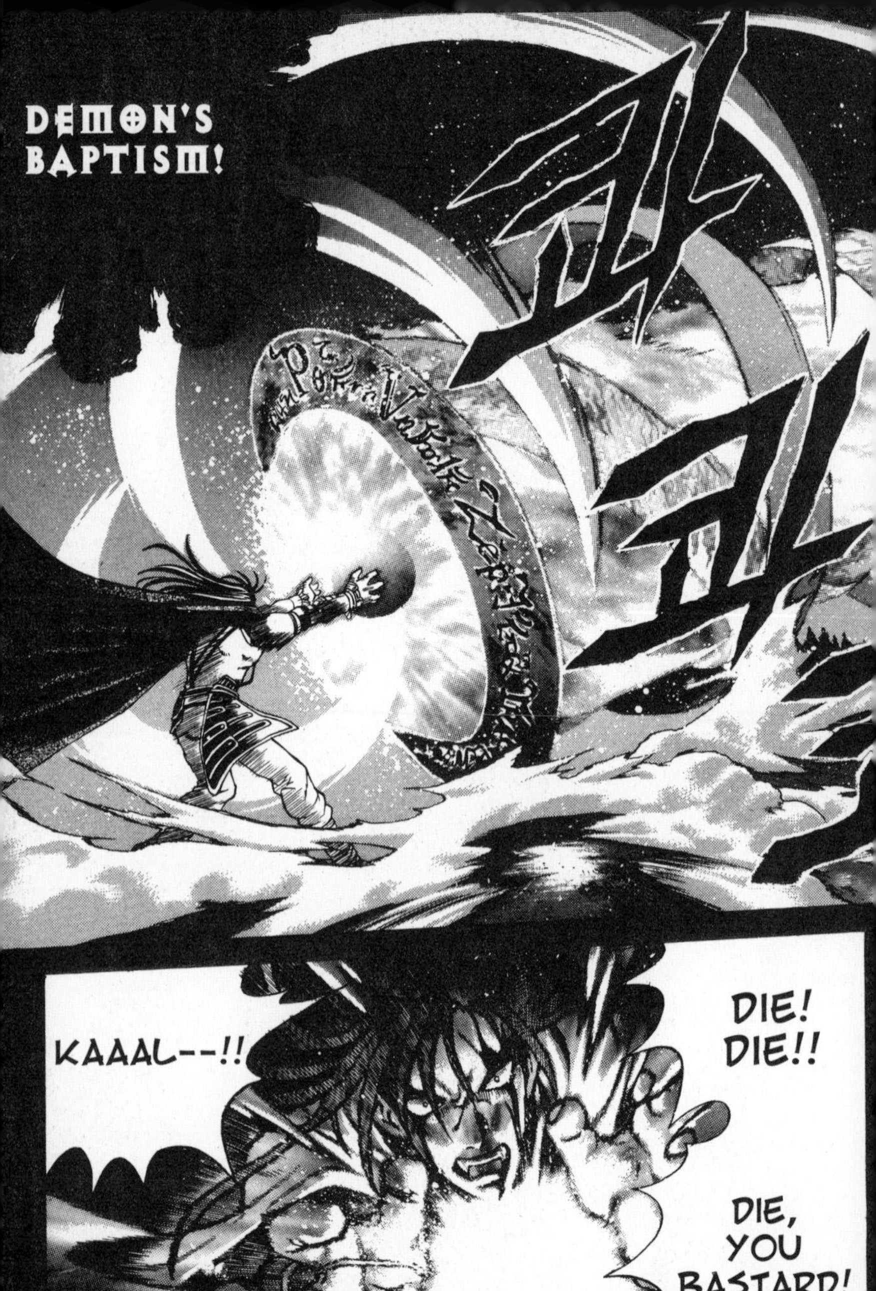
DEMON'S BAPTISM!
KAAAL--!!
DIE! DIE!!
DIE, YOU BASTARD!

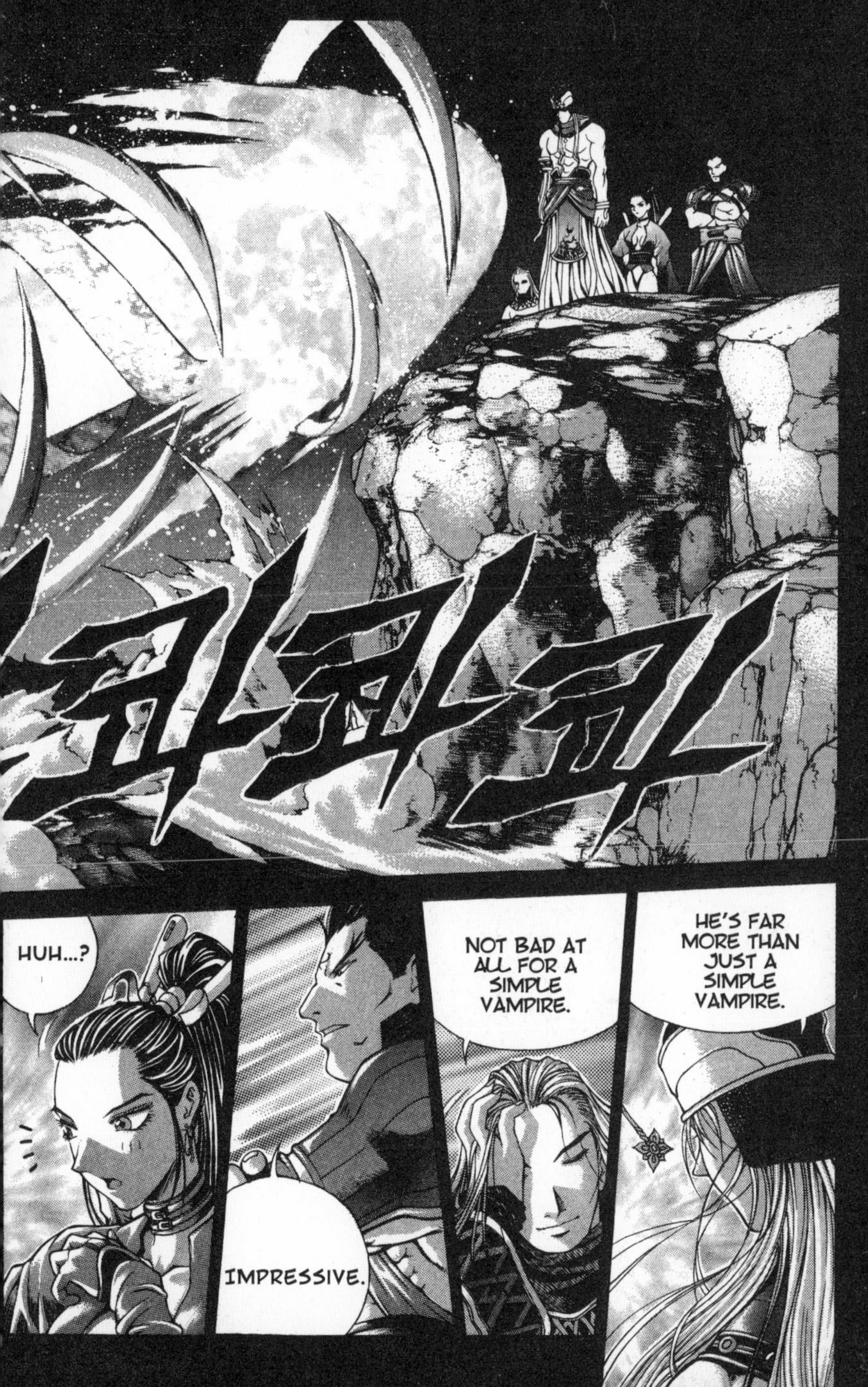
HUH...?
IMPRESSIVE.
NOT BAD AT ALL FOR A SIMPLE VAMPIRE.
HE'S FAR MORE THAN JUST A SIMPLE VAMPIRE.

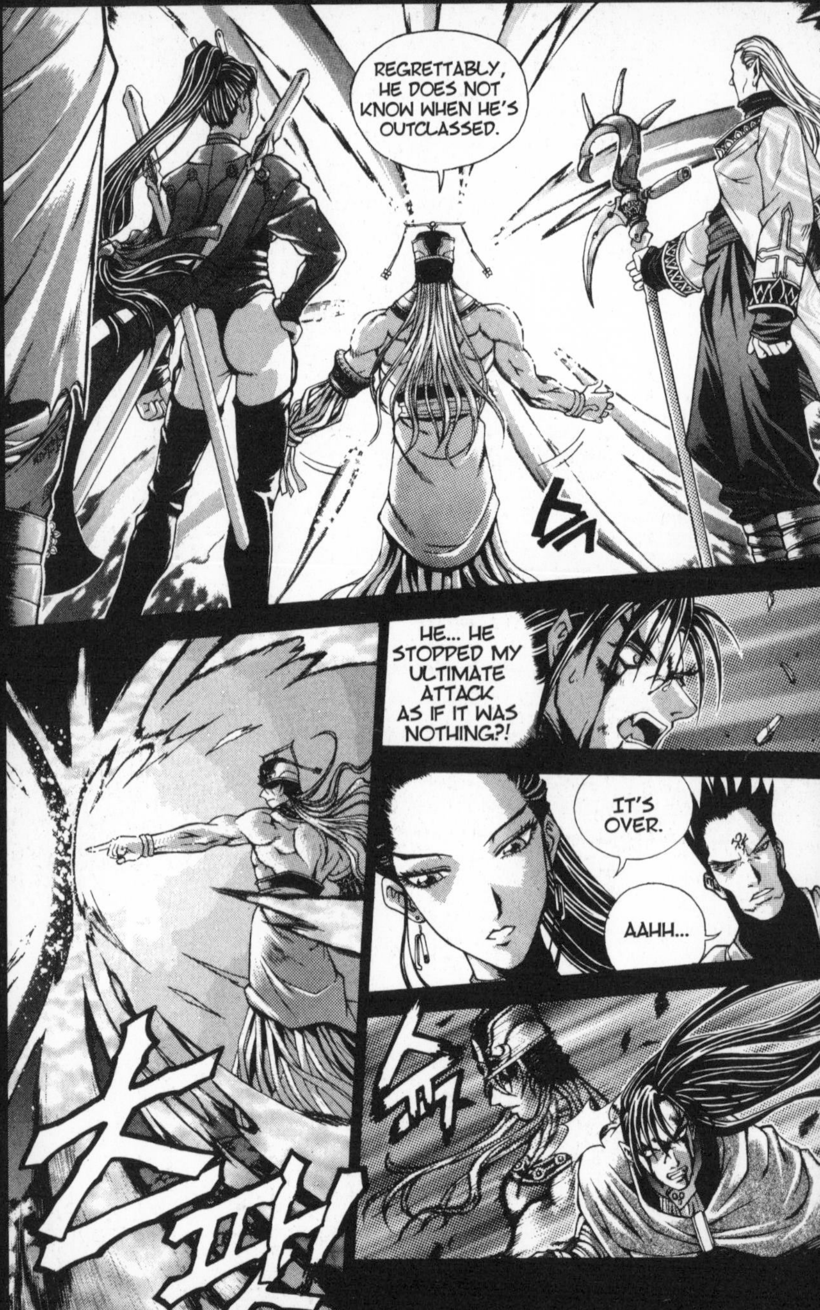
REGRETTABLY, HE DOES NOT KNOW WHEN HE'S OUTCLASSED.
HE... HE STOPPED MY ULTIMATE ATTACK AS IF IT WAS NOTHING?!
IT'S OVER.
AAHH...

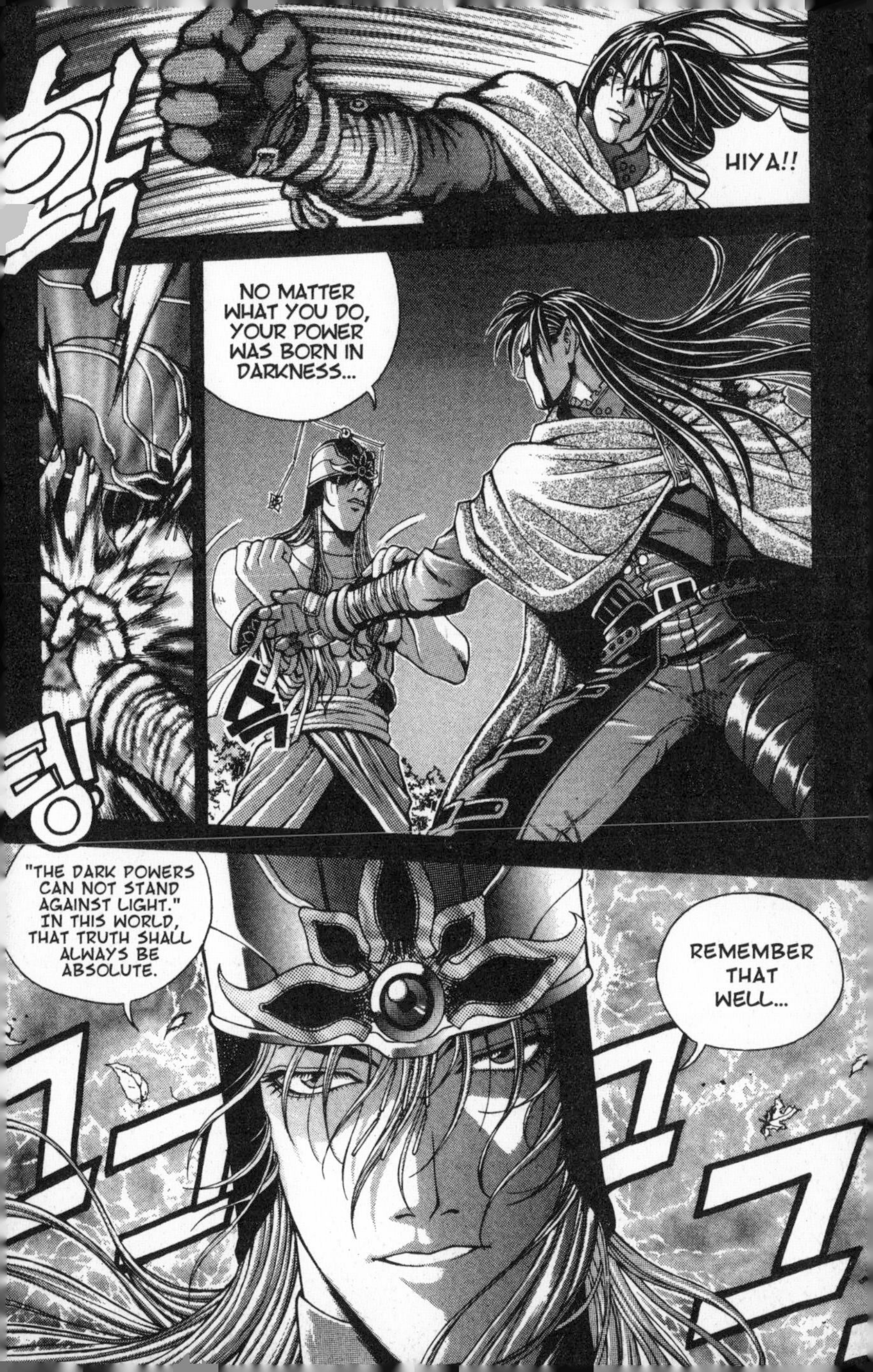
HIYA!!
NO MATTER WHAT YOU DO, YOUR POWER WAS BORN IN DARKNESS...
"THE DARK POWERS CAN NOT STAND AGAINST LIGHT." IN THIS WORLD, THAT TRUTH SHALL ALWAYS BE ABSOLUTE.
REMEMBER THAT WELL...

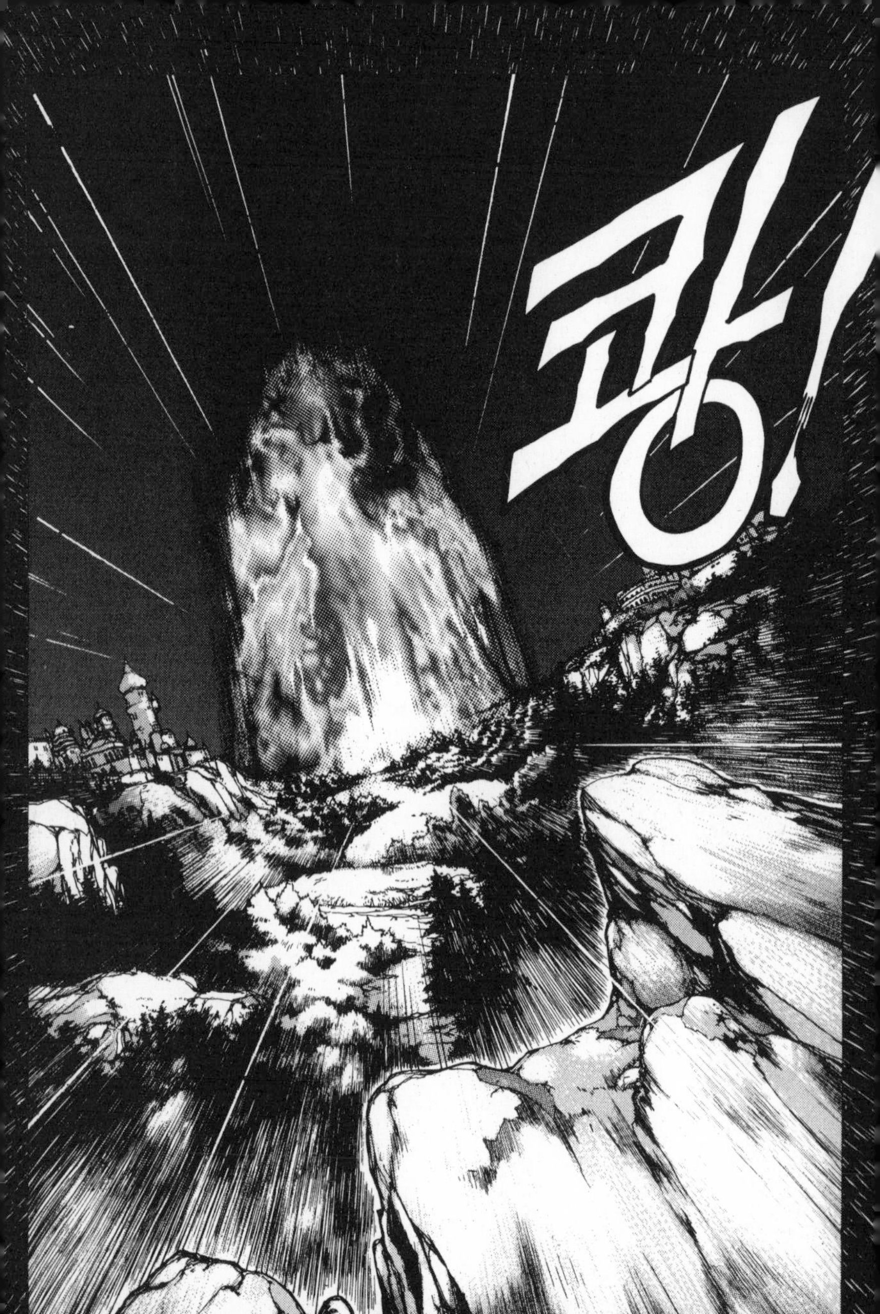
쾅!

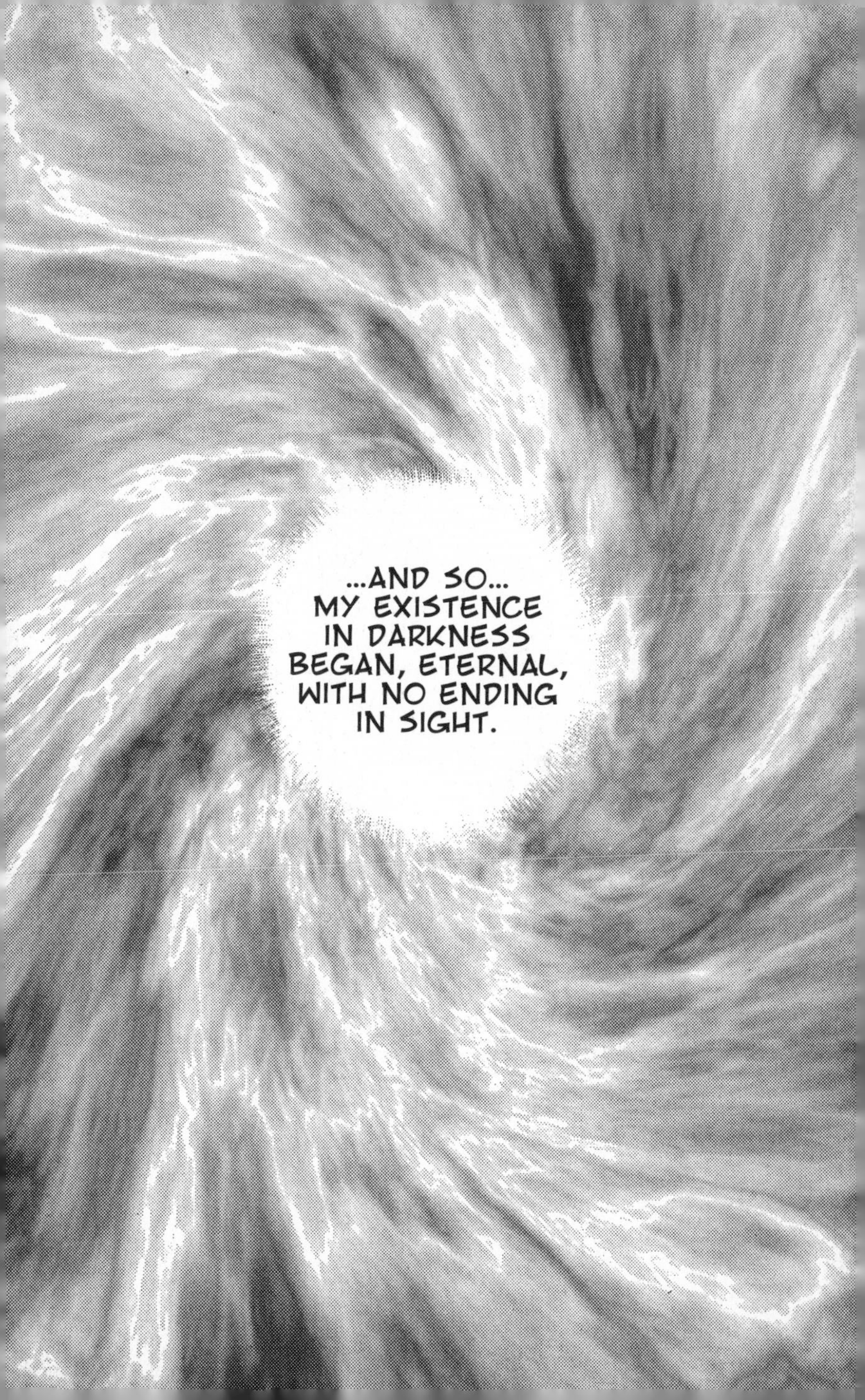
...AND SO...
MY EXISTENCE
IN DARKNESS
BEGAN, ETERNAL,
WITH NO ENDING
IN SIGHT.

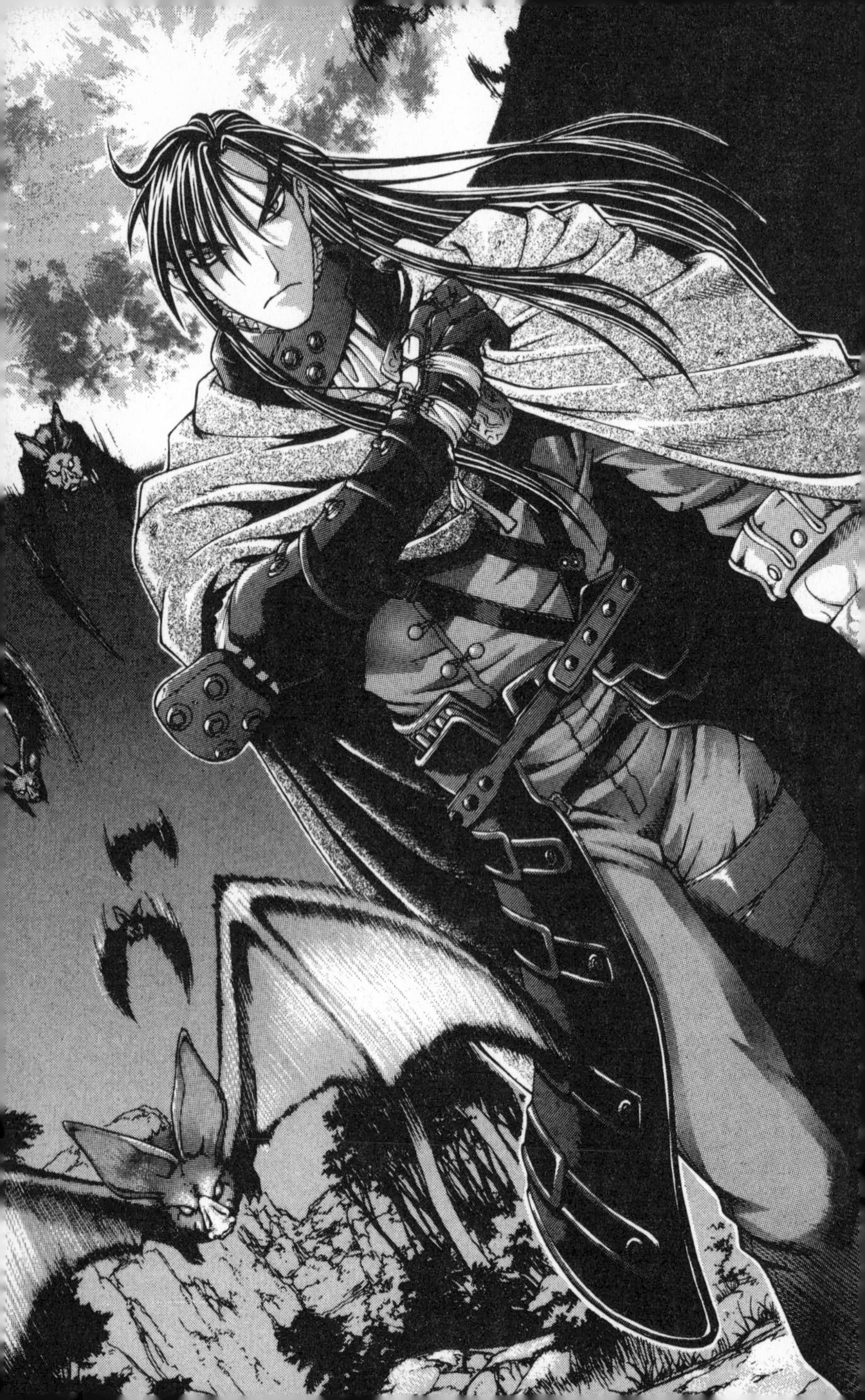

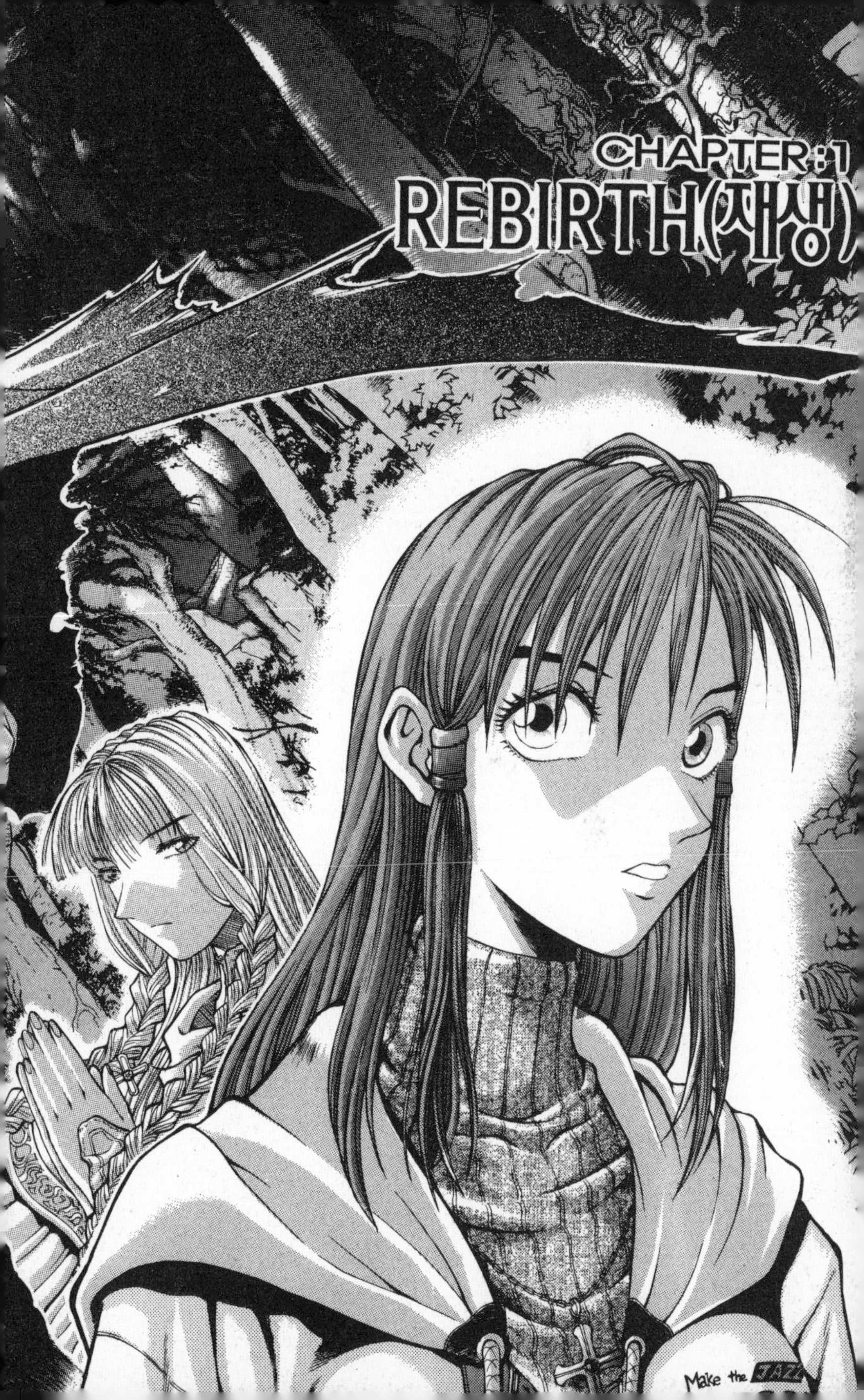
CHAPTER :1
REBIRTH(재생)
Make the JAZZ

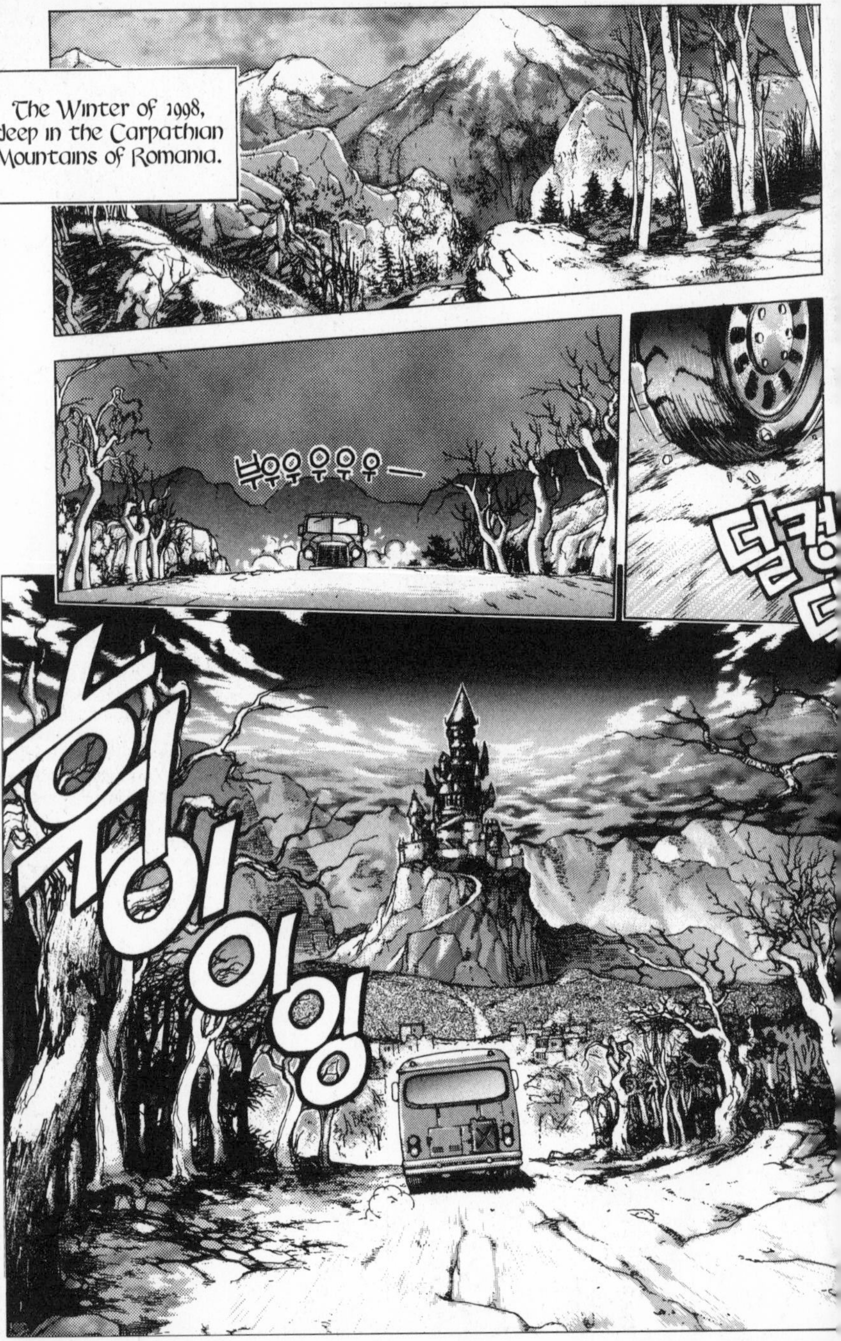

The Winter of 1998, deep in the Carpathian Mountains of Romania.
부우우우우—
덜컹
우이이잉

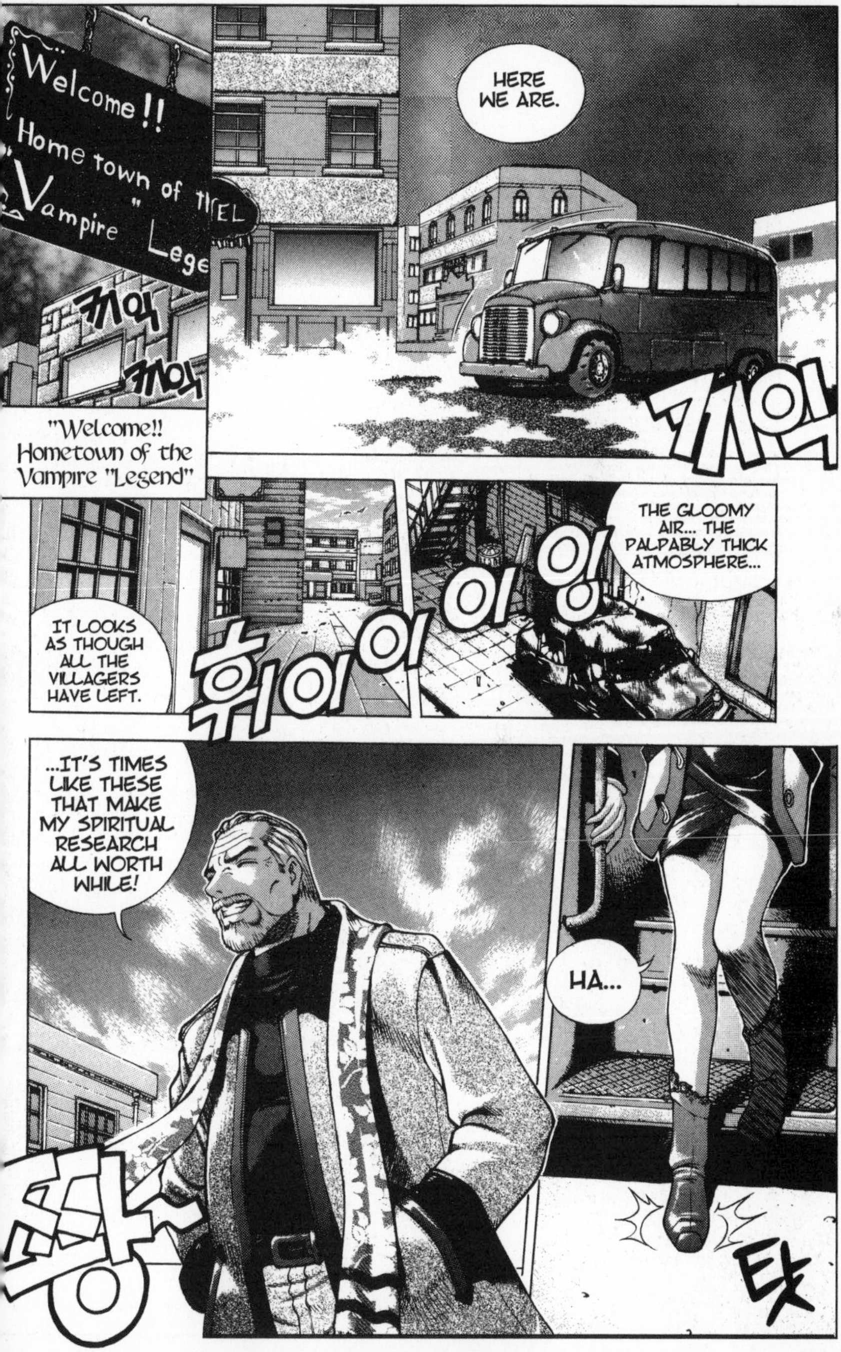
Welcome!!
Home town of th
"Vampire" Lege
끼익
끼익
"Welcome!! Hometown of the Vampire "Legend"
HERE WE ARE.
끼익
IT LOOKS AS THOUGH ALL THE VILLAGERS HAVE LEFT.
휘이이이이잉
THE GLOOMY AIR... THE PALPABLY THICK ATMOSPHERE...
...IT'S TIMES LIKE THESE THAT MAKE MY SPIRITUAL RESEARCH ALL WORTH WHILE!
HA...
탓

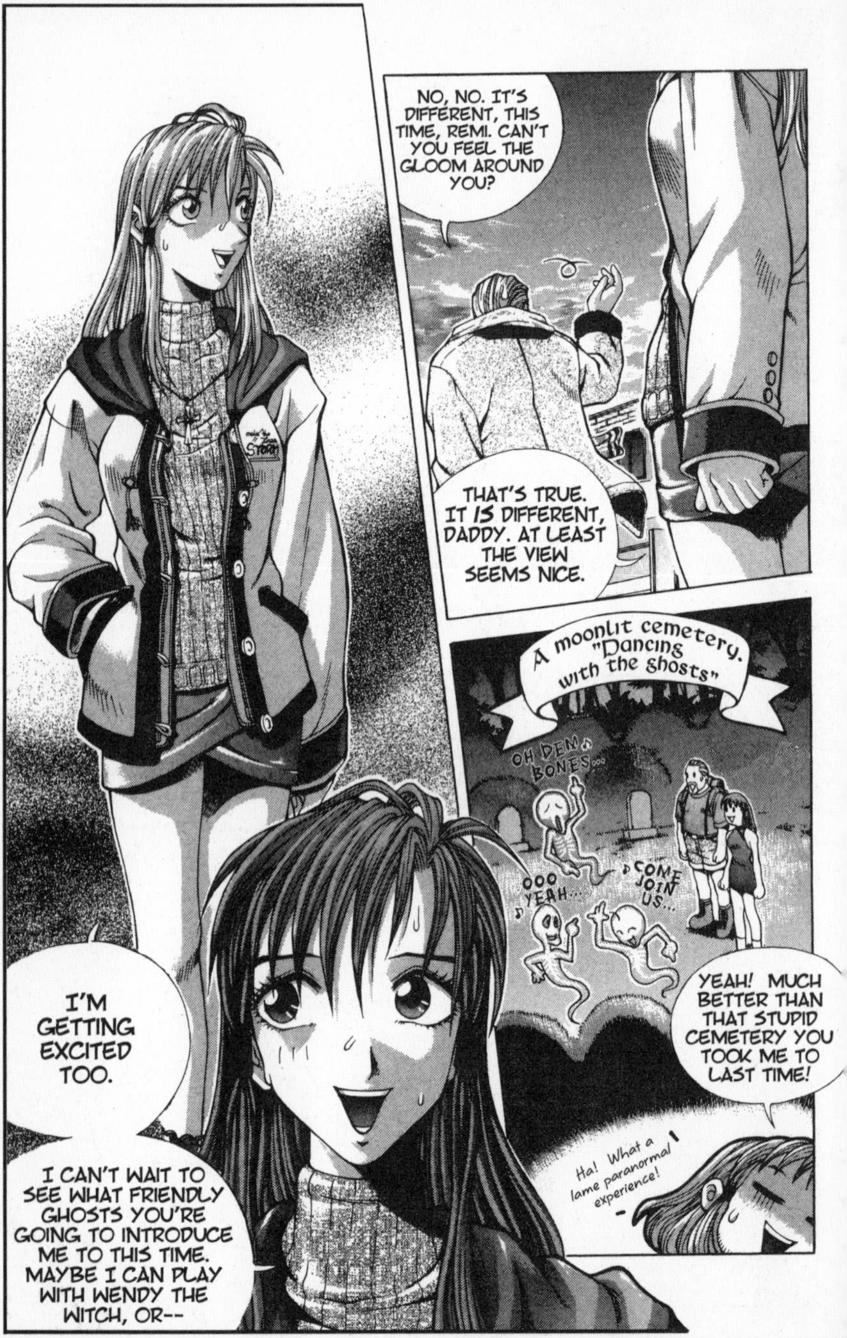
I'M GETTING EXCITED TOO.
I CAN'T WAIT TO SEE WHAT FRIENDLY GHOSTS YOU'RE GOING TO INTRODUCE ME TO THIS TIME. MAYBE I CAN PLAY WITH WENDY THE WITCH, OR--
NO, NO. IT'S DIFFERENT, THIS TIME, REMI. CAN'T YOU FEEL THE GLOOM AROUND YOU?
THAT'S TRUE. IT IS DIFFERENT, DADDY. AT LEAST THE VIEW SEEMS NICE.
A moonlit cemetery. "Dancing with the ghosts"
OH DEM BONES...
OOO YEAH...
COME JOIN US...
YEAH! MUCH BETTER THAN THAT STUPID CEMETERY YOU TOOK ME TO LAST TIME!
Ha! What a lame paranormal experience!

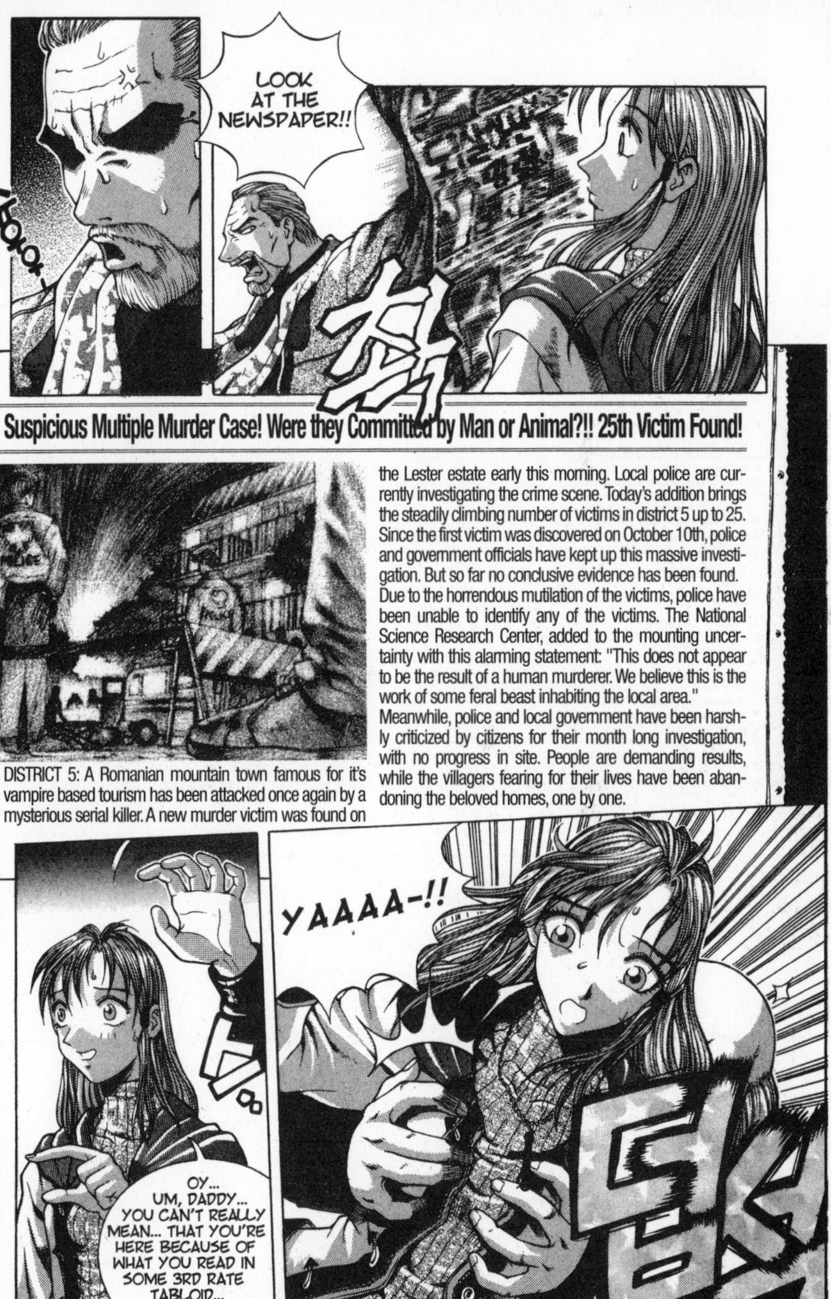
LOOK AT THE NEWSPAPER!!
Suspicious Multiple Murder Case! Were they Committed by Man or Animal?!! 25th Victim Found!
DISTRICT 5: A Romanian mountain town famous for it's vampire based tourism has been attacked once again by a mysterious serial killer. A new murder victim was found on the Lester estate early this morning. Local police are currently investigating the crime scene. Today's addition brings the steadily climbing number of victims in district 5 up to 25. Since the first victim was discovered on October 10th, police and government officials have kept up this massive investigation. But so far no conclusive evidence has been found. Due to the horrendous mutilation of the victims, police have been unable to identify any of the victims. The National Science Research Center, added to the mounting uncertainty with this alarming statement: "This does not appear to be the result of a human murderer. We believe this is the work of some feral beast inhabiting the local area." Meanwhile, police and local government have been harshly criticized by citizens for their month long investigation, with no progress in site. People are demanding results, while the villagers fearing for their lives have been abandoning the beloved homes, one by one.
OY... UM, DADDY... YOU CAN'T REALLY MEAN... THAT YOU'RE HERE BECAUSE OF WHAT YOU READ IN SOME 3RD RATE TABLOID...
YAAAA-!!

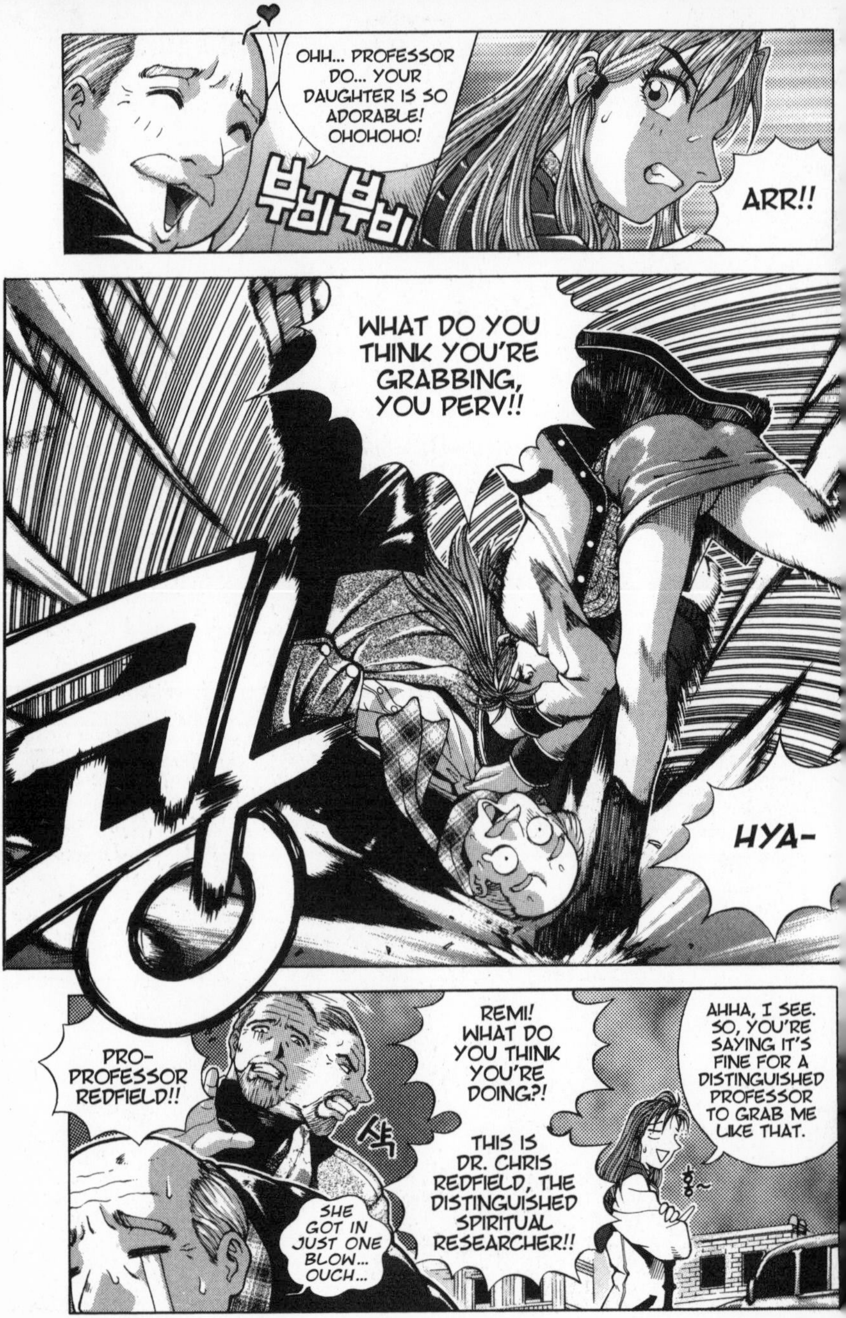
OHH... PROFESSOR DO... YOUR DAUGHTER IS SO ADORABLE! OHOHOHO!
부비부비
ARR!!
WHAT DO YOU THINK YOU'RE GRABBING, YOU PERV!!
HYA-
PRO- PROFESSOR REDFIELD!!
SHE GOT IN JUST ONE BLOW... OUCH...
REMI! WHAT DO YOU THINK YOU'RE DOING?!
THIS IS DR. CHRIS REDFIELD, THE DISTINGUISHED SPIRITUAL RESEARCHER!!
AHHA, I SEE. SO, YOU'RE SAYING IT'S FINE FOR A DISTINGUISHED PROFESSOR TO GRAB ME LIKE THAT.
흥~

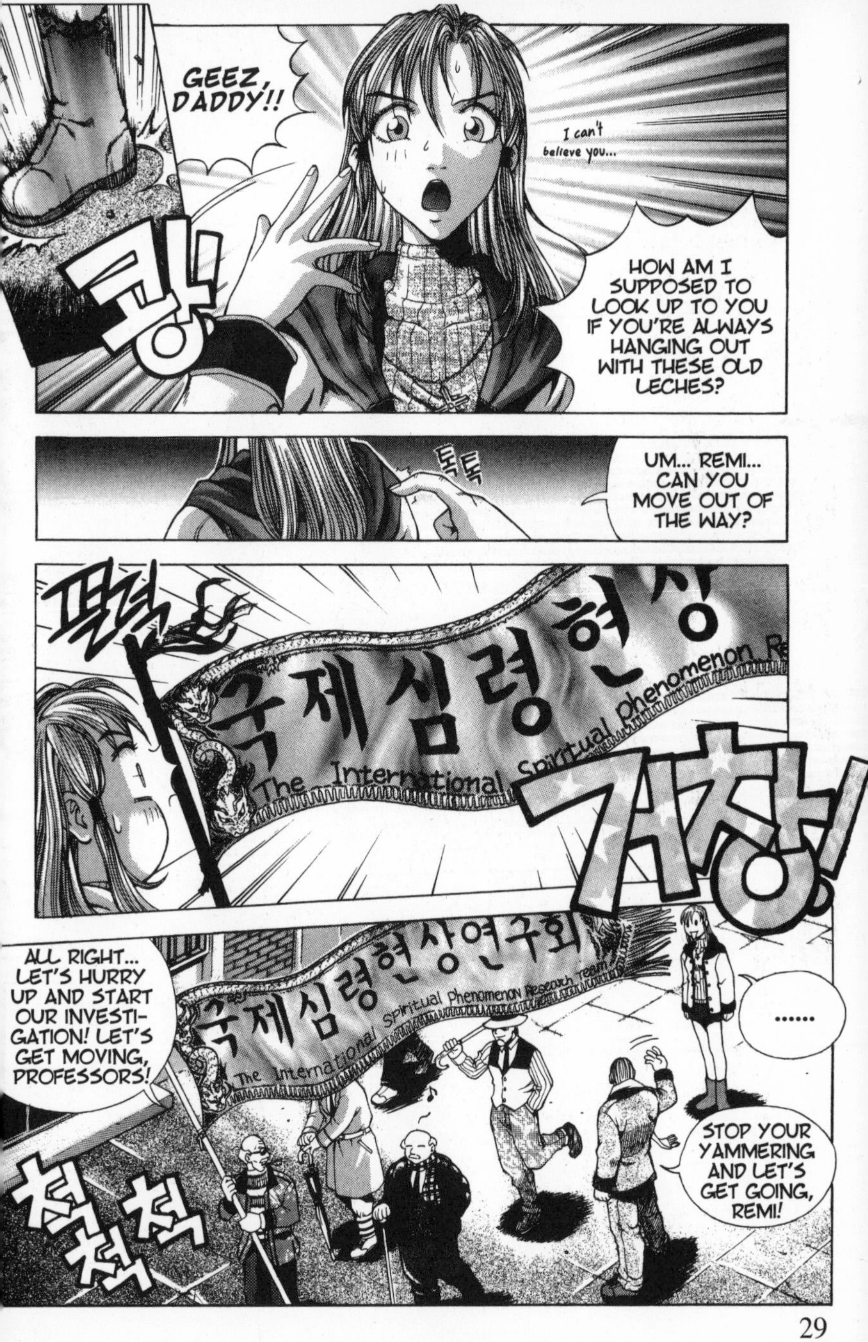
GEEZ, DADDY!!
쾅
I can't believe you...
HOW AM I SUPPOSED TO LOOK UP TO YOU IF YOU'RE ALWAYS HANGING OUT WITH THESE OLD LECHES?
톡톡
UM... REMI... CAN YOU MOVE OUT OF THE WAY?
펄럭
국제심령현상
The International Spiritual phenomenon
국제심령현상연구회
The International Spiritual Phenomenon Research Team
ALL RIGHT... LET'S HURRY UP AND START OUR INVESTI-GATION! LET'S GET MOVING, PROFESSORS!
......
STOP YOUR YAMMERING AND LET'S GET GOING, REMI!
척척척

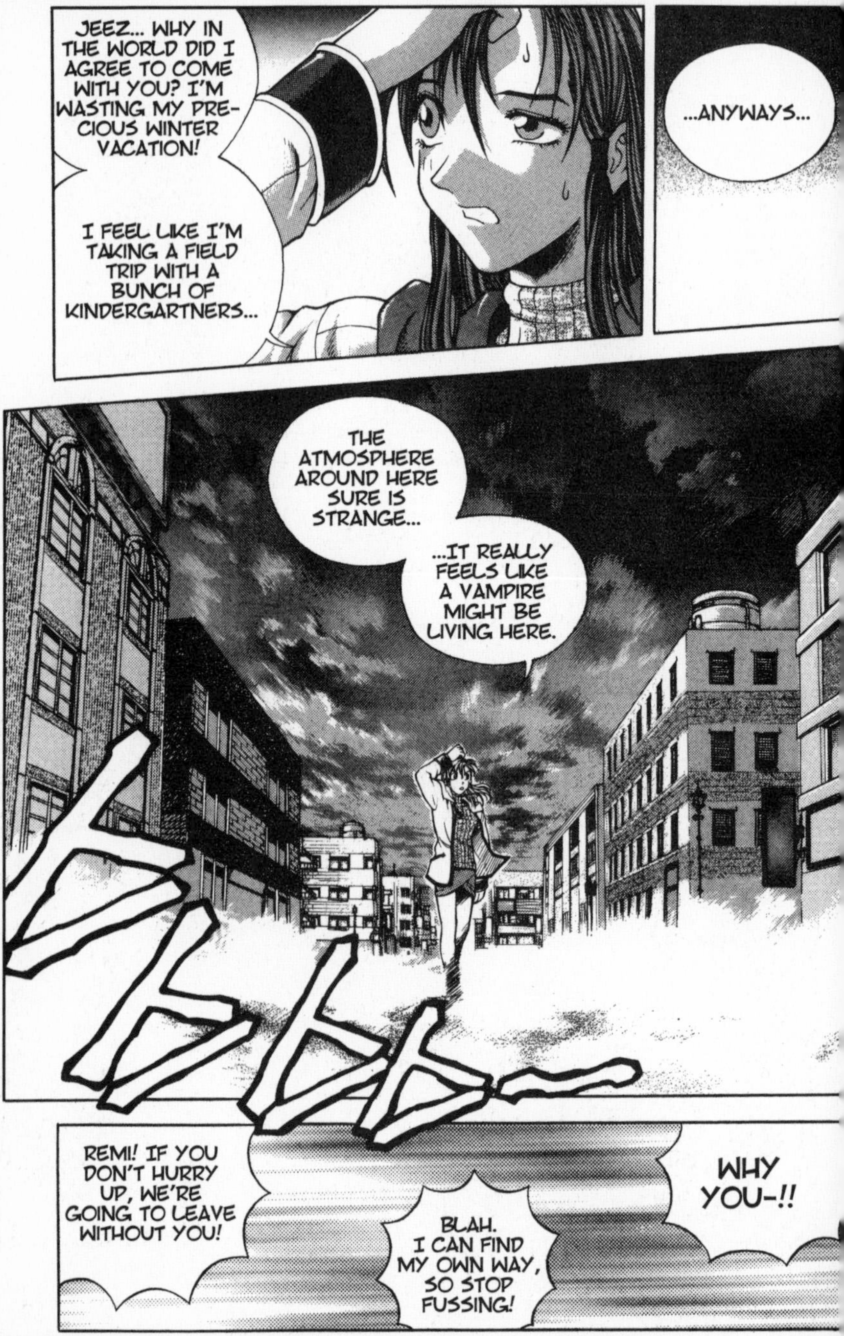
JEEZ... WHY IN THE WORLD DID I AGREE TO COME WITH YOU? I'M WASTING MY PRECIOUS WINTER VACATION!
I FEEL LIKE I'M TAKING A FIELD TRIP WITH A BUNCH OF KINDERGARTNERS...
...ANYWAYS...
THE ATMOSPHERE AROUND HERE SURE IS STRANGE...
...IT REALLY FEELS LIKE A VAMPIRE MIGHT BE LIVING HERE.
トトトー
REMI! IF YOU DON'T HURRY UP, WE'RE GOING TO LEAVE WITHOUT YOU!
BLAH. I CAN FIND MY OWN WAY, SO STOP FUSSING!
WHY YOU-!!

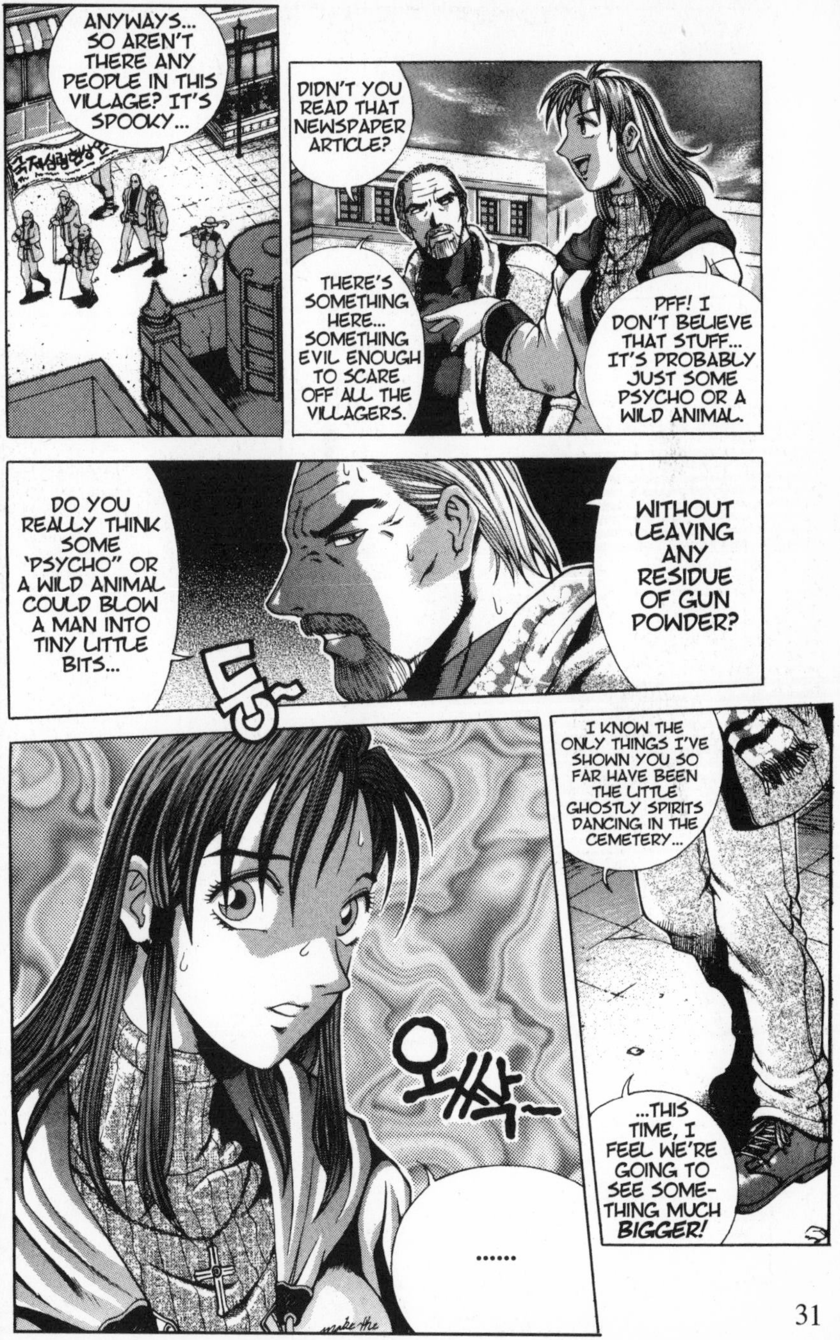
ANYWAYS... SO AREN'T THERE ANY PEOPLE IN THIS VILLAGE? IT'S SPOOKY...
DIDN'T YOU READ THAT NEWSPAPER ARTICLE?
THERE'S SOMETHING HERE... SOMETHING EVIL ENOUGH TO SCARE OFF ALL THE VILLAGERS.
PFF! I DON'T BELIEVE THAT STUFF... IT'S PROBABLY JUST SOME PSYCHO OR A WILD ANIMAL.
DO YOU REALLY THINK SOME 'PSYCHO" OR A WILD ANIMAL COULD BLOW A MAN INTO TINY LITTLE BITS...
WITHOUT LEAVING ANY RESIDUE OF GUN POWDER?
오싹~
......
I KNOW THE ONLY THINGS I'VE SHOWN YOU SO FAR HAVE BEEN THE LITTLE GHOSTLY SPIRITS DANCING IN THE CEMETERY...
...THIS TIME, I FEEL WE'RE GOING TO SEE SOME-THING MUCH *BIGGER!*

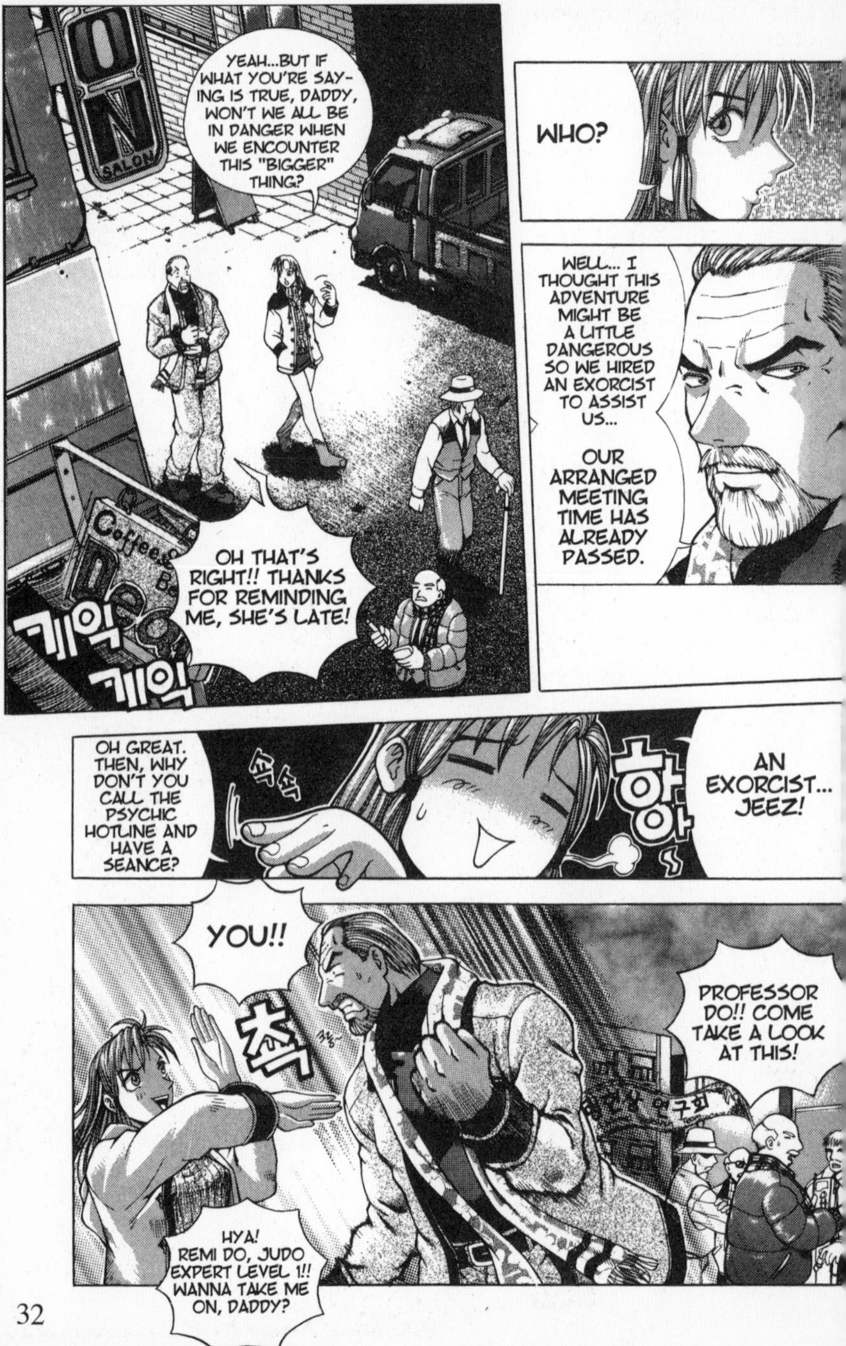
YEAH...BUT IF WHAT YOU'RE SAY-ING IS TRUE, DADDY, WON'T WE ALL BE IN DANGER WHEN WE ENCOUNTER THIS "BIGGER" THING?
OH THAT'S RIGHT!! THANKS FOR REMINDING ME, SHE'S LATE!
끼익
끼익
WHO?
WELL... I THOUGHT THIS ADVENTURE MIGHT BE A LITTLE DANGEROUS SO WE HIRED AN EXORCIST TO ASSIST US...
OUR ARRANGED MEETING TIME HAS ALREADY PASSED.
OH GREAT. THEN, WHY DON'T YOU CALL THE PSYCHIC HOTLINE AND HAVE A SEANCE?
AN EXORCIST... JEEZ!
YOU!!
HYA! REMI DO, JUDO EXPERT LEVEL 1!! WANNA TAKE ME ON, DADDY?
PROFESSOR DO!! COME TAKE A LOOK AT THIS!

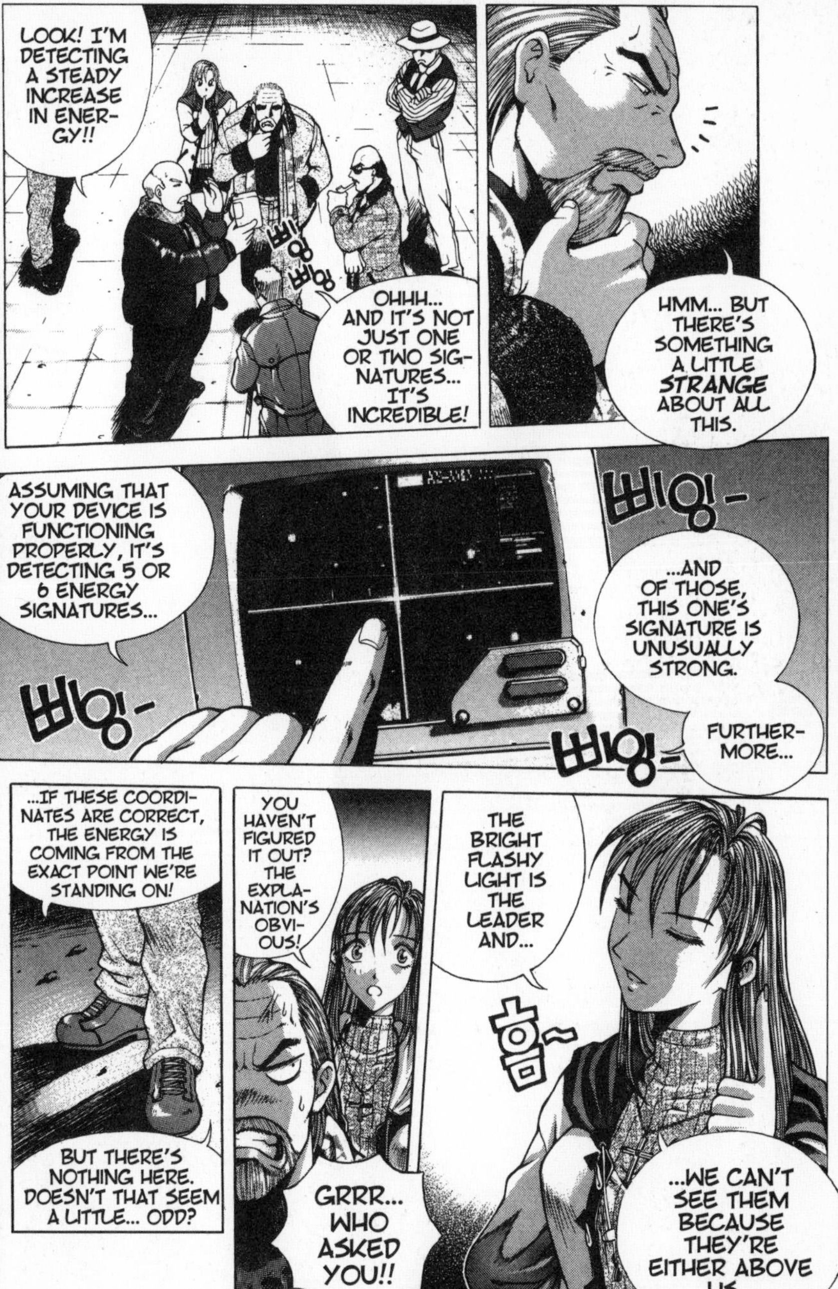
LOOK! I'M DETECTING A STEADY INCREASE IN ENER-GY!!
삐잉 삐잉
OHHH... AND IT'S NOT JUST ONE OR TWO SIG-NATURES... IT'S INCREDIBLE!
HMM... BUT THERE'S SOMETHING A LITTLE STRANGE ABOUT ALL THIS.
ASSUMING THAT YOUR DEVICE IS FUNCTIONING PROPERLY, IT'S DETECTING 5 OR 6 ENERGY SIGNATURES...
삐잉-
삐잉-
...AND OF THOSE, THIS ONE'S SIGNATURE IS UNUSUALLY STRONG.
삐잉-
FURTHER-MORE...
...IF THESE COORDI-NATES ARE CORRECT, THE ENERGY IS COMING FROM THE EXACT POINT WE'RE STANDING ON!
BUT THERE'S NOTHING HERE. DOESN'T THAT SEEM A LITTLE... ODD?
YOU HAVEN'T FIGURED IT OUT? THE EXPLA-NATION'S OBVI-OUS!
GRRR... WHO ASKED YOU!!
THE BRIGHT FLASHY LIGHT IS THE LEADER AND...
흡~
...WE CAN'T SEE THEM BECAUSE THEY'RE EITHER ABOVE US...

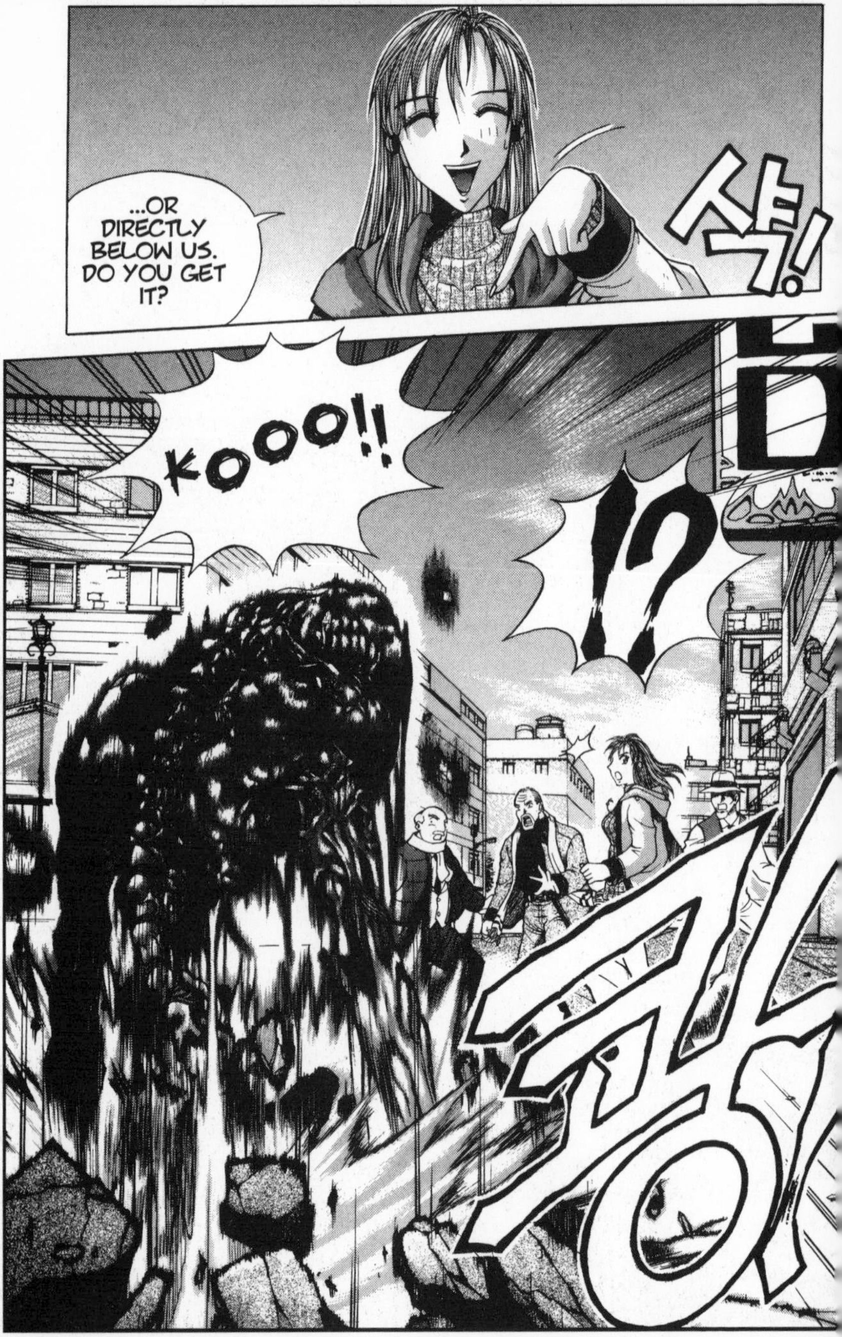
...OR DIRECTLY BELOW US. DO YOU GET IT?
KOOO!!
!?

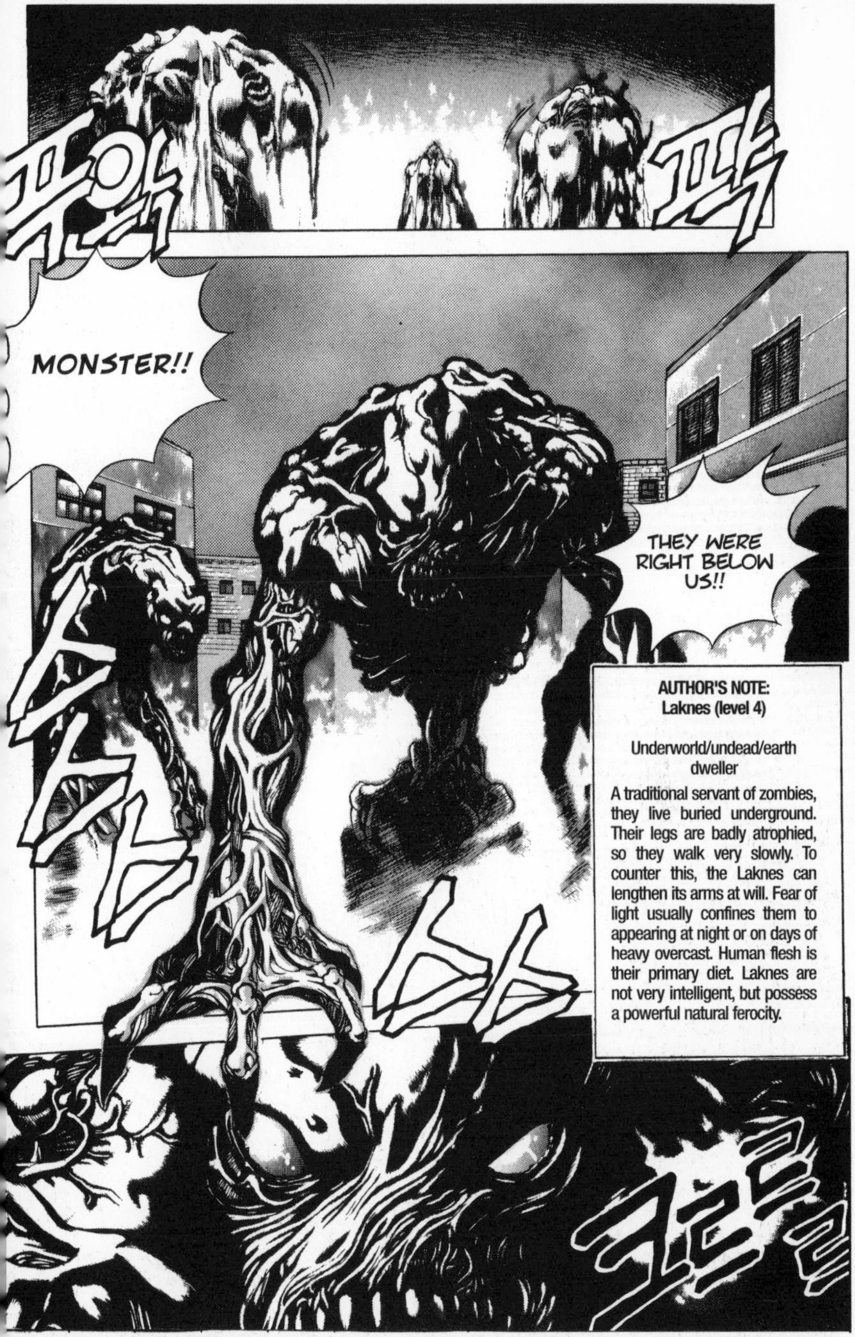
MONSTER!!
THEY WERE RIGHT BELOW US!!
AUTHOR'S NOTE: Laknes (level 4)
Underworld/undead/earth dweller
A traditional servant of zombies, they live buried underground. Their legs are badly atrophied, so they walk very slowly. To counter this, the Laknes can lengthen its arms at will. Fear of light usually confines them to appearing at night or on days of heavy overcast. Human flesh is their primary diet. Laknes are not very intelligent, but possess a powerful natural ferocity.

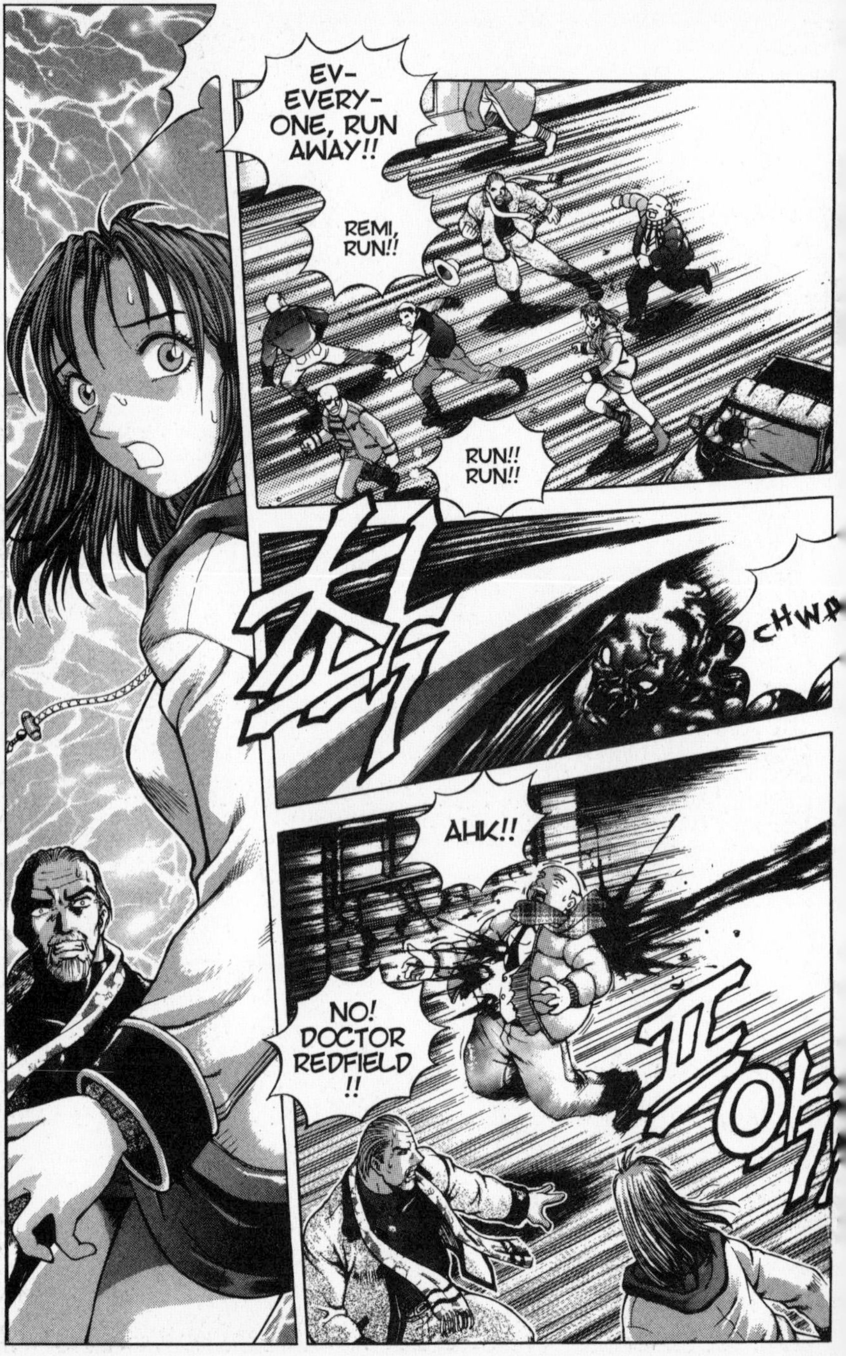
EV- EVERY- ONE, RUN AWAY!!
REMI, RUN!!
RUN!! RUN!!
CHWP
AHK!!
NO! DOCTOR REDFIELD !!

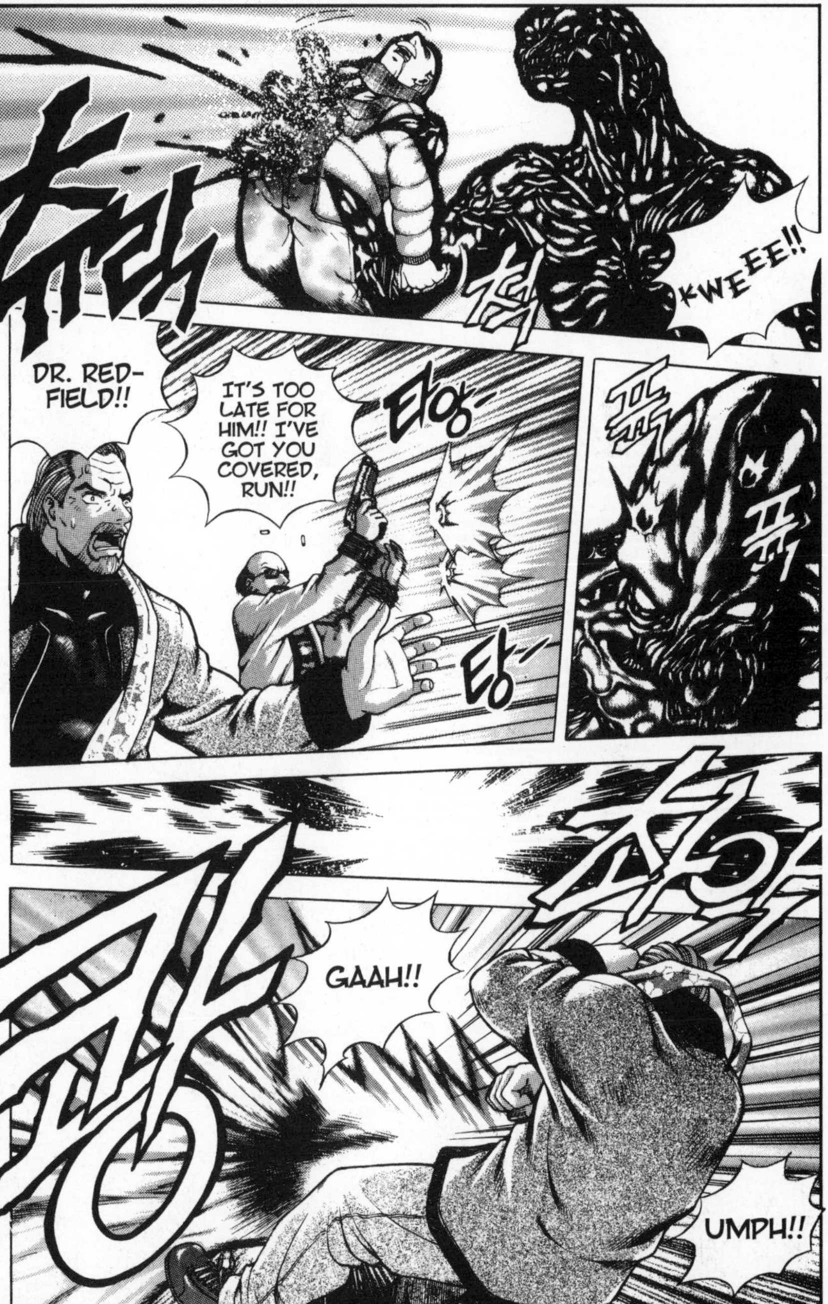
KWEEE!!
DR. RED-FIELD!!
IT'S TOO LATE FOR HIM!! I'VE GOT YOU COVERED, RUN!!
GAAH!!
UMPH!!

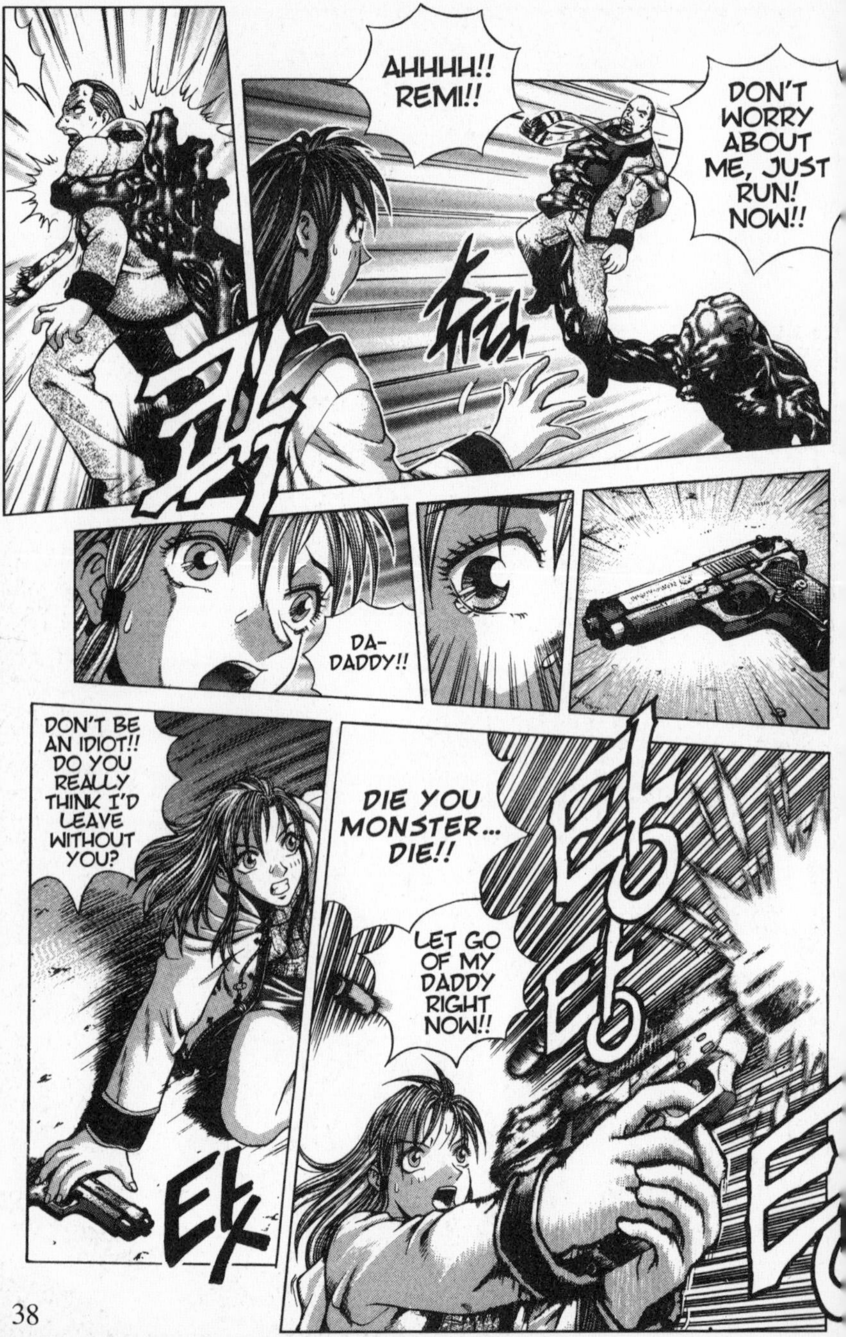

AHHHH!! REMI!!
DON'T WORRY ABOUT ME, JUST RUN! NOW!!
DA-DADDY!!
DON'T BE AN IDIOT!! DO YOU REALLY THINK I'D LEAVE WITHOUT YOU?
탁
DIE YOU MONSTER... DIE!!
LET GO OF MY DADDY RIGHT NOW!!
탕
탕

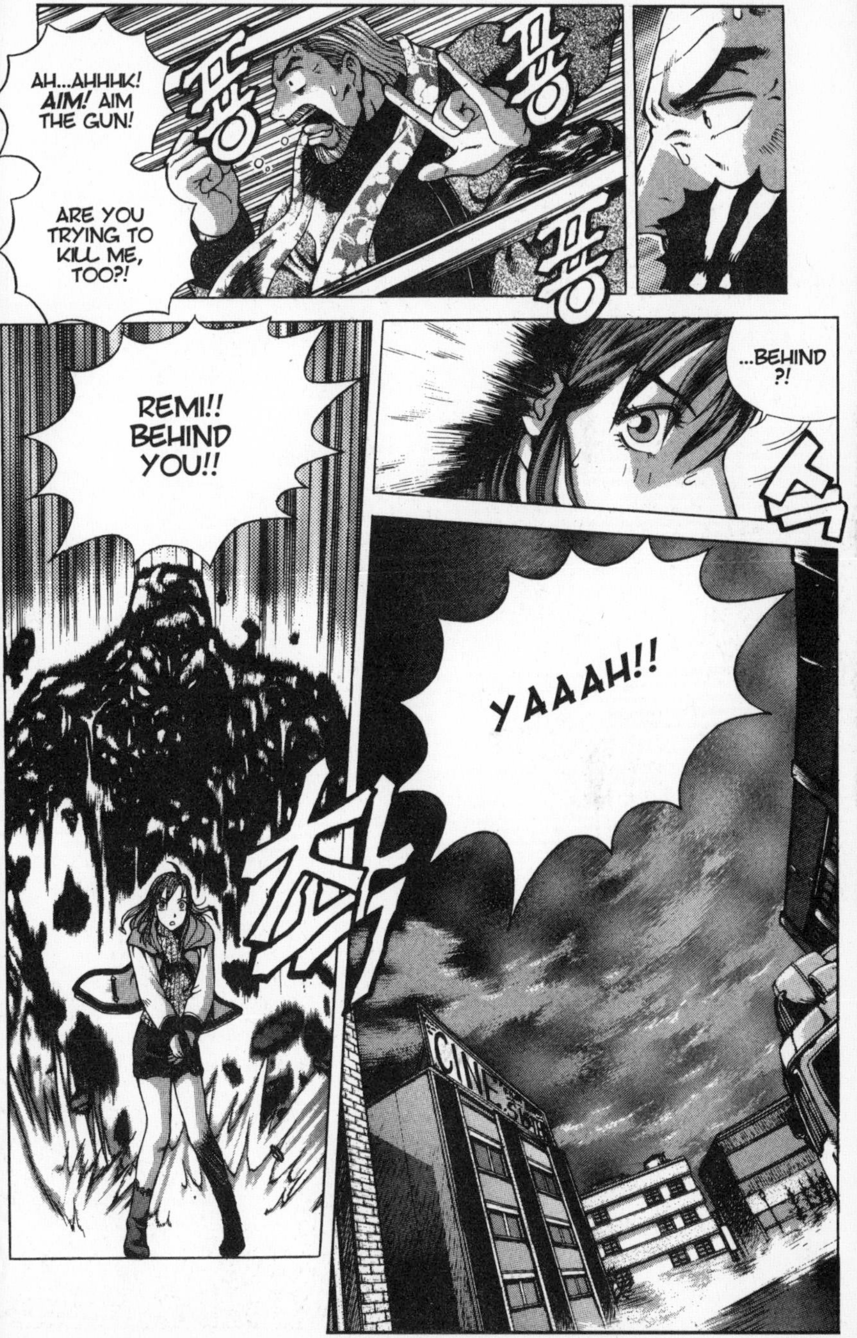
AH...AHHHK! AIM! AIM THE GUN!
ARE YOU TRYING TO KILL ME, TOO?!
REMI!! BEHIND YOU!!
...BEHIND ?!
YAAAH!!

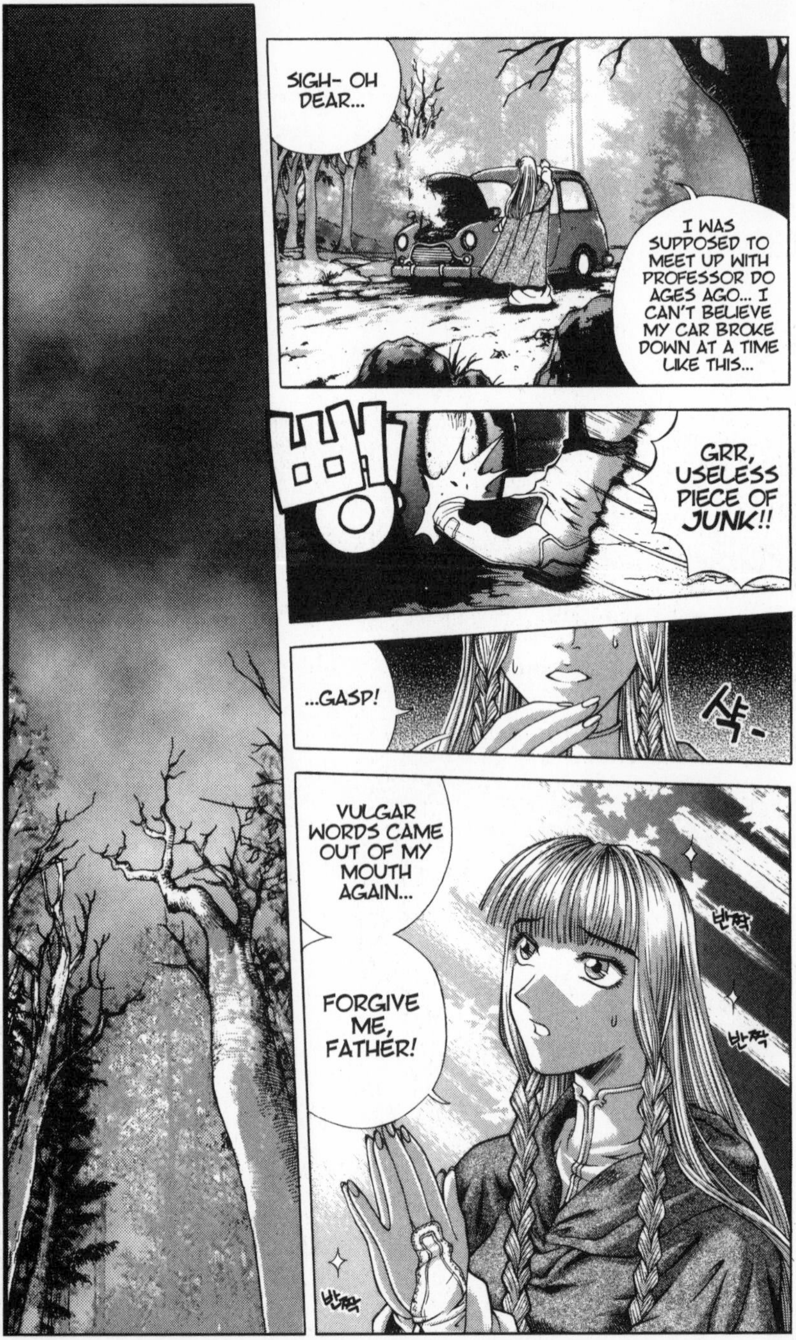
SIGH- OH DEAR...
I WAS SUPPOSED TO MEET UP WITH PROFESSOR DO AGES AGO... I CAN'T BELIEVE MY CAR BROKE DOWN AT A TIME LIKE THIS...
빵!
GRR, USELESS PIECE OF **JUNK**!!
...GASP!
삭-
VULGAR WORDS CAME OUT OF MY MOUTH AGAIN...
반짝
FORGIVE ME, FATHER!
반짝
반짝

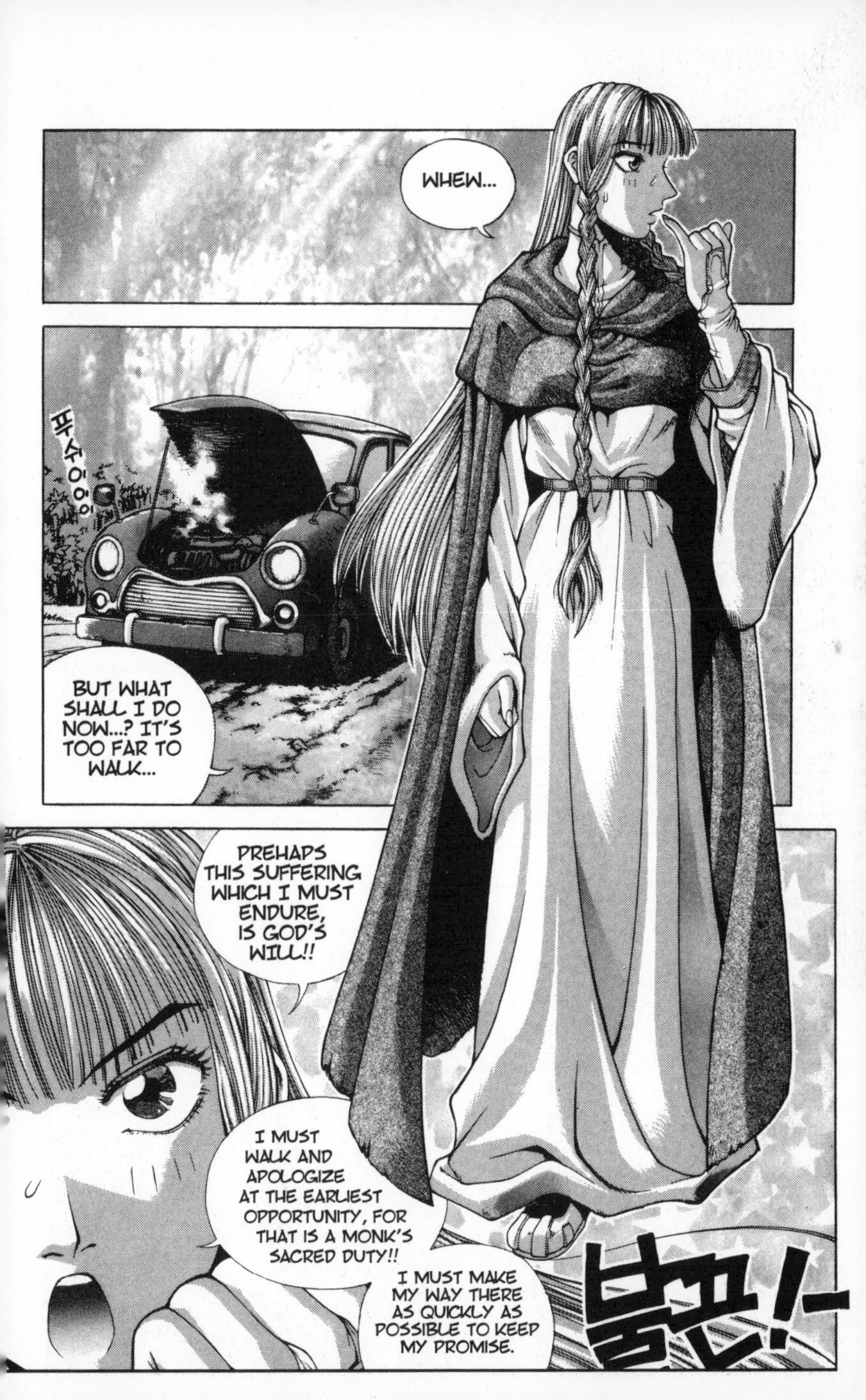
WHEW...
파사아아아
BUT WHAT SHALL I DO NOW...? IT'S TOO FAR TO WALK...
PREHAPS THIS SUFFERING WHICH I MUST ENDURE, IS GOD'S WILL!!
I MUST WALK AND APOLOGIZE AT THE EARLIEST OPPORTUNITY, FOR THAT IS A MONK'S SACRED DUTY!!
I MUST MAKE MY WAY THERE AS QUICKLY AS POSSIBLE TO KEEP MY PROMISE.

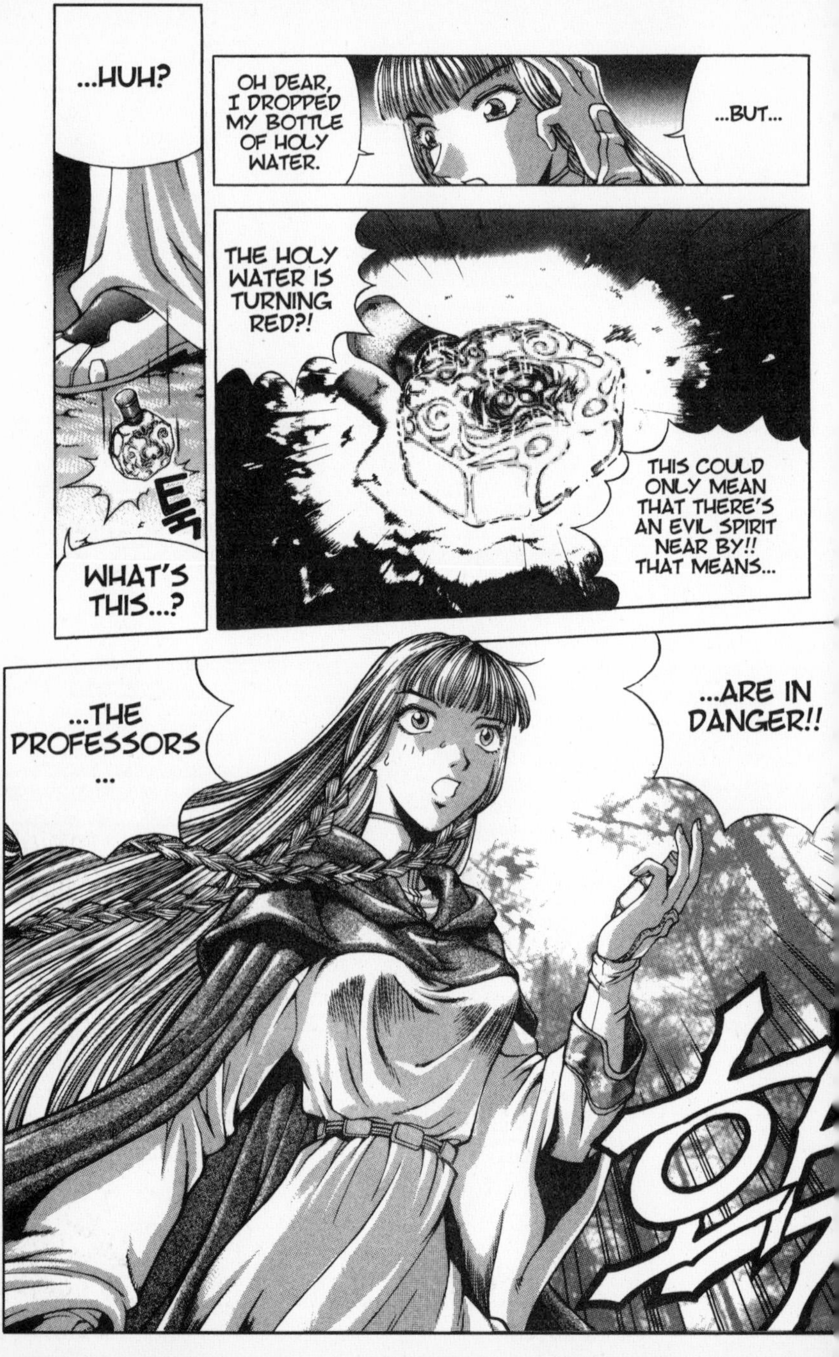
...HUH?
WHAT'S THIS...?
OH DEAR, I DROPPED MY BOTTLE OF HOLY WATER.
...BUT...
THE HOLY WATER IS TURNING RED?!
THIS COULD ONLY MEAN THAT THERE'S AN EVIL SPIRIT NEAR BY!! THAT MEANS...
...THE PROFESSORS ...
...ARE IN DANGER!!

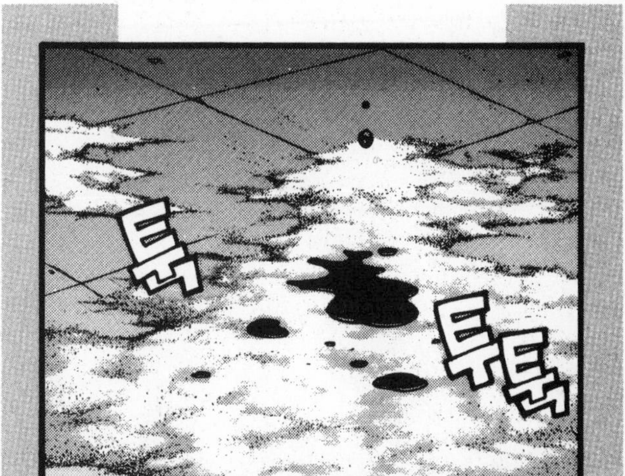
툭
투툭

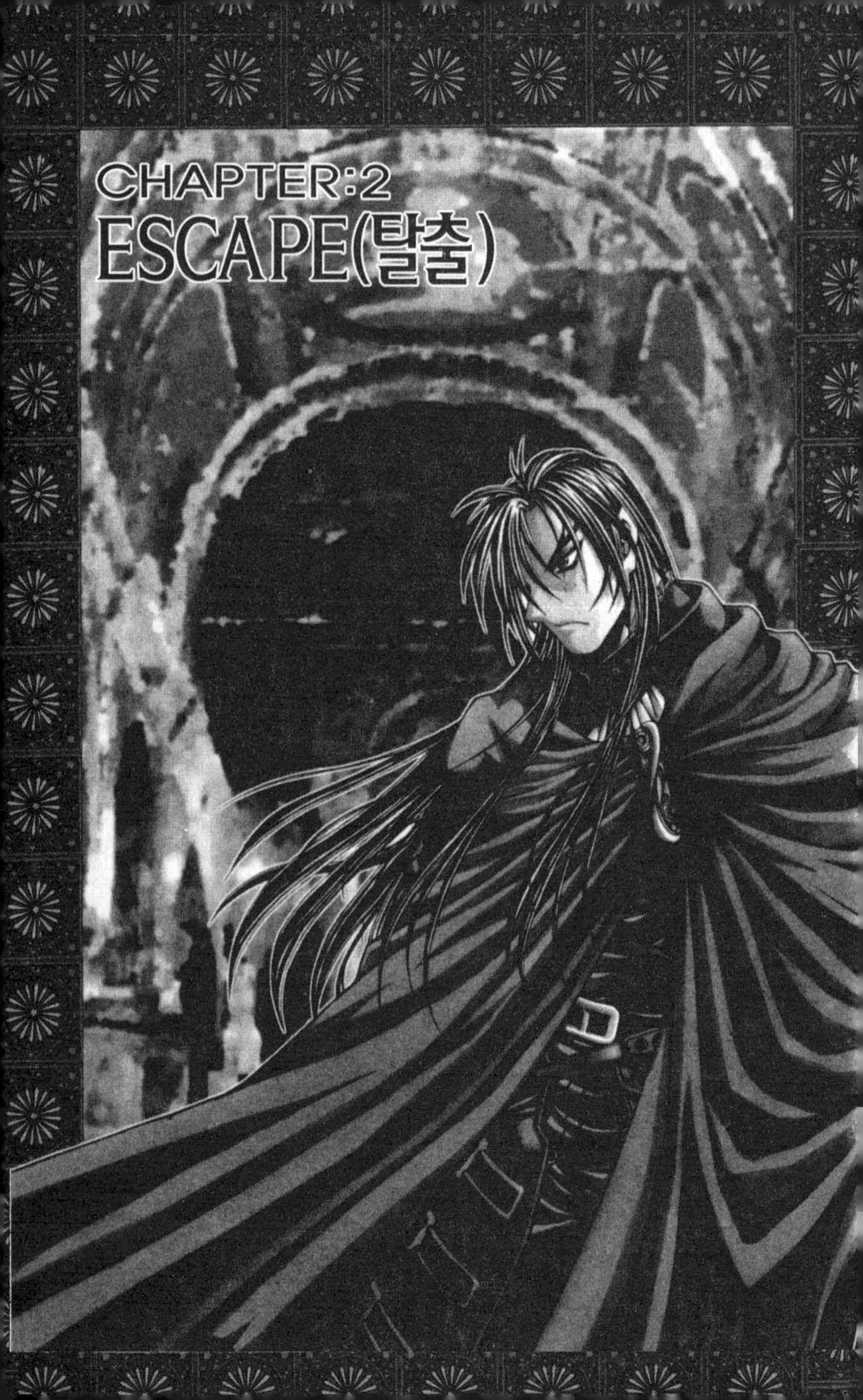
CHAPTER:2
ESCAPE(탈출)

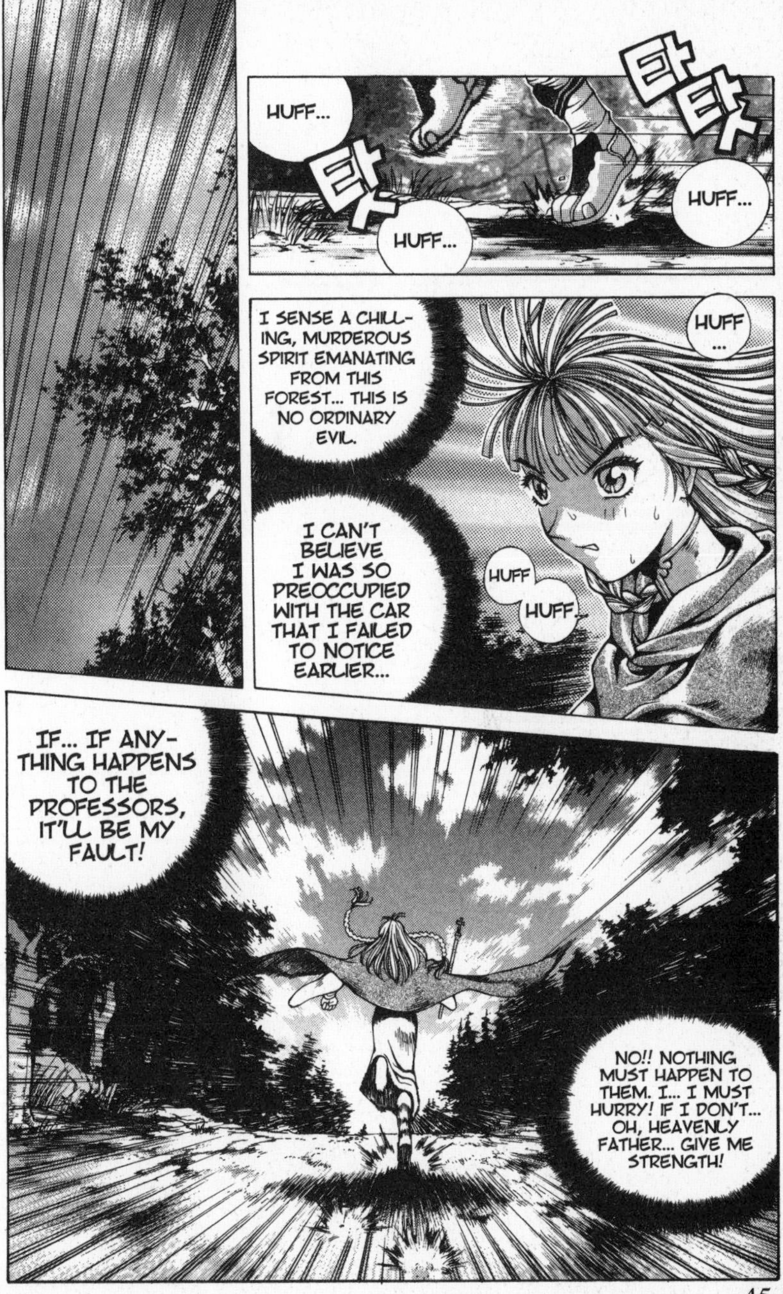
HUFF...
타 타
타
HUFF...
HUFF...
I SENSE A CHILL-ING, MURDEROUS SPIRIT EMANATING FROM THIS FOREST... THIS IS NO ORDINARY EVIL.
HUFF ...
I CAN'T BELIEVE I WAS SO PREOCCUPIED WITH THE CAR THAT I FAILED TO NOTICE EARLIER...
HUFF
HUFF...
IF... IF ANY-THING HAPPENS TO THE PROFESSORS, IT'LL BE MY FAULT!
NO!! NOTHING MUST HAPPEN TO THEM. I... I MUST HURRY! IF I DON'T... OH, HEAVENLY FATHER... GIVE ME STRENGTH!

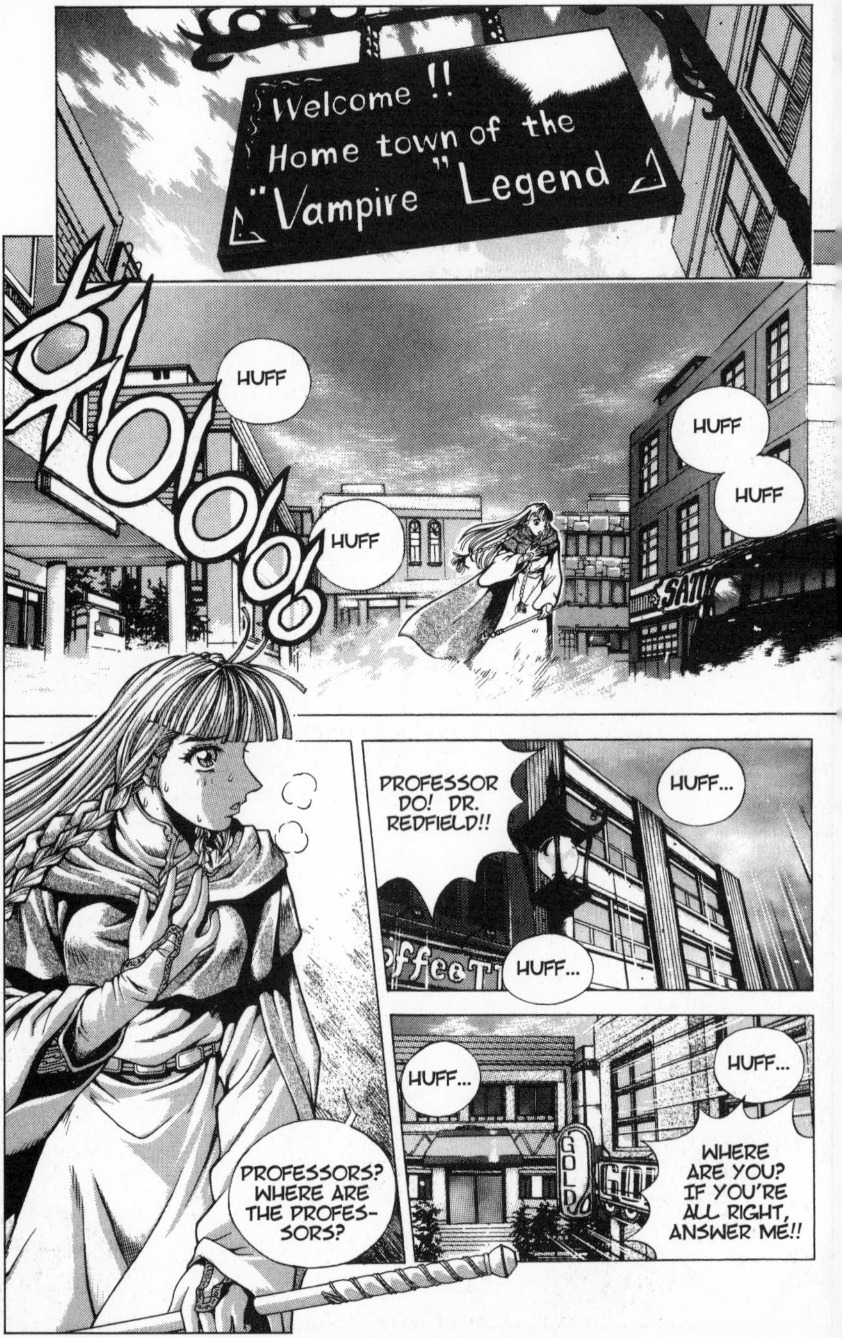
Welcome !!
Home town of the
"Vampire" Legend
HUFF
HUFF
HUFF
HUFF
PROFESSORS? WHERE ARE THE PROFES-SORS?
PROFESSOR DO! DR. REDFIELD!!
HUFF...
HUFF...
HUFF...
HUFF...
WHERE ARE YOU? IF YOU'RE ALL RIGHT, ANSWER ME!!

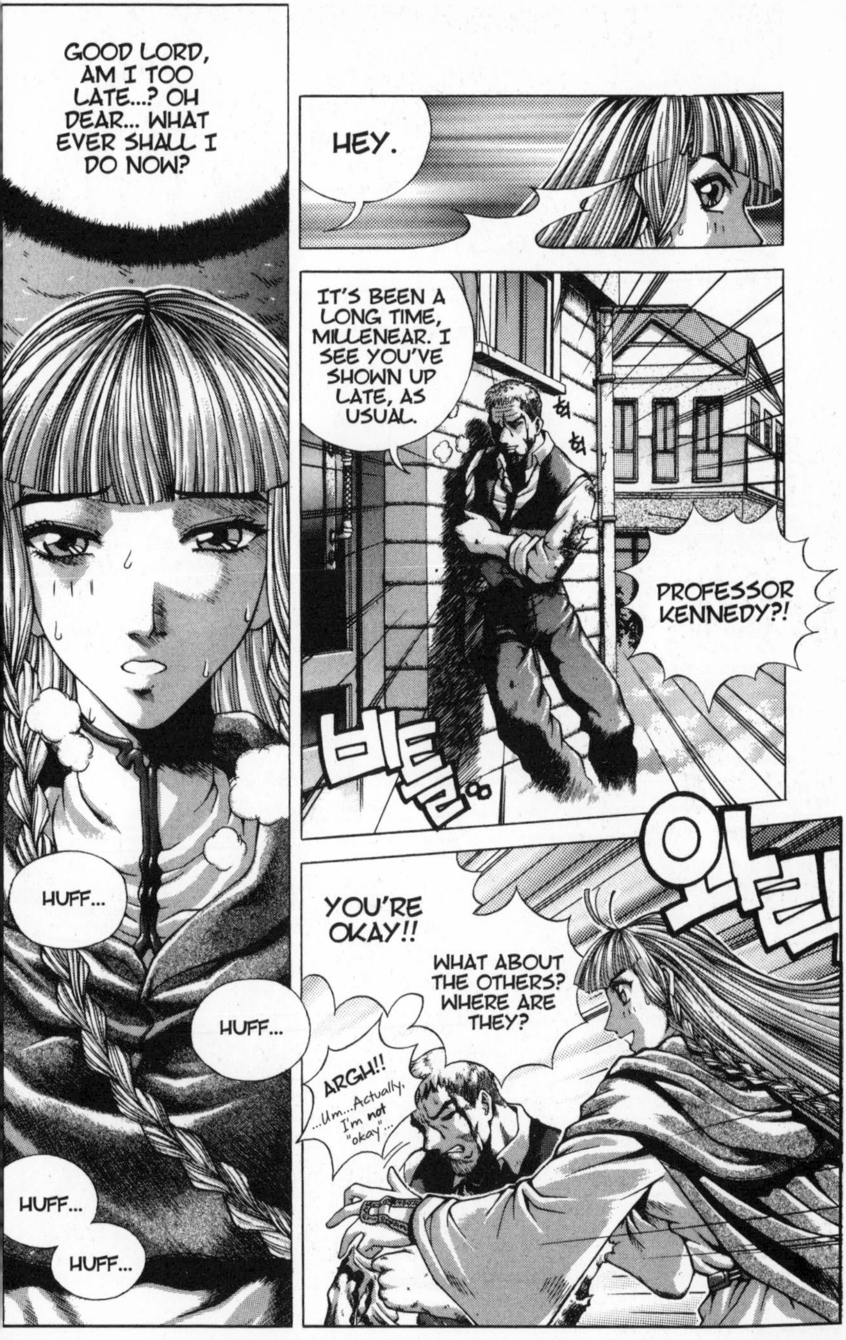
GOOD LORD, AM I TOO LATE...? OH DEAR... WHAT EVER SHALL I DO NOW?
HUFF...
HUFF...
HUFF...
HUFF...
HEY.
IT'S BEEN A LONG TIME, MILLENEAR. I SEE YOU'VE SHOWN UP LATE, AS USUAL.
헉
헉
PROFESSOR KENNEDY?!
비틀
YOU'RE OKAY!!
WHAT ABOUT THE OTHERS? WHERE ARE THEY?
ARGH!!
...Um...Actually, I'm not "okay"...

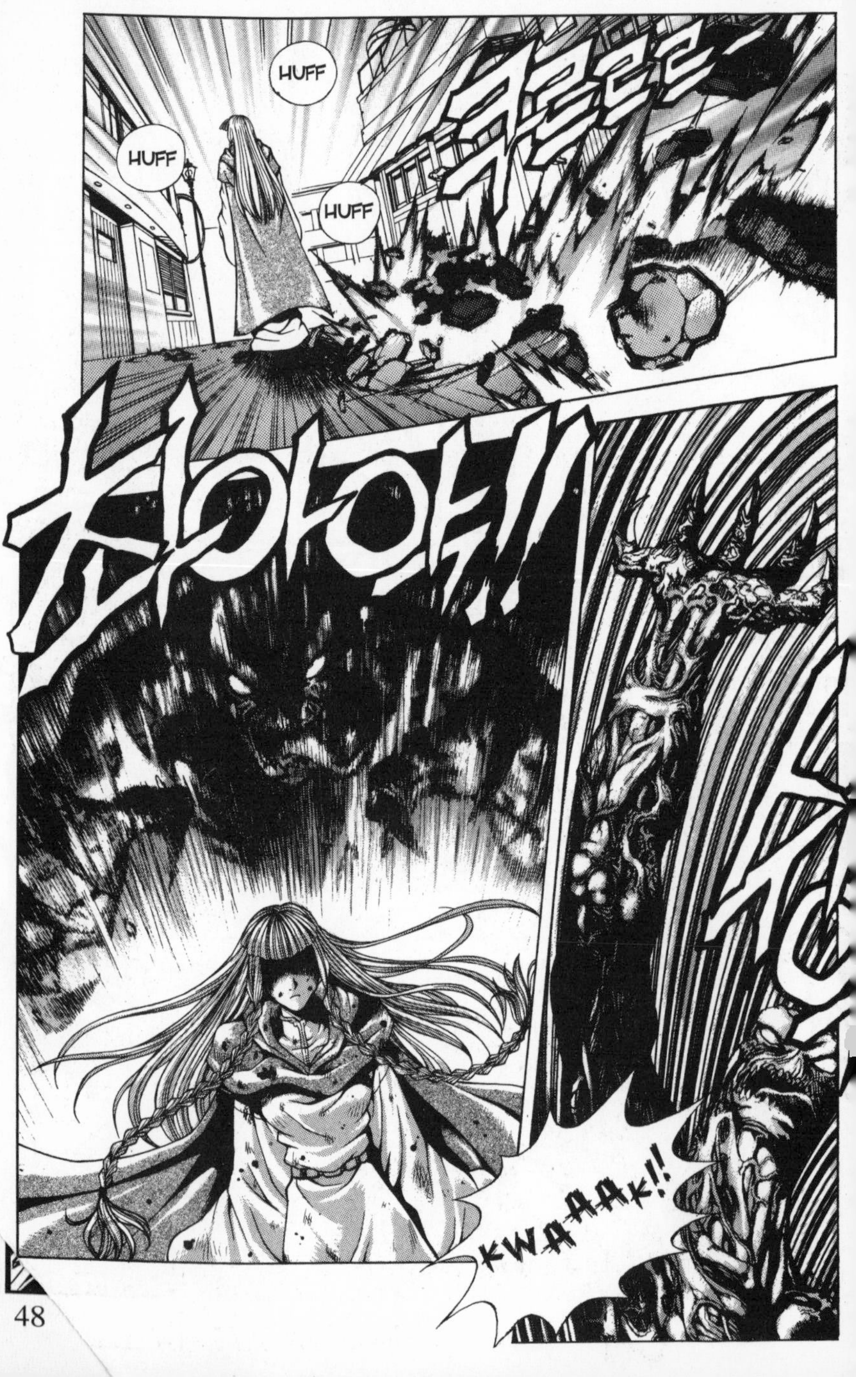
HUFF
HUFF
HUFF
KWAAAK!!

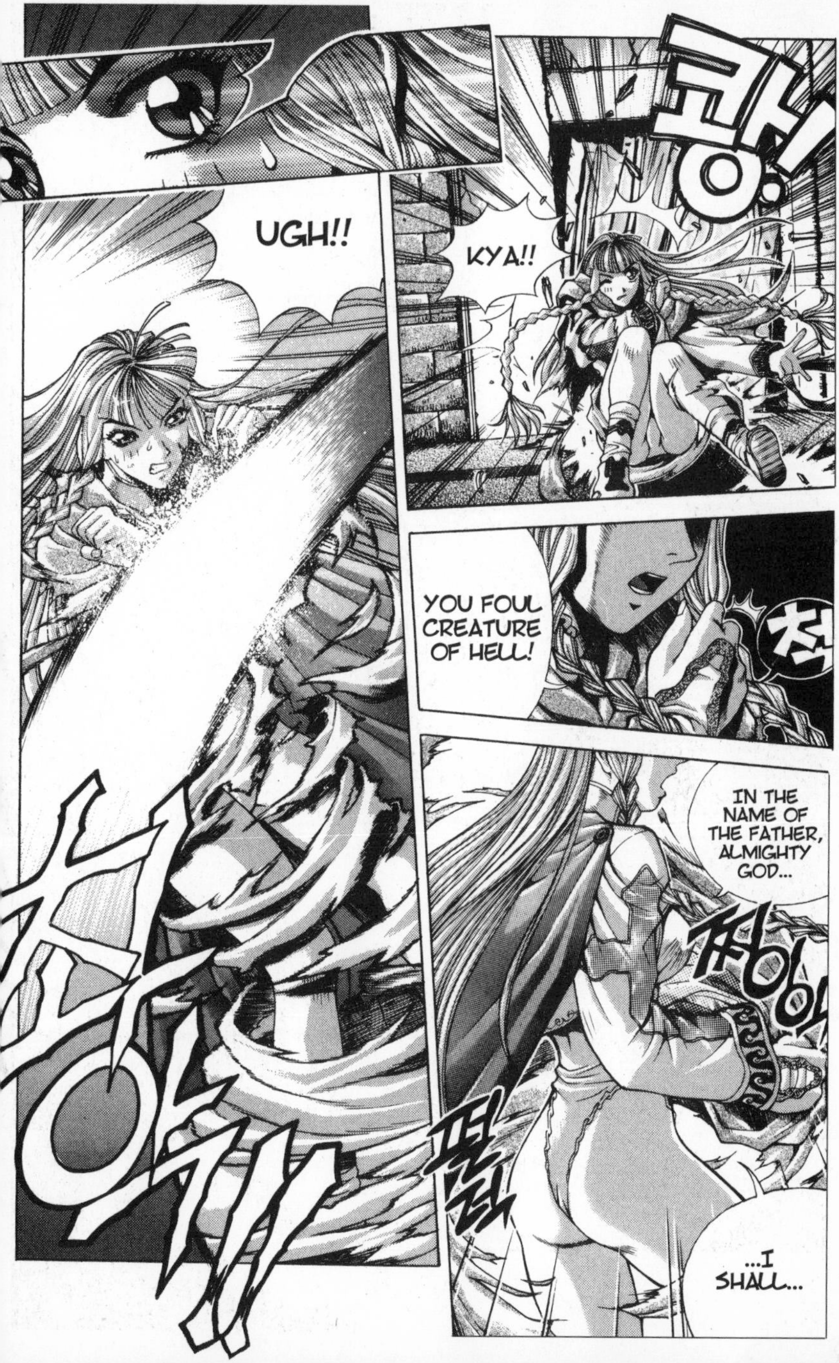
UGH!!
KYA!!
YOU FOUL CREATURE OF HELL!
IN THE NAME OF THE FATHER, ALMIGHTY GOD...
...I SHALL...

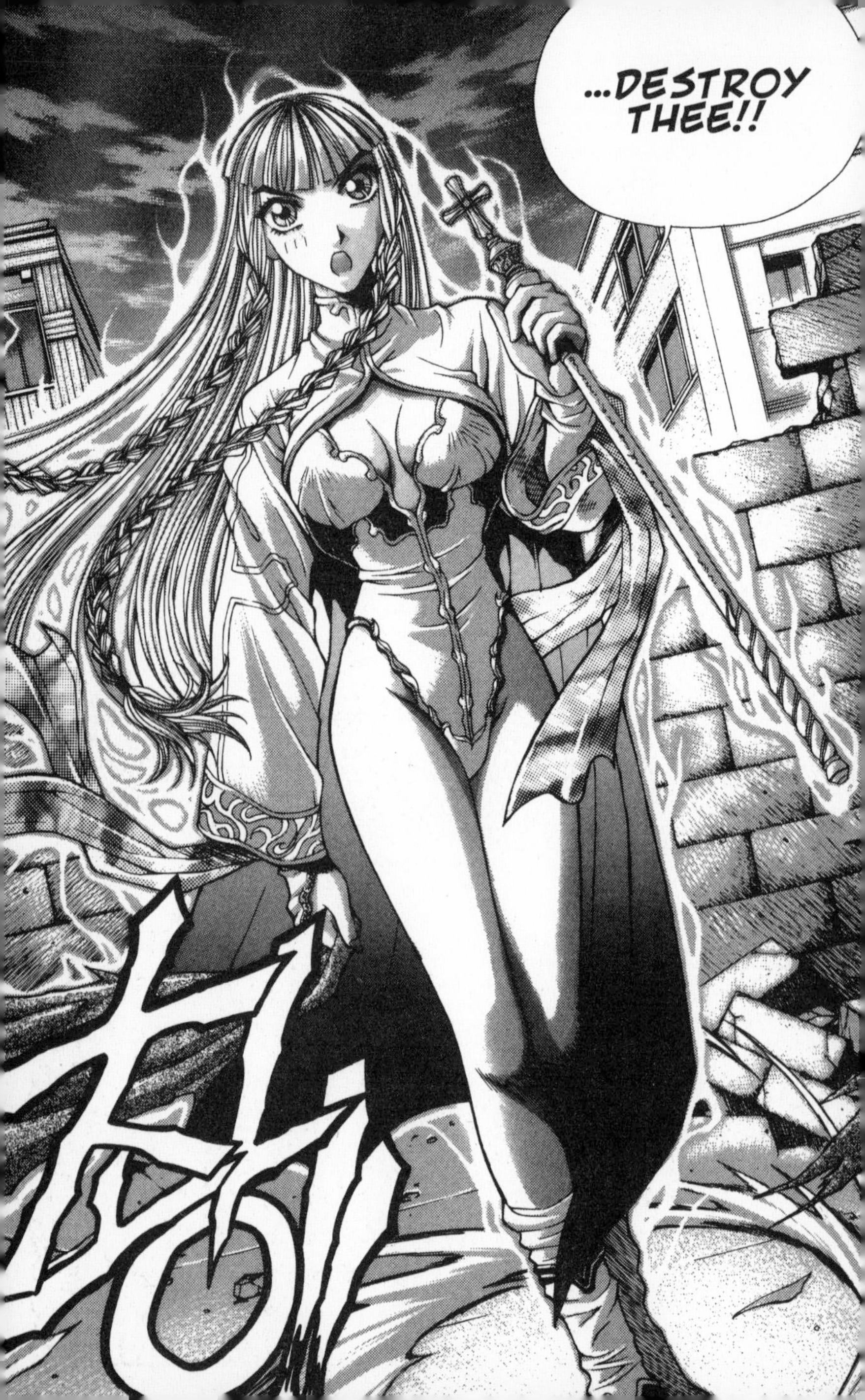
...DESTROY THEE!!

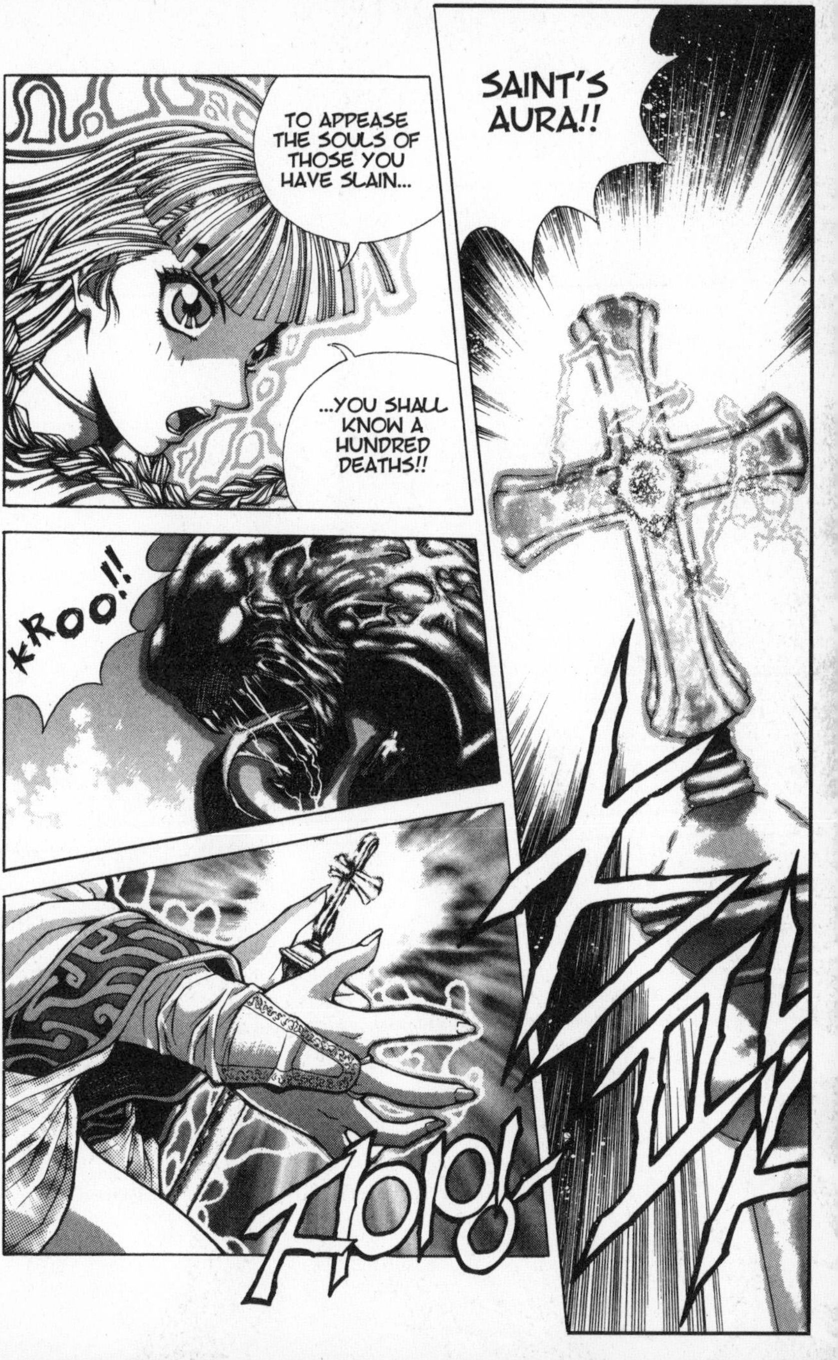
TO APPEASE THE SOULS OF THOSE YOU HAVE SLAIN...
...YOU SHALL KNOW A HUNDRED DEATHS!!
KROO!!
SAINT'S AURA!!

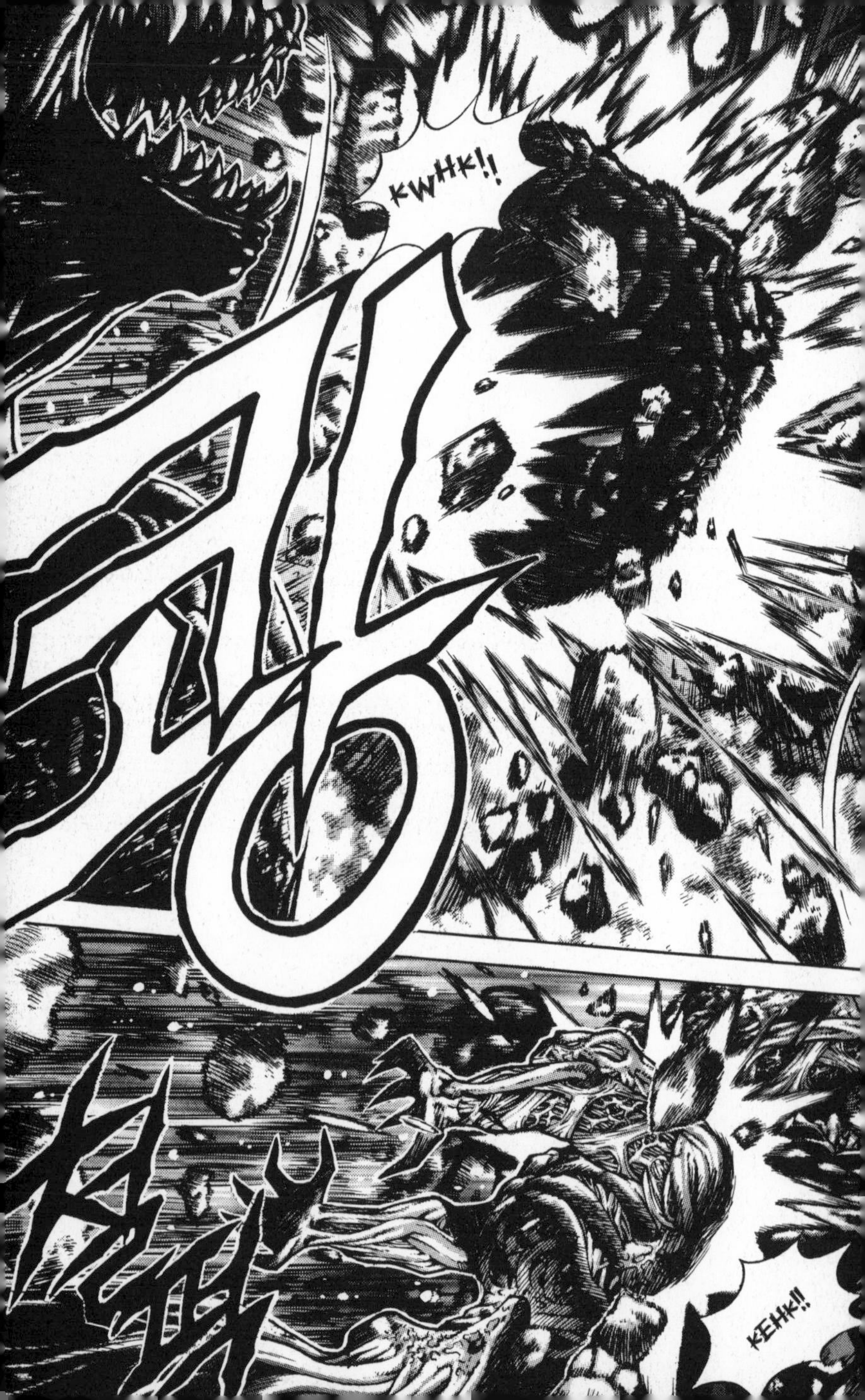
KWHK!!
KEHK!!

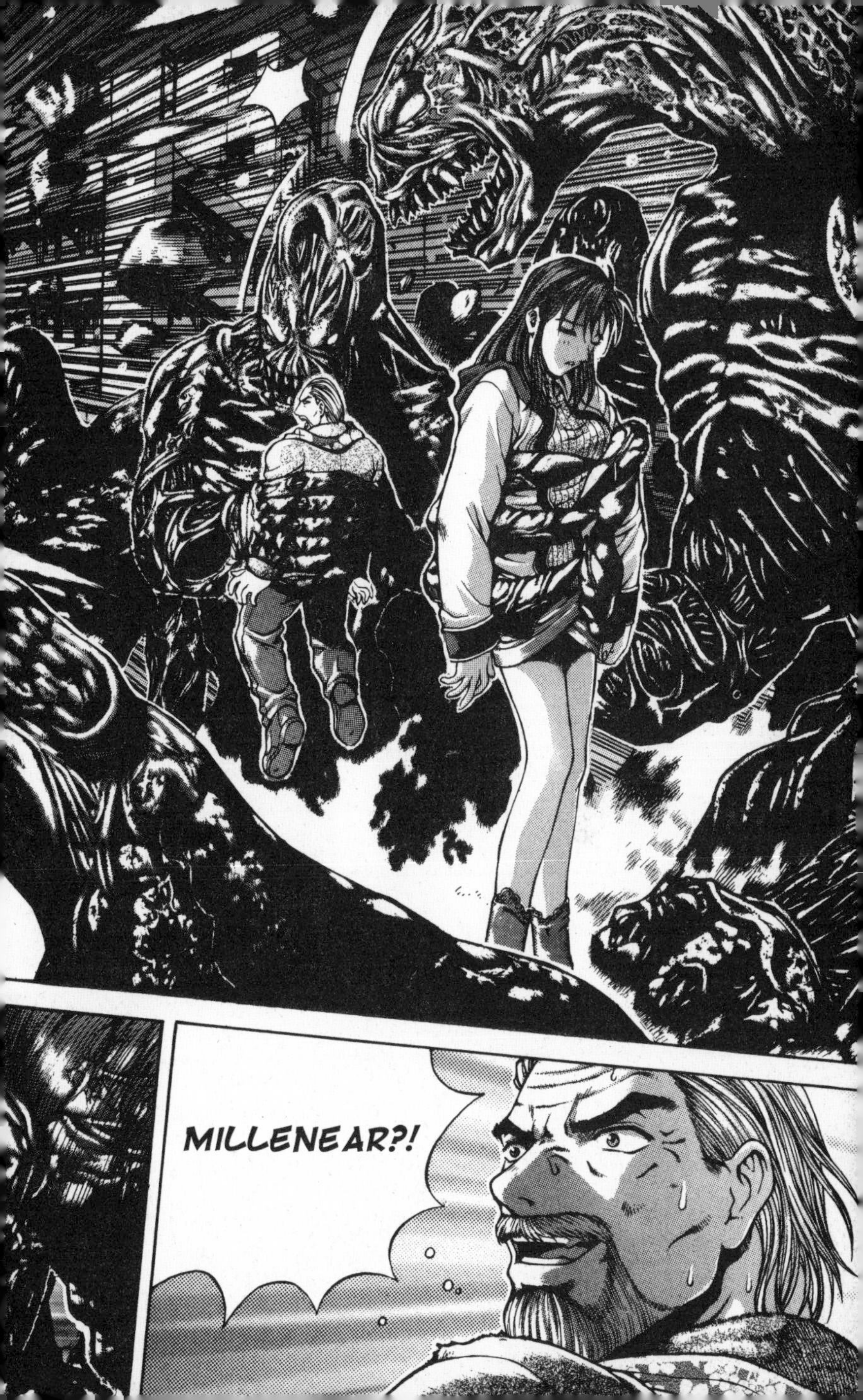
MILLENEAR?!

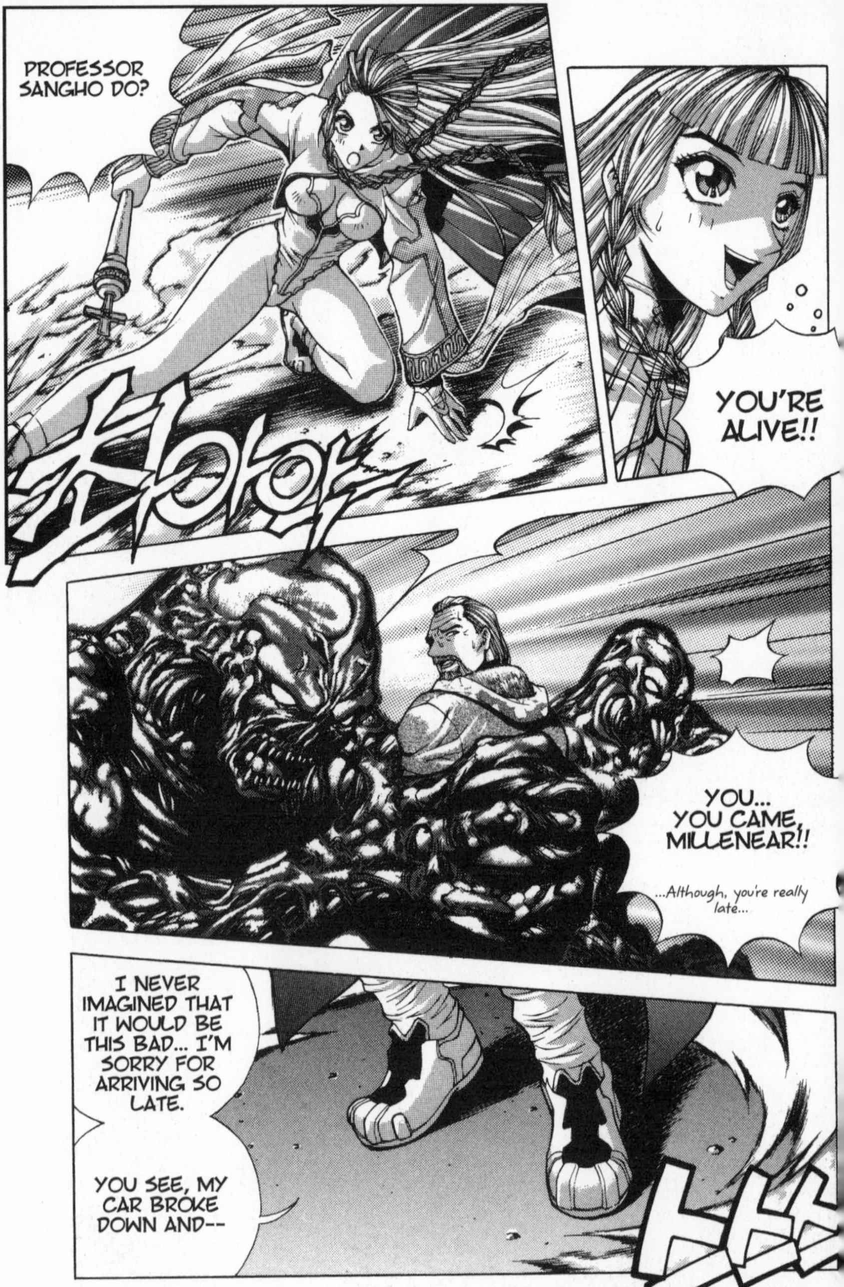
PROFESSOR SANGHO DO?
YOU'RE ALIVE!!
YOU... YOU CAME, MILLENEAR!!
...Although, you're really late...
I NEVER IMAGINED THAT IT WOULD BE THIS BAD... I'M SORRY FOR ARRIVING SO LATE.
YOU SEE, MY CAR BROKE DOWN AND--

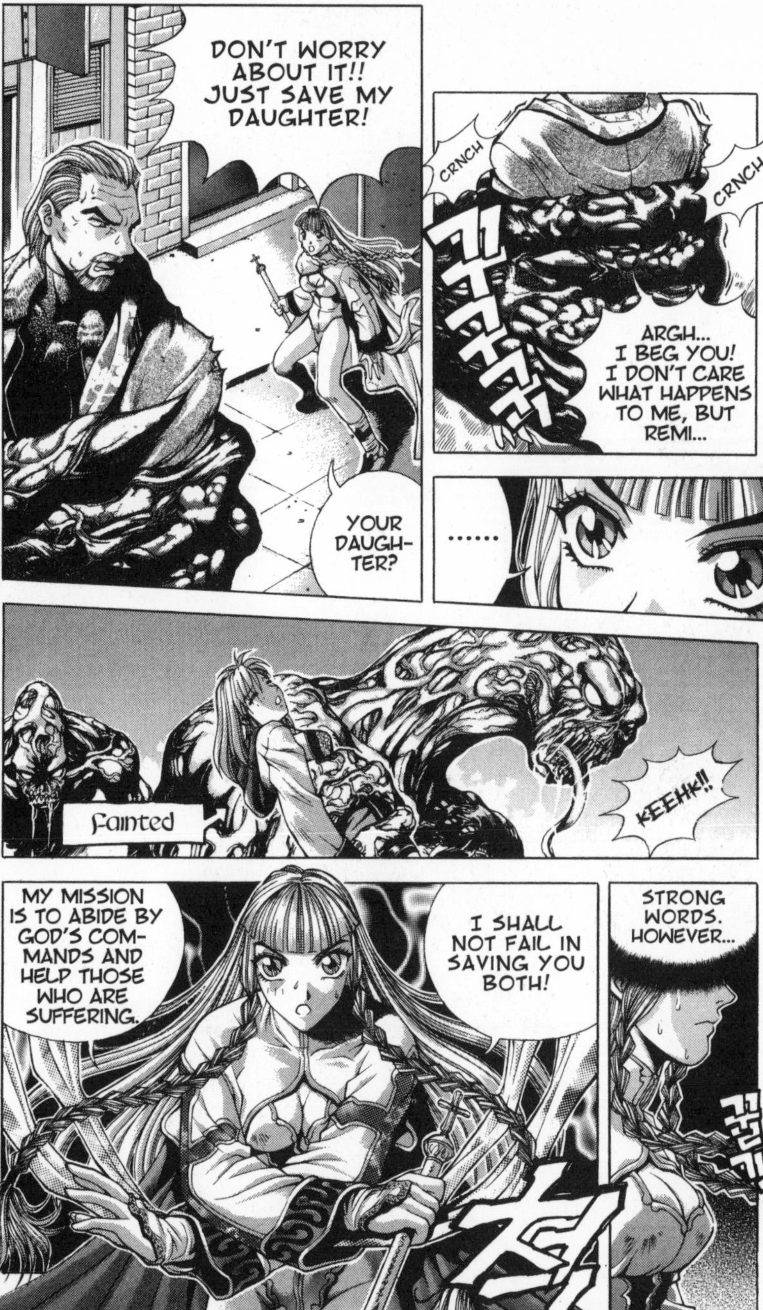
DON'T WORRY ABOUT IT!! JUST SAVE MY DAUGHTER!
YOUR DAUGHTER?
CRNCH
CRNCH
ARGH... I BEG YOU! I DON'T CARE WHAT HAPPENS TO ME, BUT REMI...
......
Fainted
KEEHK!!
MY MISSION IS TO ABIDE BY GOD'S COMMANDS AND HELP THOSE WHO ARE SUFFERING.
I SHALL NOT FAIL IN SAVING YOU BOTH!
STRONG WORDS. HOWEVER...
GULP!!

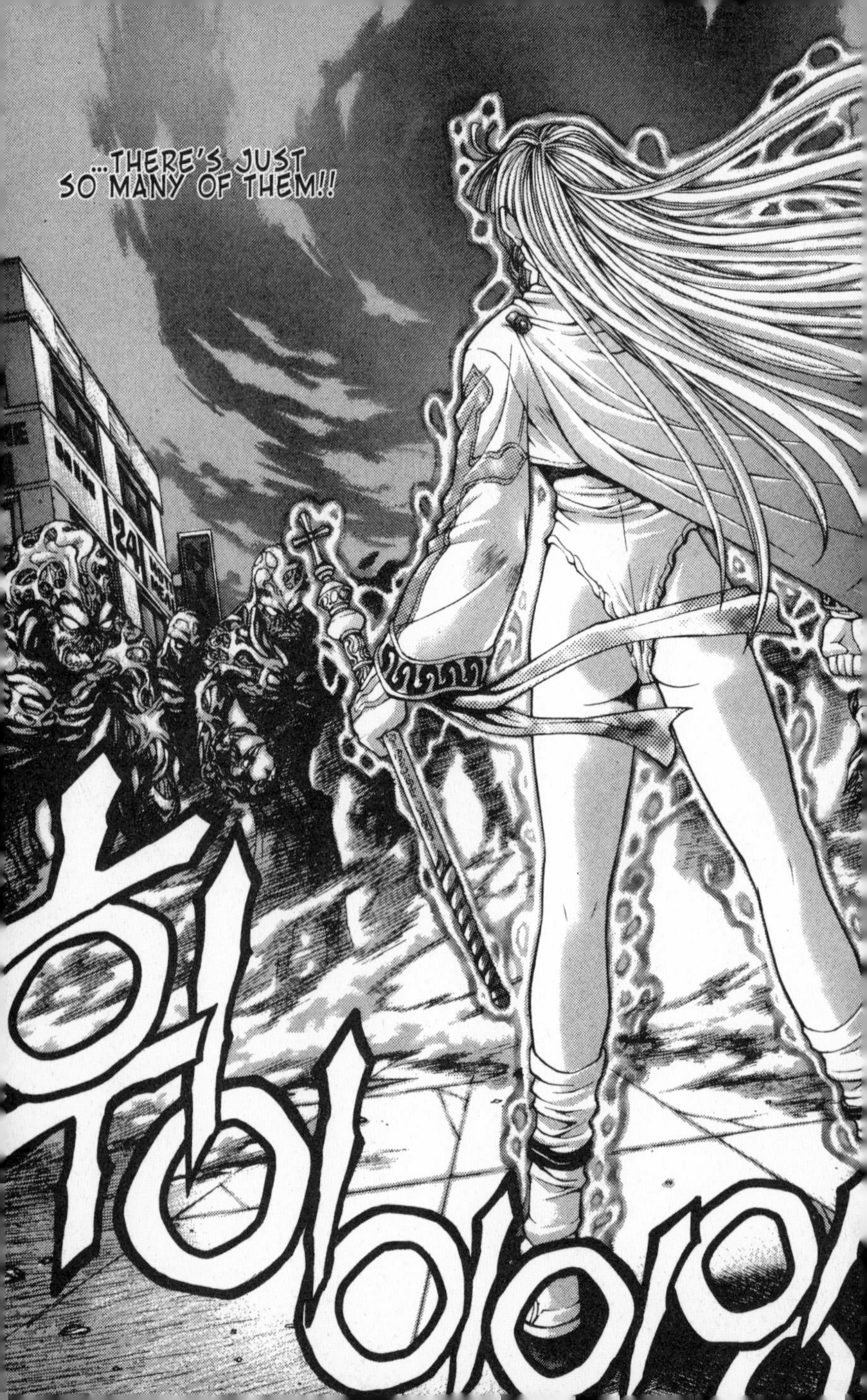
...THERE'S JUST SO MANY OF THEM!!

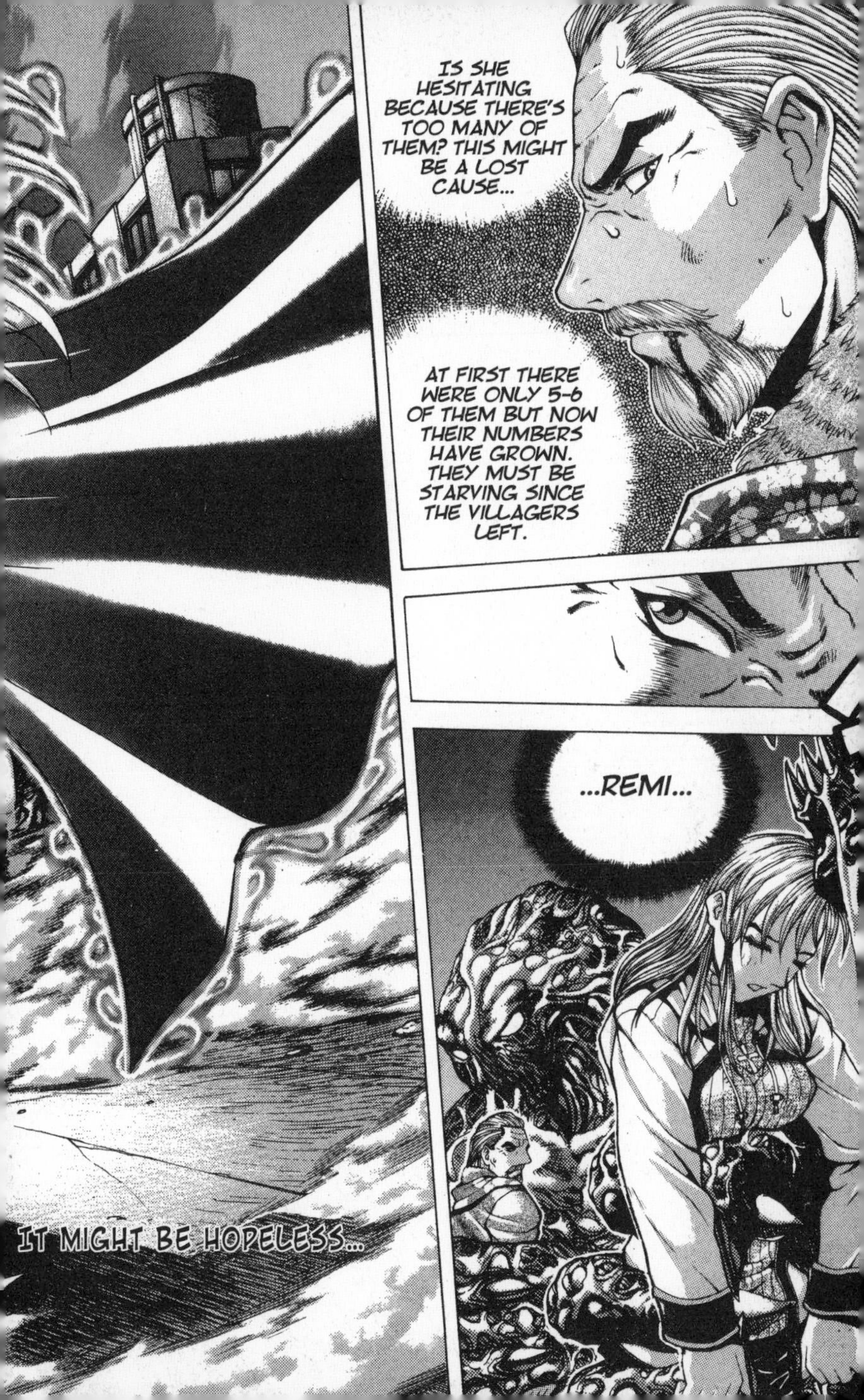
IT MIGHT BE HOPELESS...
IS SHE HESITATING BECAUSE THERE'S TOO MANY OF THEM? THIS MIGHT BE A LOST CAUSE...
AT FIRST THERE WERE ONLY 5-6 OF THEM BUT NOW THEIR NUMBERS HAVE GROWN. THEY MUST BE STARVING SINCE THE VILLAGERS LEFT.
...REMI...

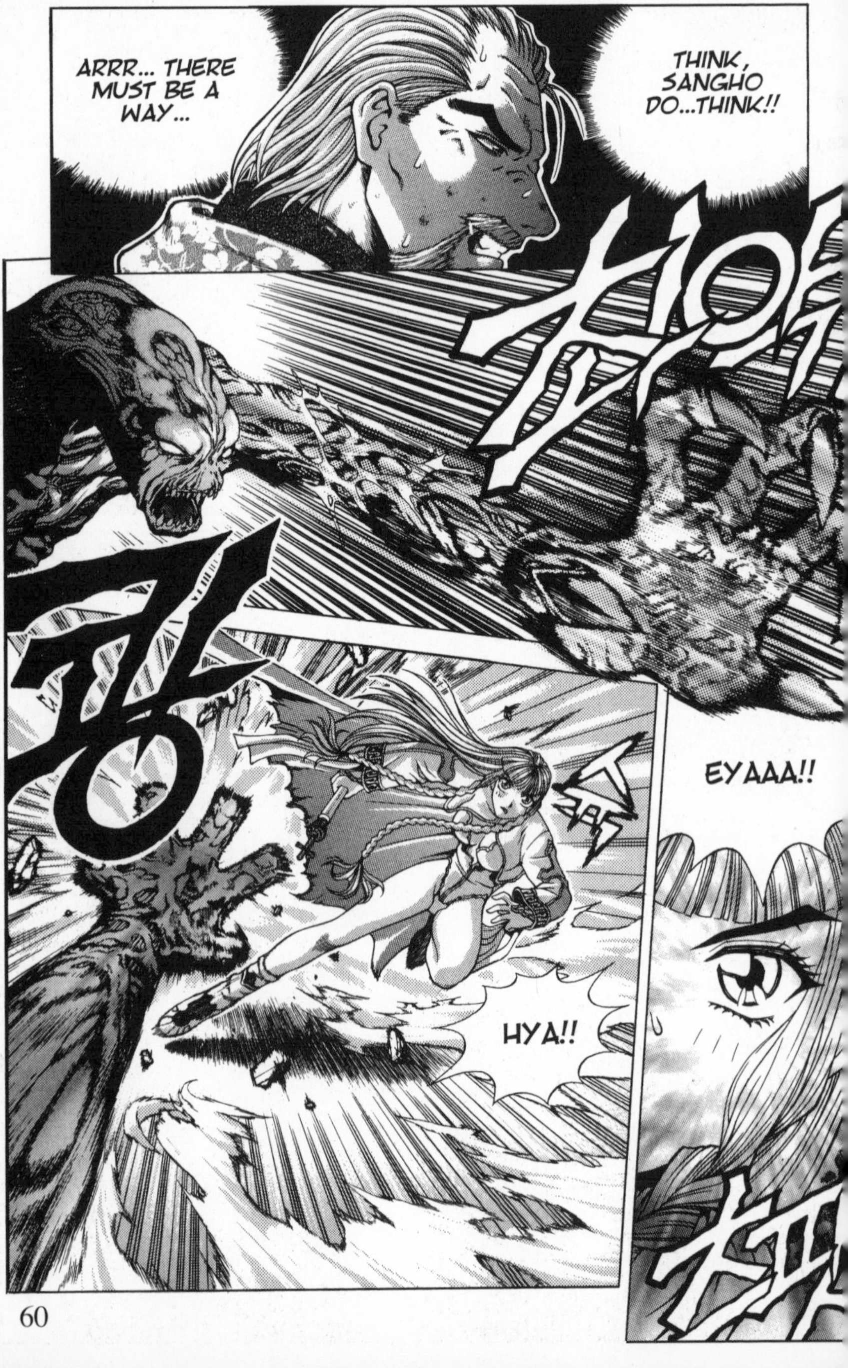
ARRR... THERE MUST BE A WAY...
THINK, SANGHO DO...THINK!!
EYAAA!!
HYA!!

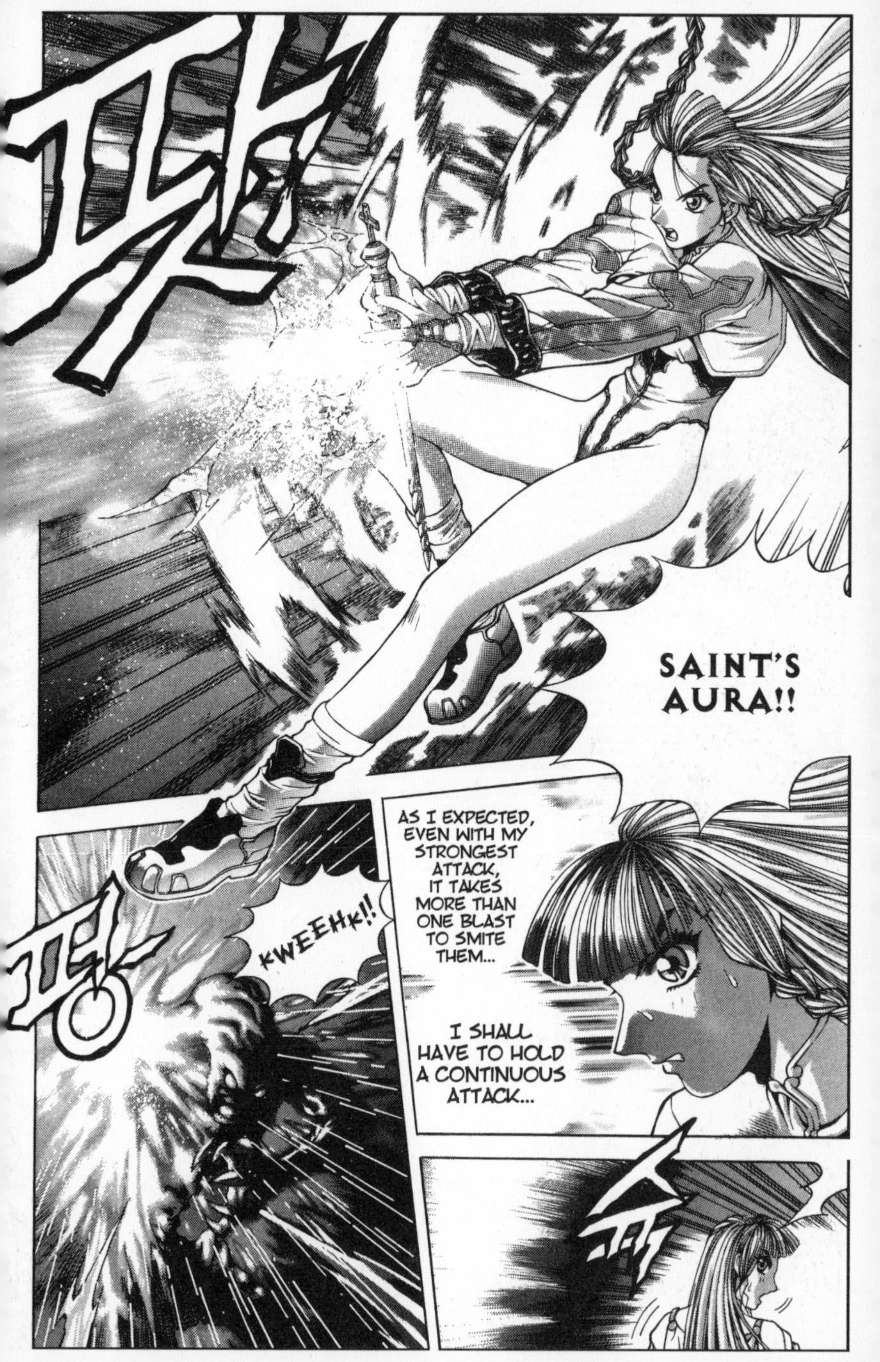
SAINT'S AURA!!
KWEEHK!!
AS I EXPECTED, EVEN WITH MY STRONGEST ATTACK, IT TAKES MORE THAN ONE BLAST TO SMITE THEM...
I SHALL HAVE TO HOLD A CONTINUOUS ATTACK...

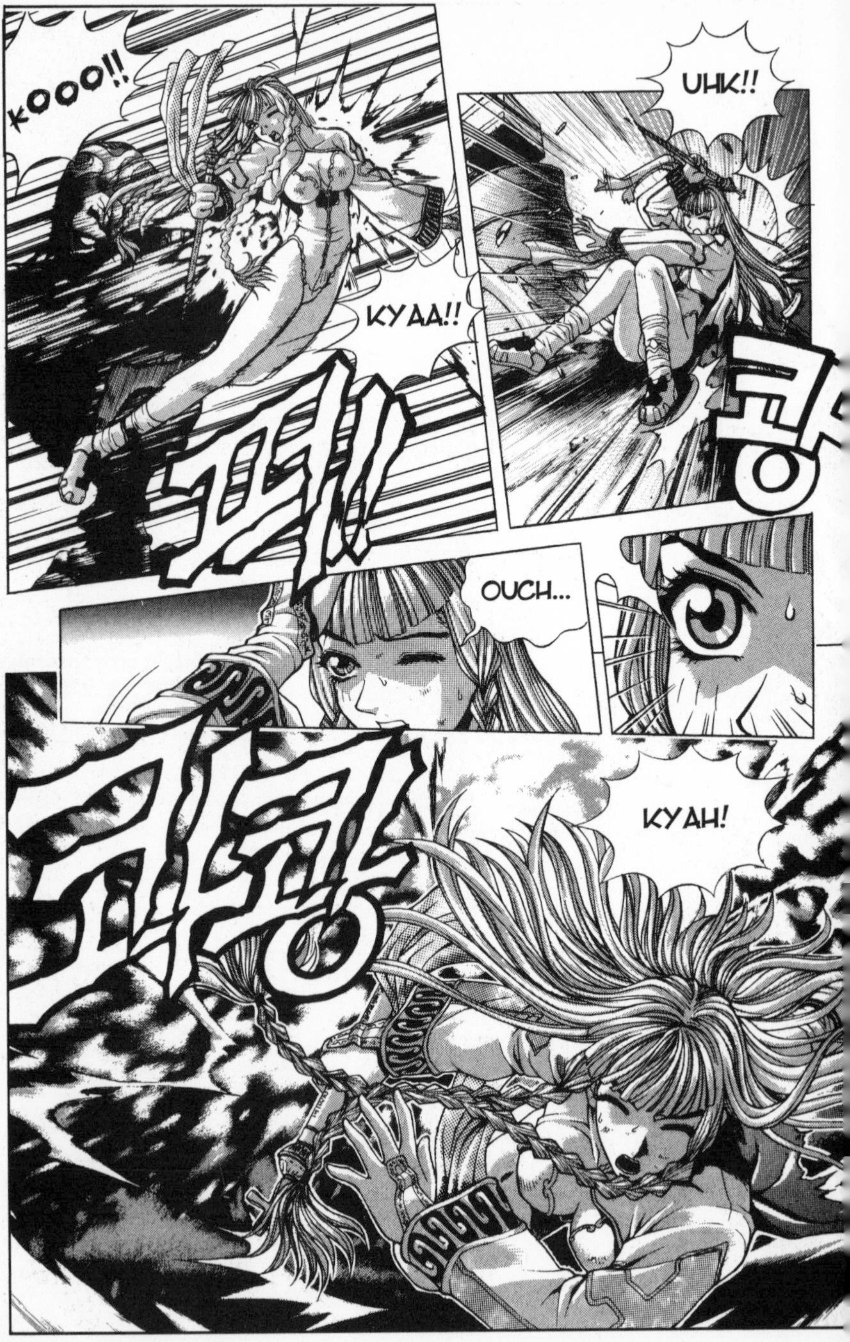
KOOO!!
KYAA!!
UHK!!
OUCH...
KYAH!

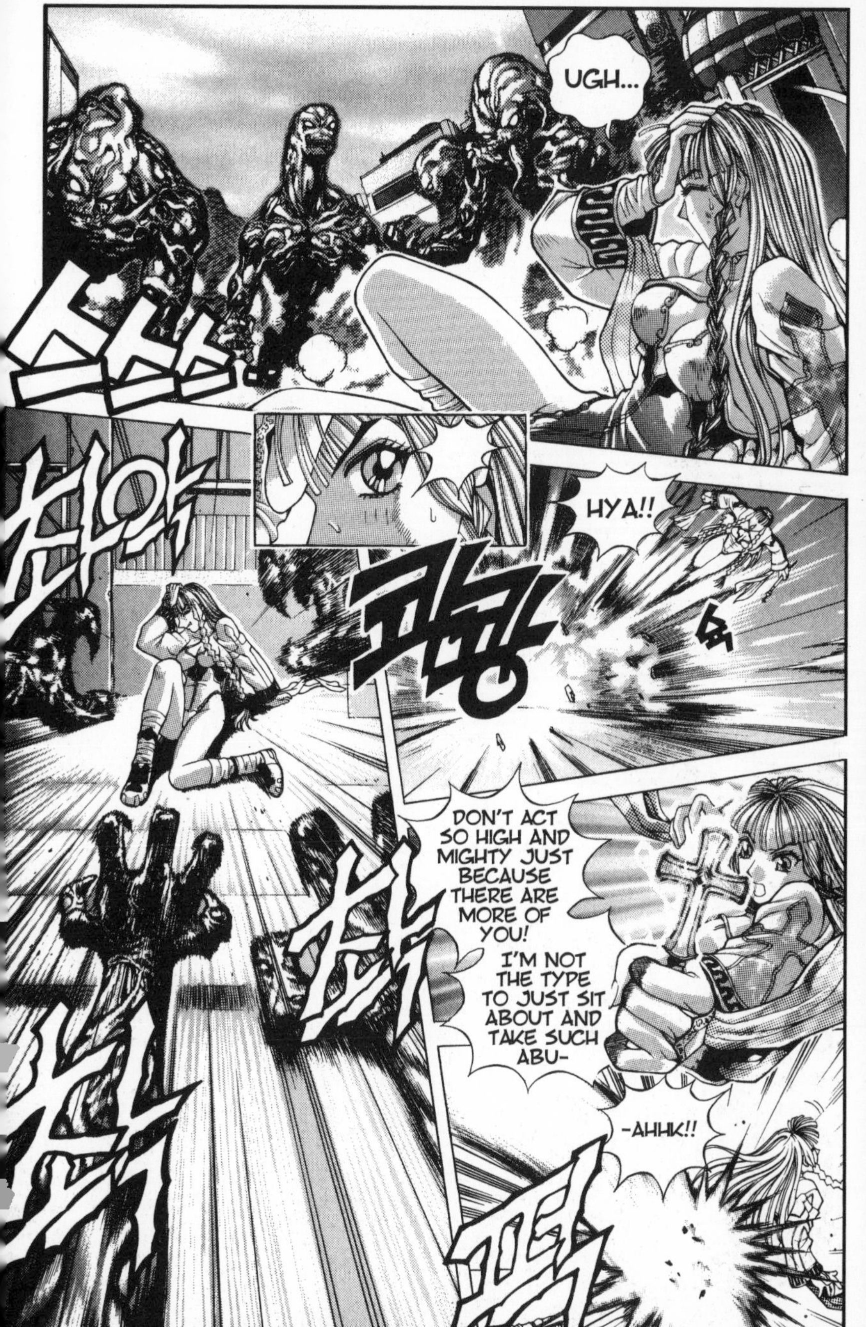
UGH...
HYA!!
DON'T ACT SO HIGH AND MIGHTY JUST BECAUSE THERE ARE MORE OF YOU!
I'M NOT THE TYPE TO JUST SIT ABOUT AND TAKE SUCH ABU-
-AHHK!!

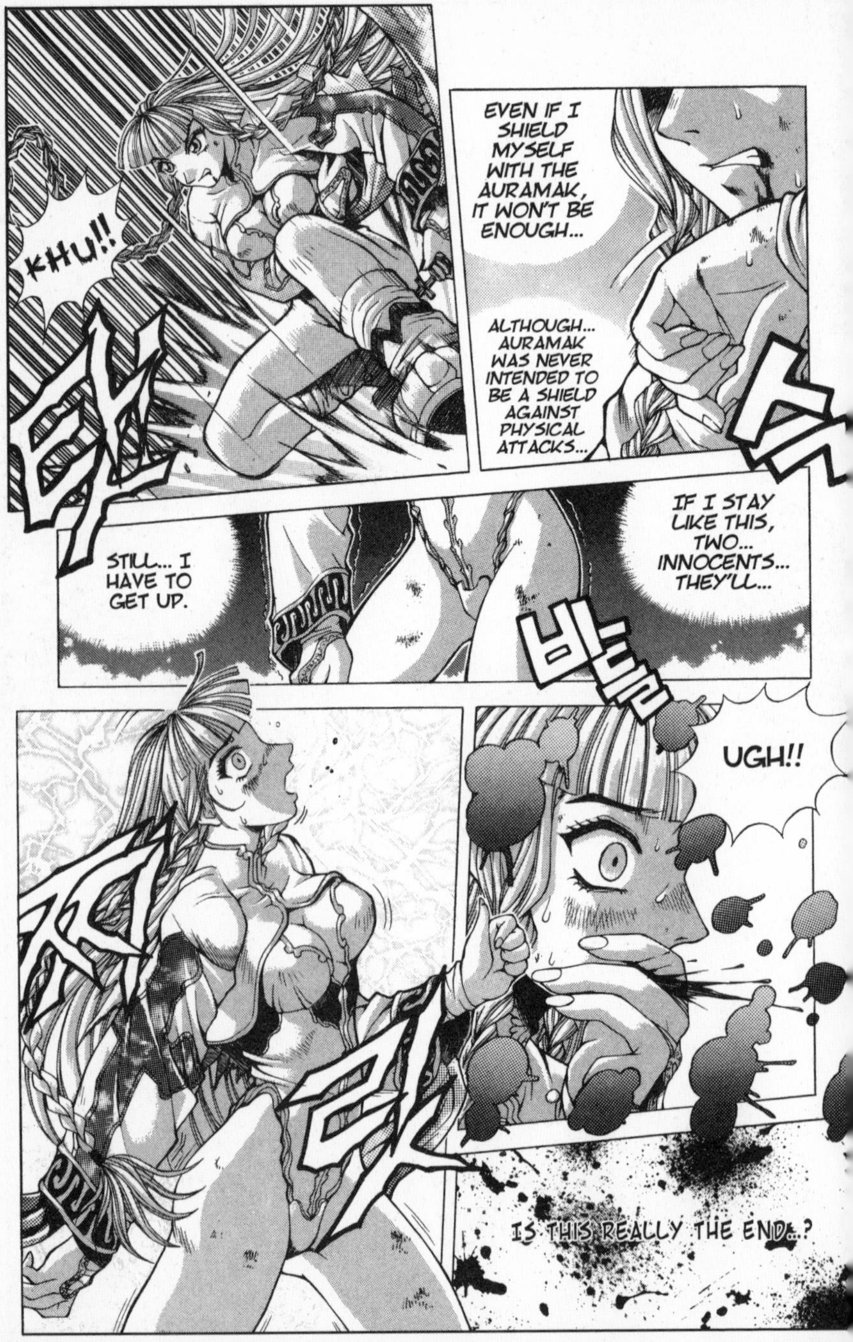
KHU!!
EVEN IF I SHIELD MYSELF WITH THE AURAMAK, IT WON'T BE ENOUGH...
ALTHOUGH... AURAMAK WAS NEVER INTENDED TO BE A SHIELD AGAINST PHYSICAL ATTACKS...
STILL... I HAVE TO GET UP.
IF I STAY LIKE THIS, TWO... INNOCENTS... THEY'LL...
UGH!!
IS THIS REALLY THE END..?

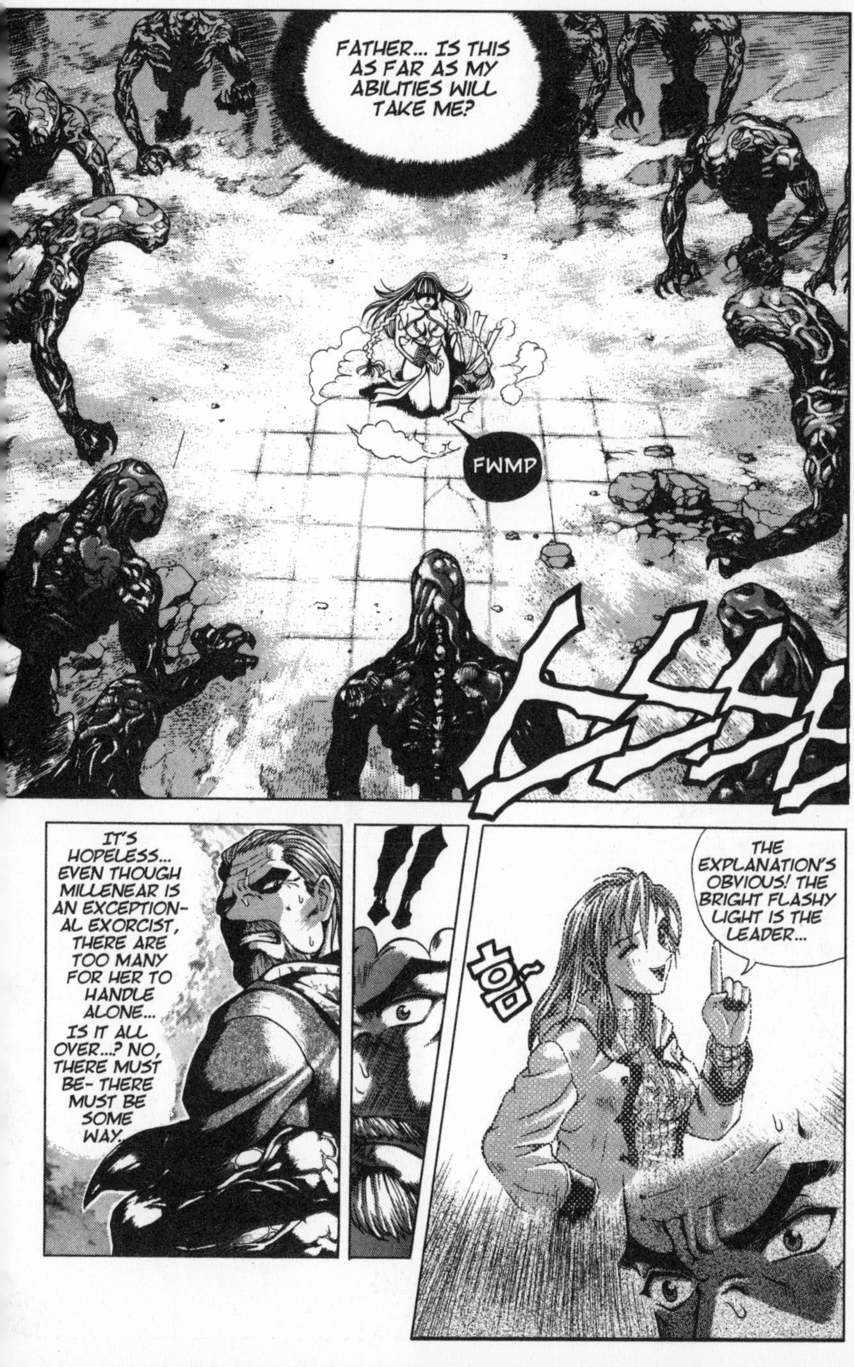
FATHER... IS THIS AS FAR AS MY ABILITIES WILL TAKE ME?
FWMP
IT'S HOPELESS... EVEN THOUGH MILLENEAR IS AN EXCEPTIONAL EXORCIST, THERE ARE TOO MANY FOR HER TO HANDLE ALONE... IS IT ALL OVER...? NO, THERE MUST BE- THERE MUST BE SOME WAY.
!!
THE EXPLANATION'S OBVIOUS! THE BRIGHT FLASHY LIGHT IS THE LEADER...

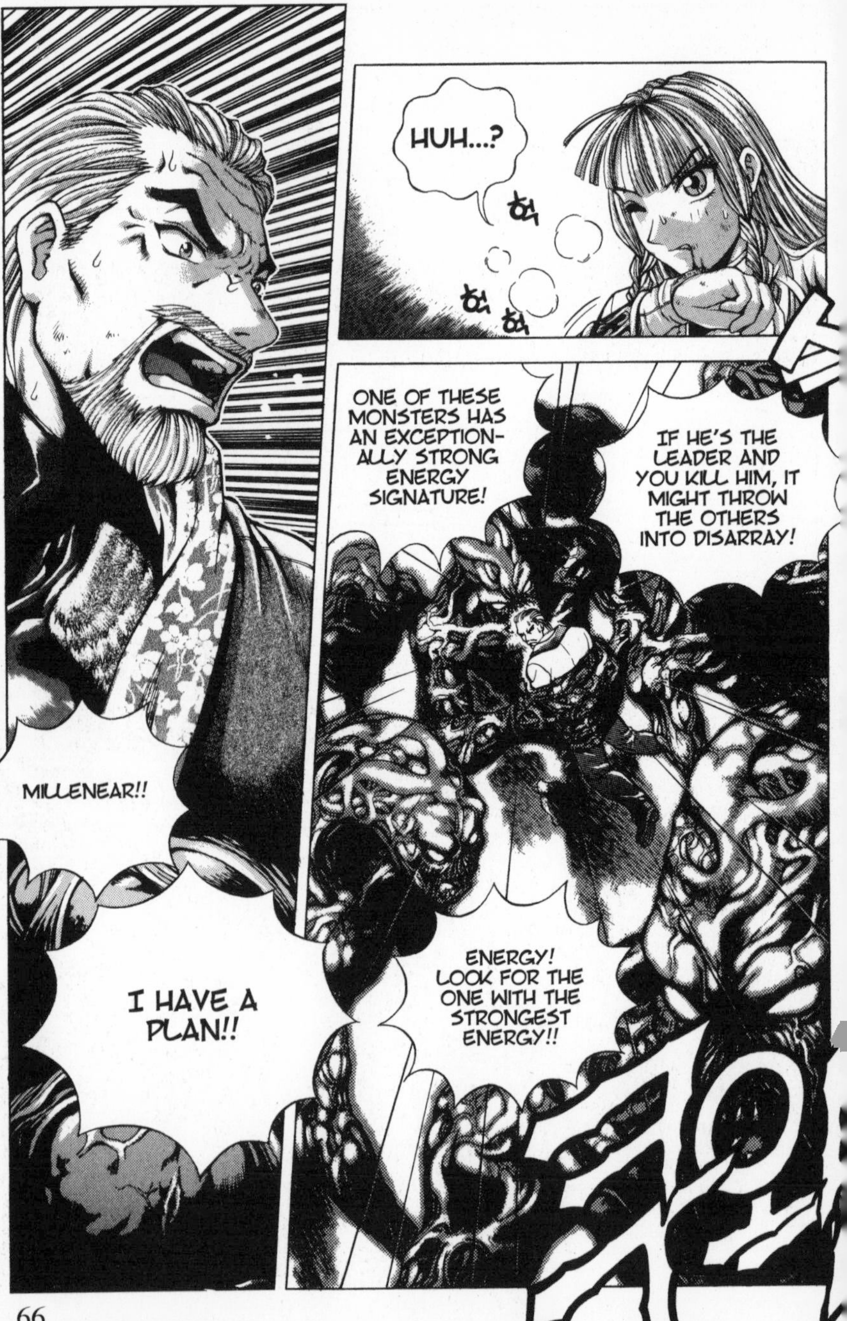
MILLENEAR!!
I HAVE A PLAN!!
HUH...?
헉
헉
헉
ONE OF THESE MONSTERS HAS AN EXCEPTION-ALLY STRONG ENERGY SIGNATURE!
IF HE'S THE LEADER AND YOU KILL HIM, IT MIGHT THROW THE OTHERS INTO DISARRAY!
ENERGY! LOOK FOR THE ONE WITH THE STRONGEST ENERGY!!

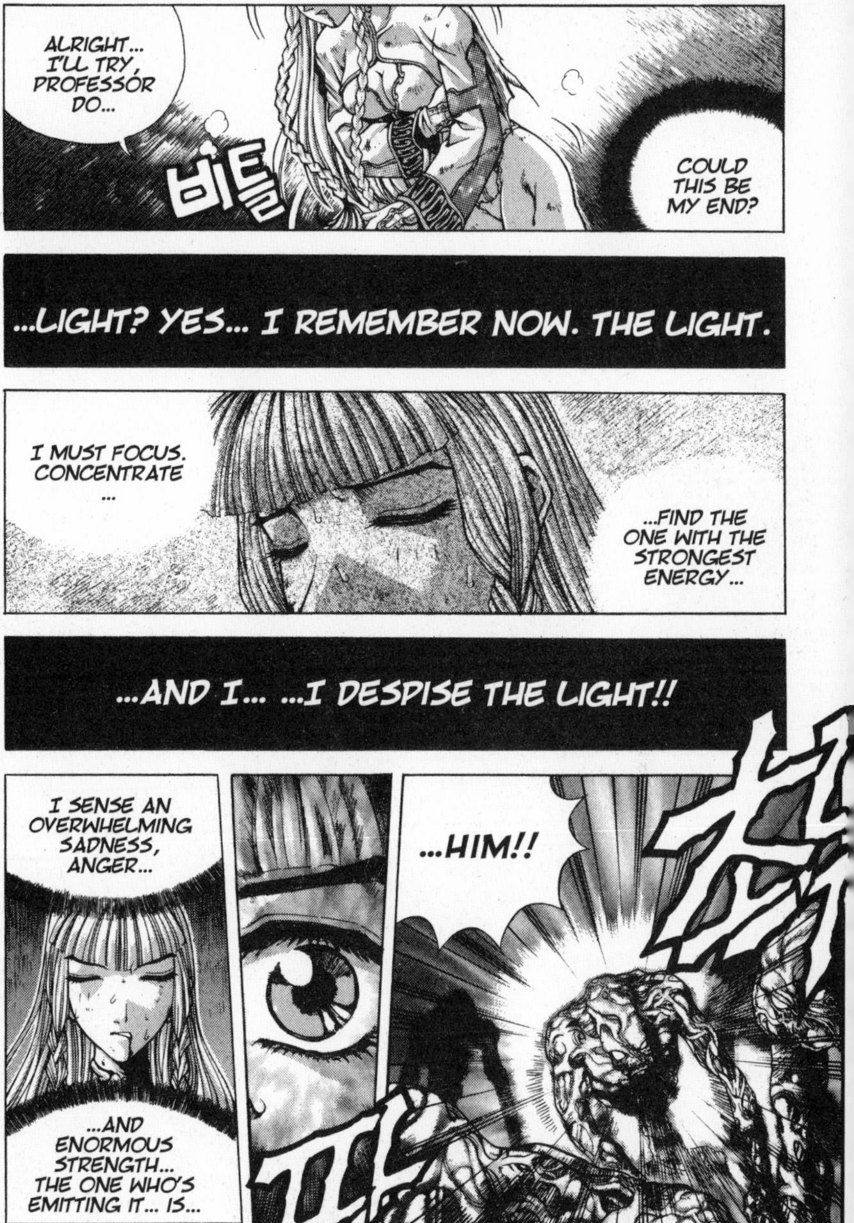
ALRIGHT... I'LL TRY, PROFESSOR DO...
비틀
COULD THIS BE MY END?
...LIGHT? YES... I REMEMBER NOW. THE LIGHT.
I MUST FOCUS. CONCENTRATE ...
...FIND THE ONE WITH THE STRONGEST ENERGY...
...AND I... ...I DESPISE THE LIGHT!!
I SENSE AN OVERWHELMING SADNESS, ANGER...
...AND ENORMOUS STRENGTH... THE ONE WHO'S EMITTING IT... IS...
...HIM!!

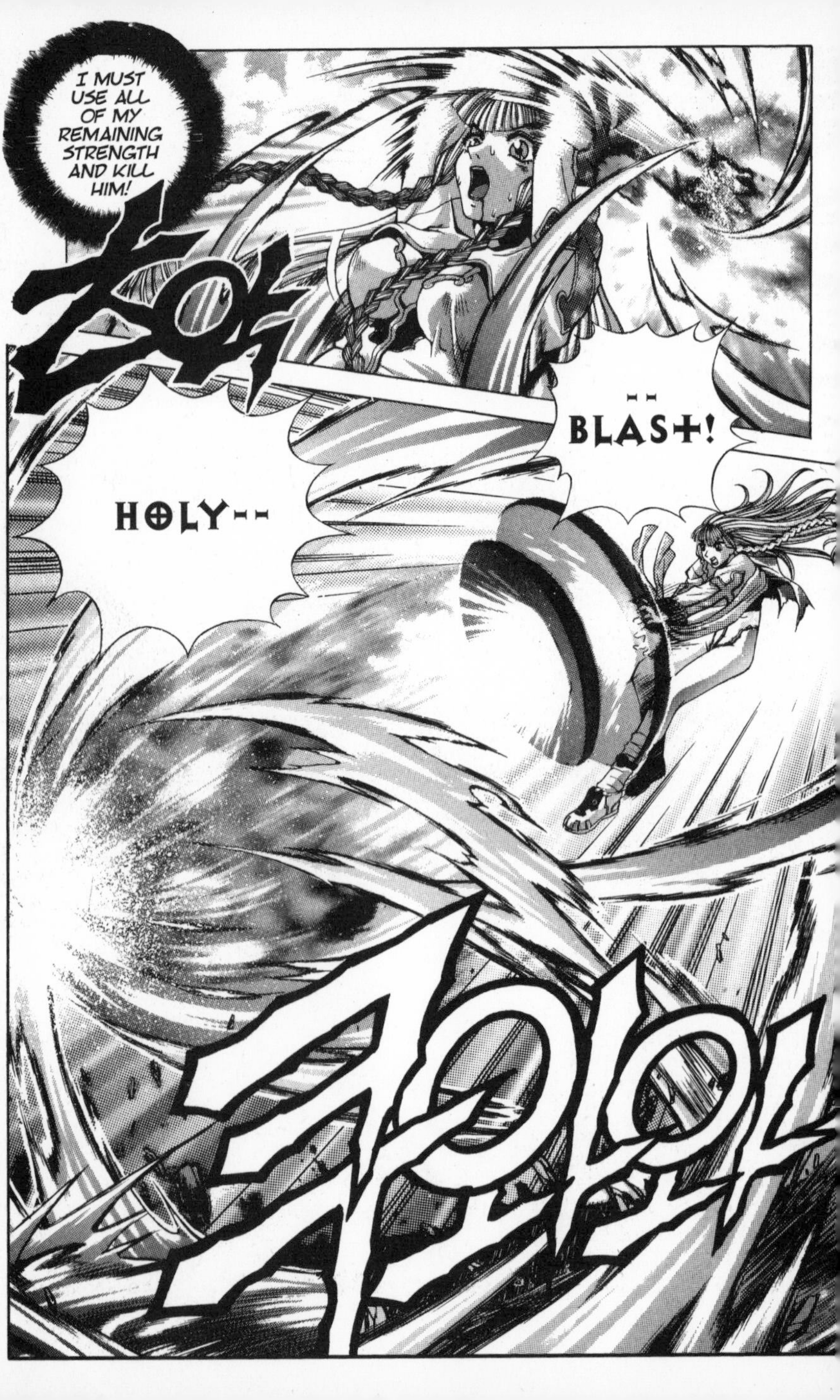
I MUST USE ALL OF MY REMAINING STRENGTH AND KILL HIM!
HOLY--
--BLAST!

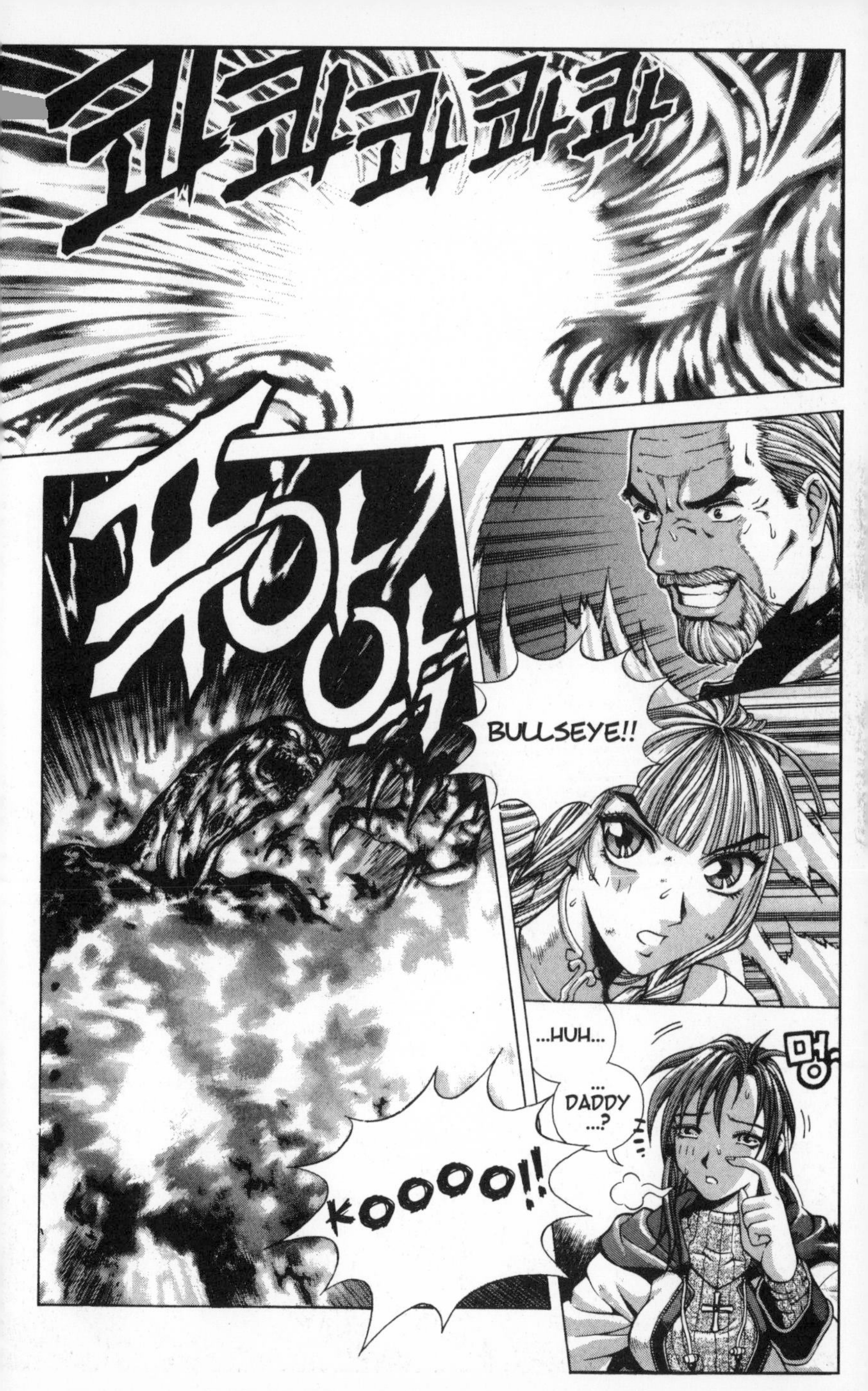
KOOOOO!!
BULLSEYE!!
...HUH...
... DADDY ...?
멍

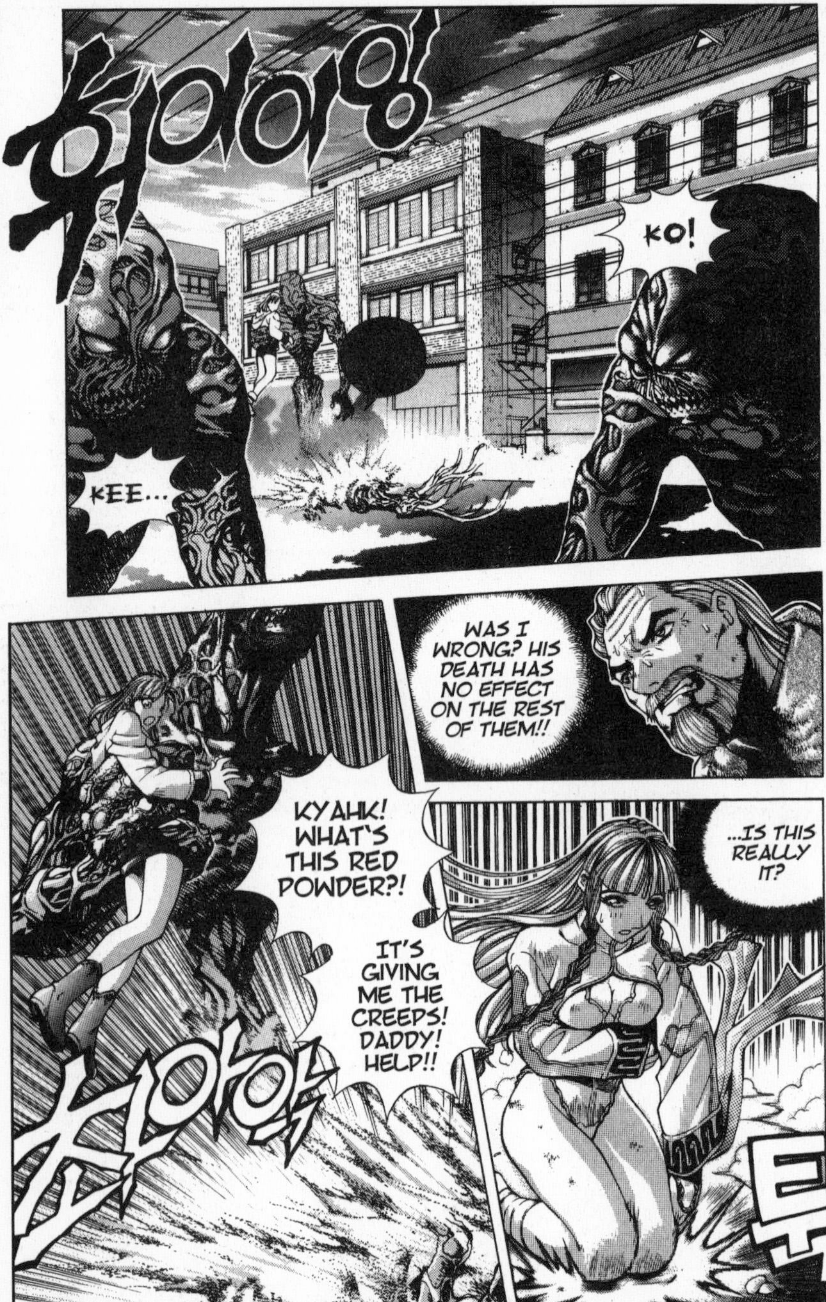
KEE...
KO!
KYAHK! WHAT'S THIS RED POWDER?!
IT'S GIVING ME THE CREEPS! DADDY! HELP!!
WAS I WRONG? HIS DEATH HAS NO EFFECT ON THE REST OF THEM!!
...IS THIS REALLY IT?

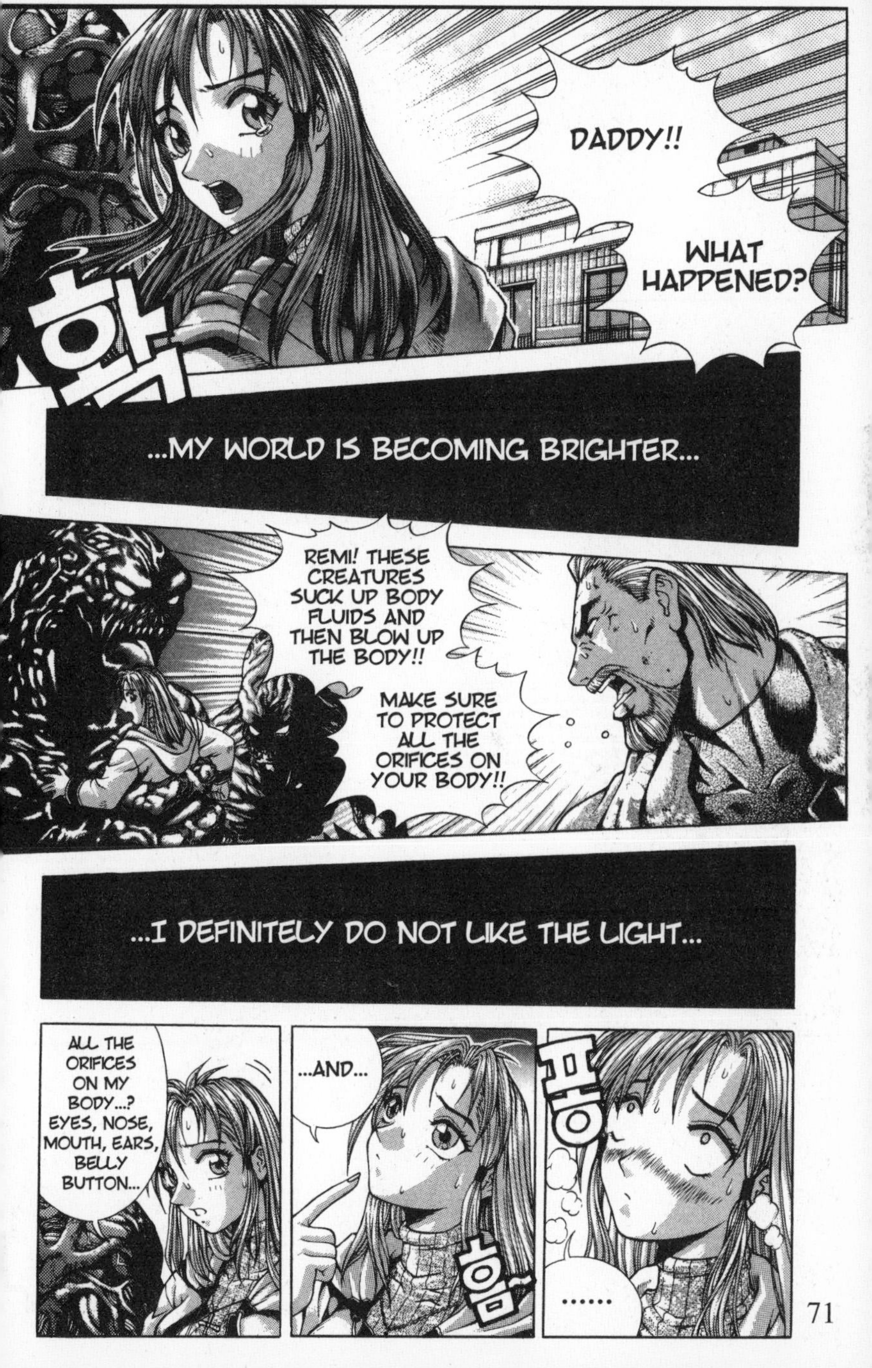
학
DADDY!!
WHAT HAPPENED?
...MY WORLD IS BECOMING BRIGHTER...
REMI! THESE CREATURES SUCK UP BODY FLUIDS AND THEN BLOW UP THE BODY!!
MAKE SURE TO PROTECT ALL THE ORIFICES ON YOUR BODY!!
...I DEFINITELY DO NOT LIKE THE LIGHT...
ALL THE ORIFICES ON MY BODY...? EYES, NOSE, MOUTH, EARS, BELLY BUTTON...
...AND...
흠
퐁
......

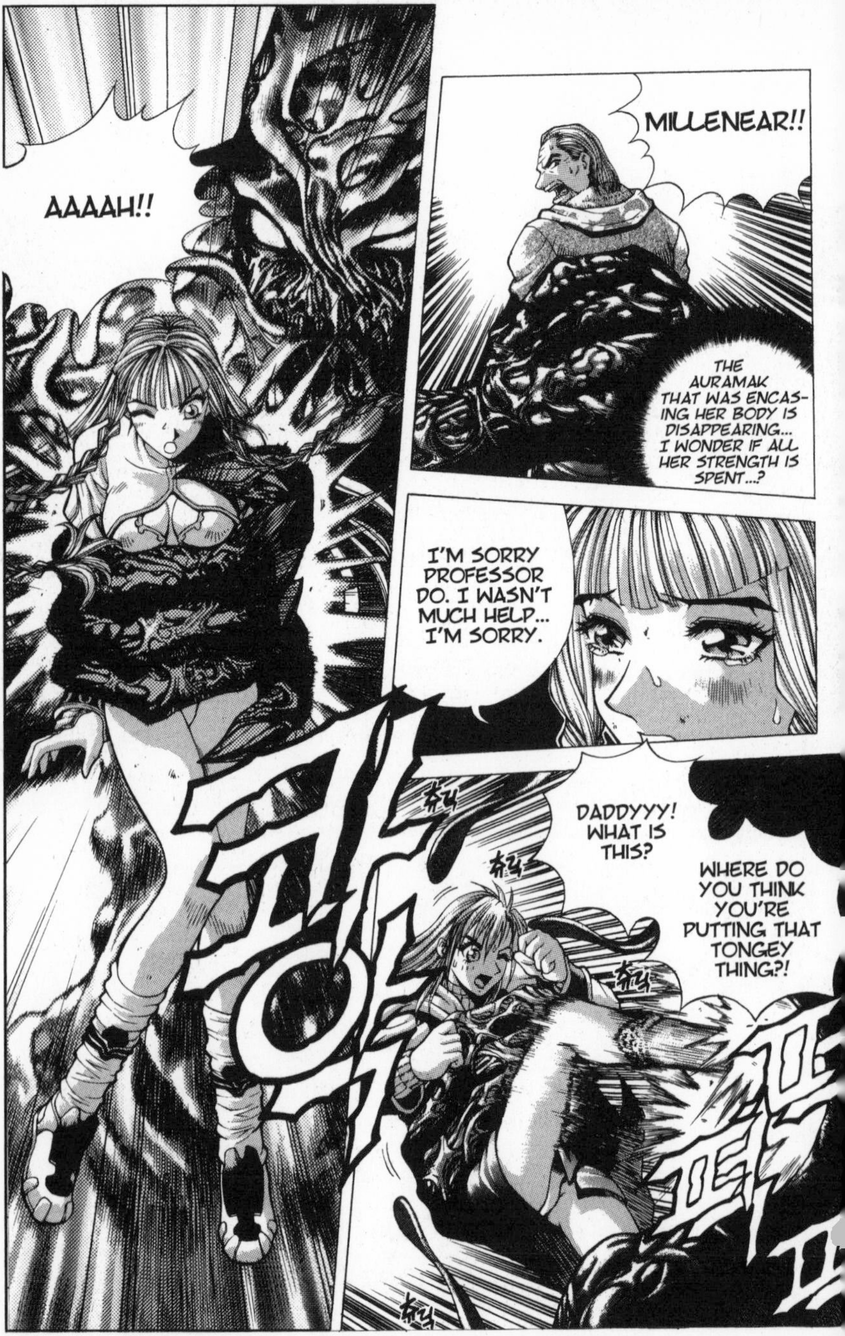
AAAAH!!
MILLENEAR!!
THE AURAMAK THAT WAS ENCASING HER BODY IS DISAPPEARING... I WONDER IF ALL HER STRENGTH IS SPENT...?
I'M SORRY PROFESSOR DO. I WASN'T MUCH HELP... I'M SORRY.
DADDYYY! WHAT IS THIS?
WHERE DO YOU THINK YOU'RE PUTTING THAT TONGEY THING?!

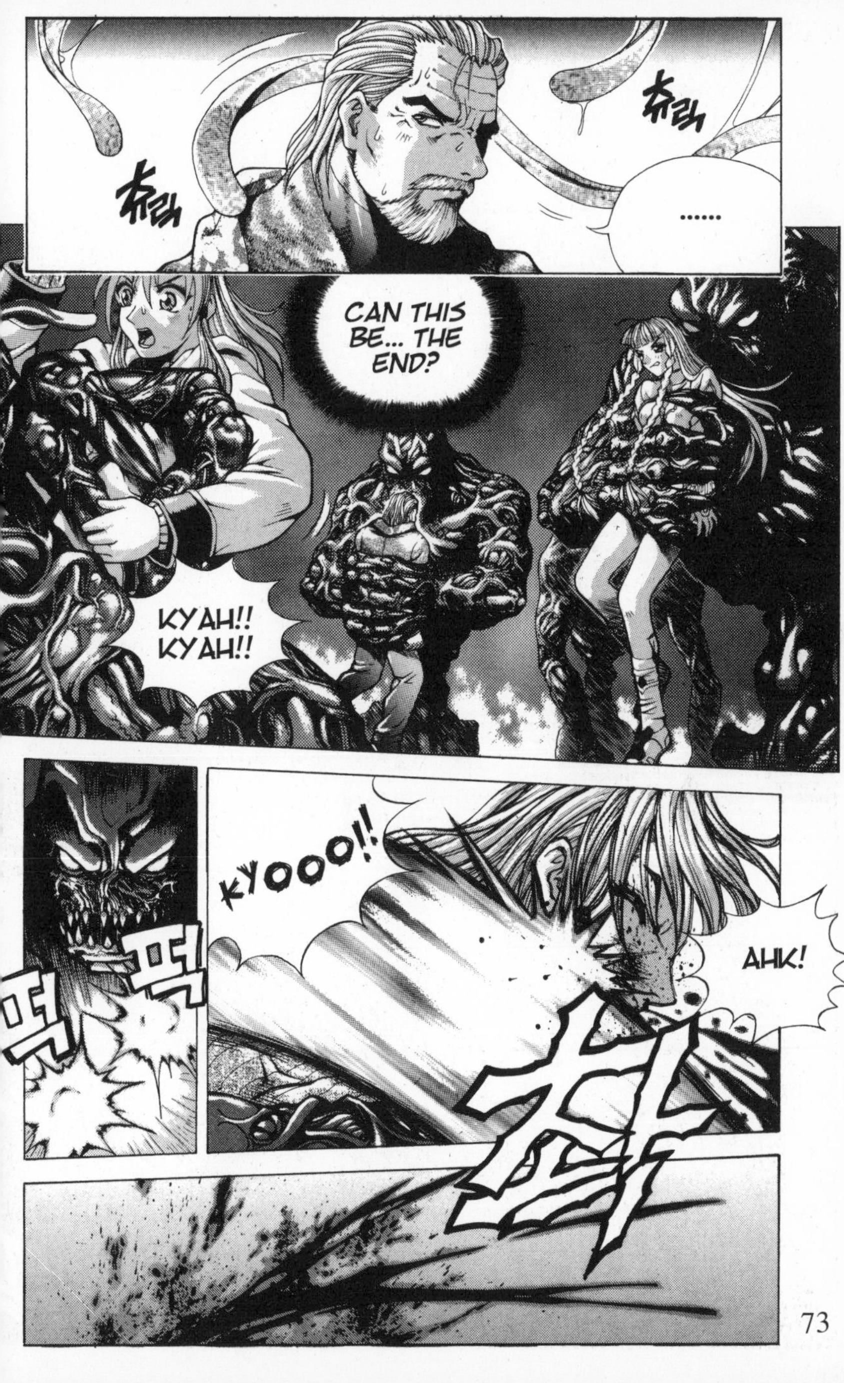
츄라
츄라
......
CAN THIS BE... THE END?
KYAH!! KYAH!!
퍽
퍽
KYOOO!!
AHK!

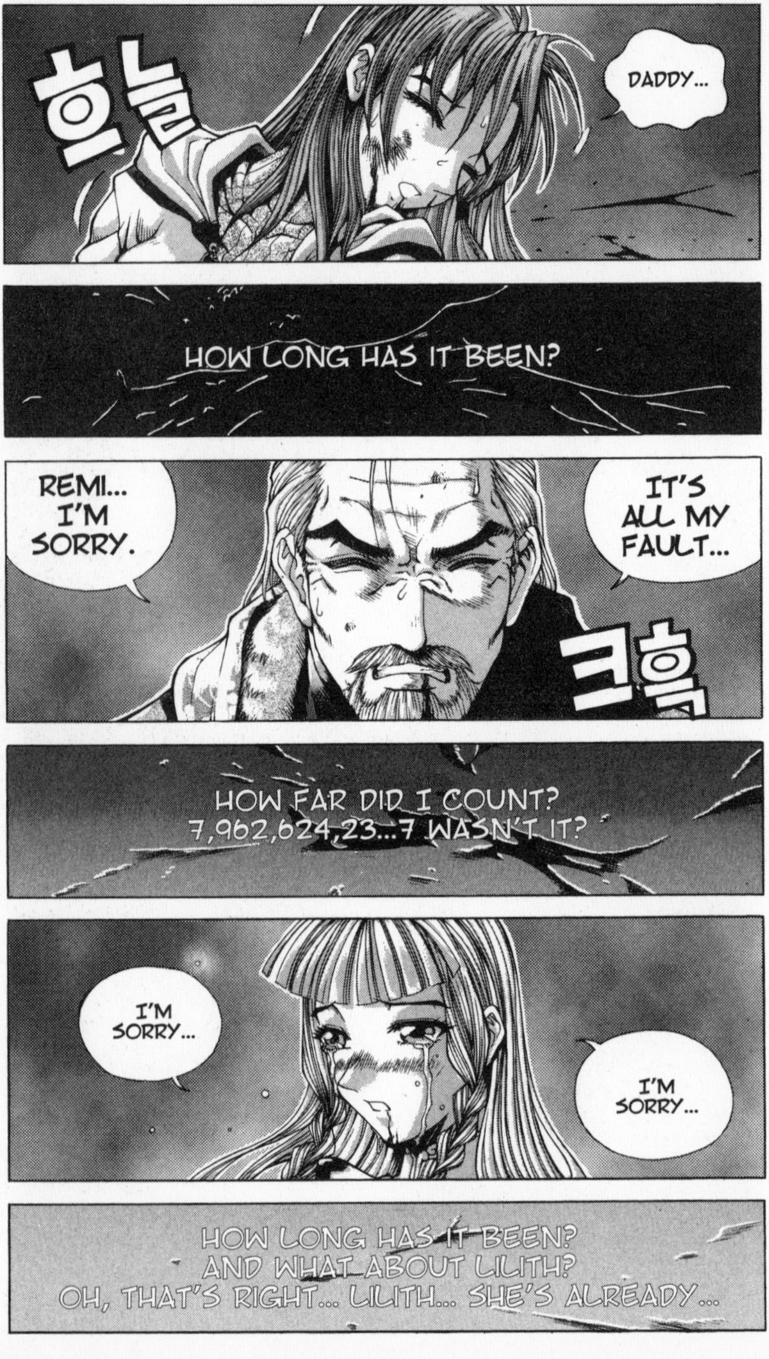
흐늘
DADDY...
HOW LONG HAS IT BEEN?
REMI... I'M SORRY.
IT'S ALL MY FAULT...
크흑
HOW FAR DID I COUNT?
7,962,624,23...7 WASN'T IT?
I'M SORRY...
I'M SORRY...
HOW LONG HAS IT BEEN?
AND WHAT ABOUT LILITH?
OH, THAT'S RIGHT... LILITH... SHE'S ALREADY...

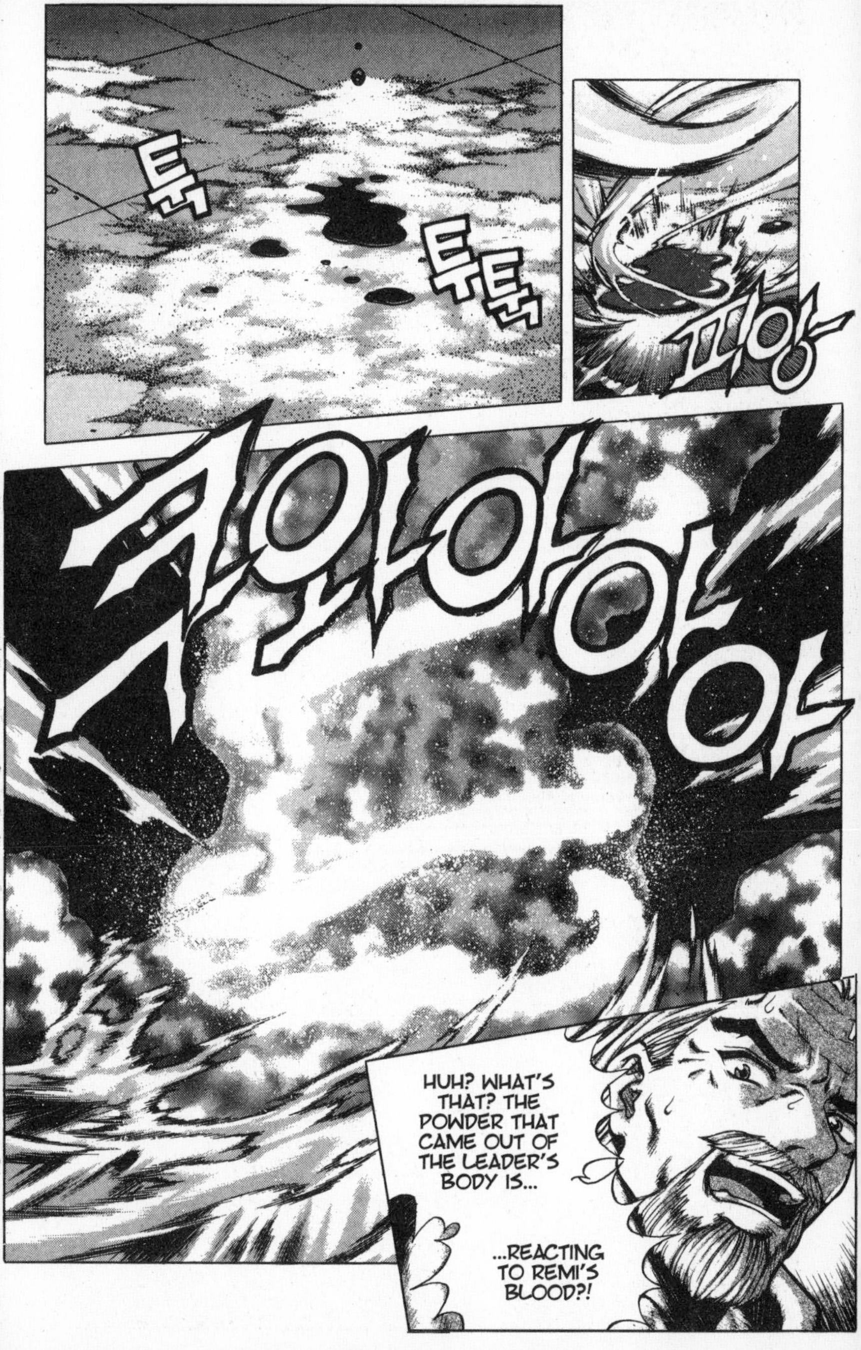
HUH? WHAT'S THAT? THE POWDER THAT CAME OUT OF THE LEADER'S BODY IS...
...REACTING TO REMI'S BLOOD?!

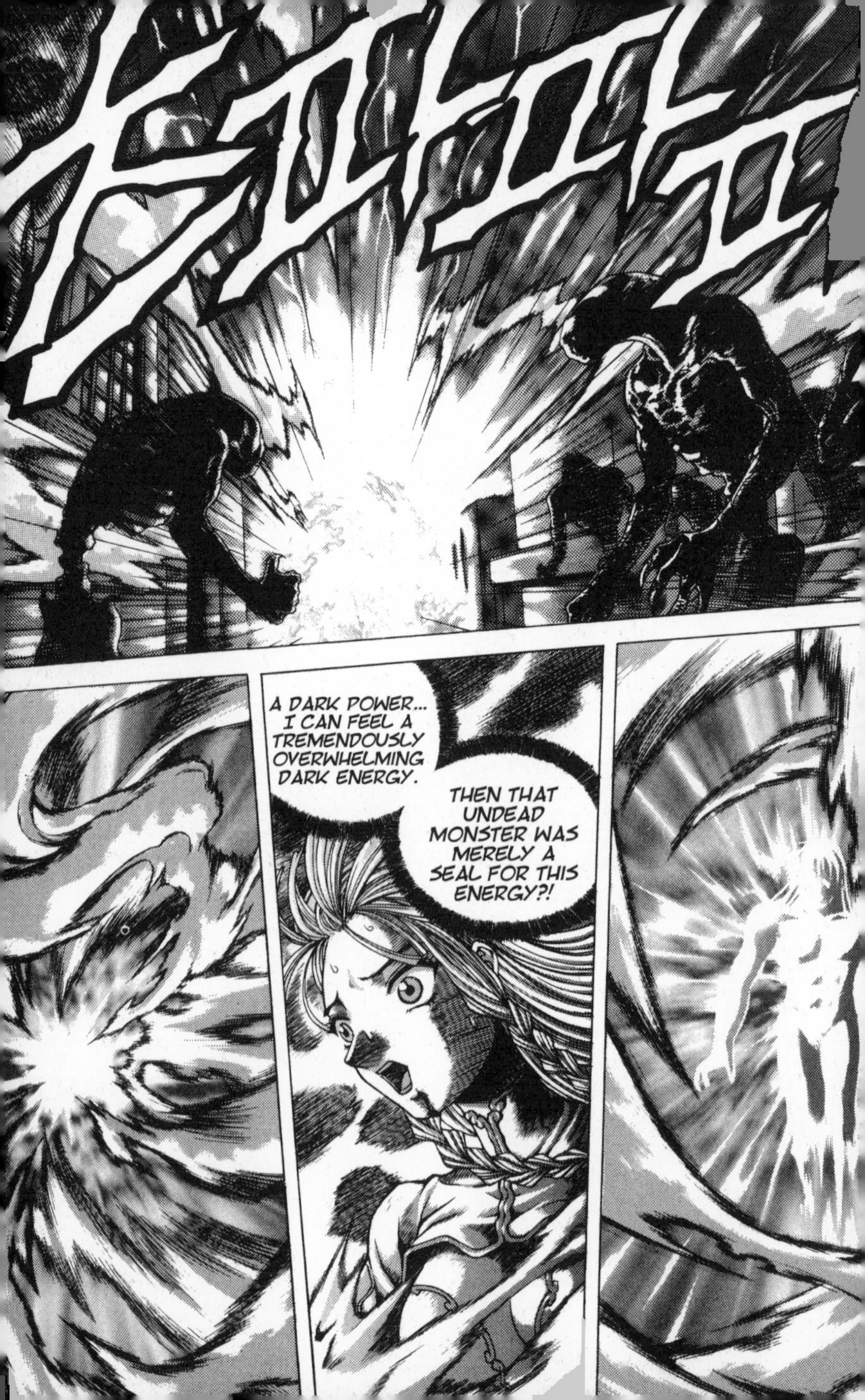
A DARK POWER... I CAN FEEL A TREMENDOUSLY OVERWHELMING DARK ENERGY.
THEN THAT UNDEAD MONSTER WAS MERELY A SEAL FOR THIS ENERGY?!

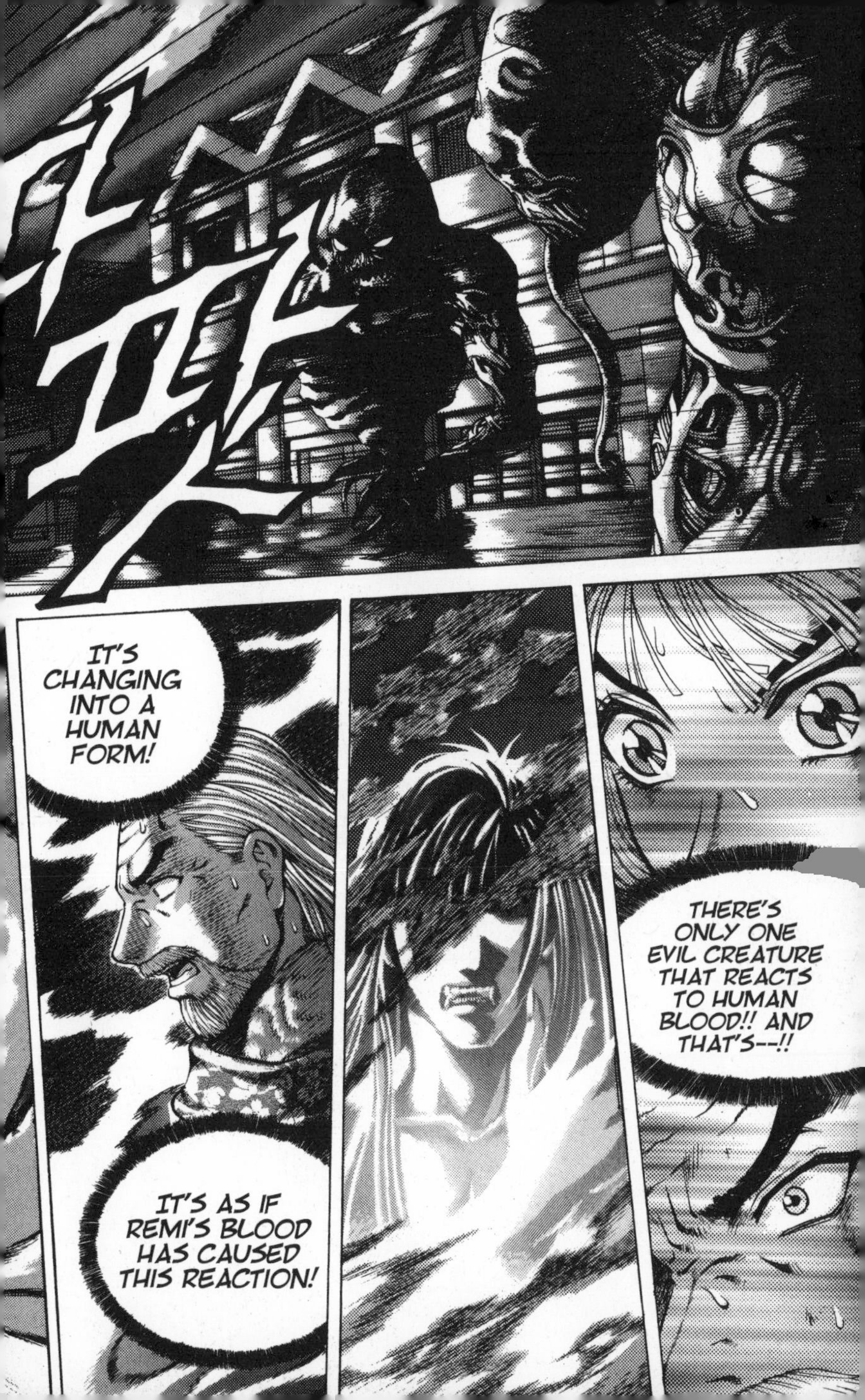
IT'S CHANGING INTO A HUMAN FORM!
IT'S AS IF REMI'S BLOOD HAS CAUSED THIS REACTION!
THERE'S ONLY ONE EVIL CREATURE THAT REACTS TO HUMAN BLOOD!! AND THAT'S--!!

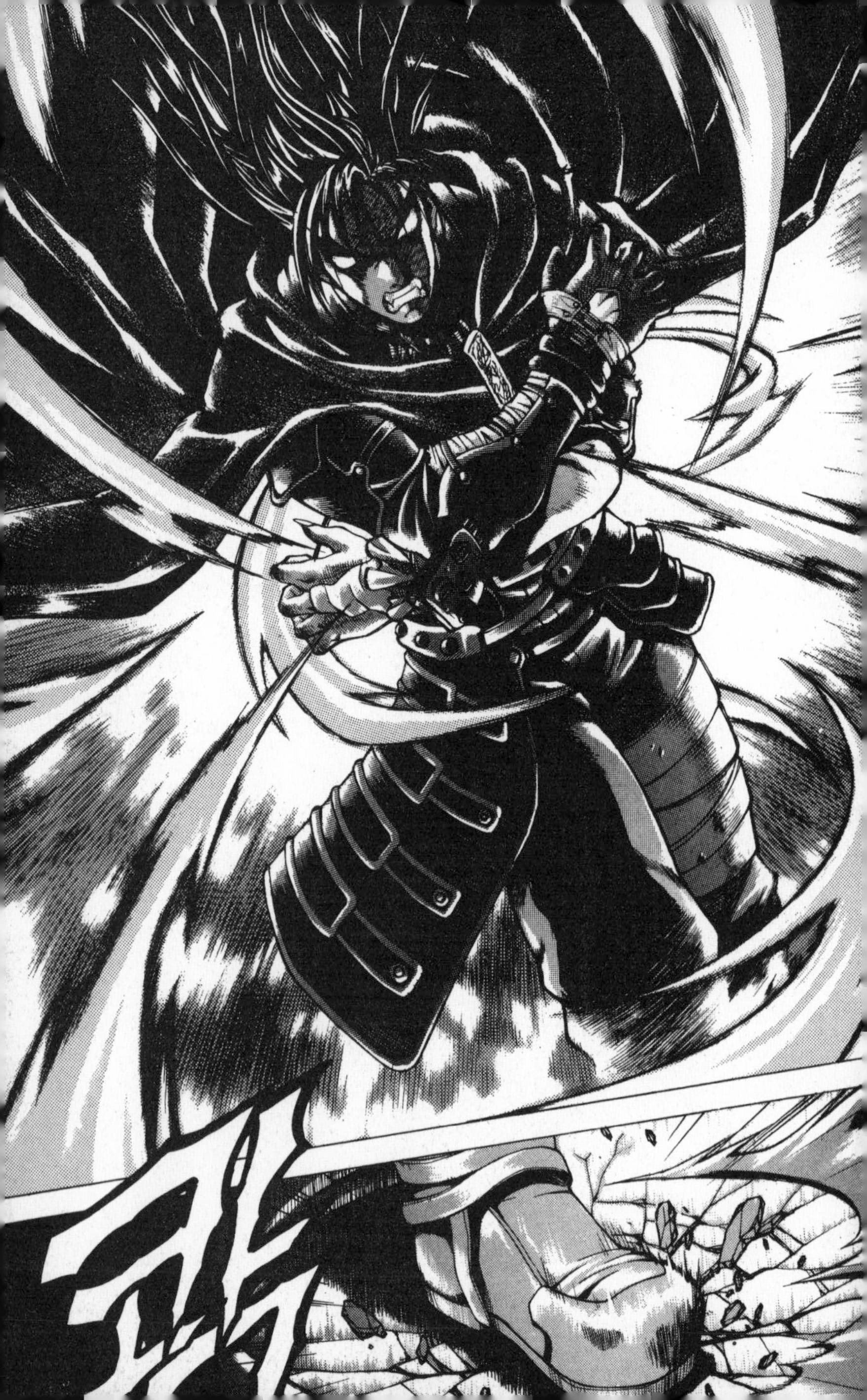

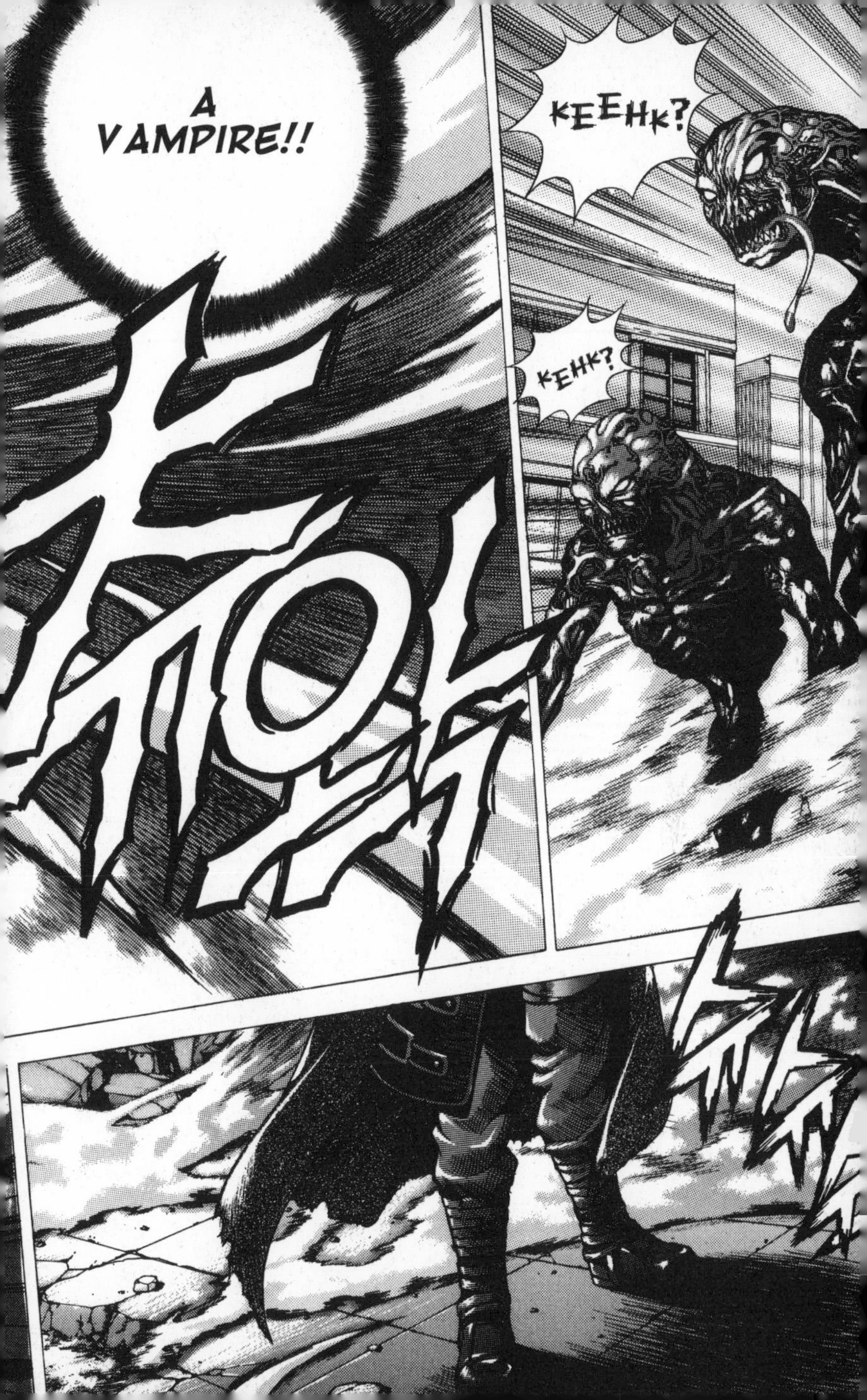
A VAMPIRE!!
KEEHK?
KEHK?

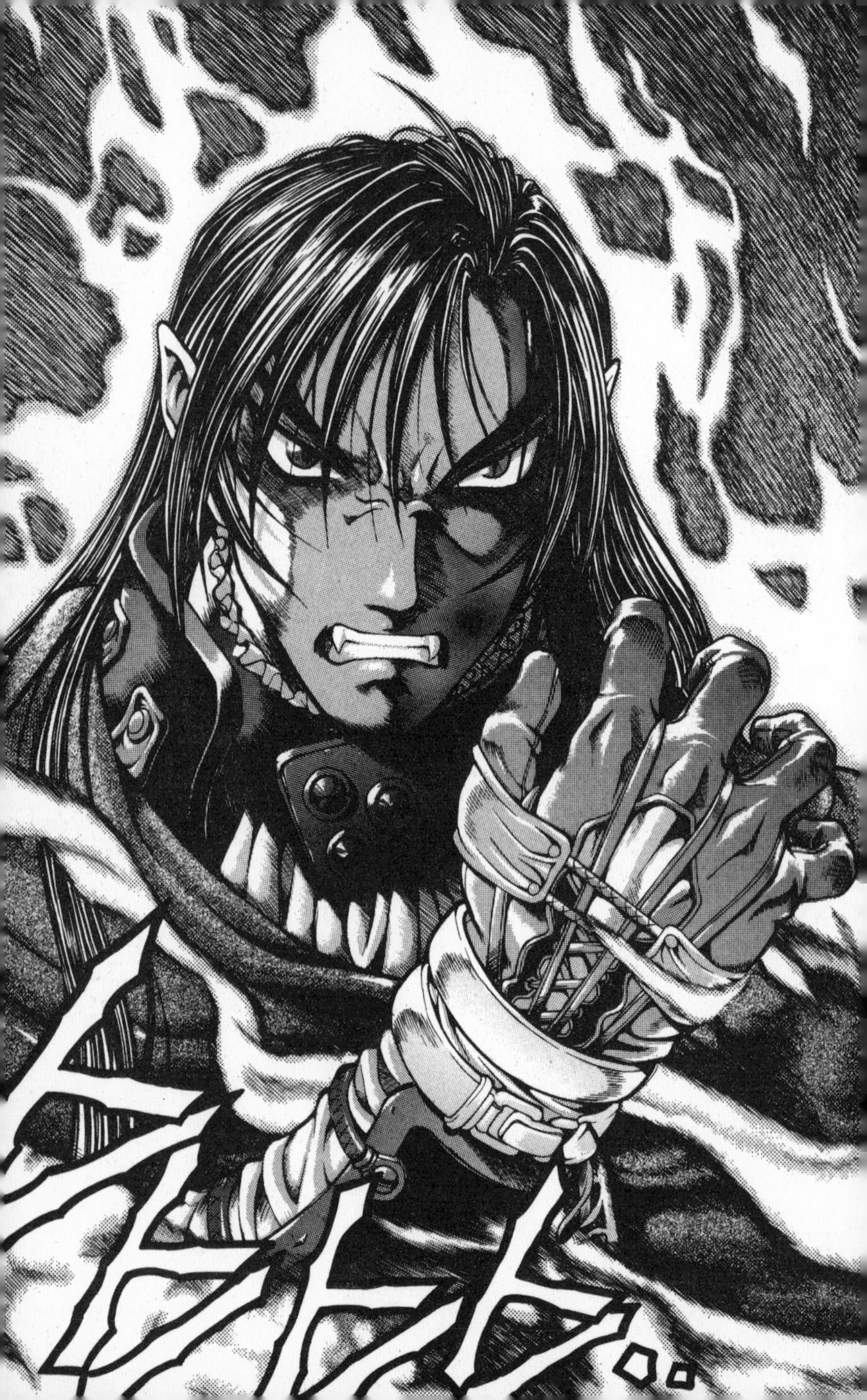

Chapter 3: Sacrifice

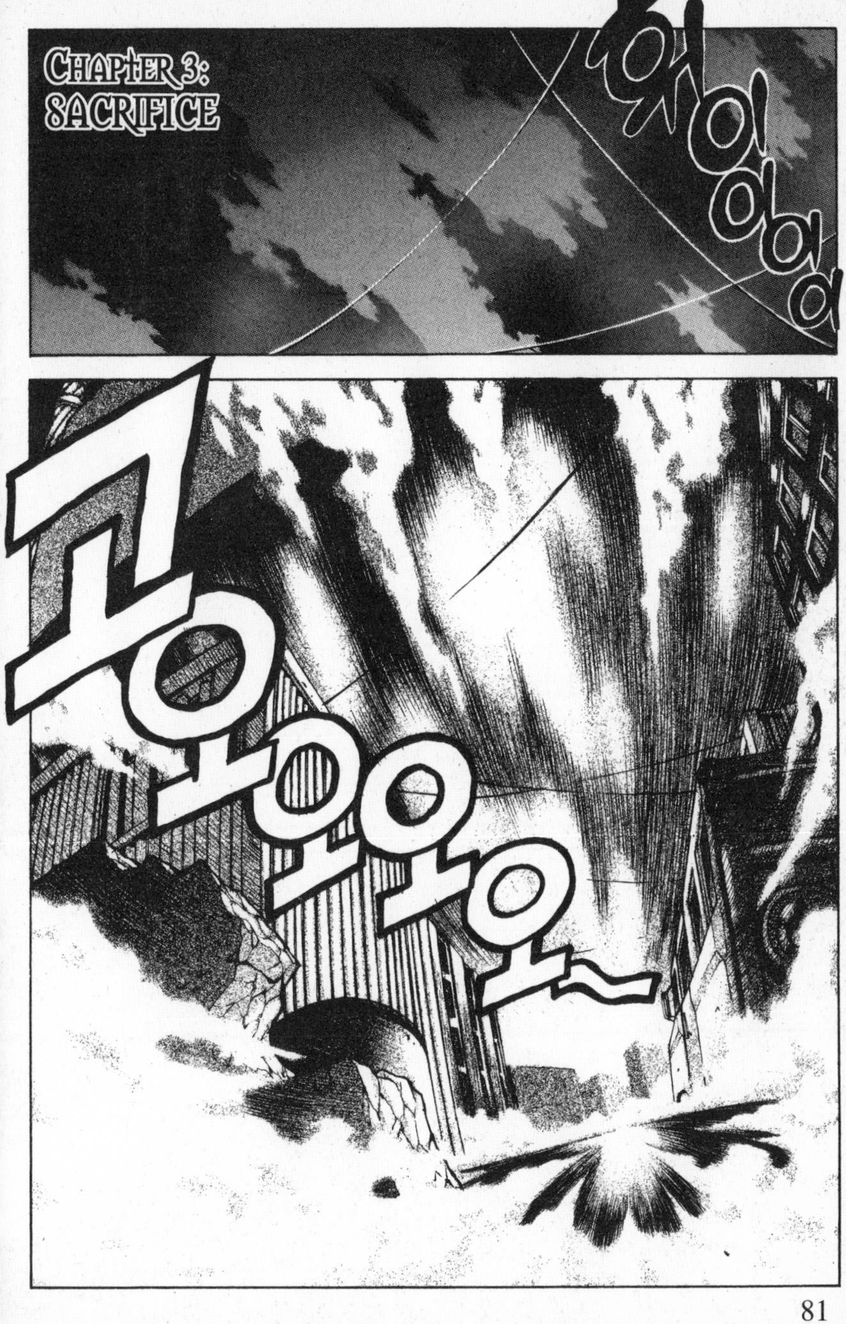

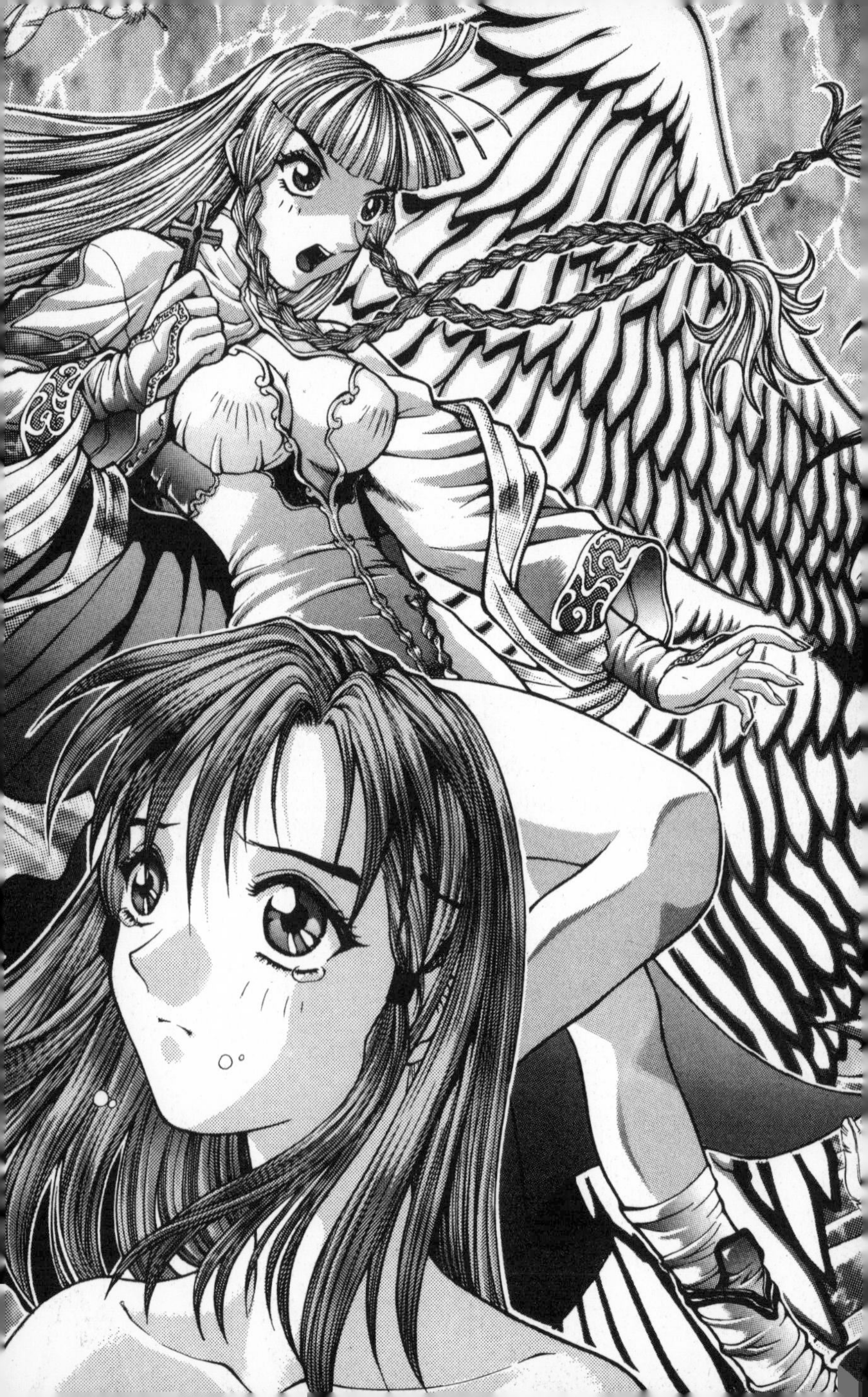

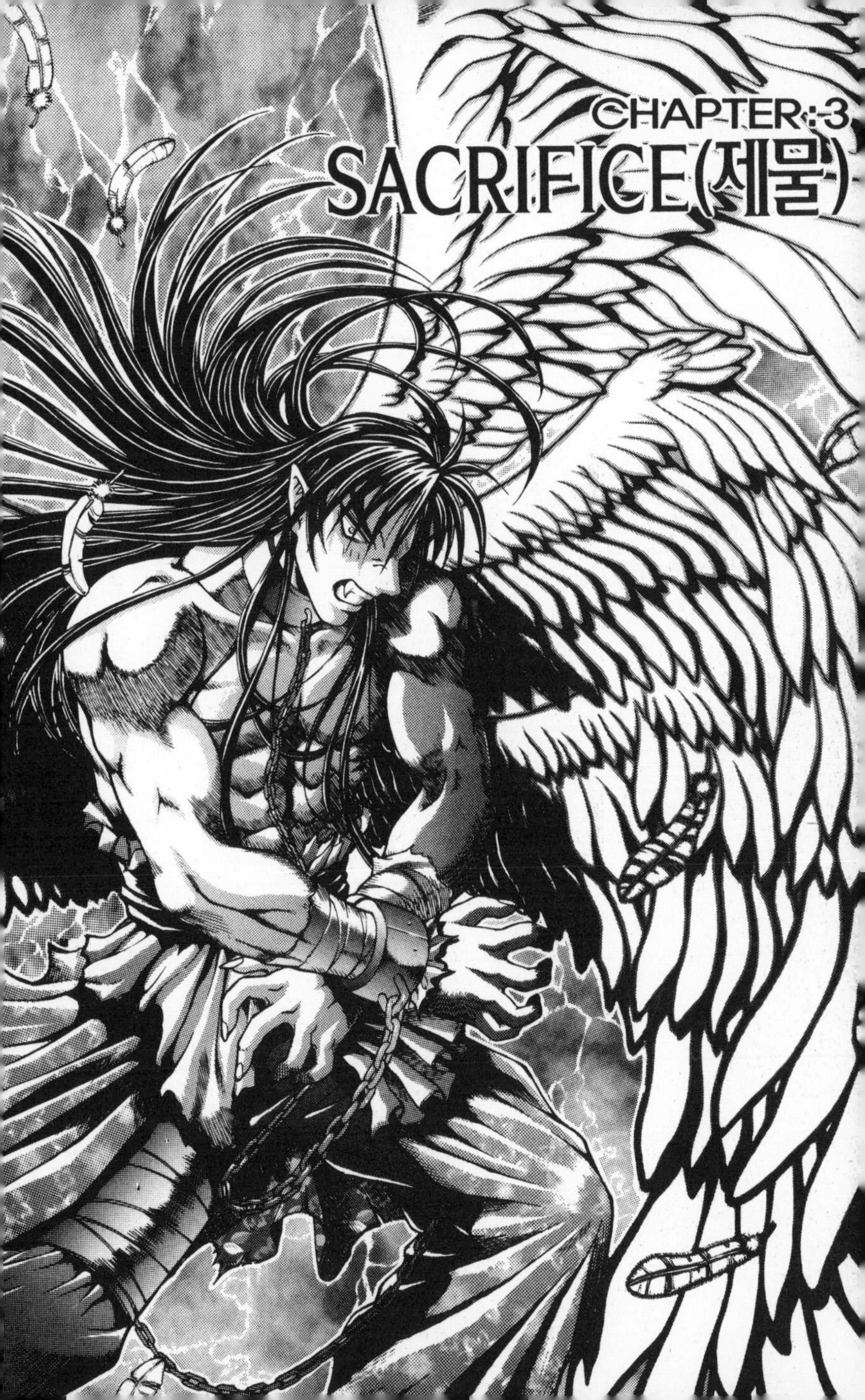
CHAPTER:3
SACRIFICE(제물)

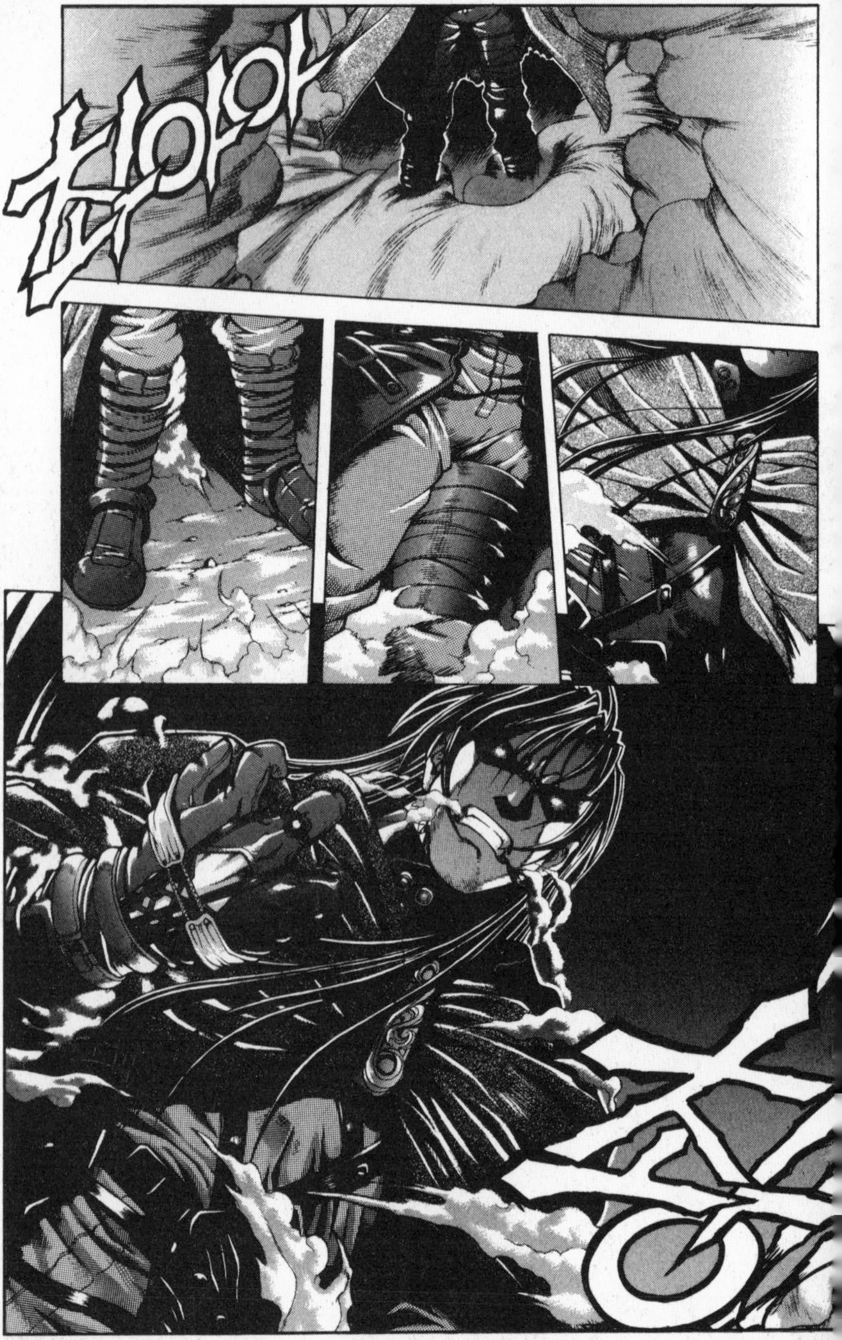
촤아아

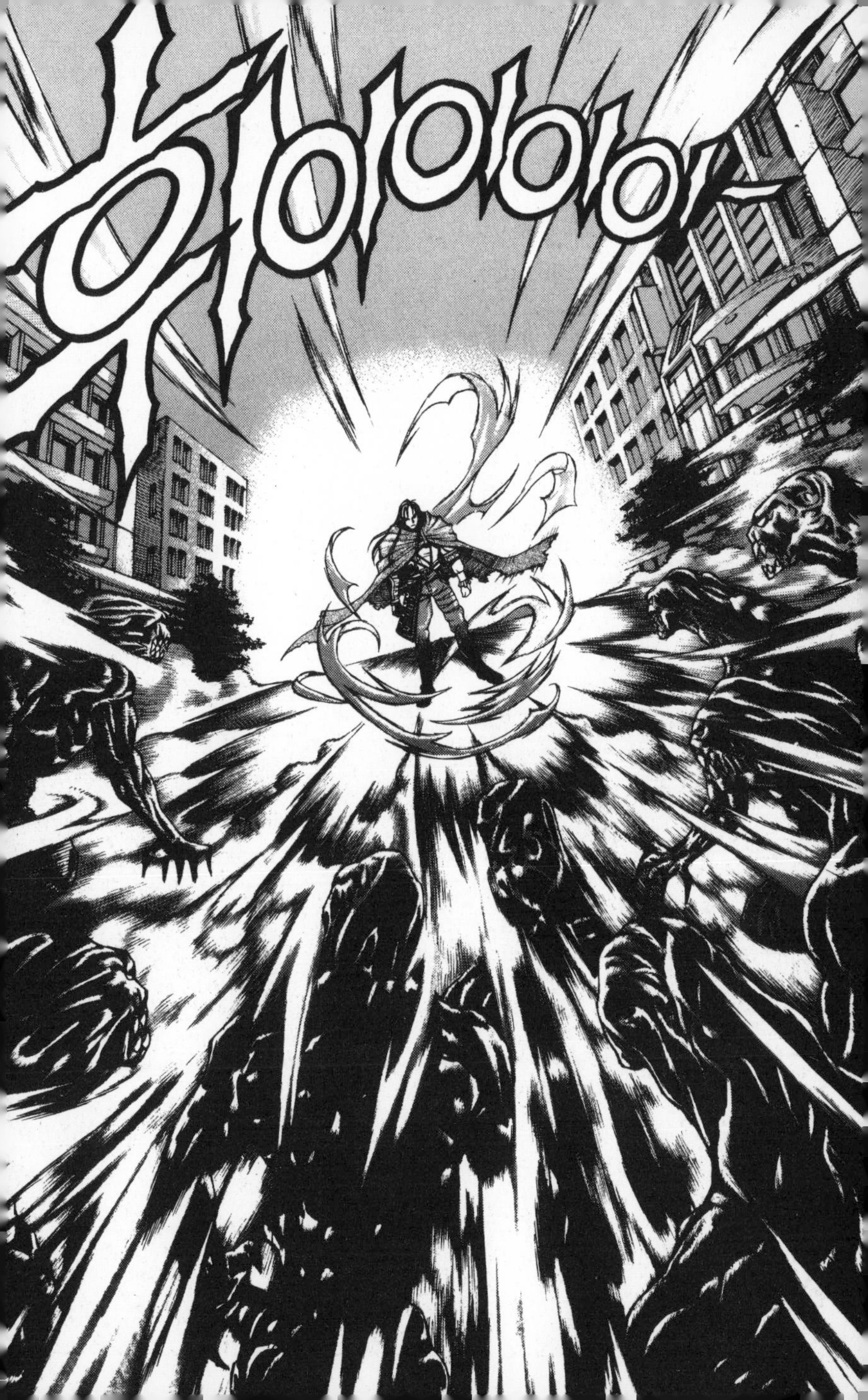

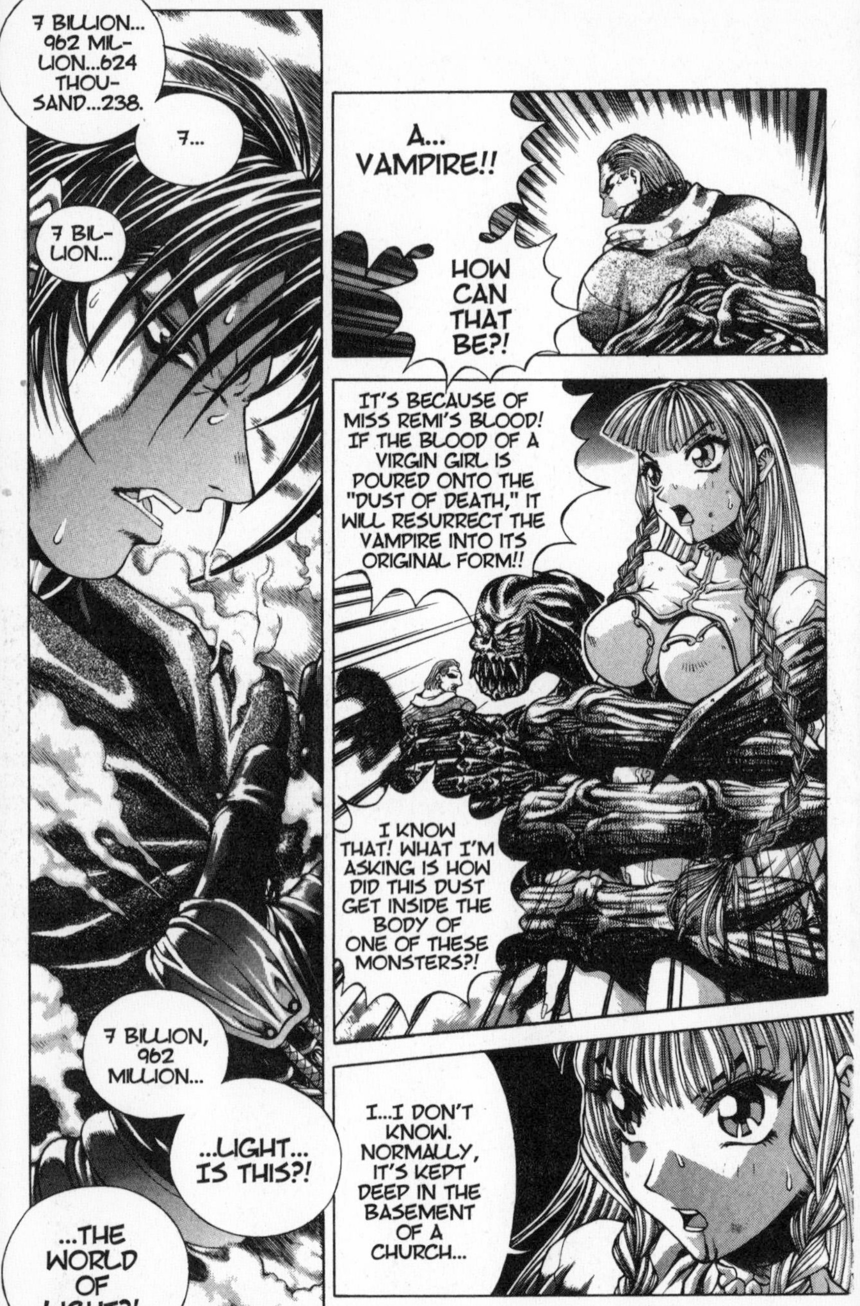

7 BILLION... 962 MIL-LION...624 THOU-SAND...238.
7...
7 BIL-LION...
7 BILLION, 962 MILLION...
...LIGHT... IS THIS?!
...THE WORLD OF LIGHT?!
A... VAMPIRE!!
HOW CAN THAT BE?!
IT'S BECAUSE OF MISS REMI'S BLOOD! IF THE BLOOD OF A VIRGIN GIRL IS POURED ONTO THE "DUST OF DEATH," IT WILL RESURRECT THE VAMPIRE INTO ITS ORIGINAL FORM!!
I KNOW THAT! WHAT I'M ASKING IS HOW DID THIS DUST GET INSIDE THE BODY OF ONE OF THESE MONSTERS?!
I...I DON'T KNOW. NORMALLY, IT'S KEPT DEEP IN THE BASEMENT OF A CHURCH...

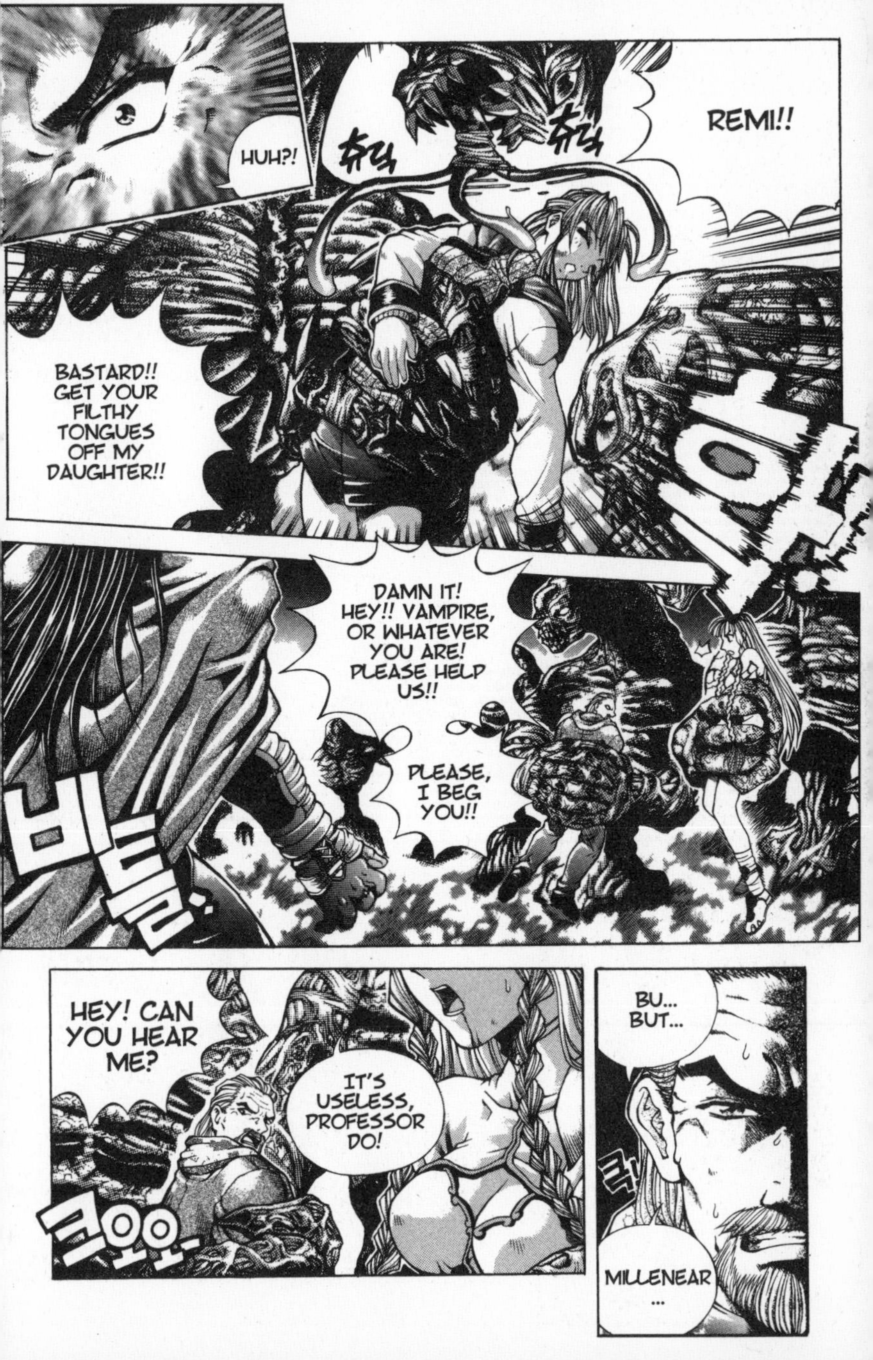
HUH?!
REMI!!
BASTARD!! GET YOUR FILTHY TONGUES OFF MY DAUGHTER!!
DAMN IT! HEY!! VAMPIRE, OR WHATEVER YOU ARE! PLEASE HELP US!!
PLEASE, I BEG YOU!!
HEY! CAN YOU HEAR ME?
IT'S USELESS, PROFESSOR DO!
BU... BUT...
MILLENEAR ...

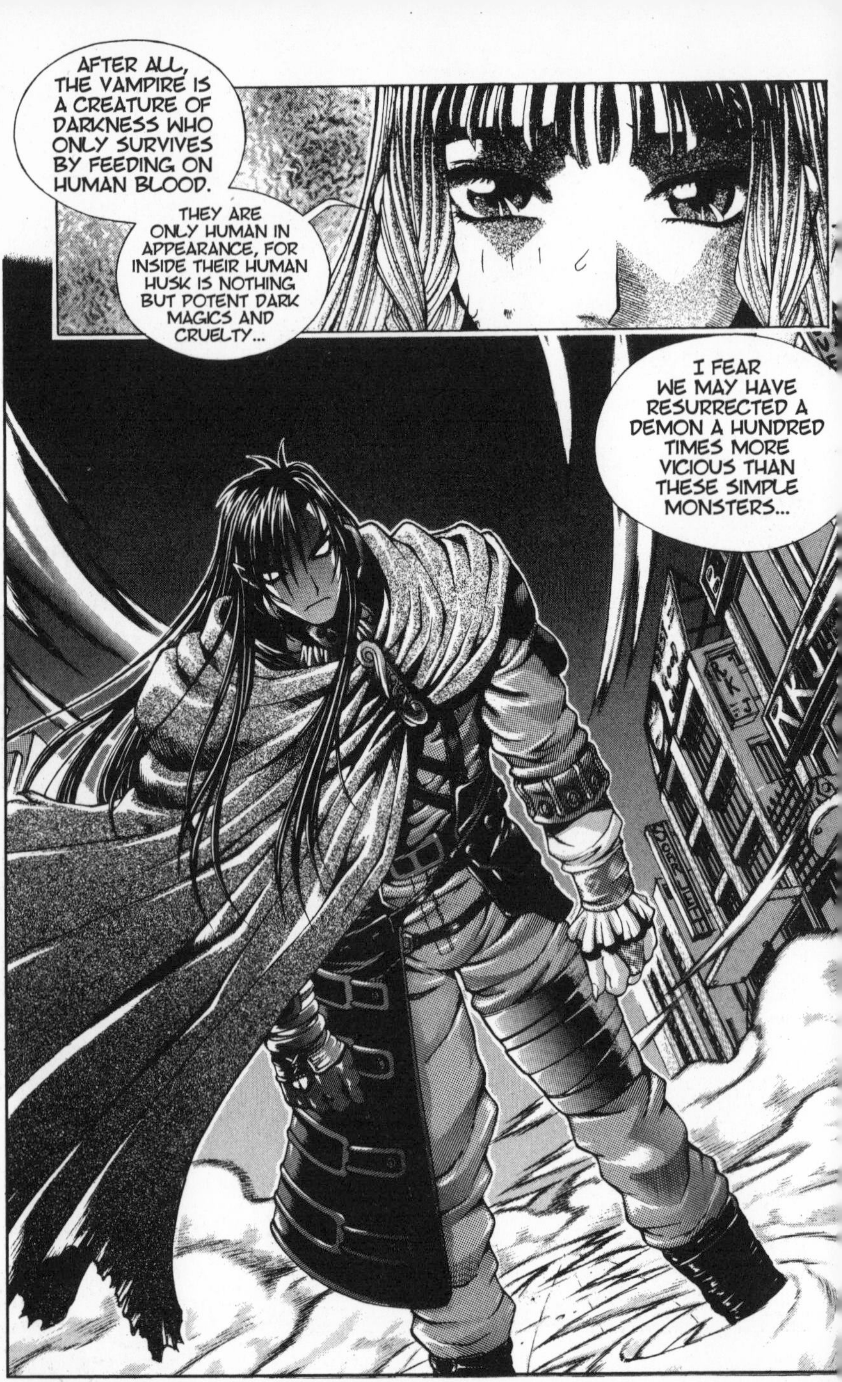
AFTER ALL, THE VAMPIRE IS A CREATURE OF DARKNESS WHO ONLY SURVIVES BY FEEDING ON HUMAN BLOOD.
THEY ARE ONLY HUMAN IN APPEARANCE, FOR INSIDE THEIR HUMAN HUSK IS NOTHING BUT POTENT DARK MAGICS AND CRUELTY...
I FEAR WE MAY HAVE RESURRECTED A DEMON A HUNDRED TIMES MORE VICIOUS THAN THESE SIMPLE MONSTERS...

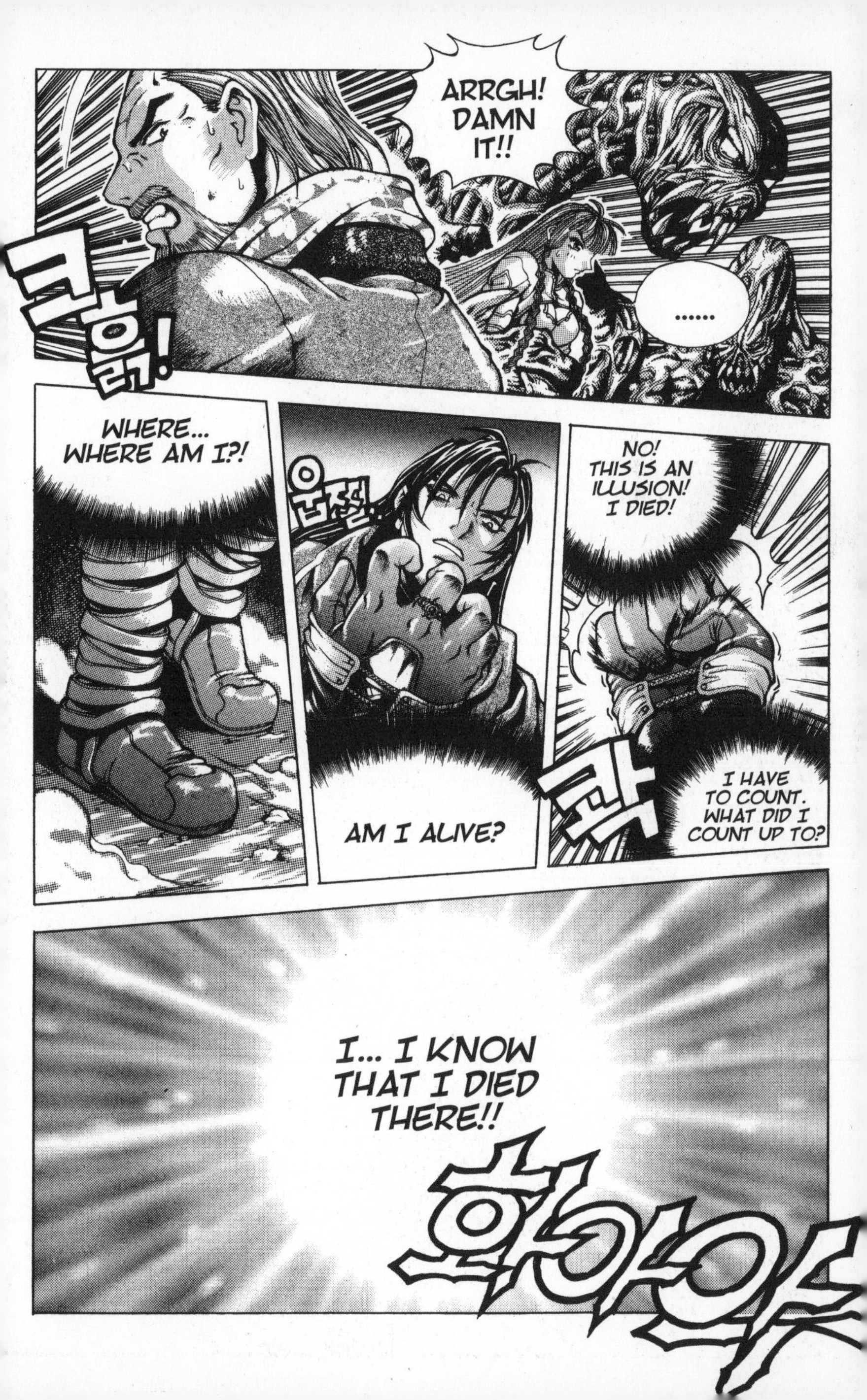
ARRGH! DAMN IT!!
......
WHERE... WHERE AM I?!
움찔
AM I ALIVE?
NO! THIS IS AN ILLUSION! I DIED!
콱
I HAVE TO COUNT. WHAT DID I COUNT UP TO?
I... I KNOW THAT I DIED THERE!!

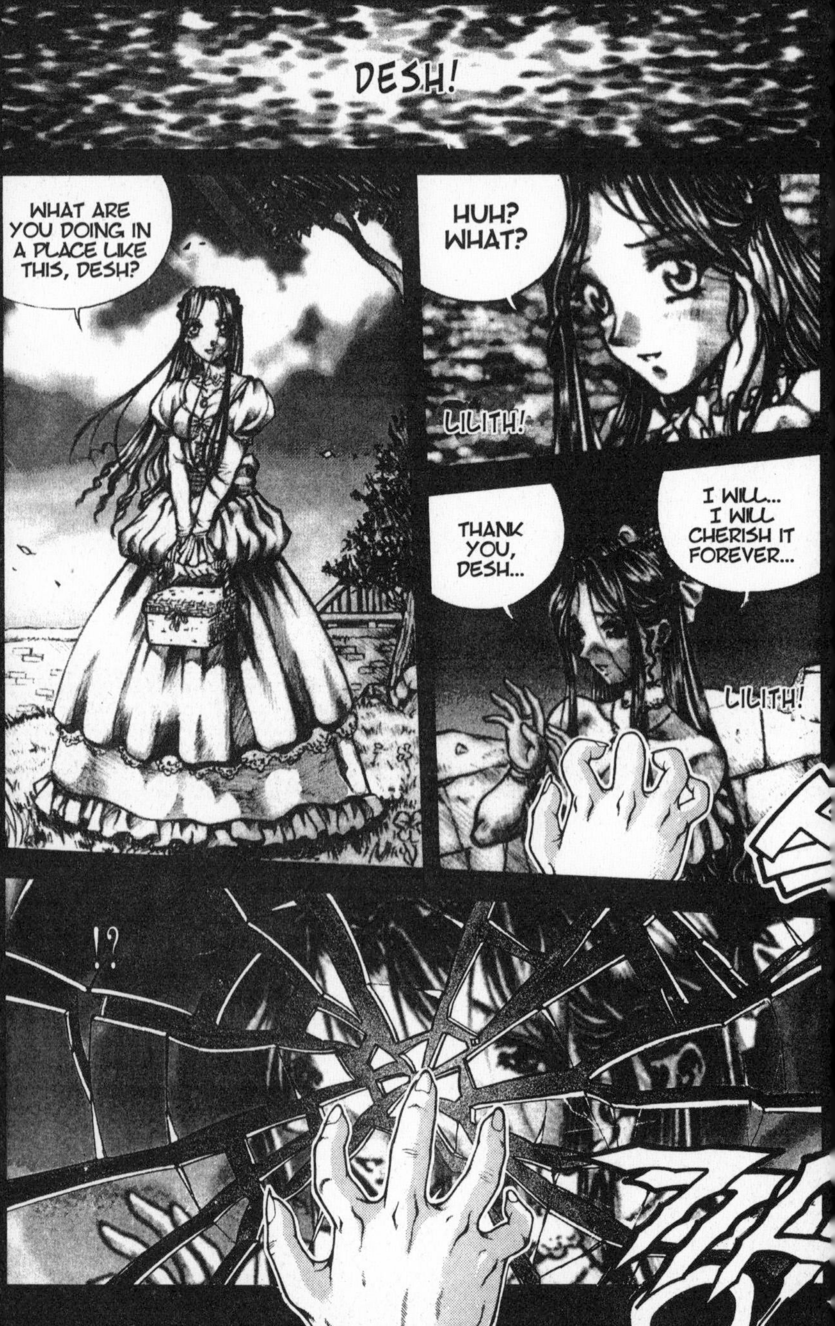
DESH!
WHAT ARE YOU DOING IN A PLACE LIKE THIS, DESH?
HUH? WHAT?
LILITH!
THANK YOU, DESH...
I WILL... I WILL CHERISH IT FOREVER...
LILITH!
!?

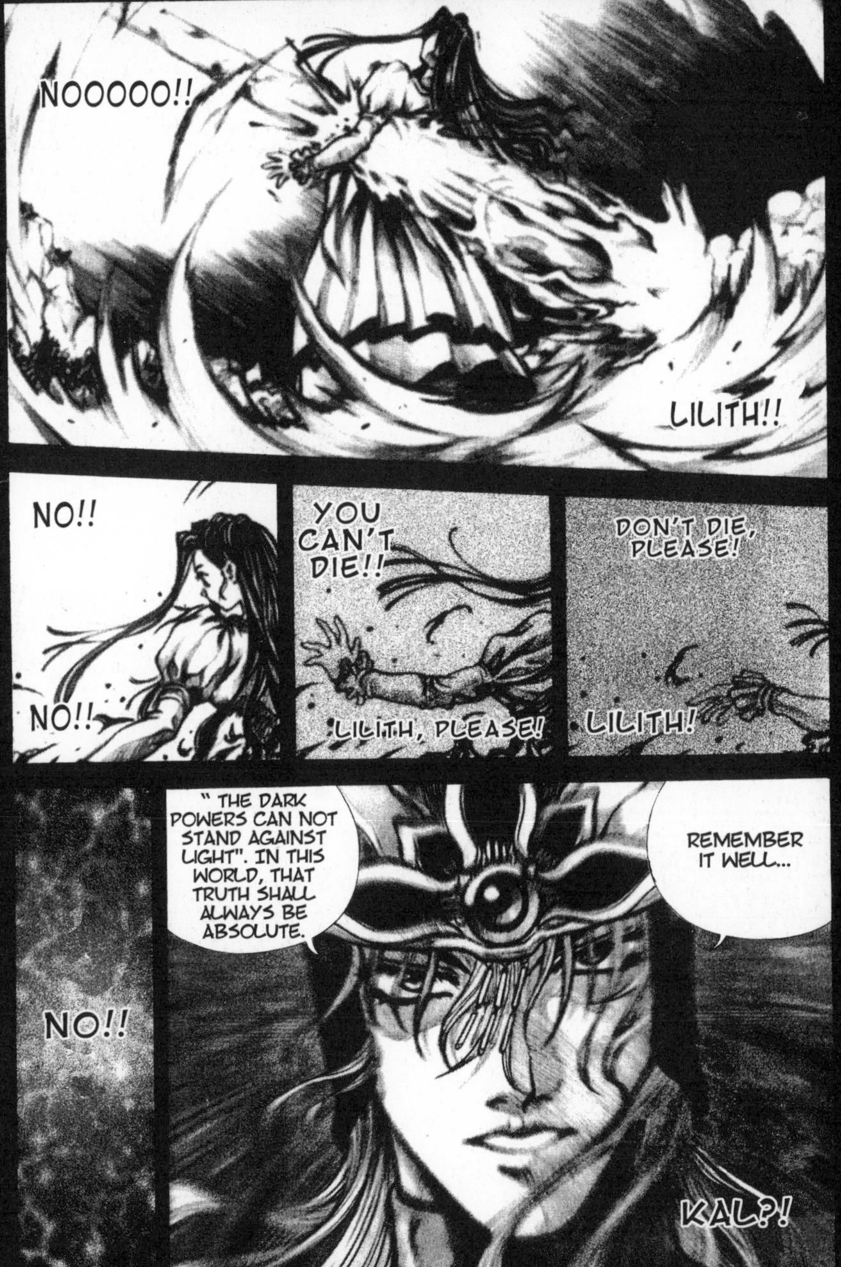
NOOOOO!!
LILITH!!
NO!!
NO!!
YOU CAN'T DIE!!
LILITH, PLEASE!
DON'T DIE, PLEASE!
LILITH!
NO!!
" THE DARK POWERS CAN NOT STAND AGAINST LIGHT". IN THIS WORLD, THAT TRUTH SHALL ALWAYS BE ABSOLUTE.
REMEMBER IT WELL...
KAL?!

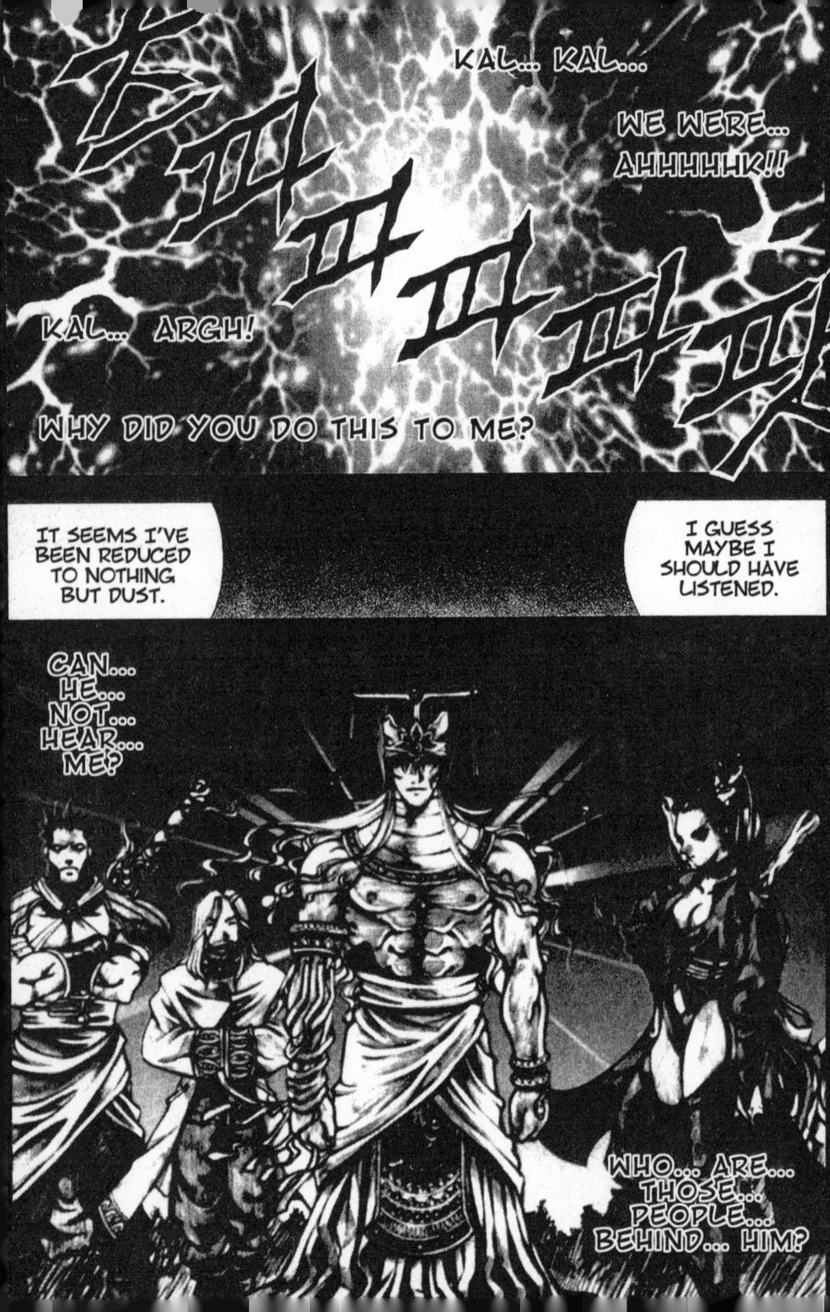
KAL... KAL...
WE WERE... AHHHHHK!!
KAL... ARGH!
WHY DID YOU DO THIS TO ME?
IT SEEMS I'VE BEEN REDUCED TO NOTHING BUT DUST.
I GUESS MAYBE I SHOULD HAVE LISTENED.
CAN... HE... NOT... HEAR... ME?
WHO... ARE... THOSE... PEOPLE... BEHIND... HIM?

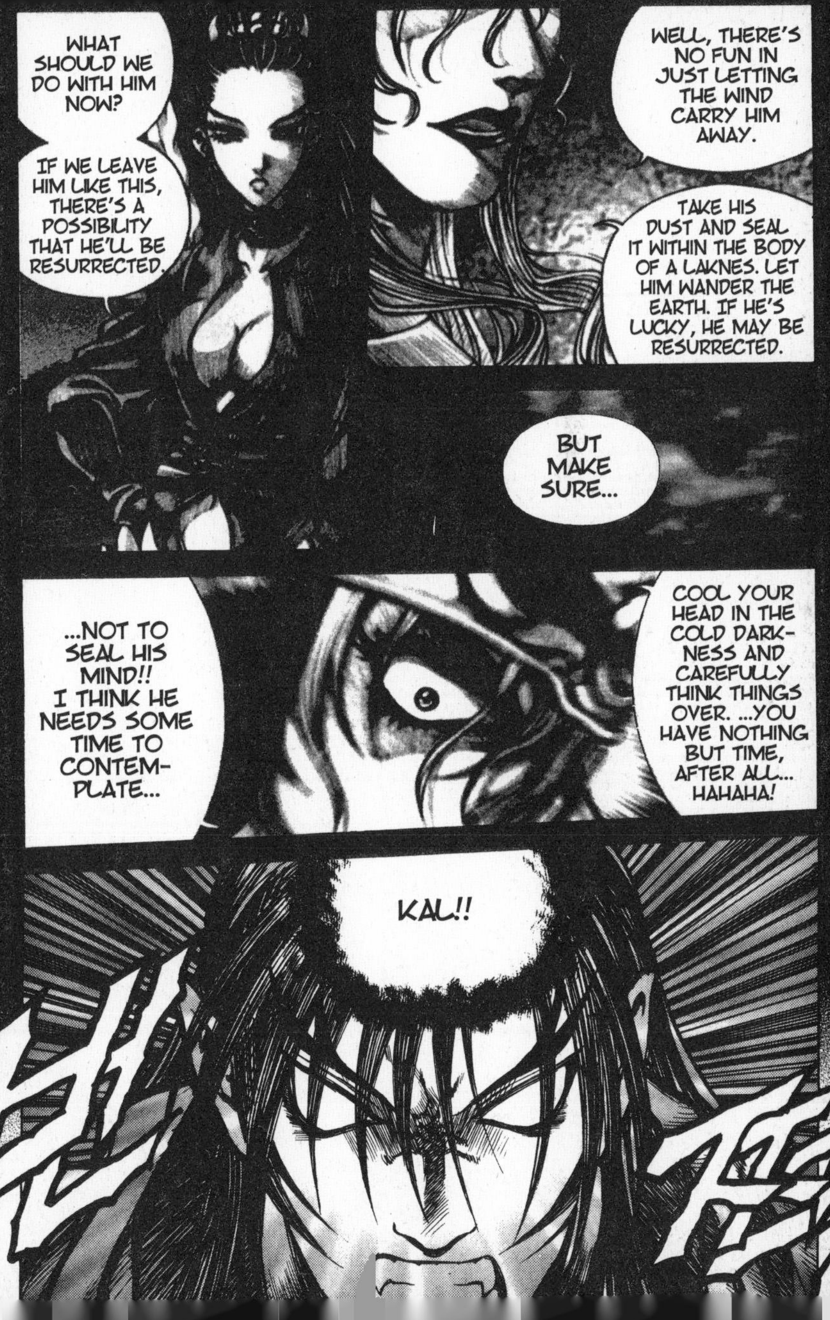
WHAT SHOULD WE DO WITH HIM NOW?
IF WE LEAVE HIM LIKE THIS, THERE'S A POSSIBILITY THAT HE'LL BE RESURRECTED.
WELL, THERE'S NO FUN IN JUST LETTING THE WIND CARRY HIM AWAY.
TAKE HIS DUST AND SEAL IT WITHIN THE BODY OF A LAKNES. LET HIM WANDER THE EARTH. IF HE'S LUCKY, HE MAY BE RESURRECTED.
BUT MAKE SURE...
...NOT TO SEAL HIS MIND!! I THINK HE NEEDS SOME TIME TO CONTEM-PLATE...
COOL YOUR HEAD IN THE COLD DARK-NESS AND CAREFULLY THINK THINGS OVER. ...YOU HAVE NOTHING BUT TIME, AFTER ALL... HAHAHA!
KAL!!

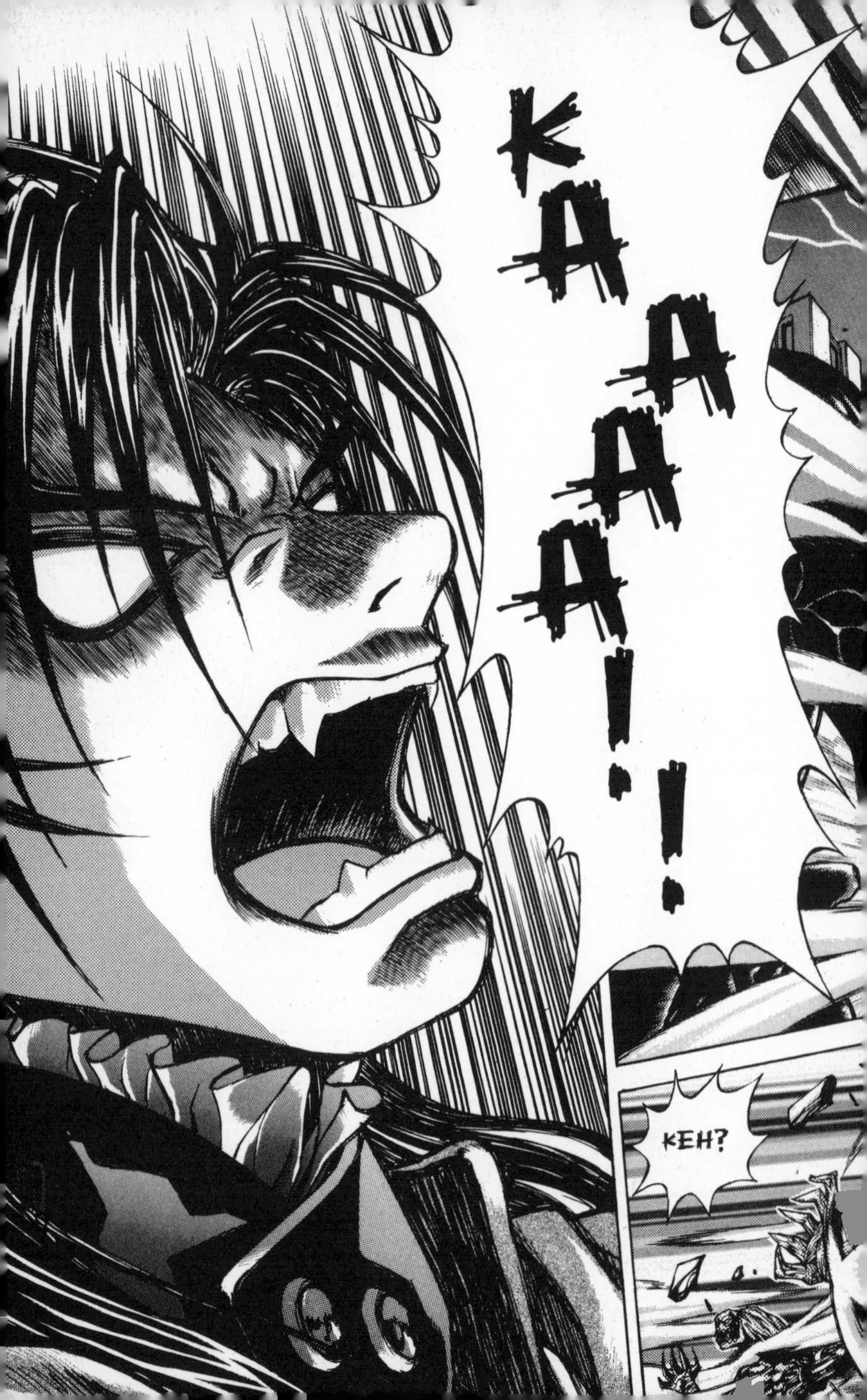
KAAAA!!!
KEH?

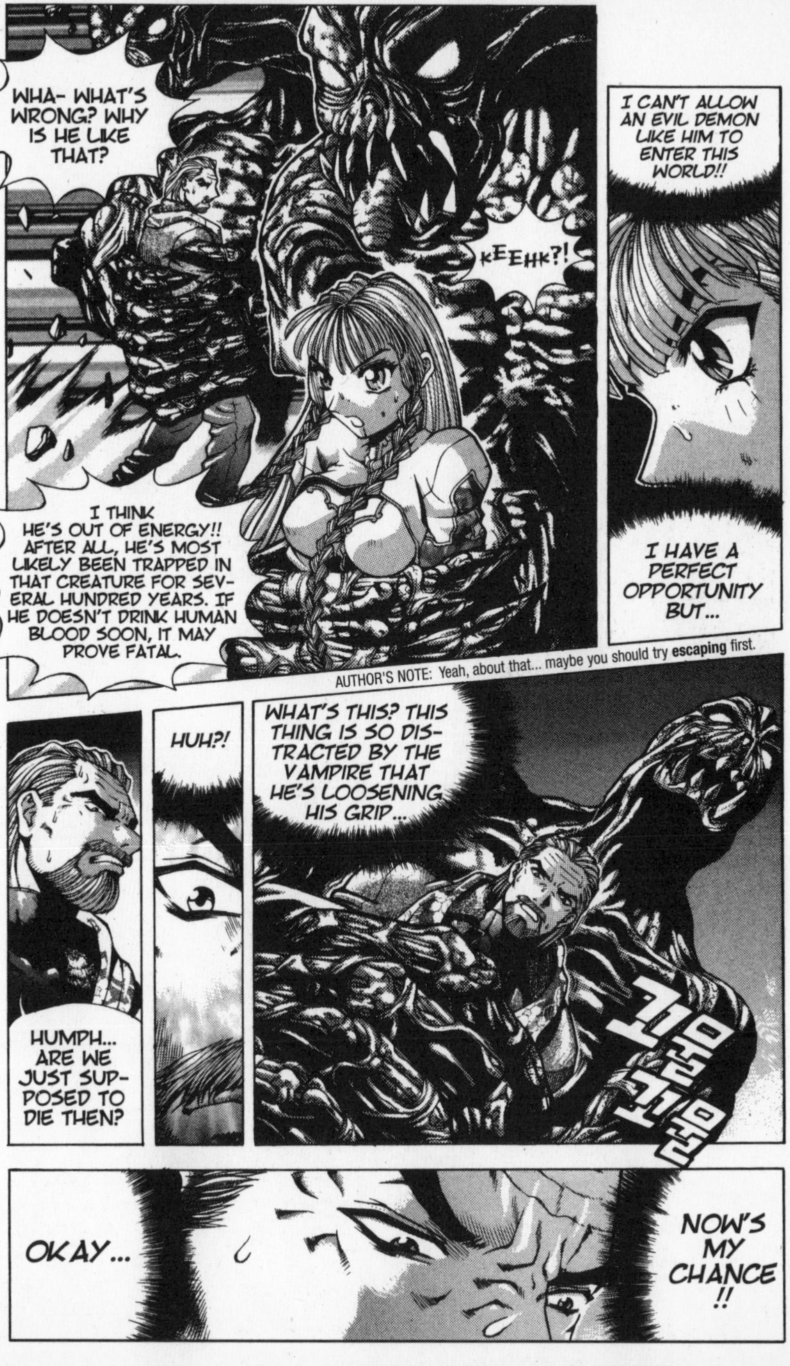
WHA- WHAT'S WRONG? WHY IS HE LIKE THAT?
KEEHK?!
I THINK HE'S OUT OF ENERGY!! AFTER ALL, HE'S MOST LIKELY BEEN TRAPPED IN THAT CREATURE FOR SEVERAL HUNDRED YEARS. IF HE DOESN'T DRINK HUMAN BLOOD SOON, IT MAY PROVE FATAL.
I CAN'T ALLOW AN EVIL DEMON LIKE HIM TO ENTER THIS WORLD!!
I HAVE A PERFECT OPPORTUNITY BUT...
AUTHOR'S NOTE: Yeah, about that... maybe you should try **escaping** first.
HUMPH... ARE WE JUST SUPPOSED TO DIE THEN?
HUH?!
WHAT'S THIS? THIS THING IS SO DISTRACTED BY THE VAMPIRE THAT HE'S LOOSENING HIS GRIP...
OKAY...
NOW'S MY CHANCE!!

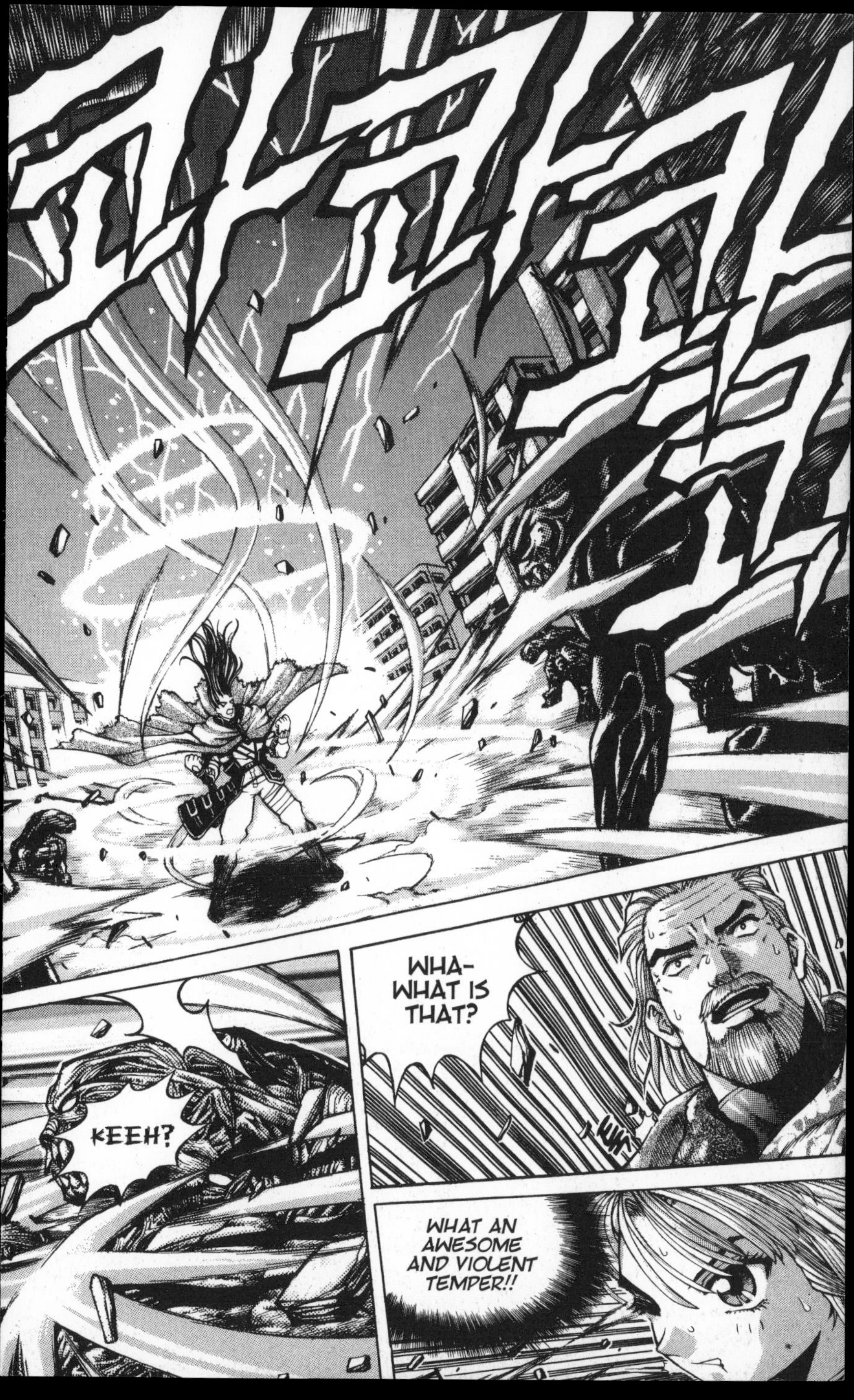
KEEH?
WHA- WHAT IS THAT?
WHAT AN AWESOME AND VIOLENT TEMPER!!

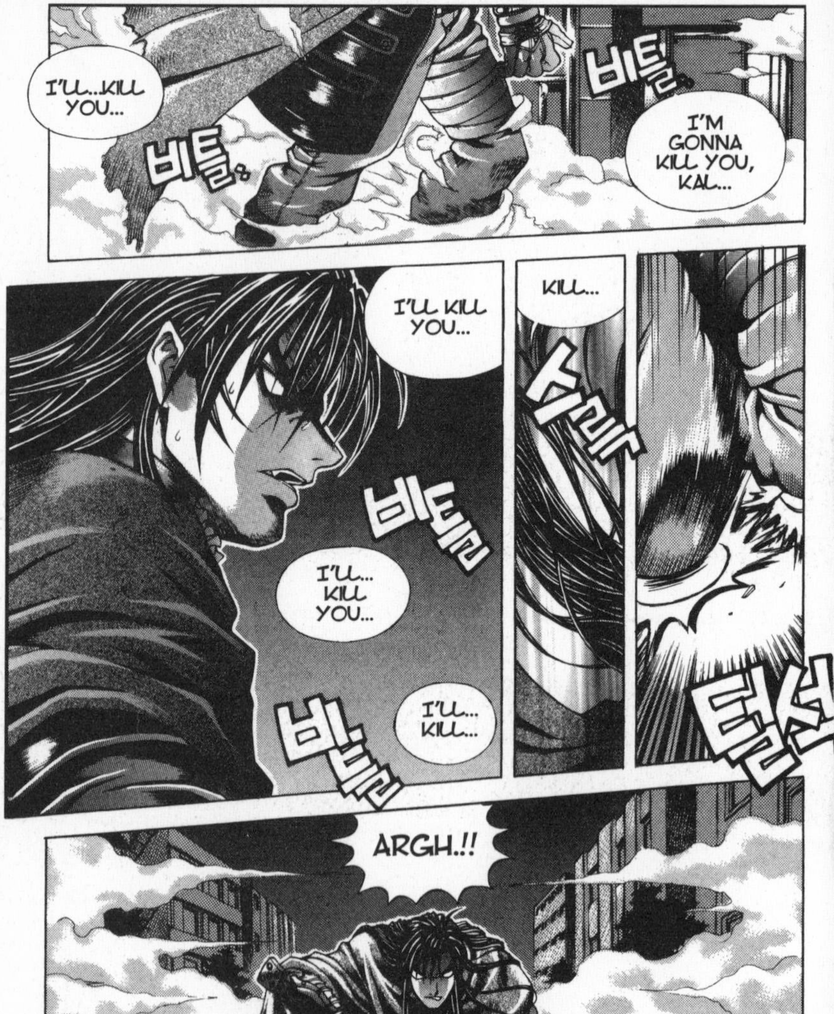
I'LL...KILL YOU...
비틀
비틀,
I'M GONNA KILL YOU, KAL...
I'LL KILL YOU...
비틀
I'LL... KILL YOU...
비틀
I'LL... KILL...
KILL...
털썩
ARGH!!

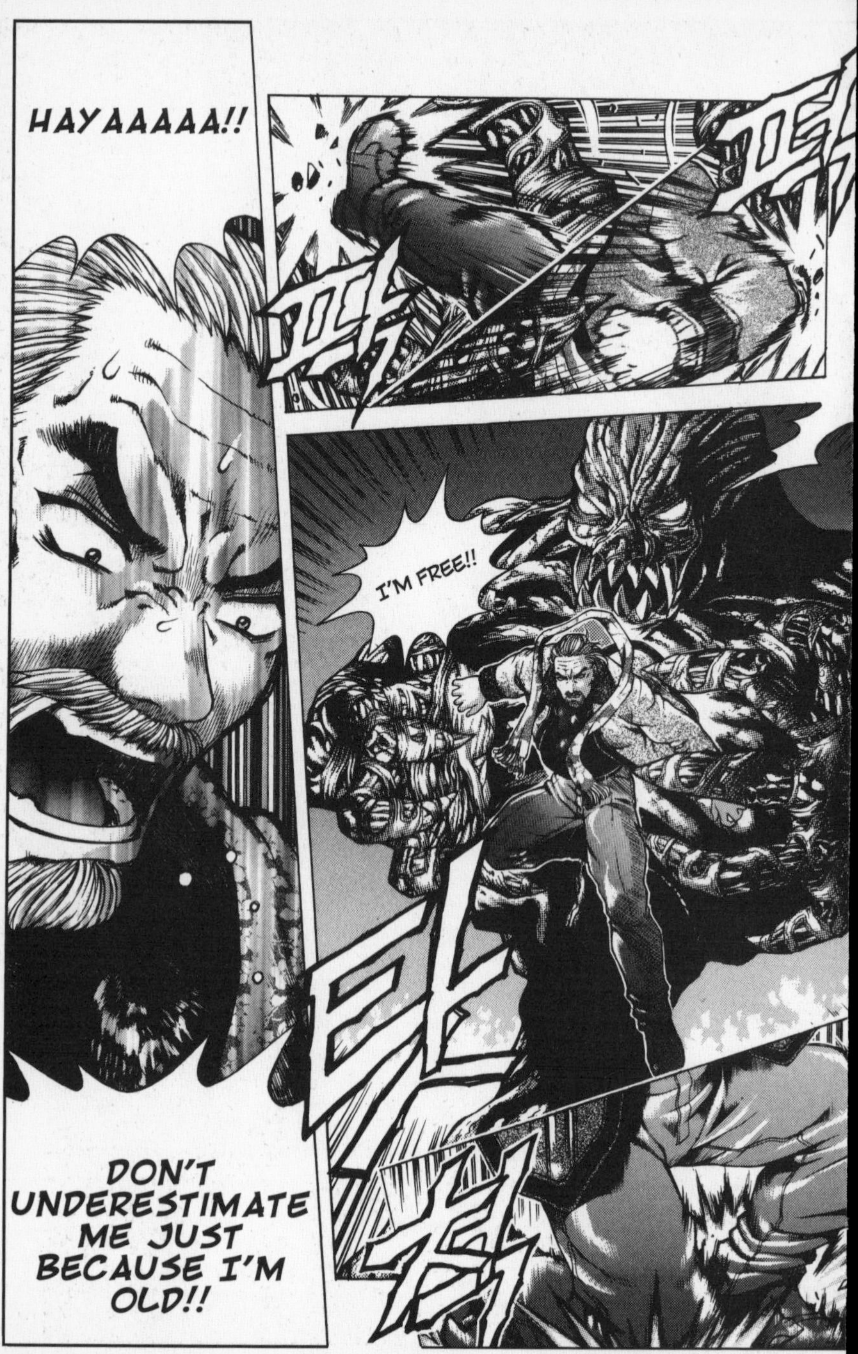
HAYAAAAA!!
DON'T UNDERESTIMATE ME JUST BECAUSE I'M OLD!!
I'M FREE!!

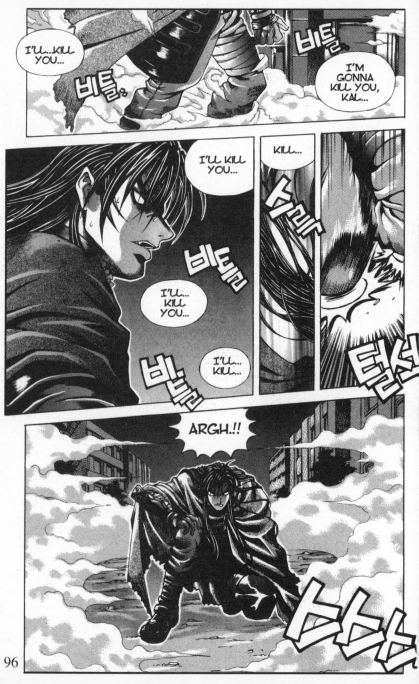

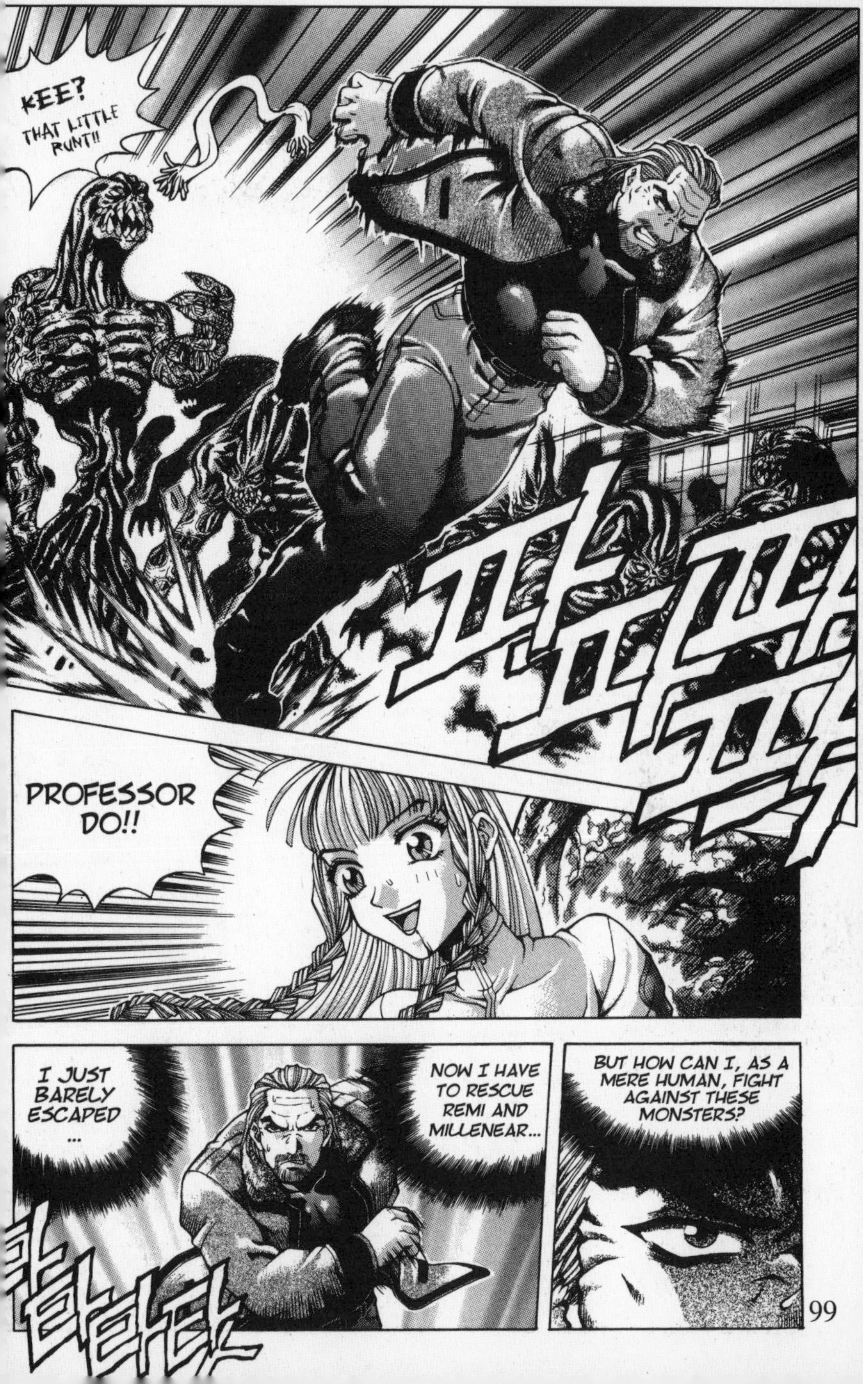
KEE?
THAT LITTLE RUNT!!
PROFESSOR DO!!
I JUST BARELY ESCAPED ...
NOW I HAVE TO RESCUE REMI AND MILLENEAR...
BUT HOW CAN I, AS A MERE HUMAN, FIGHT AGAINST THESE MONSTERS?

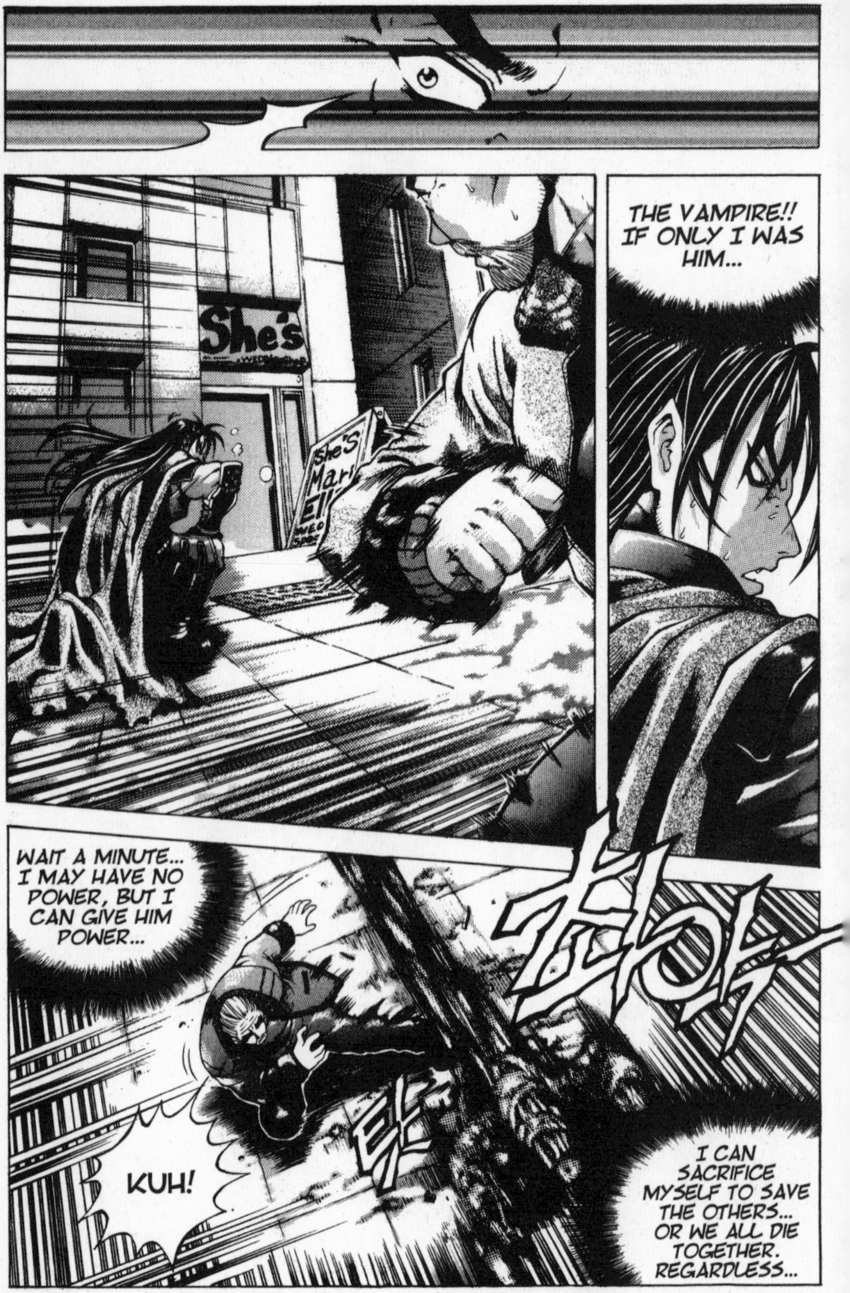
She's
THE VAMPIRE!! IF ONLY I WAS HIM...
WAIT A MINUTE... I MAY HAVE NO POWER, BUT I CAN GIVE HIM POWER...
KUH!
I CAN SACRIFICE MYSELF TO SAVE THE OTHERS... OR WE ALL DIE TOGETHER. REGARDLESS...

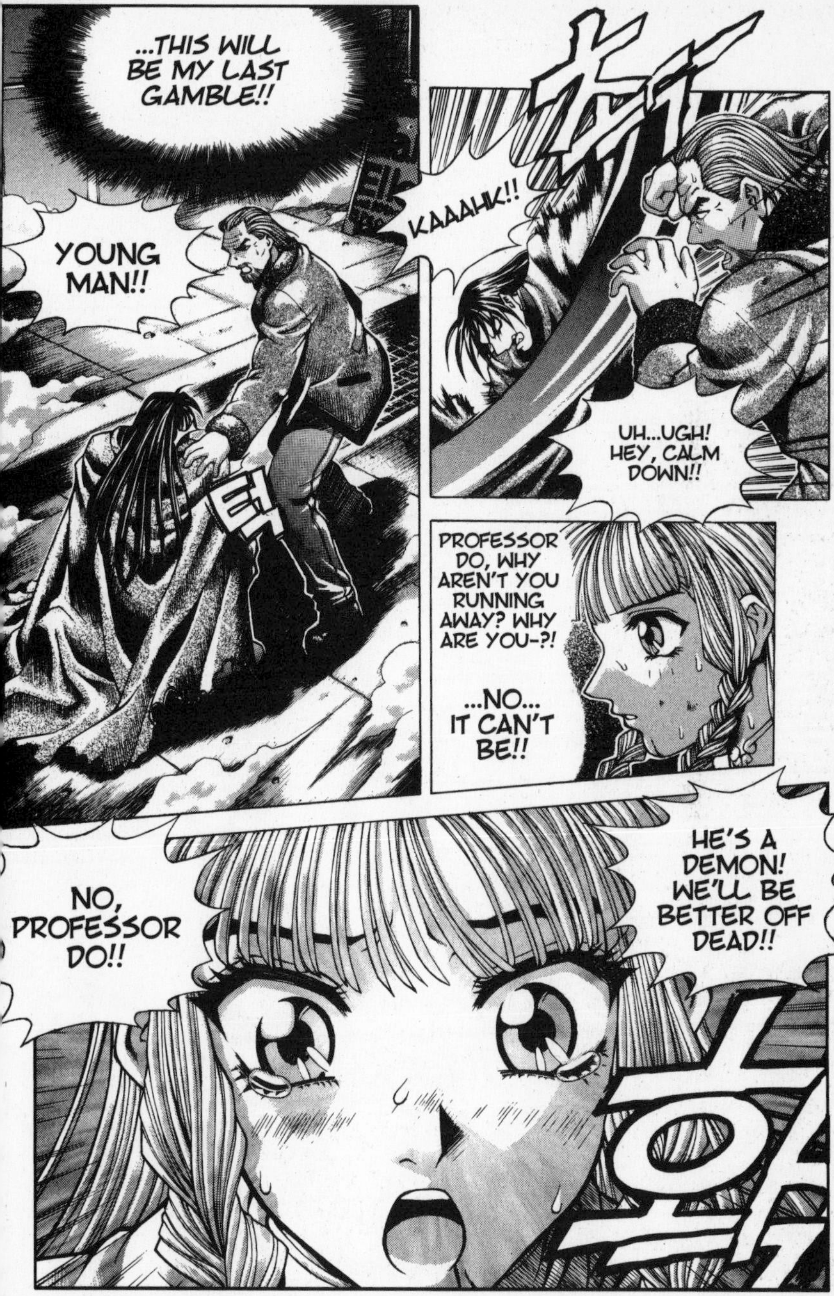
...THIS WILL BE MY LAST GAMBLE!!
YOUNG MAN!!
KAAAHK!!
UH...UGH! HEY, CALM DOWN!!
PROFESSOR DO, WHY AREN'T YOU RUNNING AWAY? WHY ARE YOU-?!
...NO... IT CAN'T BE!!
NO, PROFESSOR DO!!
HE'S A DEMON! WE'LL BE BETTER OFF DEAD!!

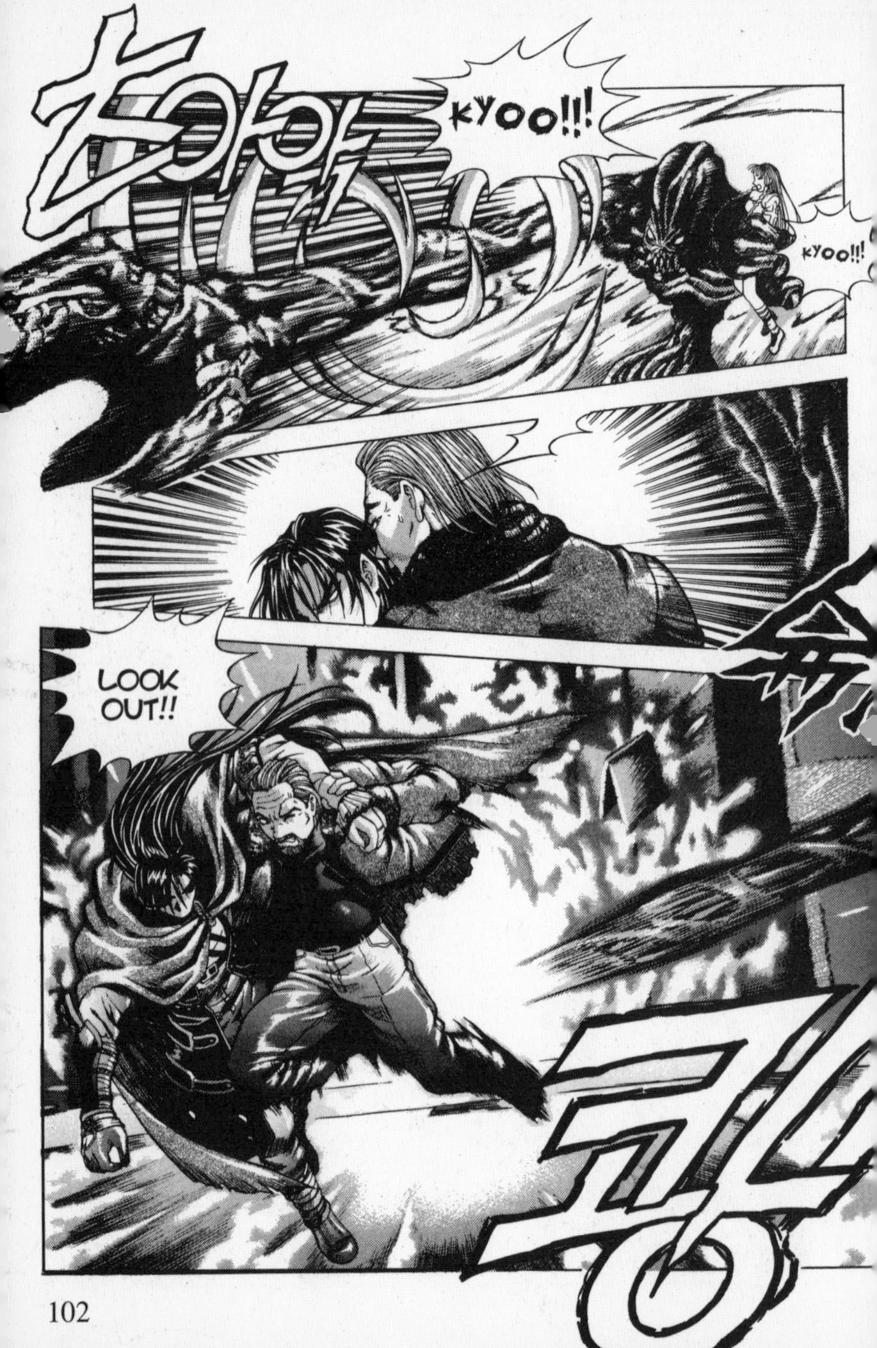

KYOO!!!
KYOO!!!
LOOK OUT!!

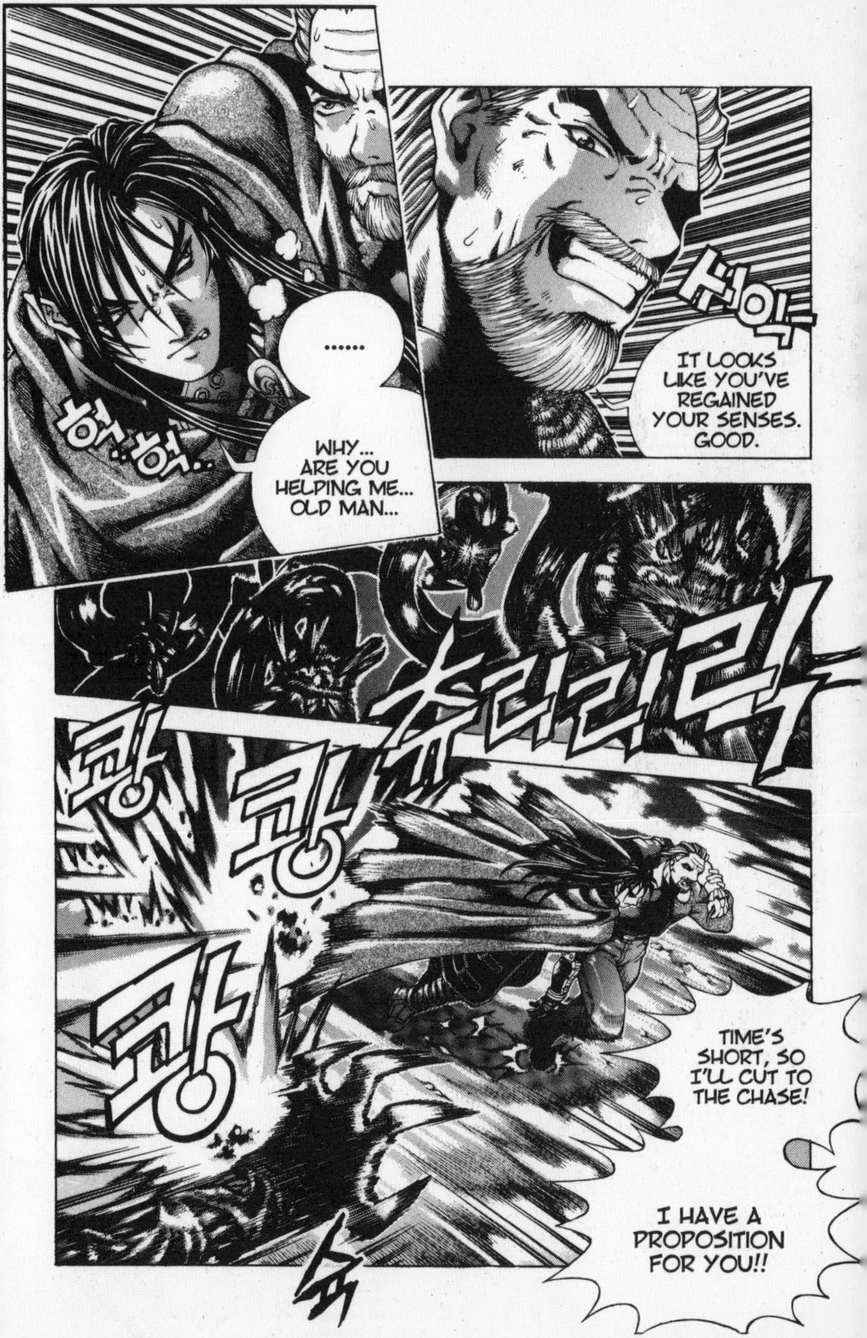
......
WHY... ARE YOU HELPING ME... OLD MAN...
IT LOOKS LIKE YOU'VE REGAINED YOUR SENSES. GOOD.
TIME'S SHORT, SO I'LL CUT TO THE CHASE!
I HAVE A PROPOSITION FOR YOU!!

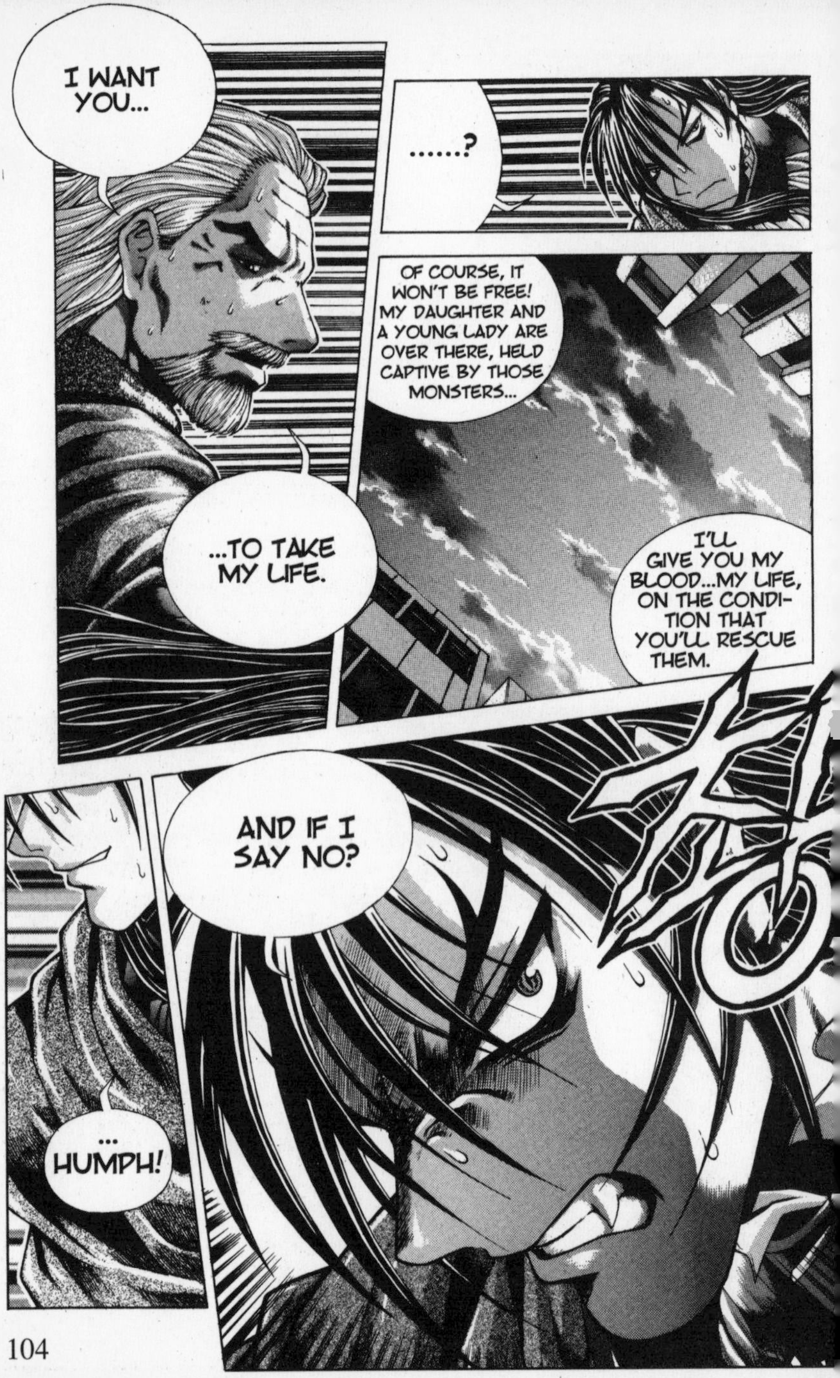
I WANT YOU...
......?
OF COURSE, IT WON'T BE FREE! MY DAUGHTER AND A YOUNG LADY ARE OVER THERE, HELD CAPTIVE BY THOSE MONSTERS...
...TO TAKE MY LIFE.
I'LL GIVE YOU MY BLOOD...MY LIFE, ON THE CONDITION THAT YOU'LL RESCUE THEM.
... HUMPH!
AND IF I SAY NO?

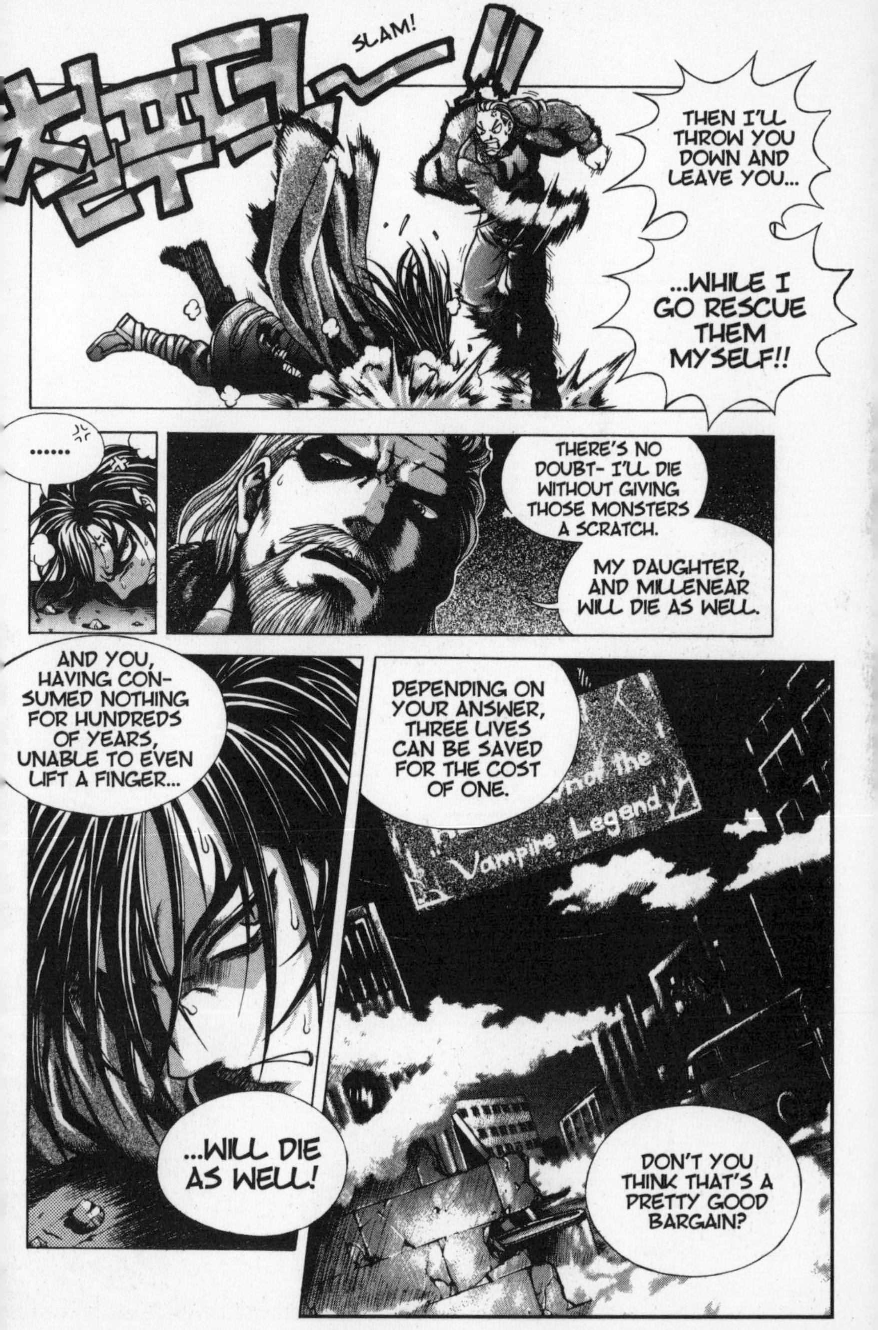
SLAM!
THEN I'LL THROW YOU DOWN AND LEAVE YOU...
...WHILE I GO RESCUE THEM MYSELF!!
......
THERE'S NO DOUBT- I'LL DIE WITHOUT GIVING THOSE MONSTERS A SCRATCH.
MY DAUGHTER, AND MILLENEAR WILL DIE AS WELL.
AND YOU, HAVING CON-SUMED NOTHING FOR HUNDREDS OF YEARS, UNABLE TO EVEN LIFT A FINGER...
...WILL DIE AS WELL!
DEPENDING ON YOUR ANSWER, THREE LIVES CAN BE SAVED FOR THE COST OF ONE.
DON'T YOU THINK THAT'S A PRETTY GOOD BARGAIN?

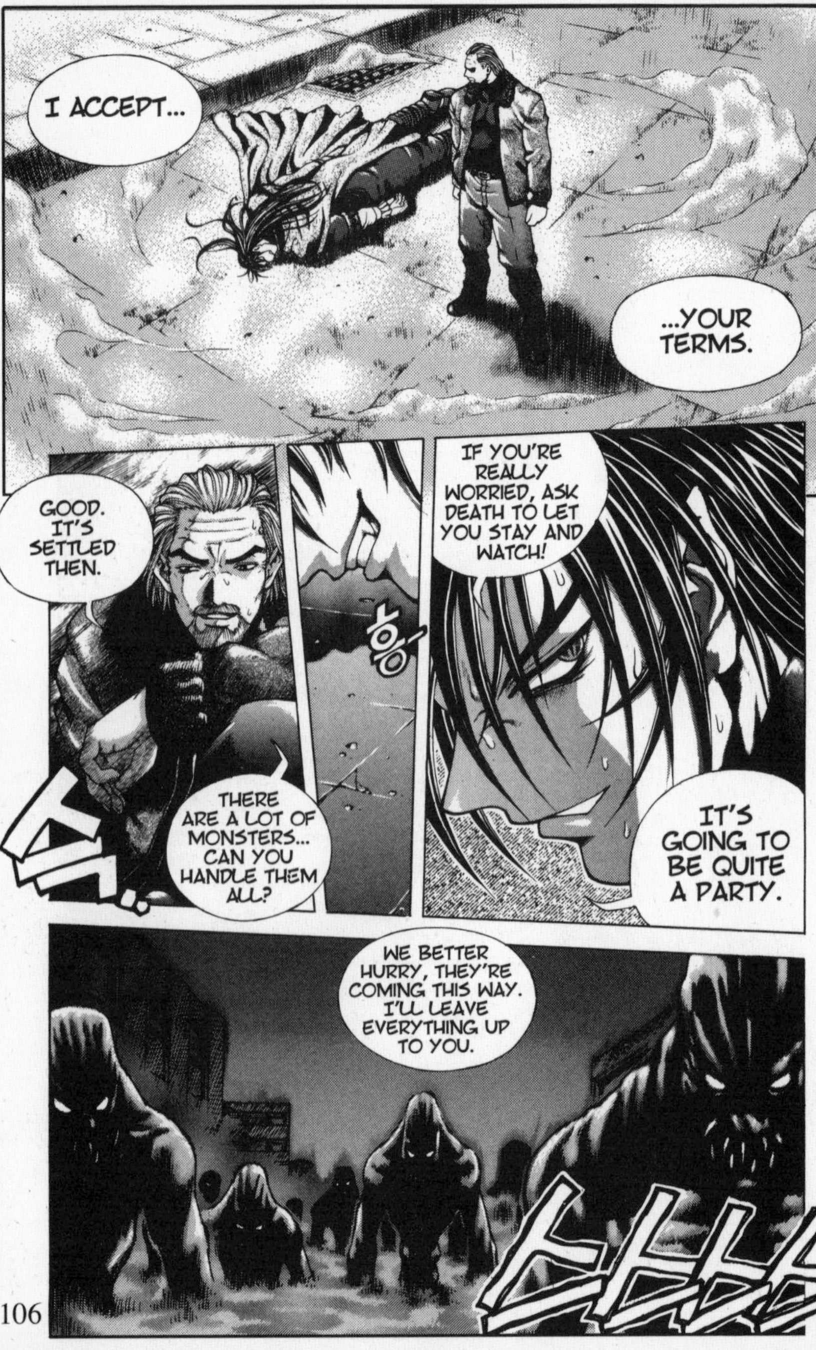
I ACCEPT...
...YOUR TERMS.
GOOD. IT'S SETTLED THEN.
THERE ARE A LOT OF MONSTERS... CAN YOU HANDLE THEM ALL?
IF YOU'RE REALLY WORRIED, ASK DEATH TO LET YOU STAY AND WATCH!
IT'S GOING TO BE QUITE A PARTY.
WE BETTER HURRY, THEY'RE COMING THIS WAY. I'LL LEAVE EVERYTHING UP TO YOU.

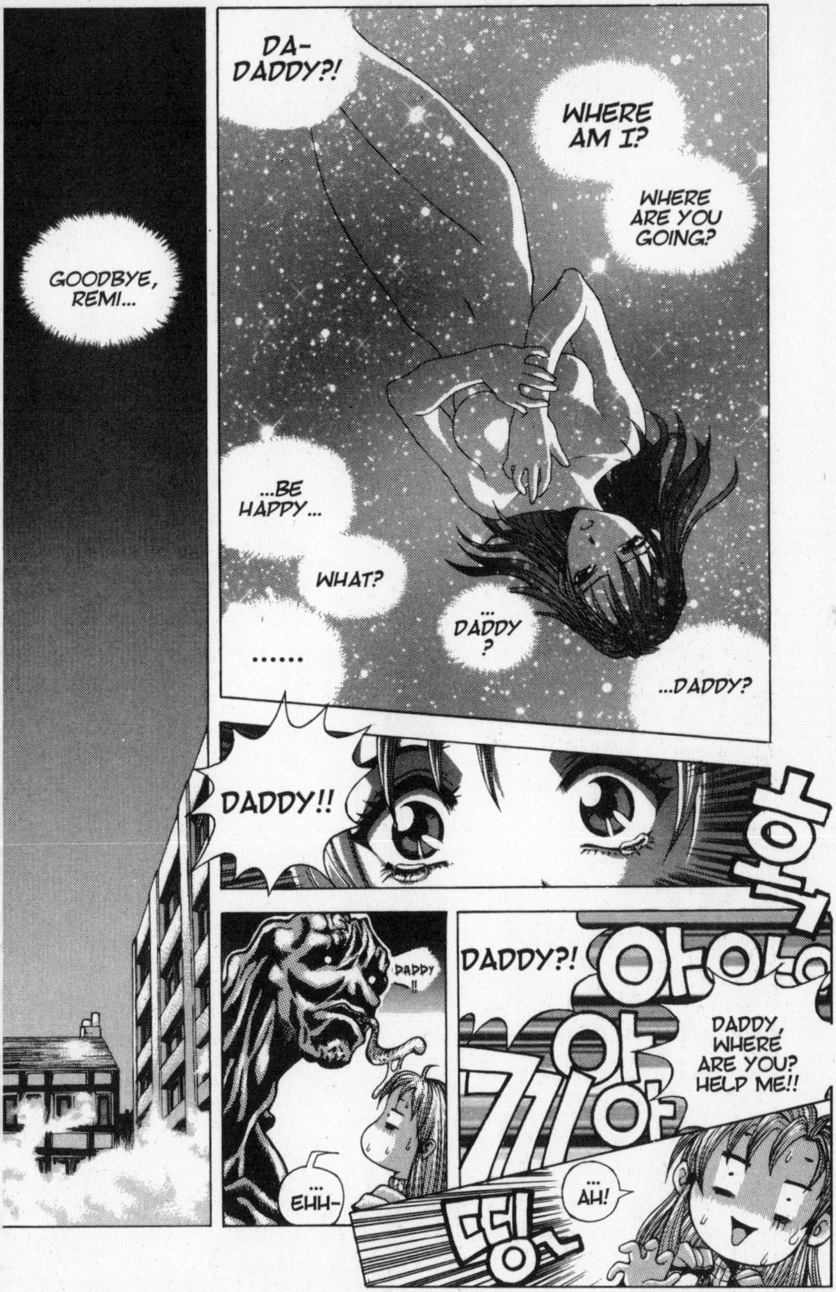
GOODBYE, REMI...
DA- DADDY?!
WHERE AM I?
WHERE ARE YOU GOING?
...BE HAPPY...
WHAT?
......
... DADDY ?
...DADDY?
DADDY!!
DADDY !!
... EHH-
DADDY?!
DADDY, WHERE ARE YOU? HELP ME!!
... AH!

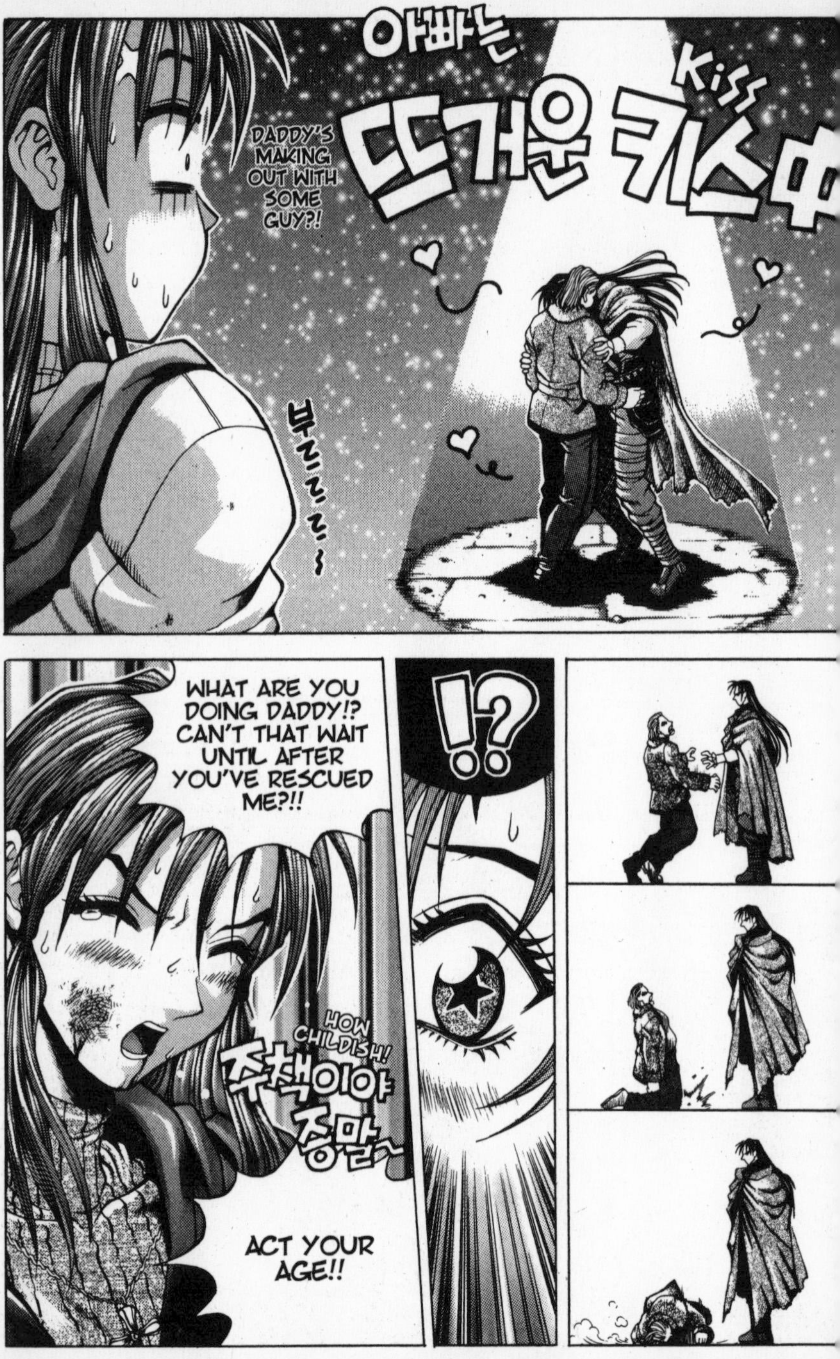
아빠는
DADDY'S MAKING OUT WITH SOME GUY?!
Kiss
뜨거운 키스中
부르르르르~
WHAT ARE YOU DOING DADDY!? CAN'T THAT WAIT UNTIL AFTER YOU'VE RESCUED ME?!!
HOW CHILDISH!
주책이야 정말~
ACT YOUR AGE!!
!?

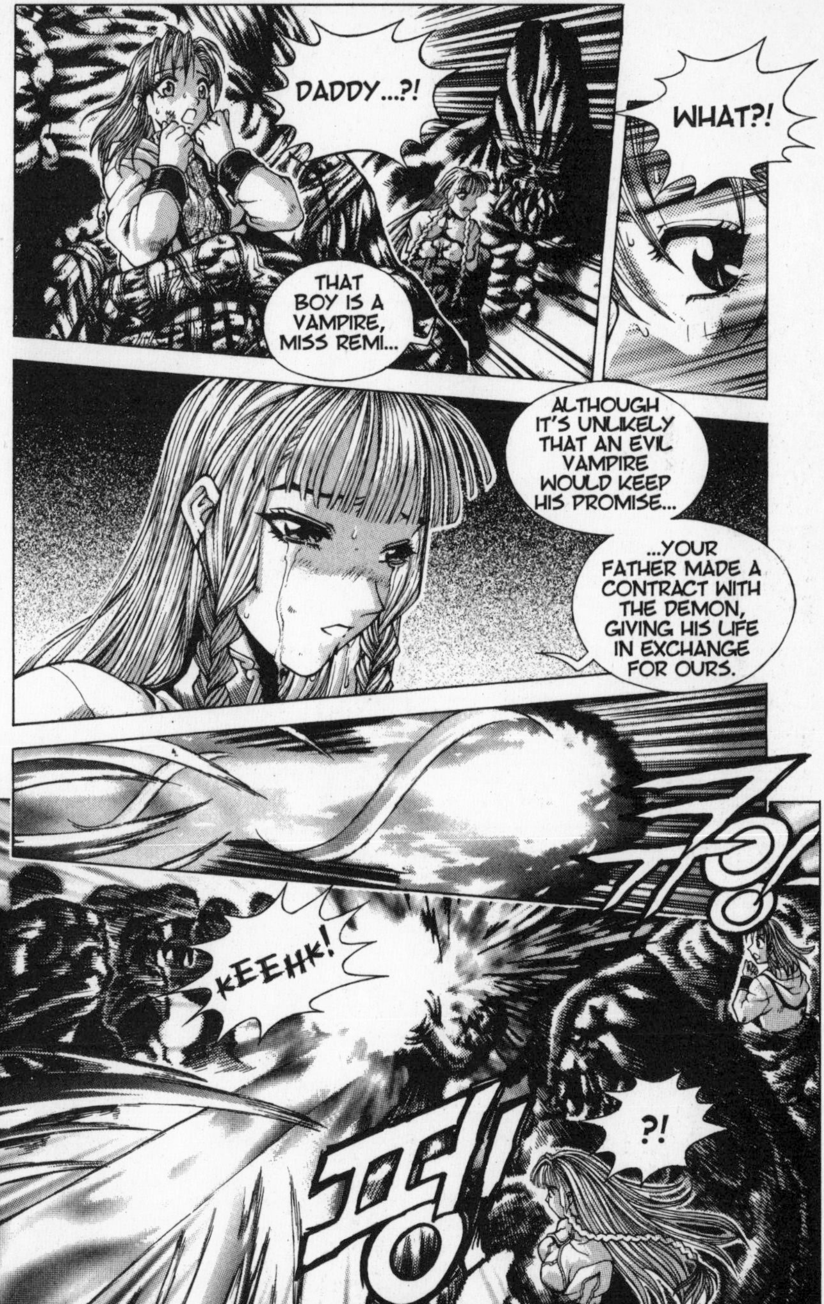
DADDY...?!
THAT BOY IS A VAMPIRE, MISS REMI...
WHAT?!
ALTHOUGH IT'S UNLIKELY THAT AN EVIL VAMPIRE WOULD KEEP HIS PROMISE...
...YOUR FATHER MADE A CONTRACT WITH THE DEMON, GIVING HIS LIFE IN EXCHANGE FOR OURS.
KEEHK!
?!

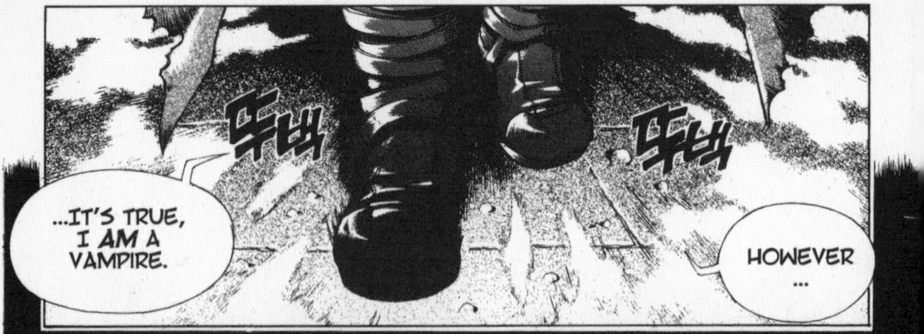
뚜벅
...IT'S TRUE, I *AM* A VAMPIRE.
뚜벅
HOWEVER ...

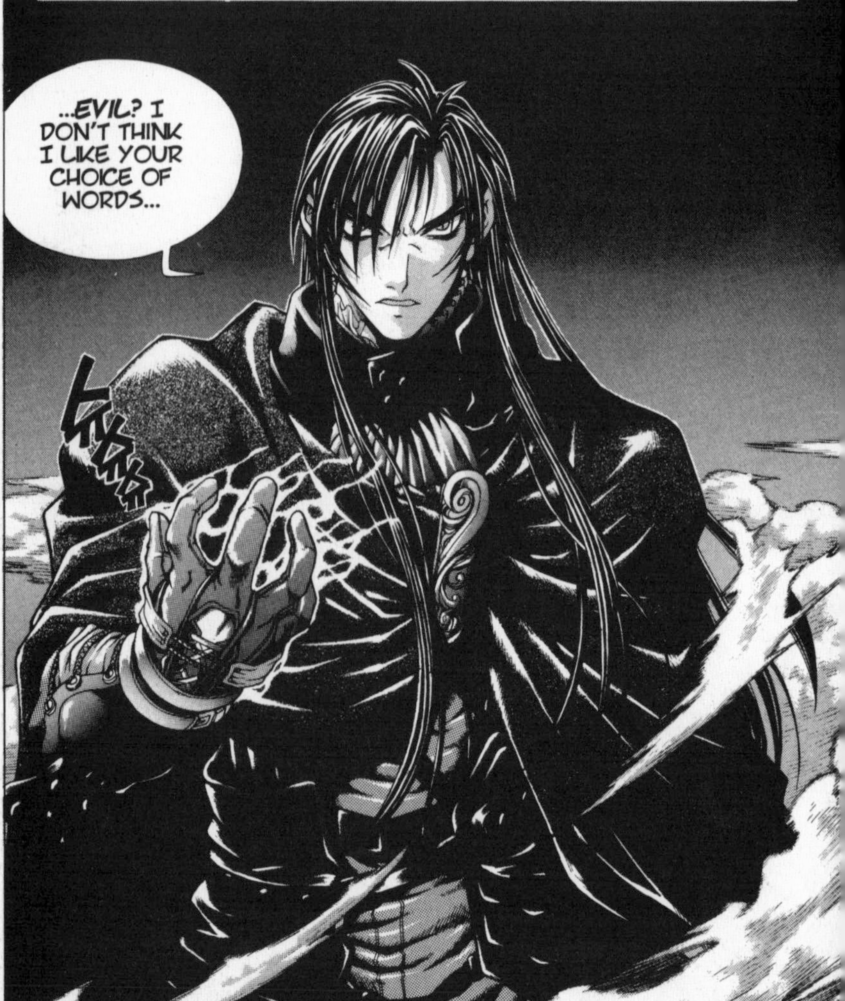
...*EVIL*? I DON'T THINK I LIKE YOUR CHOICE OF WORDS...

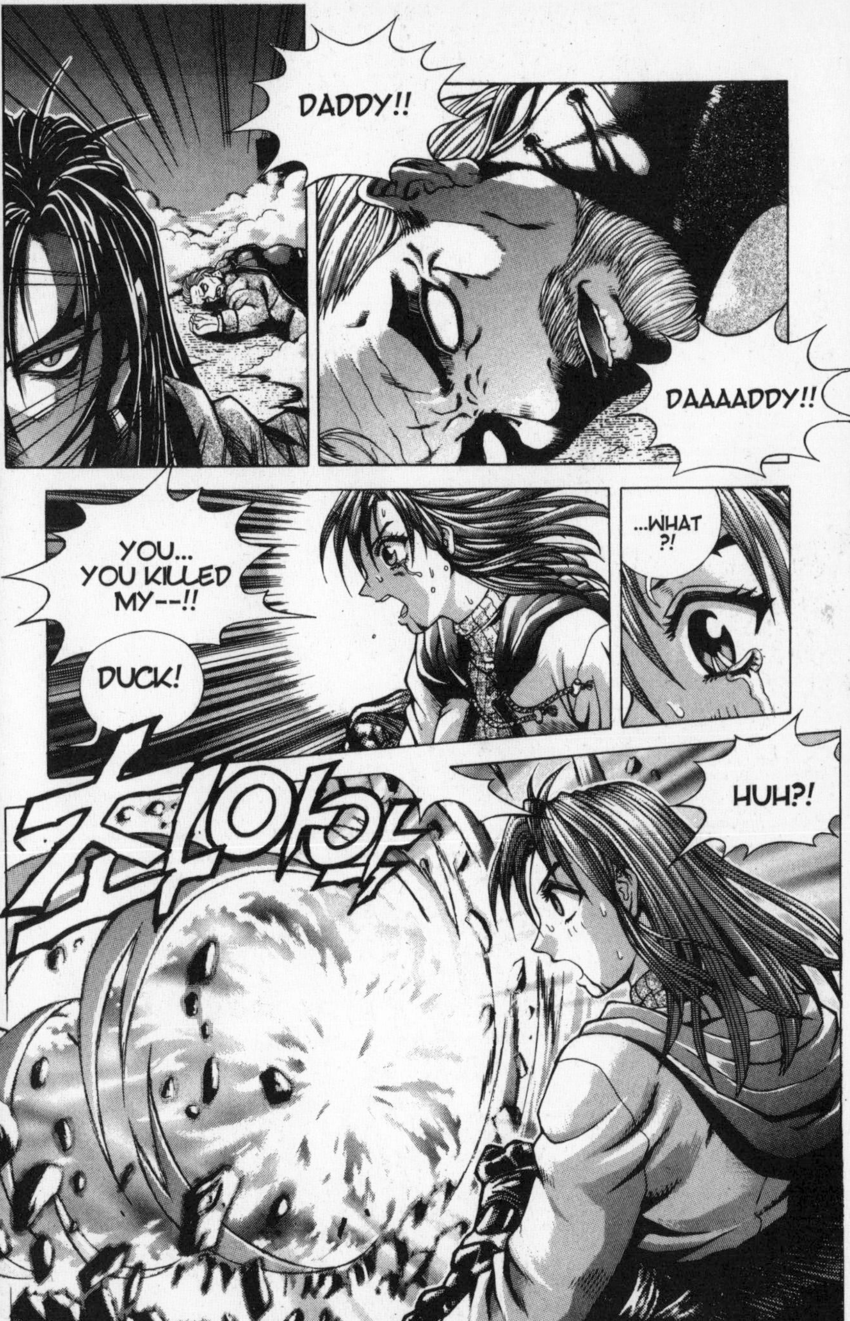
DADDY!!
DAAAADDY!!
YOU... YOU KILLED MY--!!
DUCK!
...WHAT ?!
HUH?!

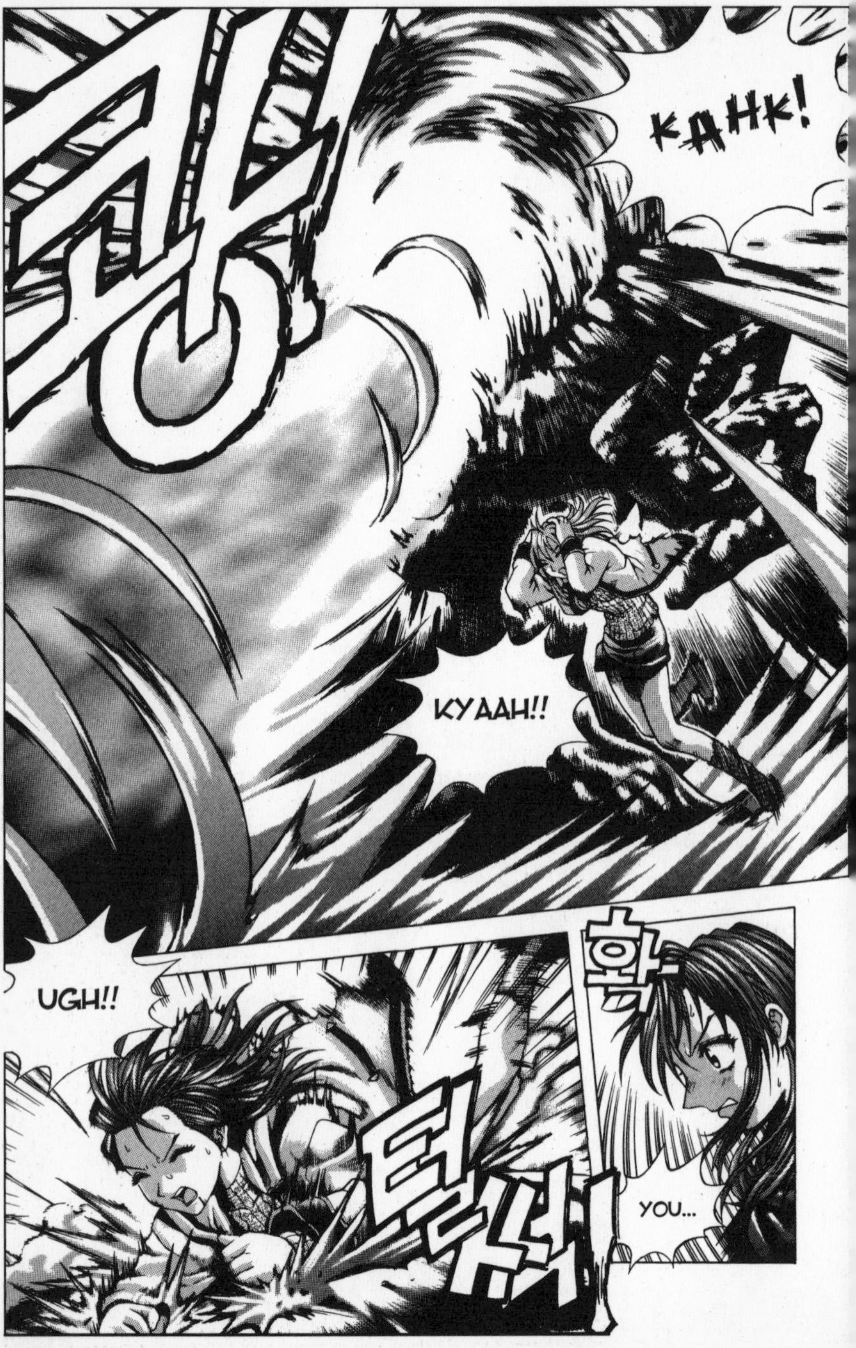
KAHK!
KYAAH!!
UGH!!
YOU...

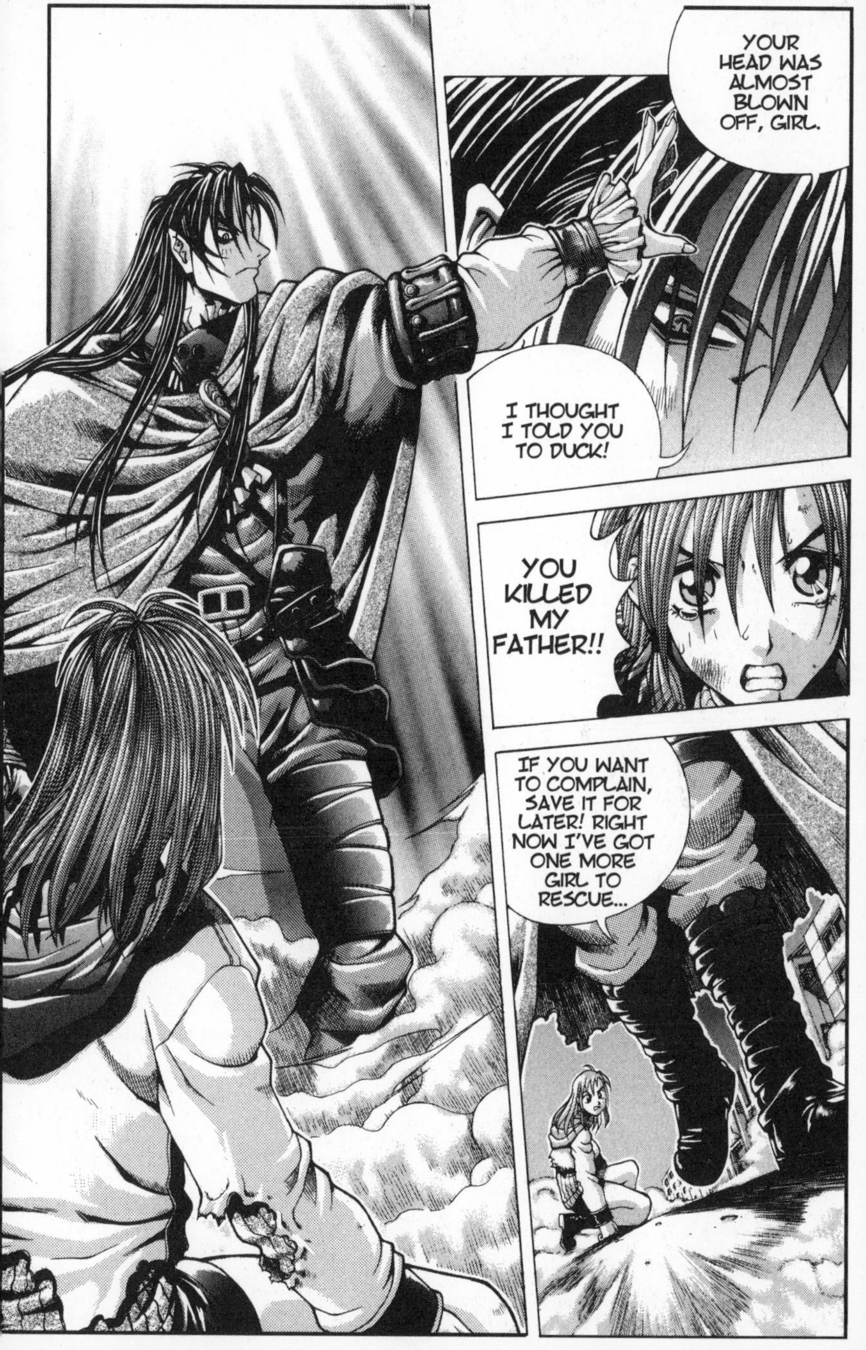
YOUR HEAD WAS ALMOST BLOWN OFF, GIRL.
I THOUGHT I TOLD YOU TO DUCK!
YOU KILLED MY FATHER!!
IF YOU WANT TO COMPLAIN, SAVE IT FOR LATER! RIGHT NOW I'VE GOT ONE MORE GIRL TO RESCUE...

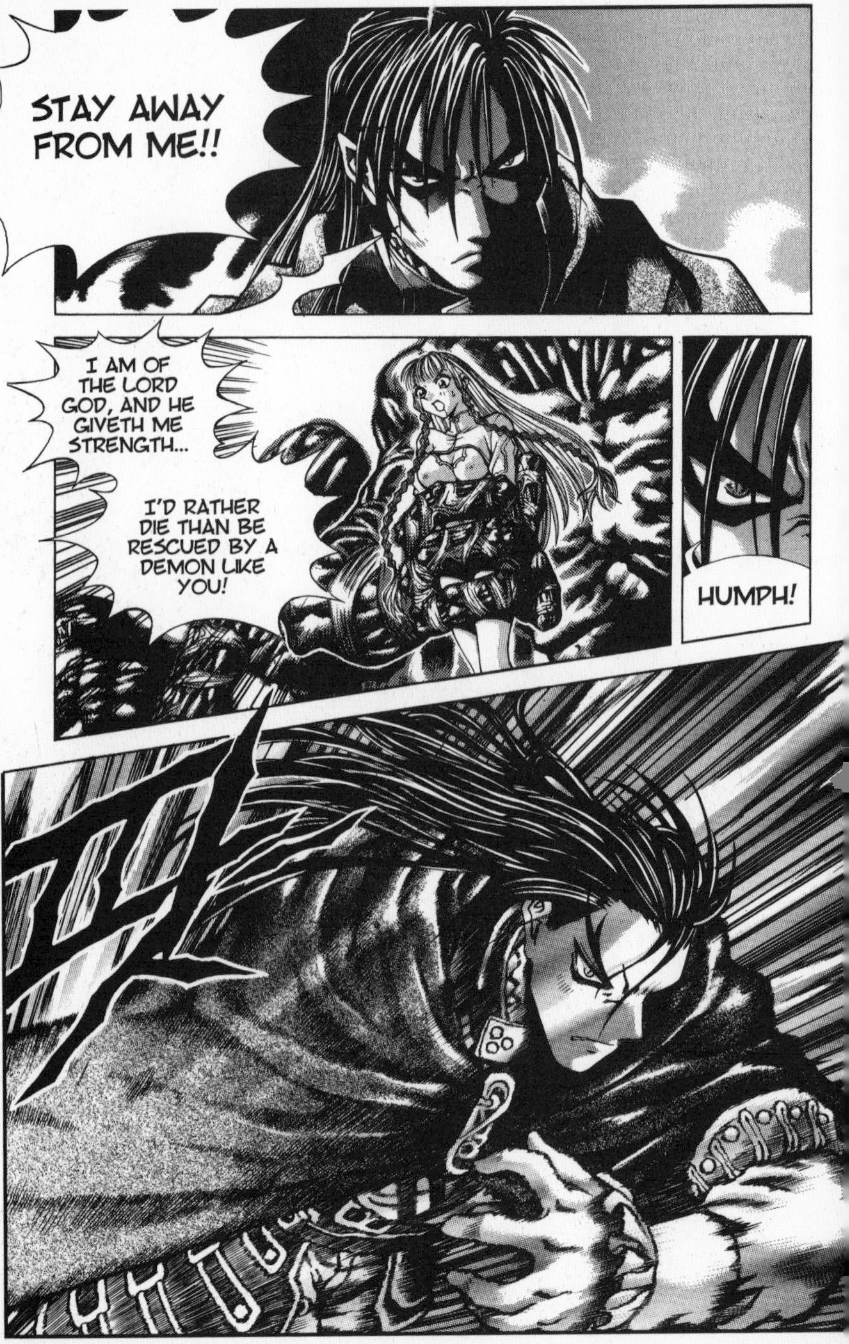
STAY AWAY FROM ME!!
I AM OF THE LORD GOD, AND HE GIVETH ME STRENGTH...
I'D RATHER DIE THAN BE RESCUED BY A DEMON LIKE YOU!
HUMPH!

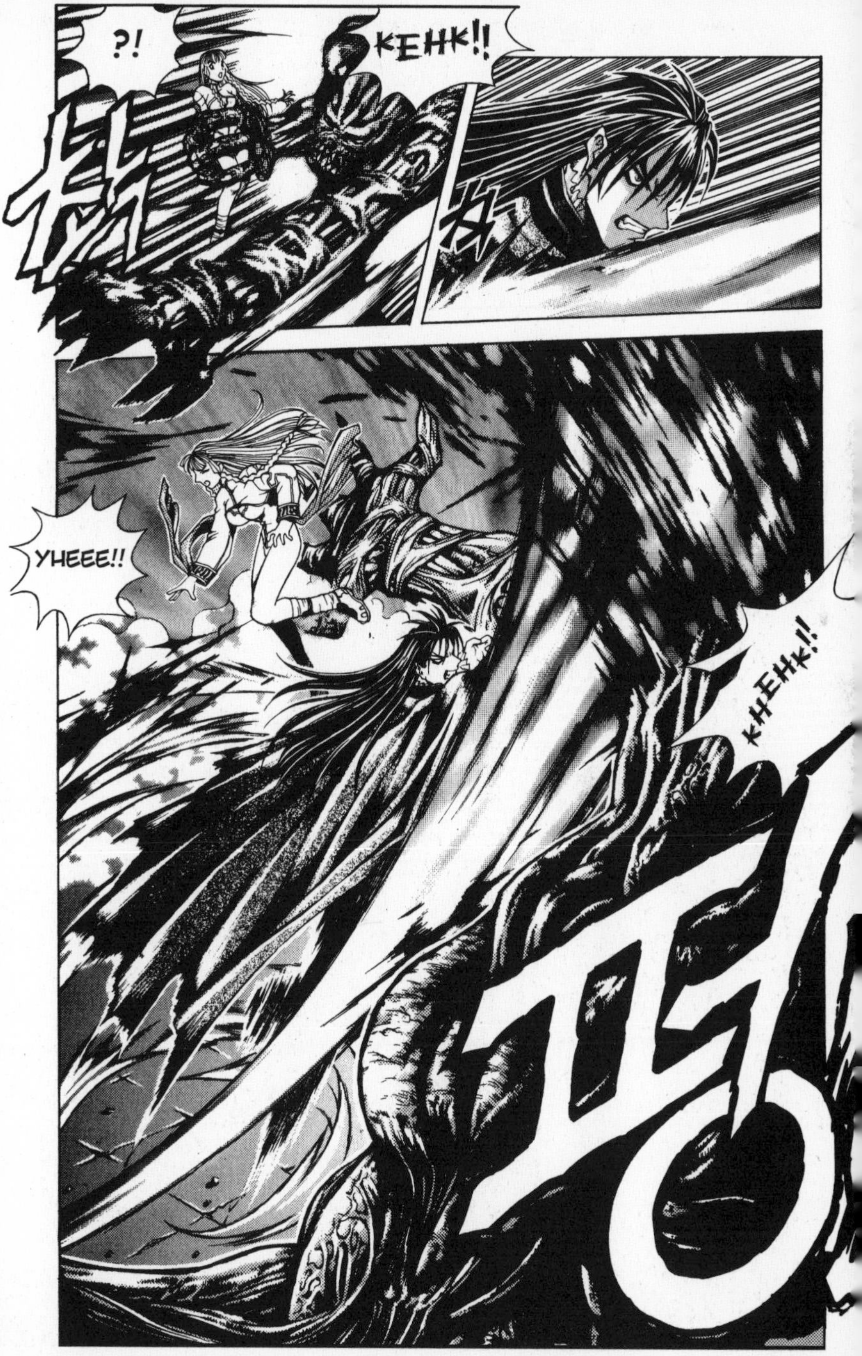
?!
KEHK!!
YHEEE!!
KHEHK!!

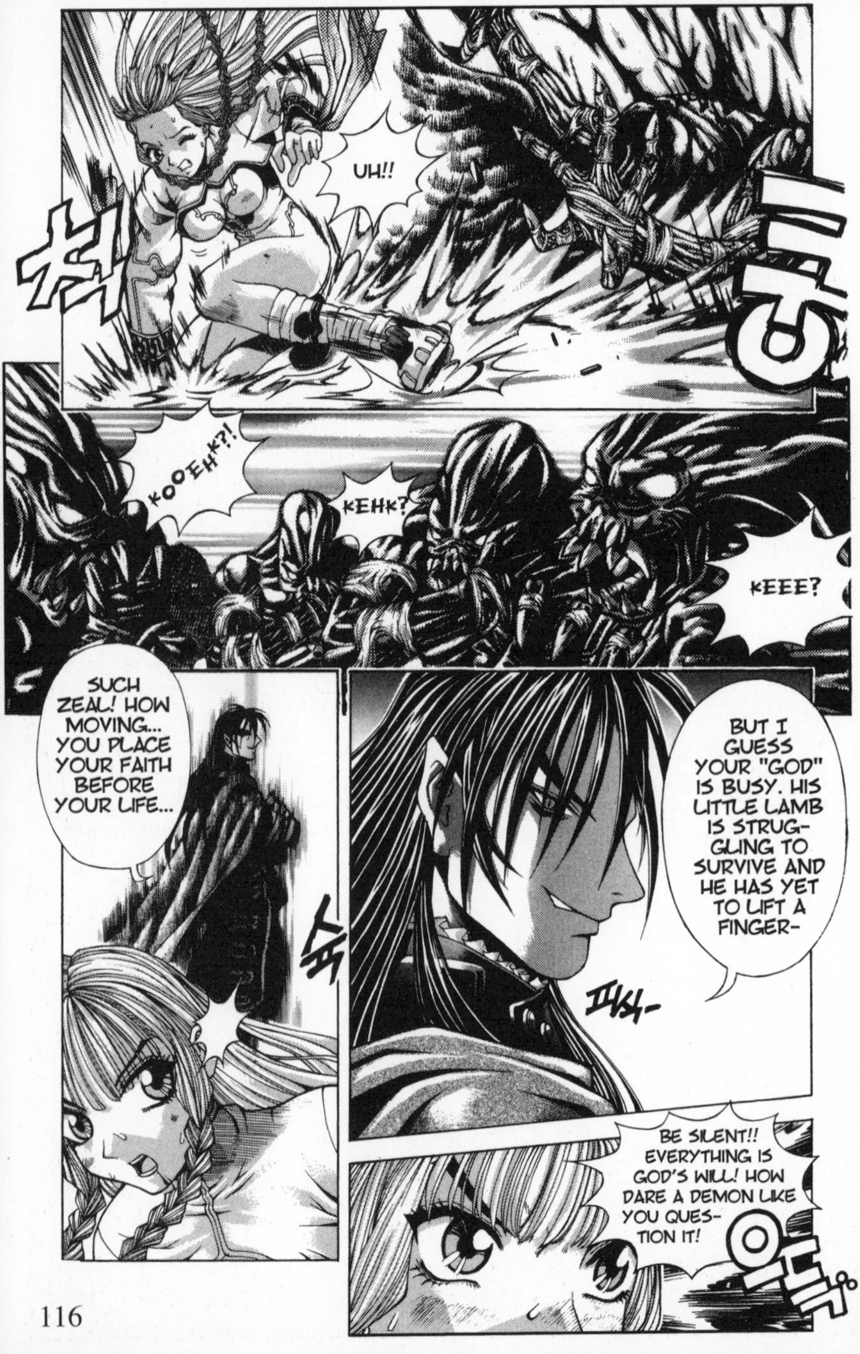
UH!!
KOOEHK?!
KEHK?
KEEE?
SUCH ZEAL! HOW MOVING... YOU PLACE YOUR FAITH BEFORE YOUR LIFE...
BUT I GUESS YOUR "GOD" IS BUSY. HIS LITTLE LAMB IS STRUG-GLING TO SURVIVE AND HE HAS YET TO LIFT A FINGER-
BE SILENT!! EVERYTHING IS GOD'S WILL! HOW DARE A DEMON LIKE YOU QUES-TION IT!

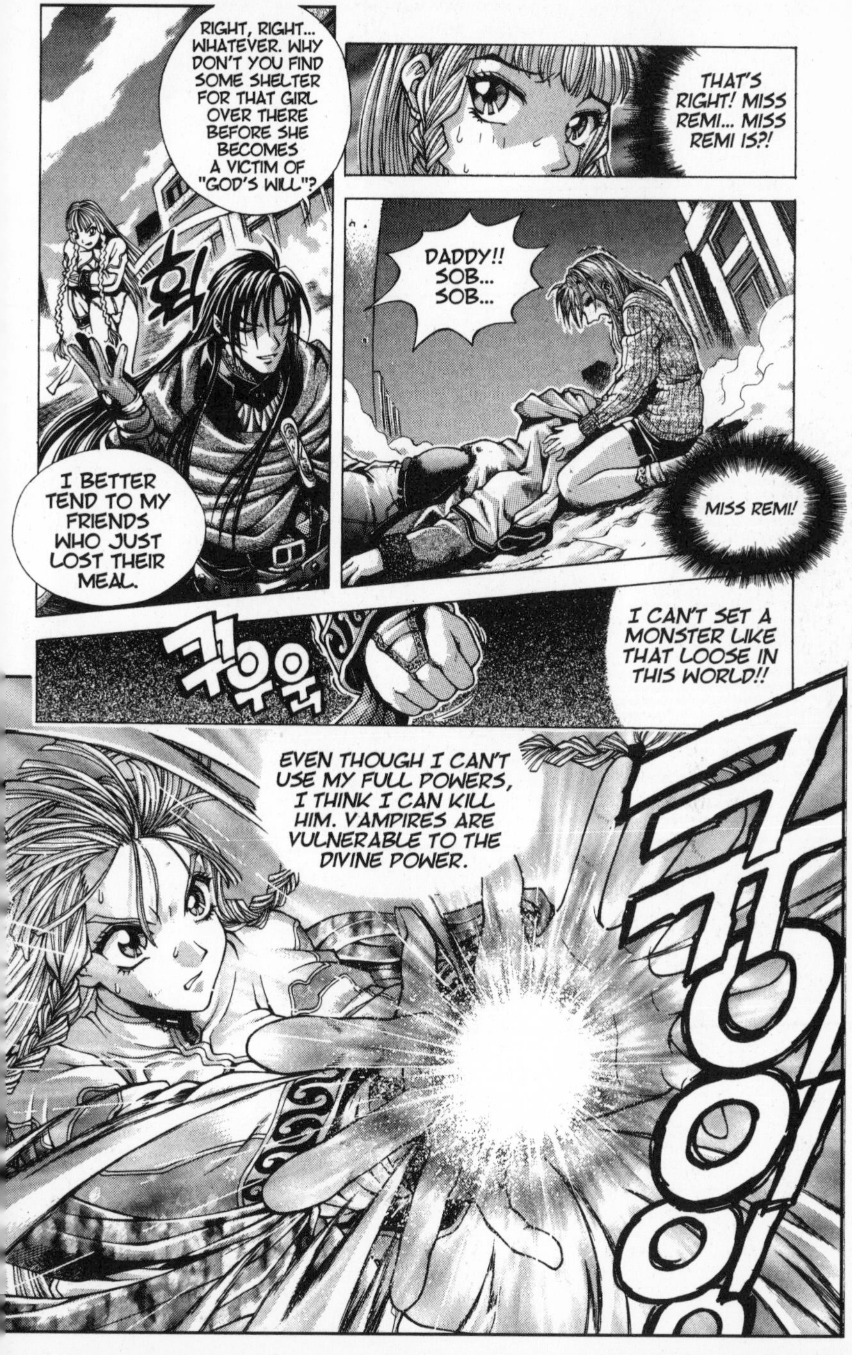
RIGHT, RIGHT... WHATEVER. WHY DON'T YOU FIND SOME SHELTER FOR THAT GIRL OVER THERE BEFORE SHE BECOMES A VICTIM OF "GOD'S WILL"?
I BETTER TEND TO MY FRIENDS WHO JUST LOST THEIR MEAL.
THAT'S RIGHT! MISS REMI... MISS REMI IS?!
DADDY!! SOB... SOB...
MISS REMI!
I CAN'T SET A MONSTER LIKE THAT LOOSE IN THIS WORLD!!
EVEN THOUGH I CAN'T USE MY FULL POWERS, I THINK I CAN KILL HIM. VAMPIRES ARE VULNERABLE TO THE DIVINE POWER.

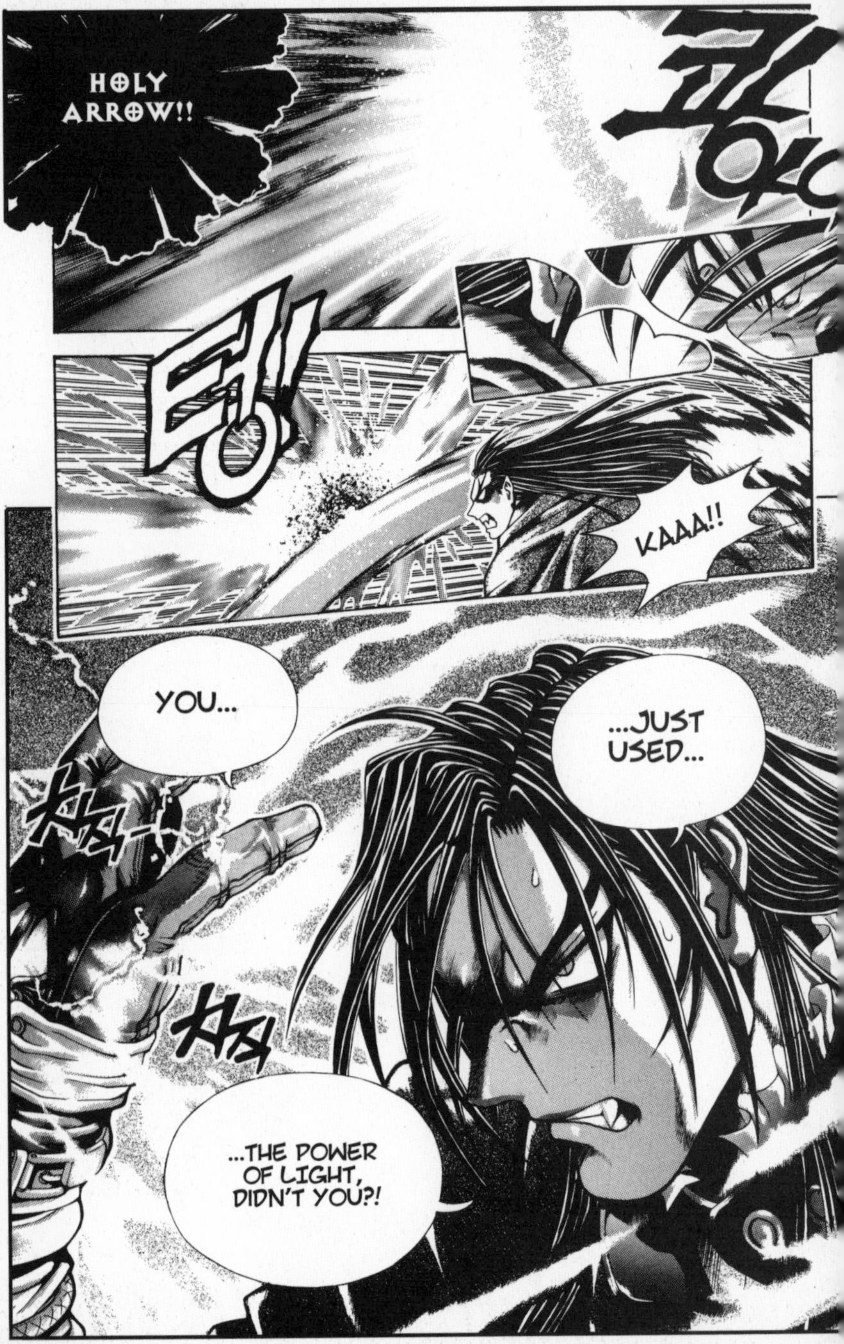
HOLY ARROW!!
KAAA!!
YOU...
...JUST USED...
...THE POWER OF LIGHT, DIDN'T YOU?!

Chapter 4: The Sands of Death

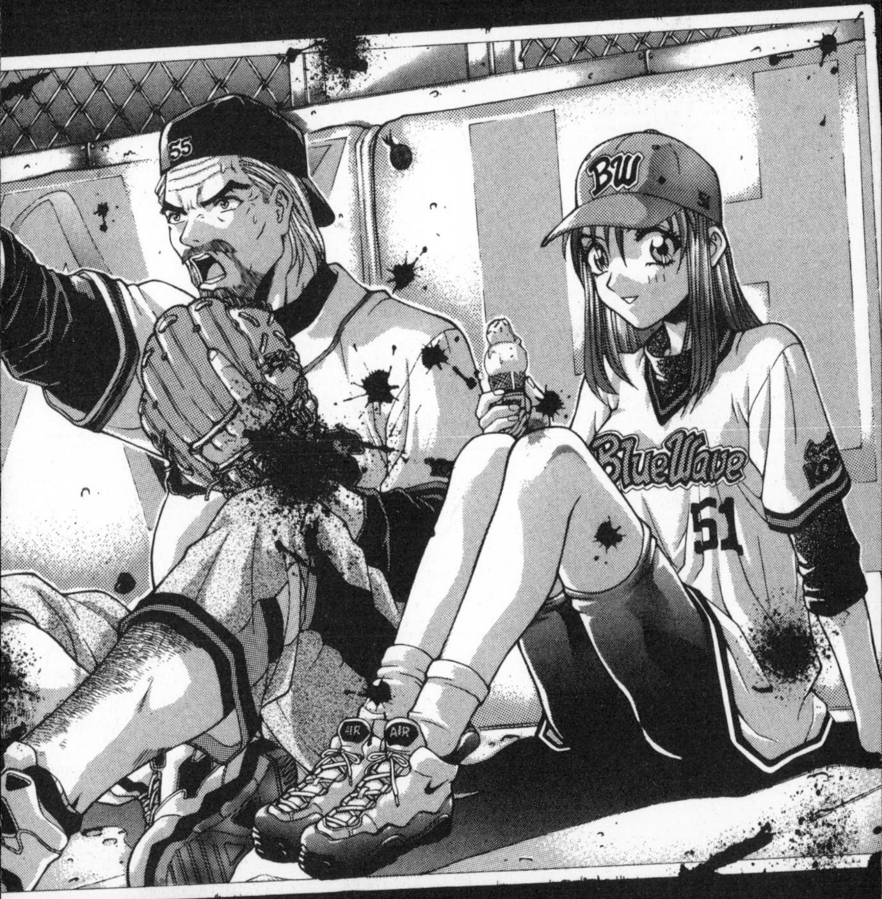
BlueWave

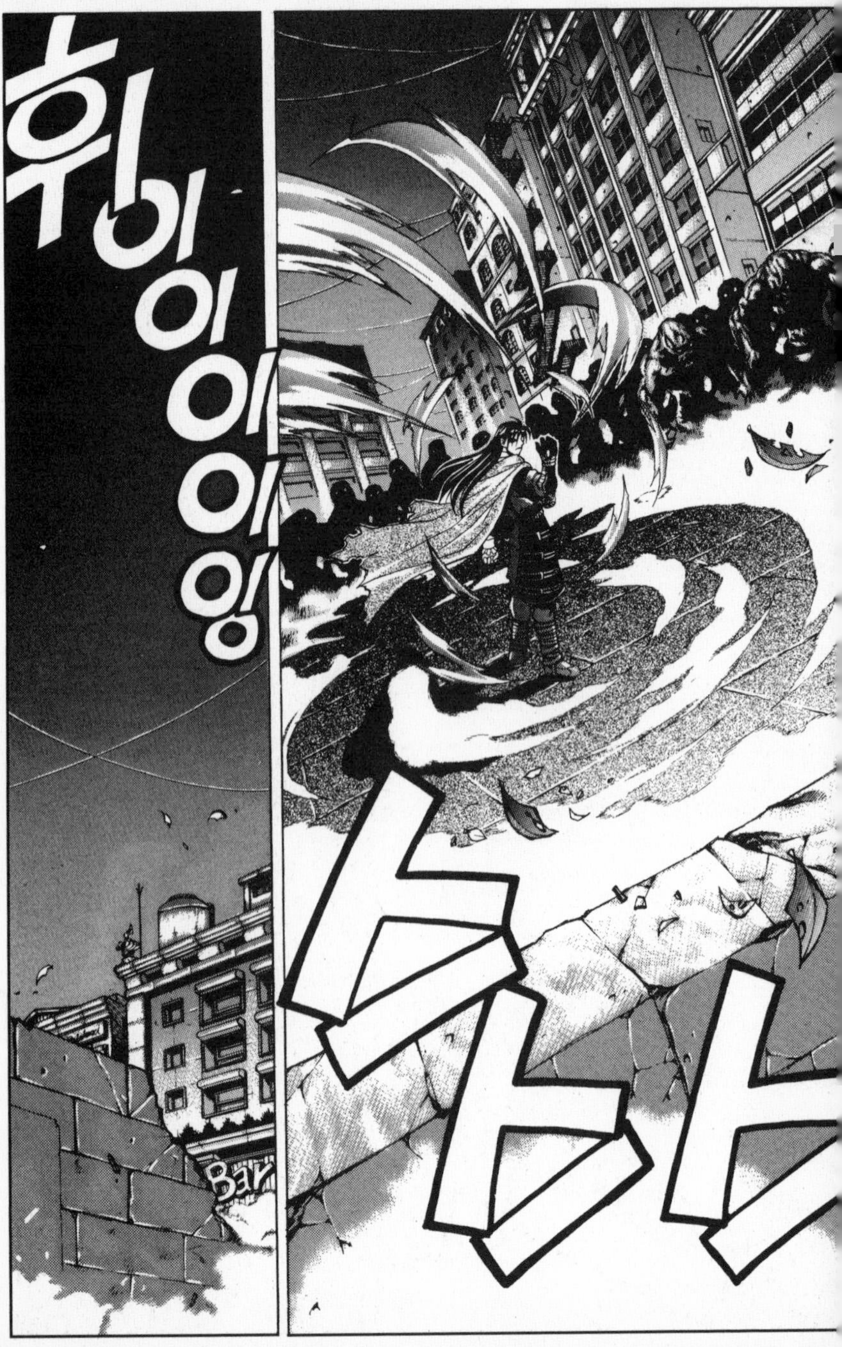
후이이이이잉!
Bar

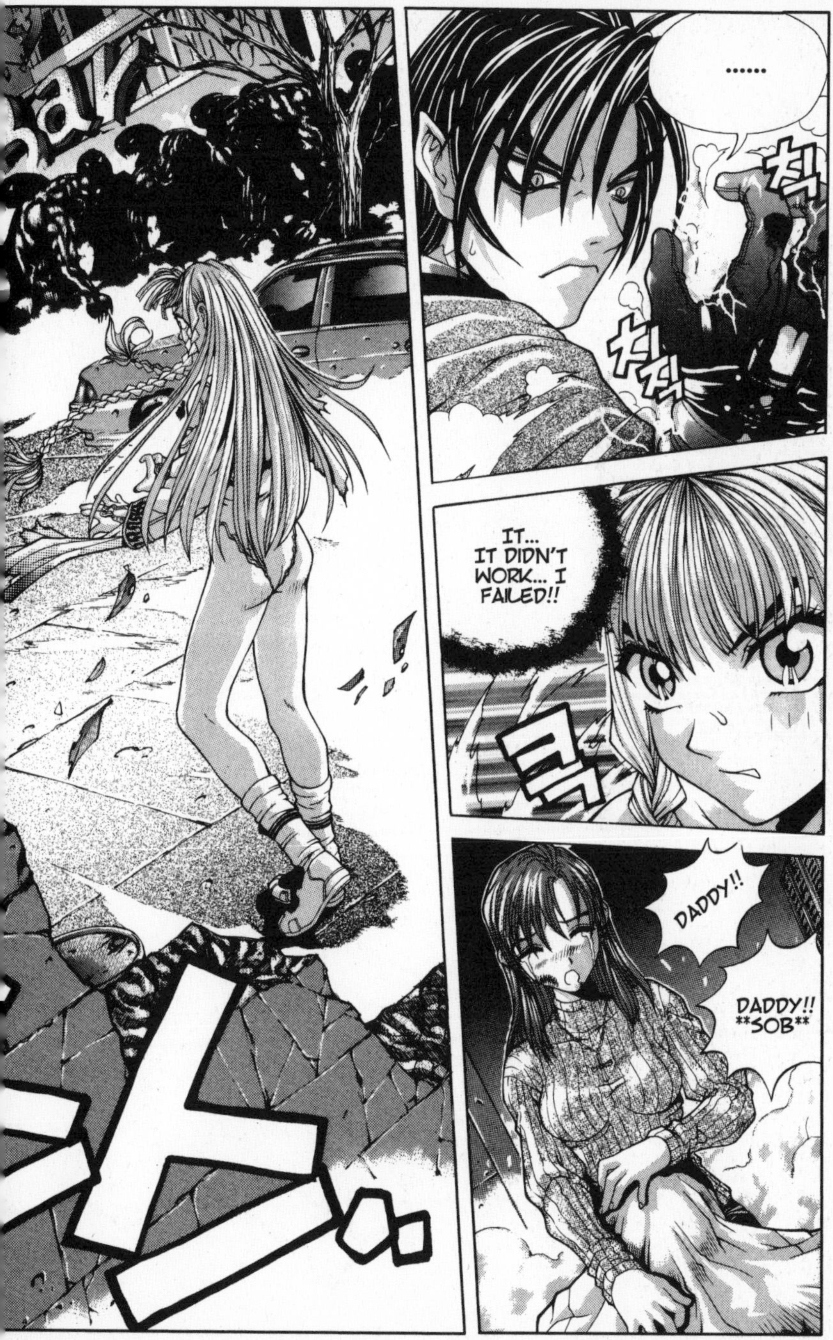
......
IT... IT DIDN'T WORK... I FAILED!!
DADDY!!
DADDY!! **SOB**

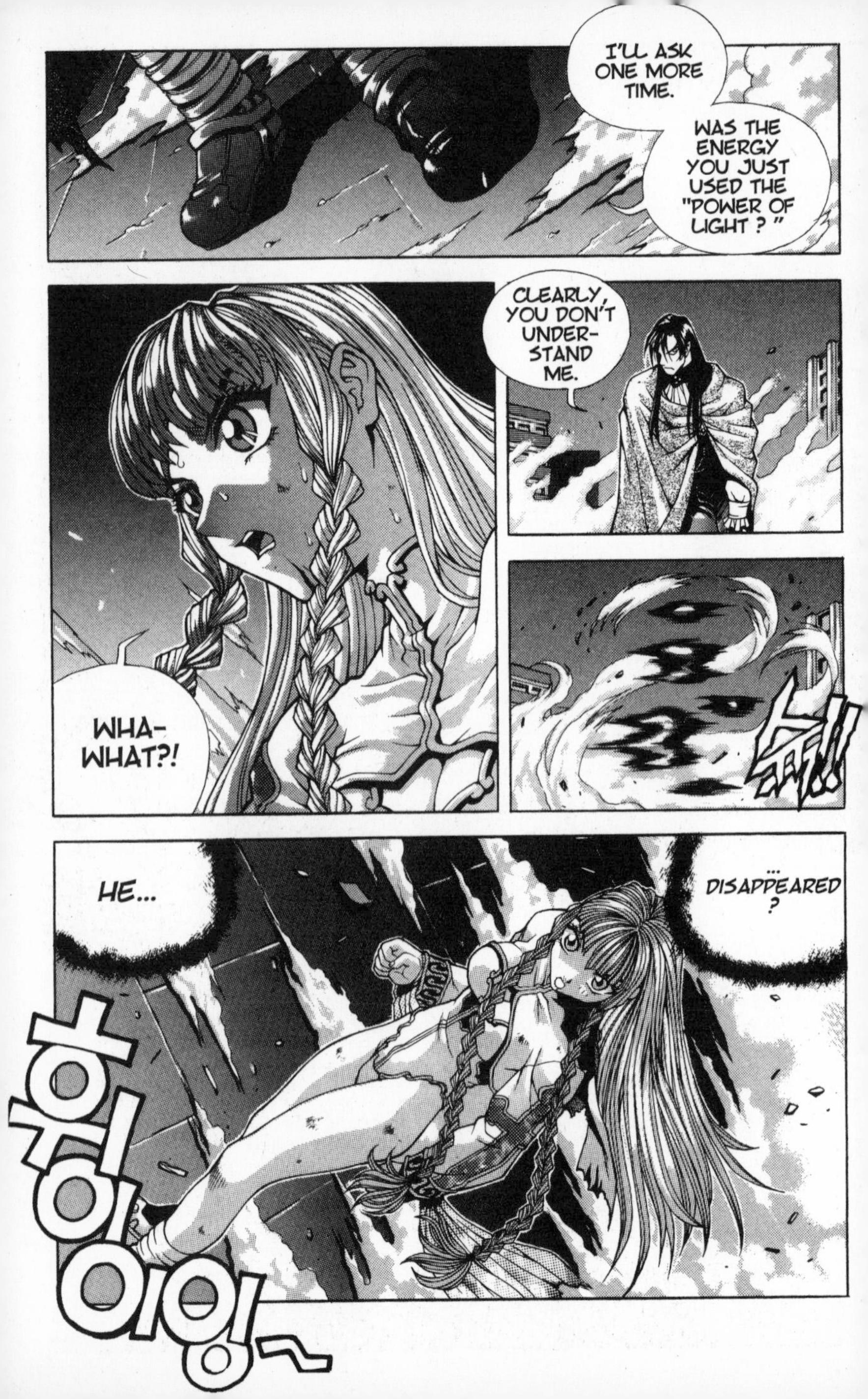
I'LL ASK ONE MORE TIME.
WAS THE ENERGY YOU JUST USED THE "POWER OF LIGHT ? "
WHA-WHAT?!
CLEARLY, YOU DON'T UNDER-STAND ME.
HE...
... DISAPPEARED ?
하이이잉~

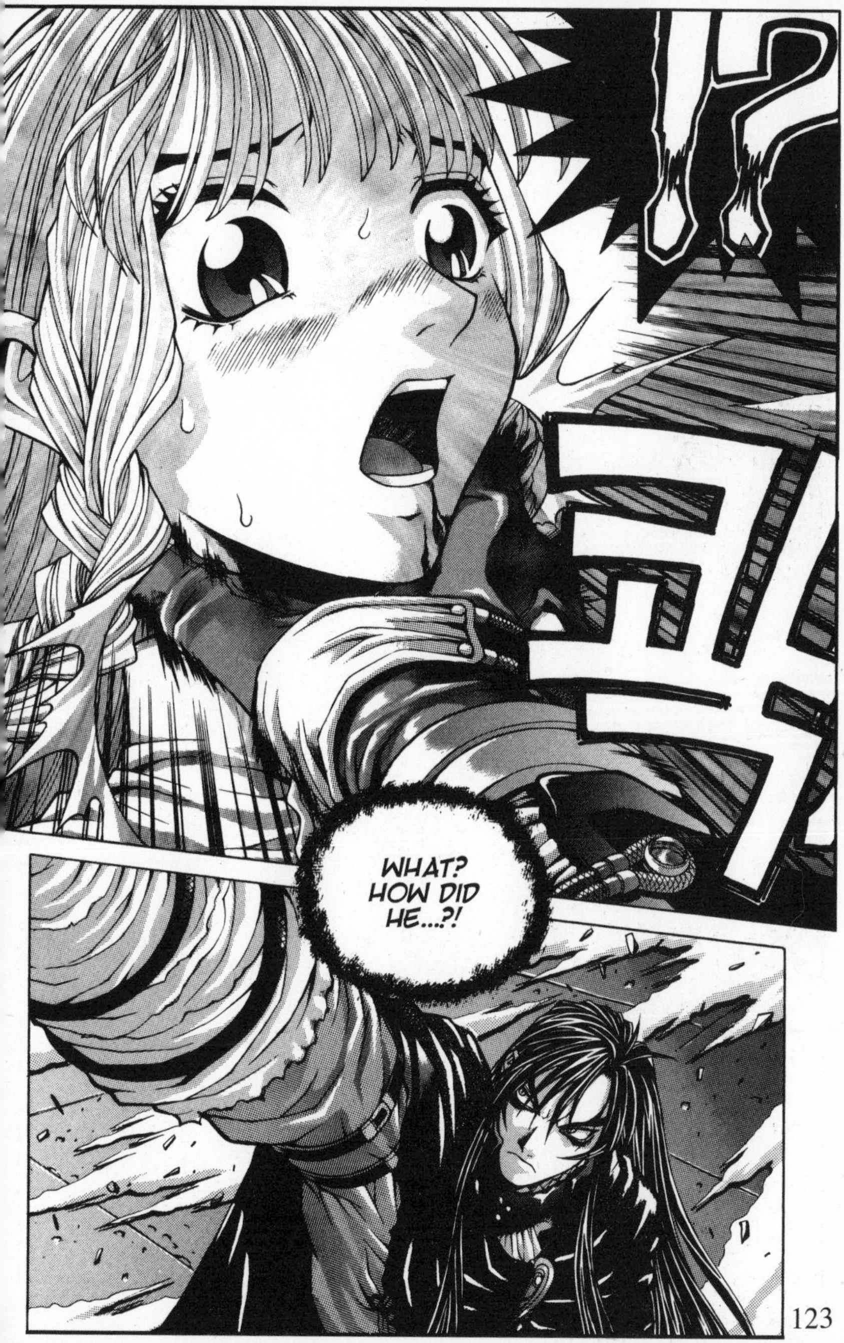
!?
WHAT? HOW DID HE...?!

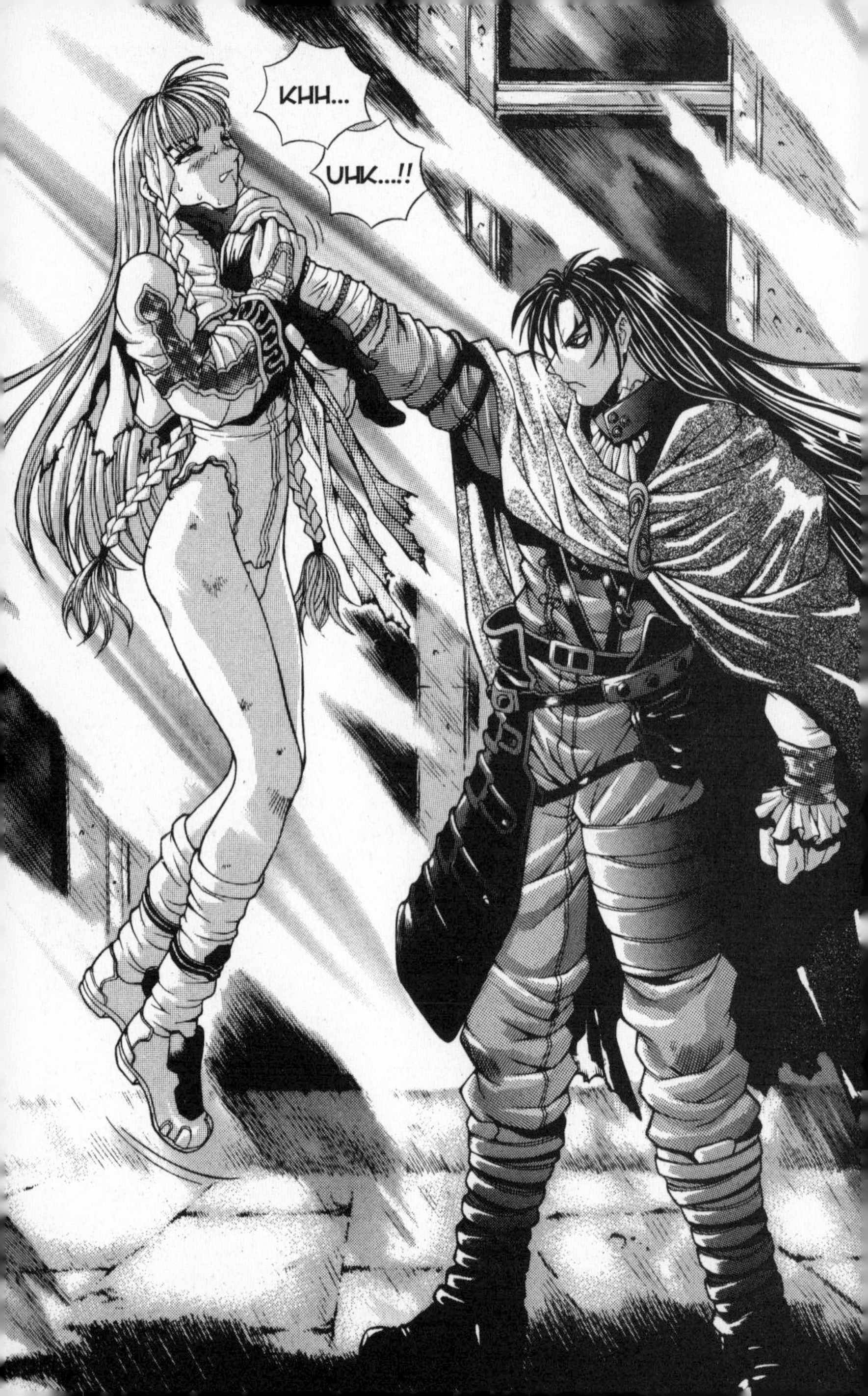
KHH...
UHK...!!

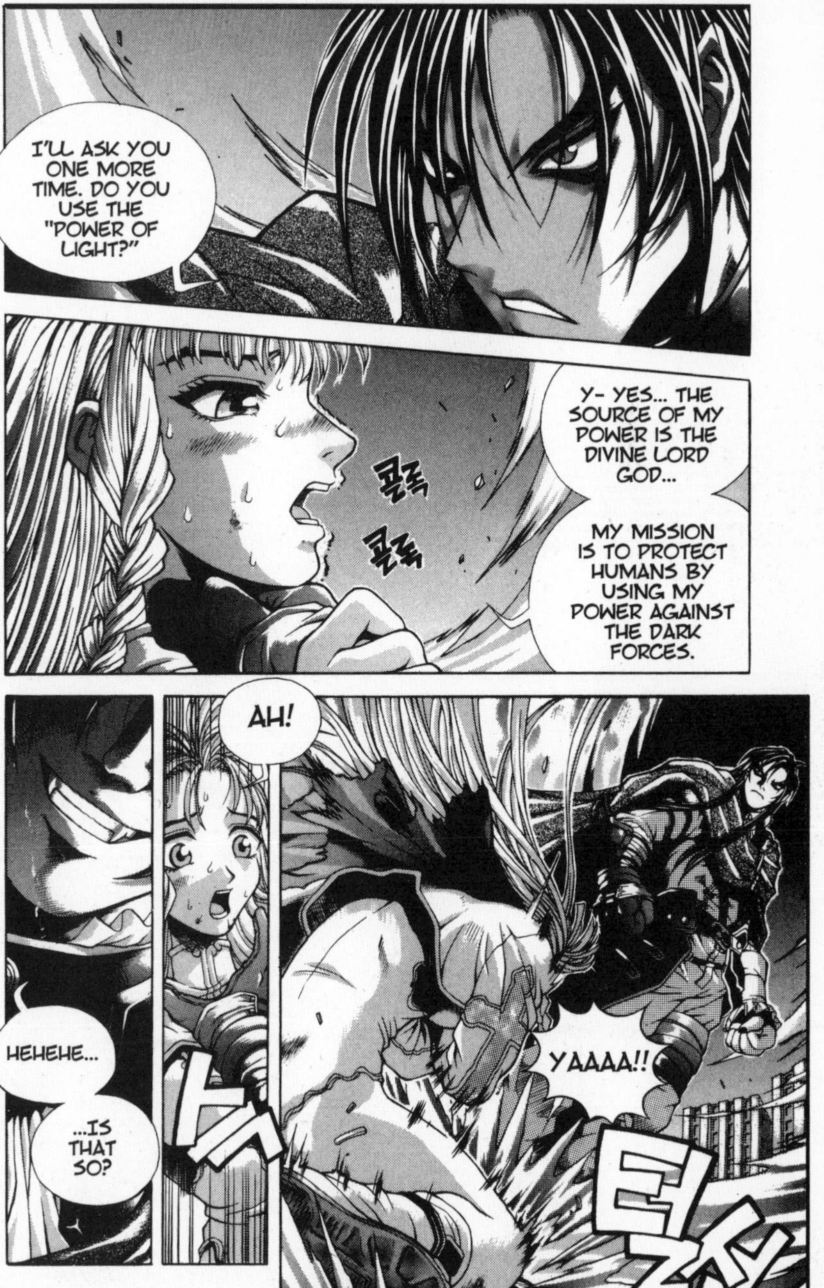
I'LL ASK YOU ONE MORE TIME. DO YOU USE THE "POWER OF LIGHT?"
Y- YES... THE SOURCE OF MY POWER IS THE DIVINE LORD GOD...
MY MISSION IS TO PROTECT HUMANS BY USING MY POWER AGAINST THE DARK FORCES.
HEHEHE...
...IS THAT SO?
AH!
YAAAA!!

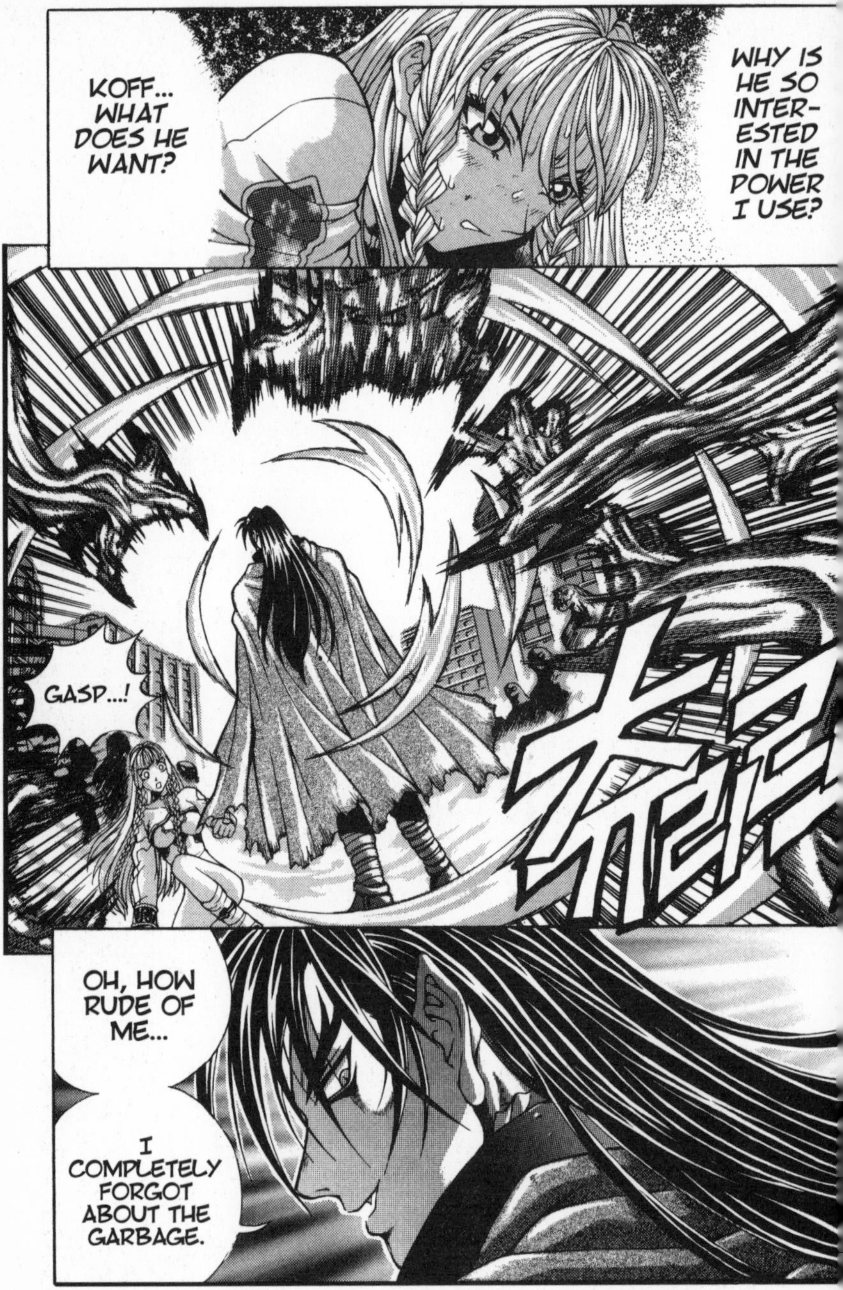
KOFF... WHAT DOES HE WANT?
WHY IS HE SO INTER-ESTED IN THE POWER I USE?
GASP...!
OH, HOW RUDE OF ME...
I COMPLETELY FORGOT ABOUT THE GARBAGE.

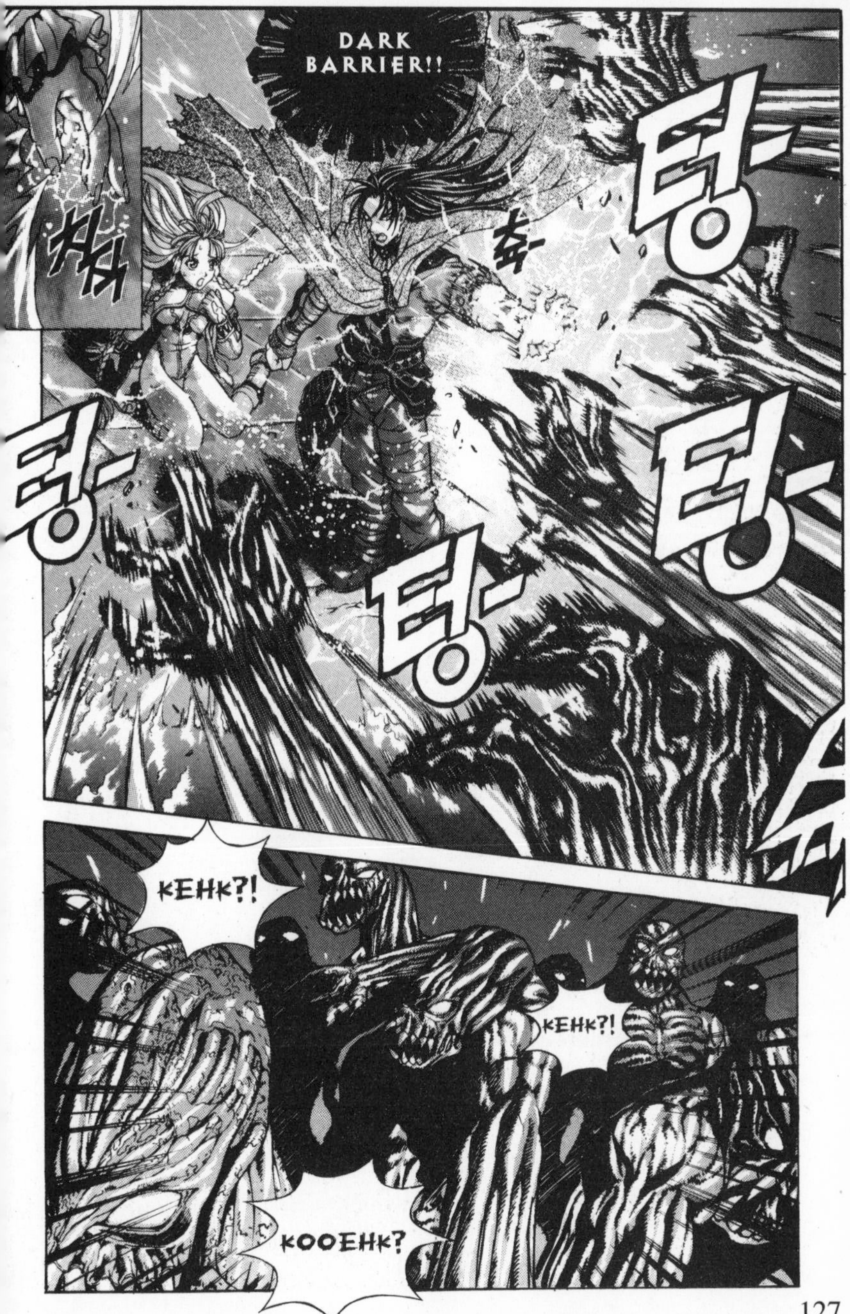
DARK BARRIER!!
KEHK?!
KEHK?!
KOOEHK?

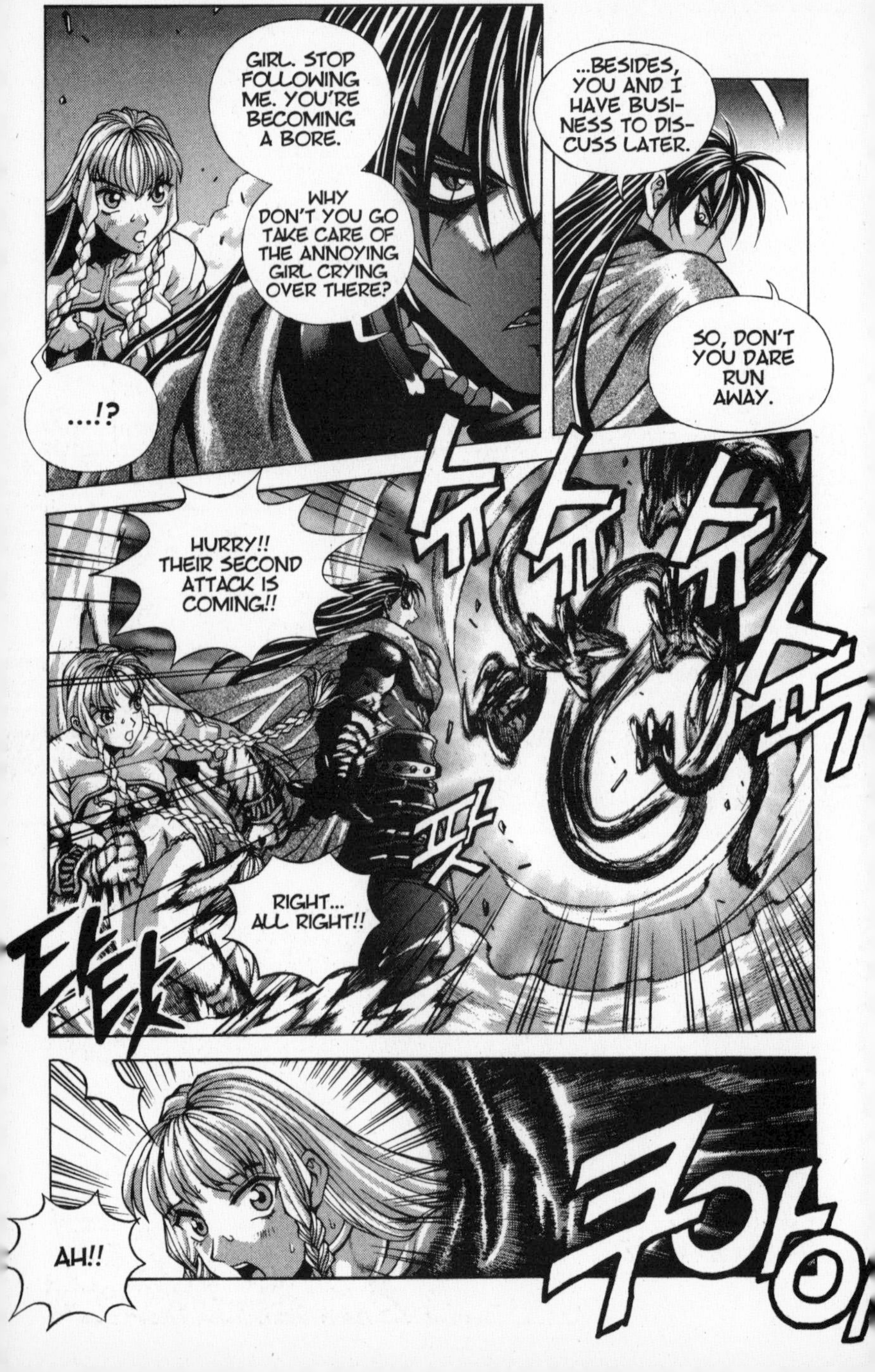
GIRL. STOP FOLLOWING ME. YOU'RE BECOMING A BORE.
WHY DON'T YOU GO TAKE CARE OF THE ANNOYING GIRL CRYING OVER THERE?
...!?
...BESIDES, YOU AND I HAVE BUSI-NESS TO DIS-CUSS LATER.
SO, DON'T YOU DARE RUN AWAY.
HURRY!! THEIR SECOND ATTACK IS COMING!!
RIGHT... ALL RIGHT!!
AH!!

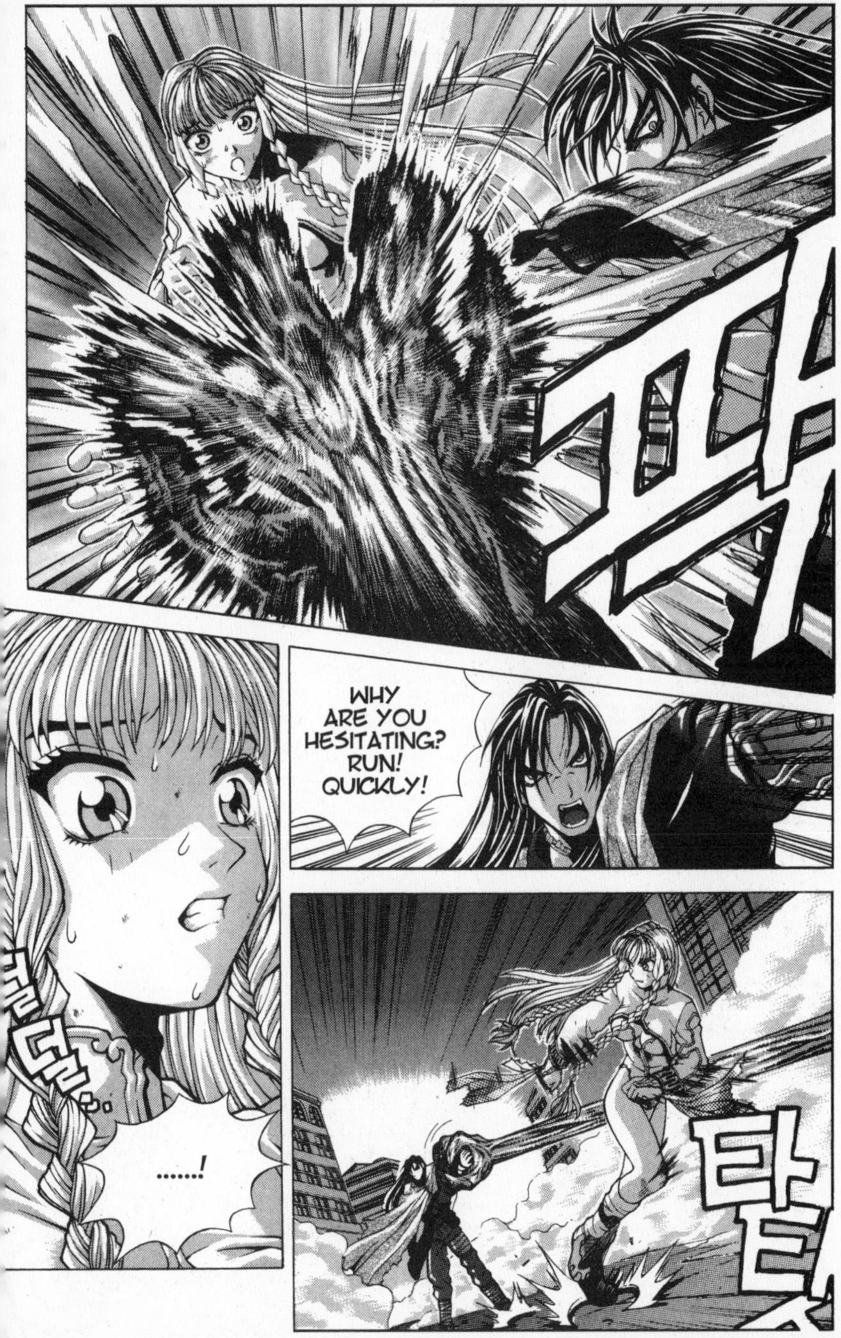
......!
WHY ARE YOU HESITATING? RUN! QUICKLY!

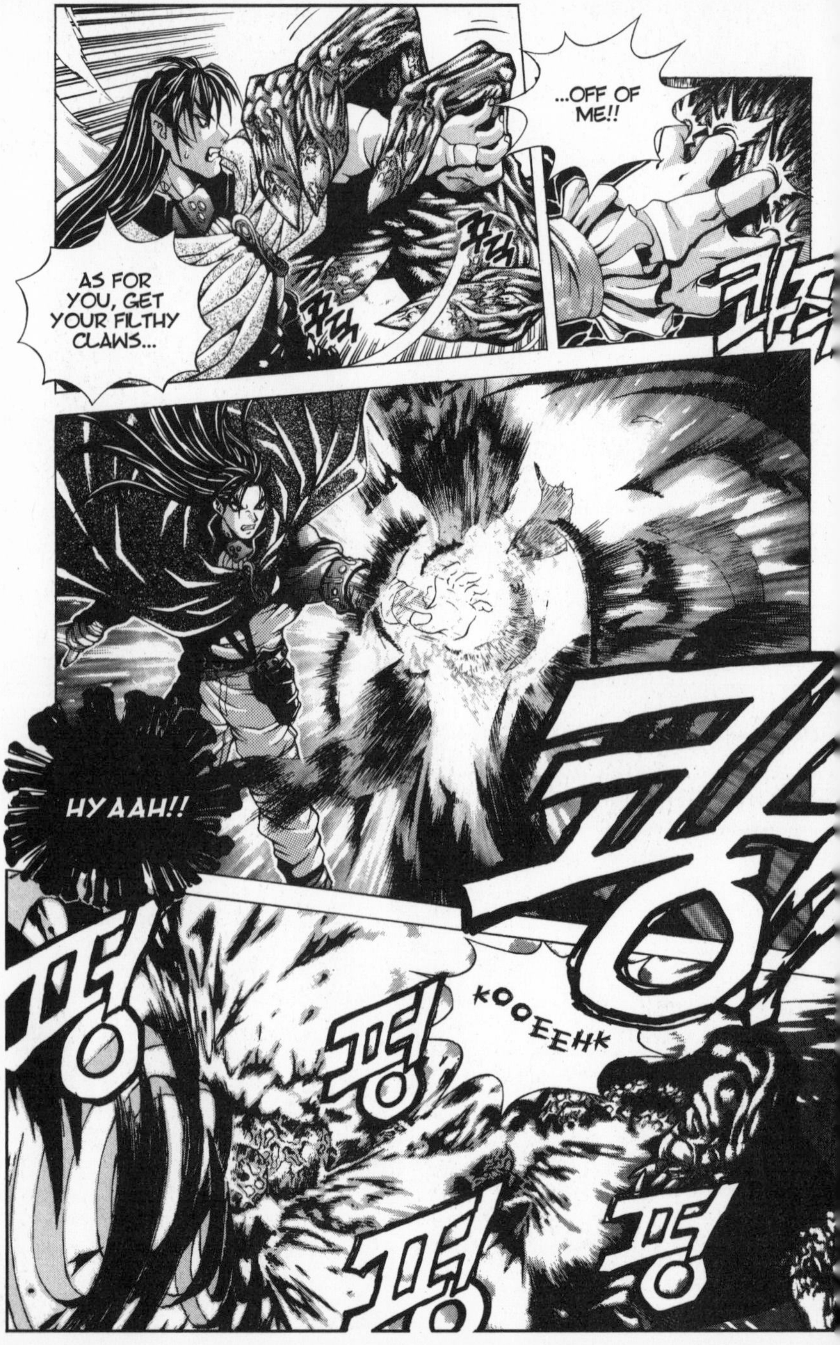
AS FOR YOU, GET YOUR FILTHY CLAWS...
...OFF OF ME!!
HYAAH!!
KOOEEHK

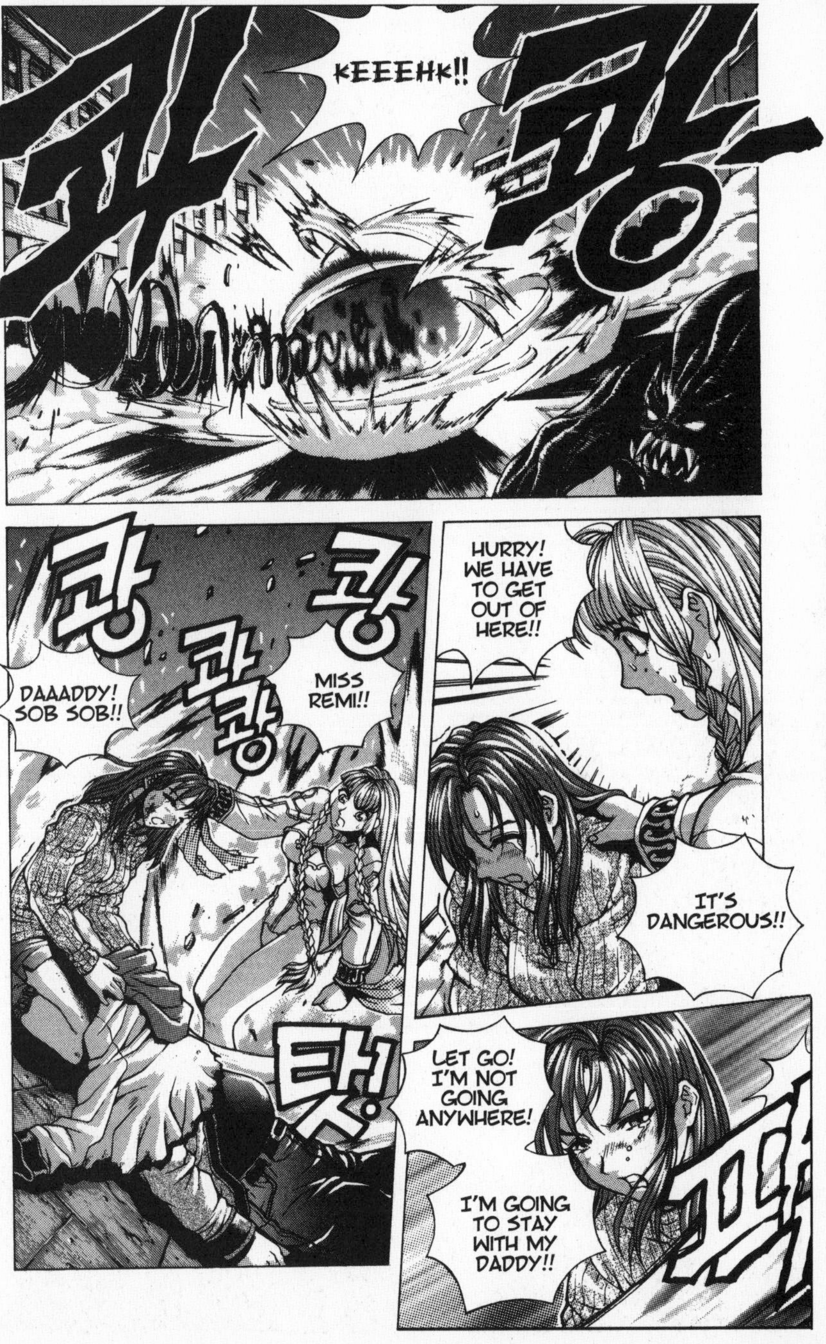
KEEEHK!!
DAAAADDY! SOB SOB!!
콰광
MISS REMI!!
HURRY! WE HAVE TO GET OUT OF HERE!!
IT'S DANGEROUS!!
탁!
LET GO! I'M NOT GOING ANYWHERE!
I'M GOING TO STAY WITH MY DADDY!!

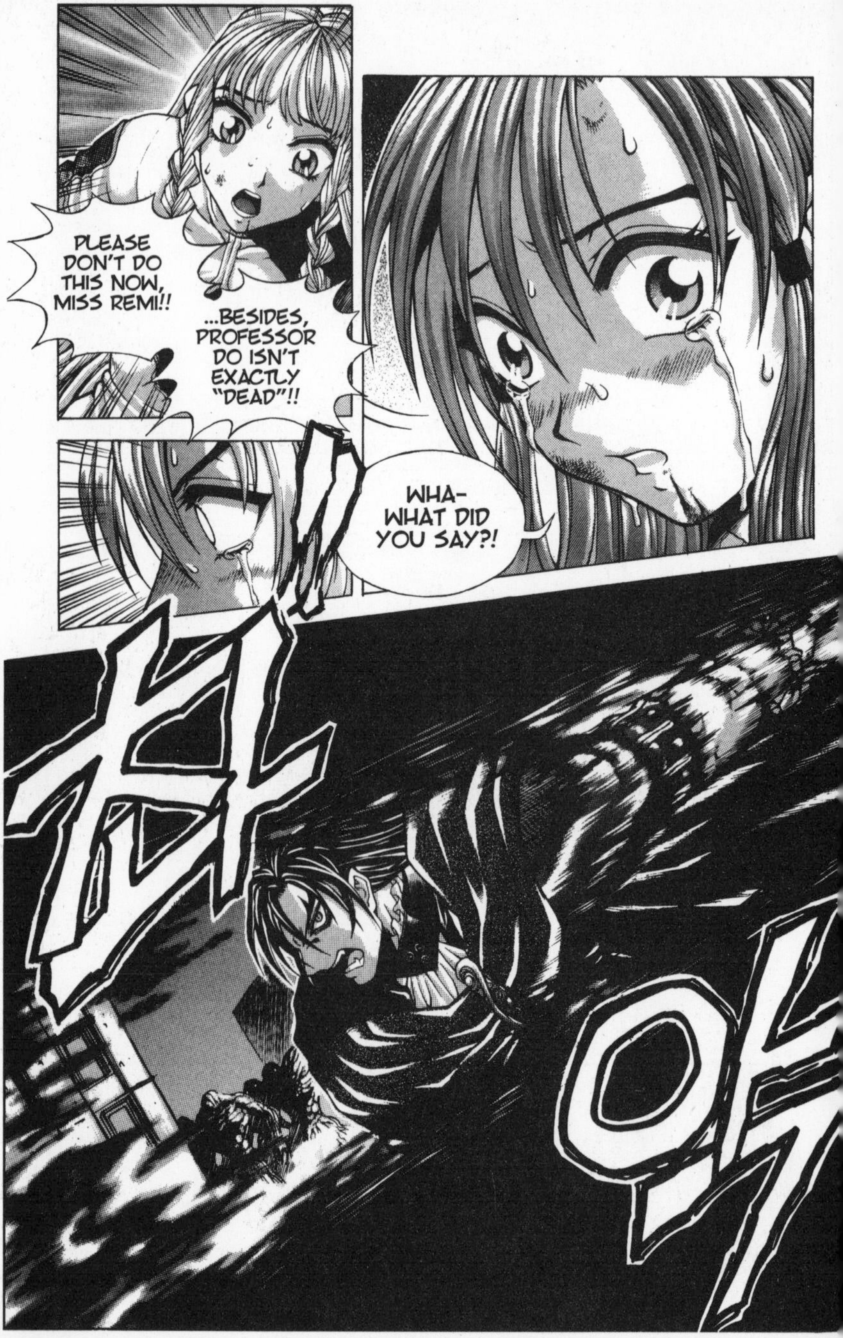
PLEASE DON'T DO THIS NOW, MISS REMI!!
...BESIDES, PROFESSOR DO ISN'T EXACTLY "DEAD"!!
WHA-WHAT DID YOU SAY?!

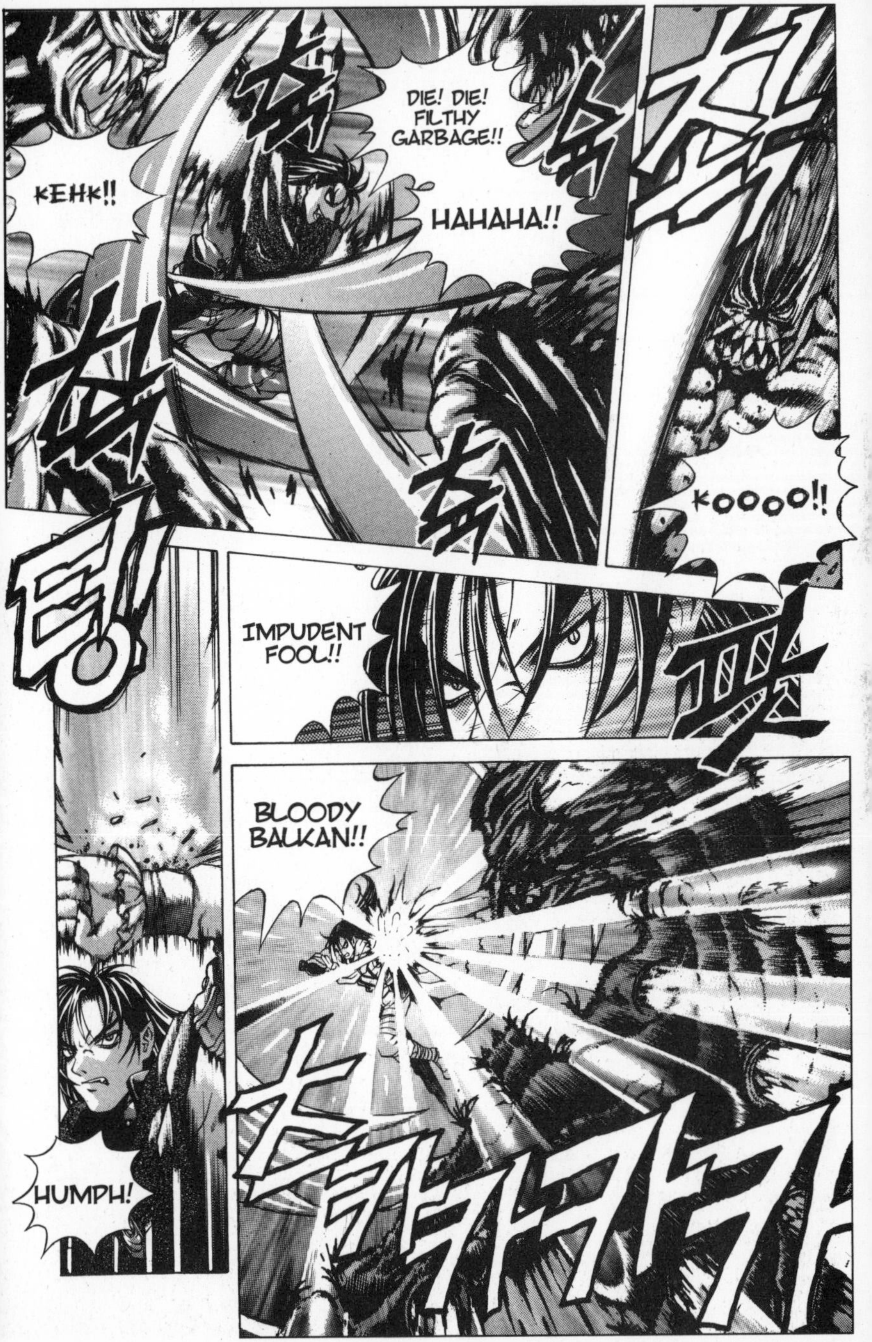
KEHK!!
DIE! DIE! FILTHY GARBAGE!!
HAHAHA!!
KOOOO!!
HUMPH!
IMPUDENT FOOL!!
BLOODY BALKAN!!

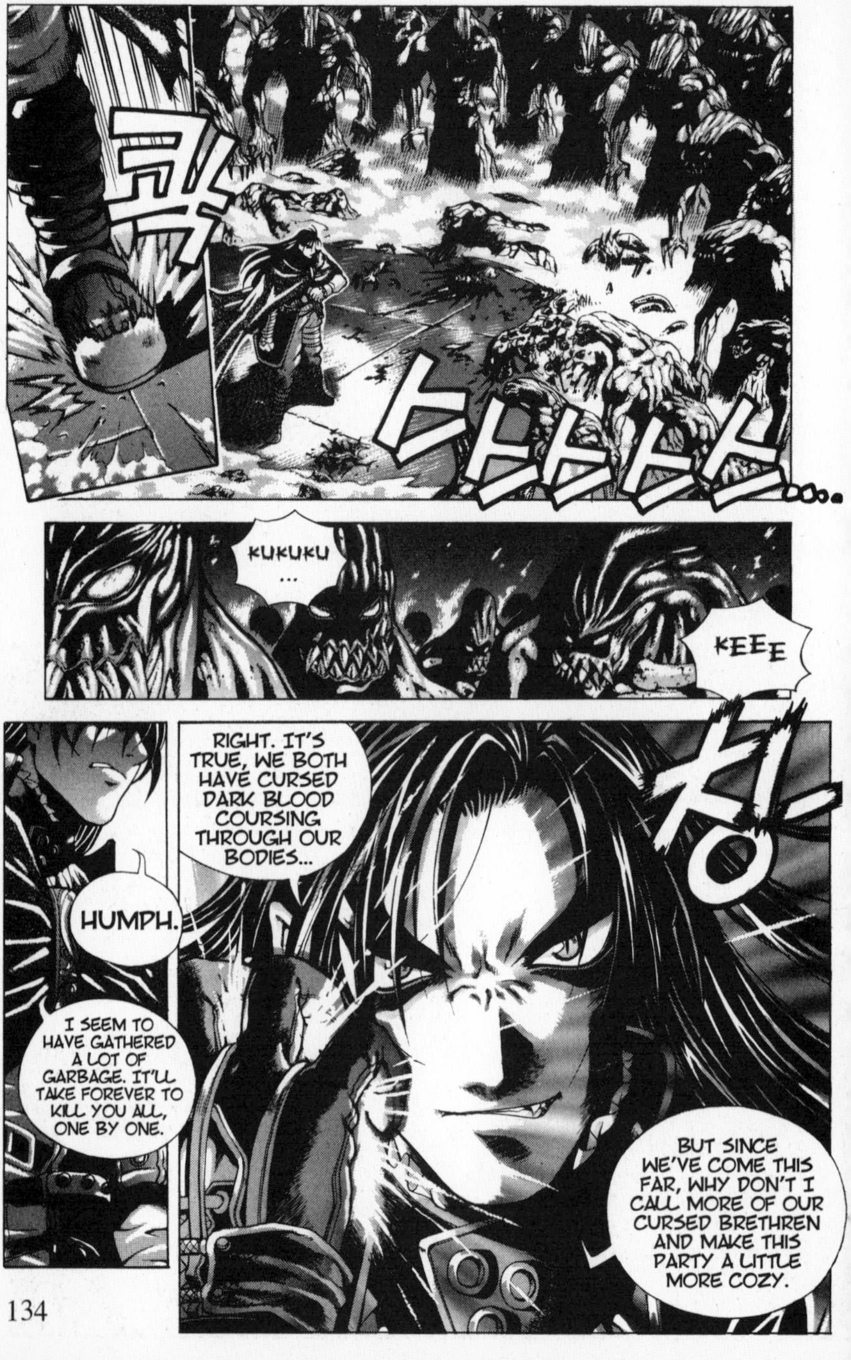
KUKUKU ...
KEEE
RIGHT. IT'S TRUE, WE BOTH HAVE CURSED DARK BLOOD COURSING THROUGH OUR BODIES...
HUMPH.
I SEEM TO HAVE GATHERED A LOT OF GARBAGE. IT'LL TAKE FOREVER TO KILL YOU ALL, ONE BY ONE.
BUT SINCE WE'VE COME THIS FAR, WHY DON'T I CALL MORE OF OUR CURSED BRETHREN AND MAKE THIS PARTY A LITTLE MORE COZY.

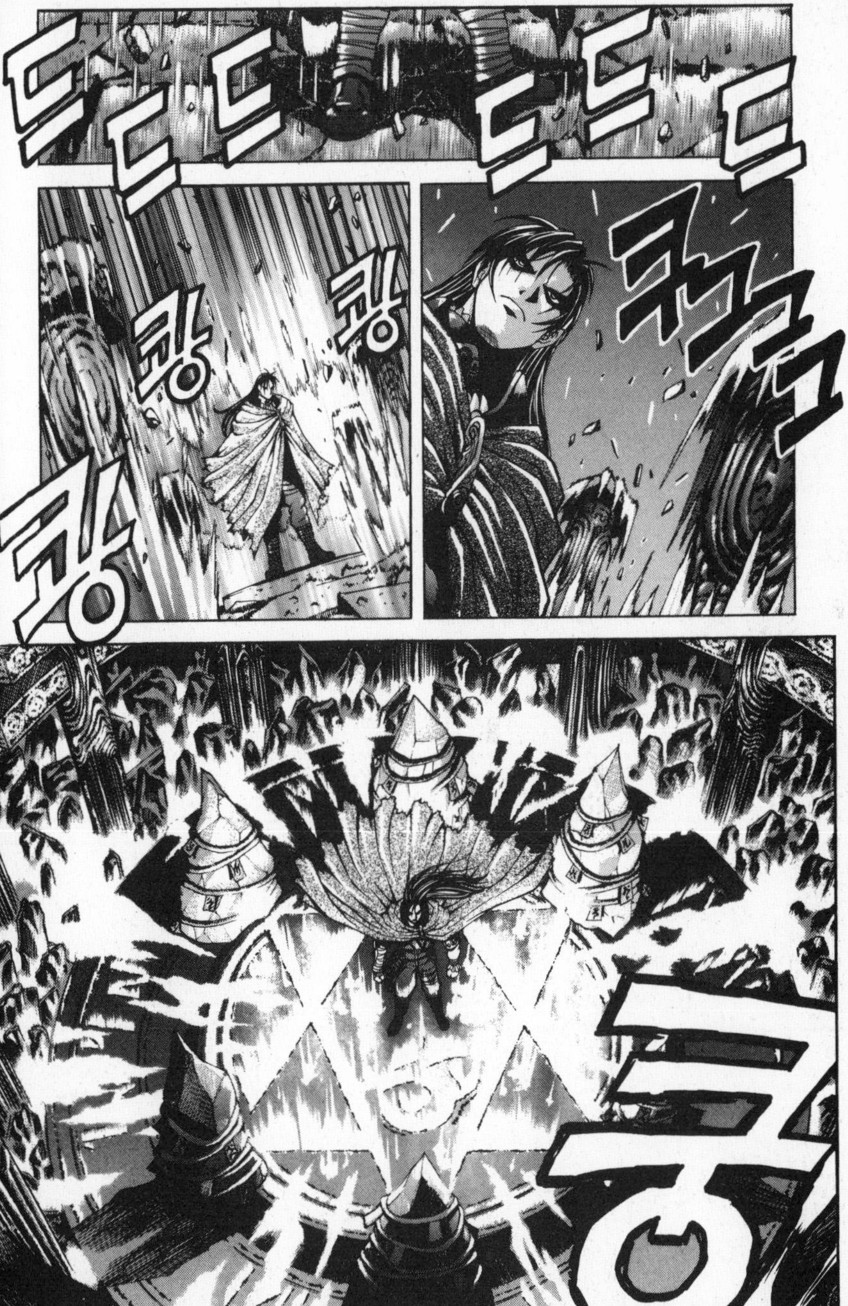
드드드
드드드
쾅
쾅
쾅
쿠그그그

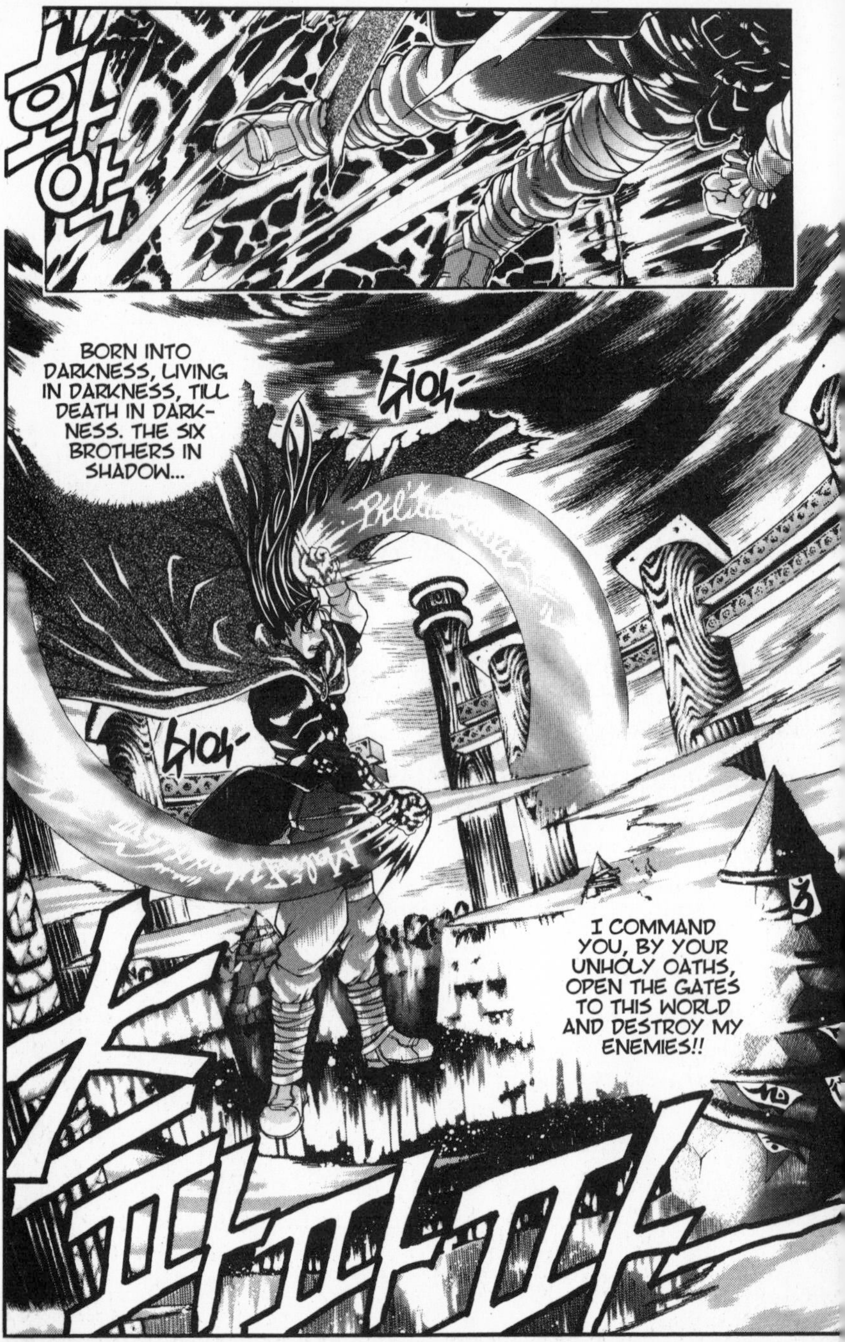
BORN INTO DARKNESS, LIVING IN DARKNESS, TILL DEATH IN DARKNESS. THE SIX BROTHERS IN SHADOW...
I COMMAND YOU, BY YOUR UNHOLY OATHS, OPEN THE GATES TO THIS WORLD AND DESTROY MY ENEMIES!!

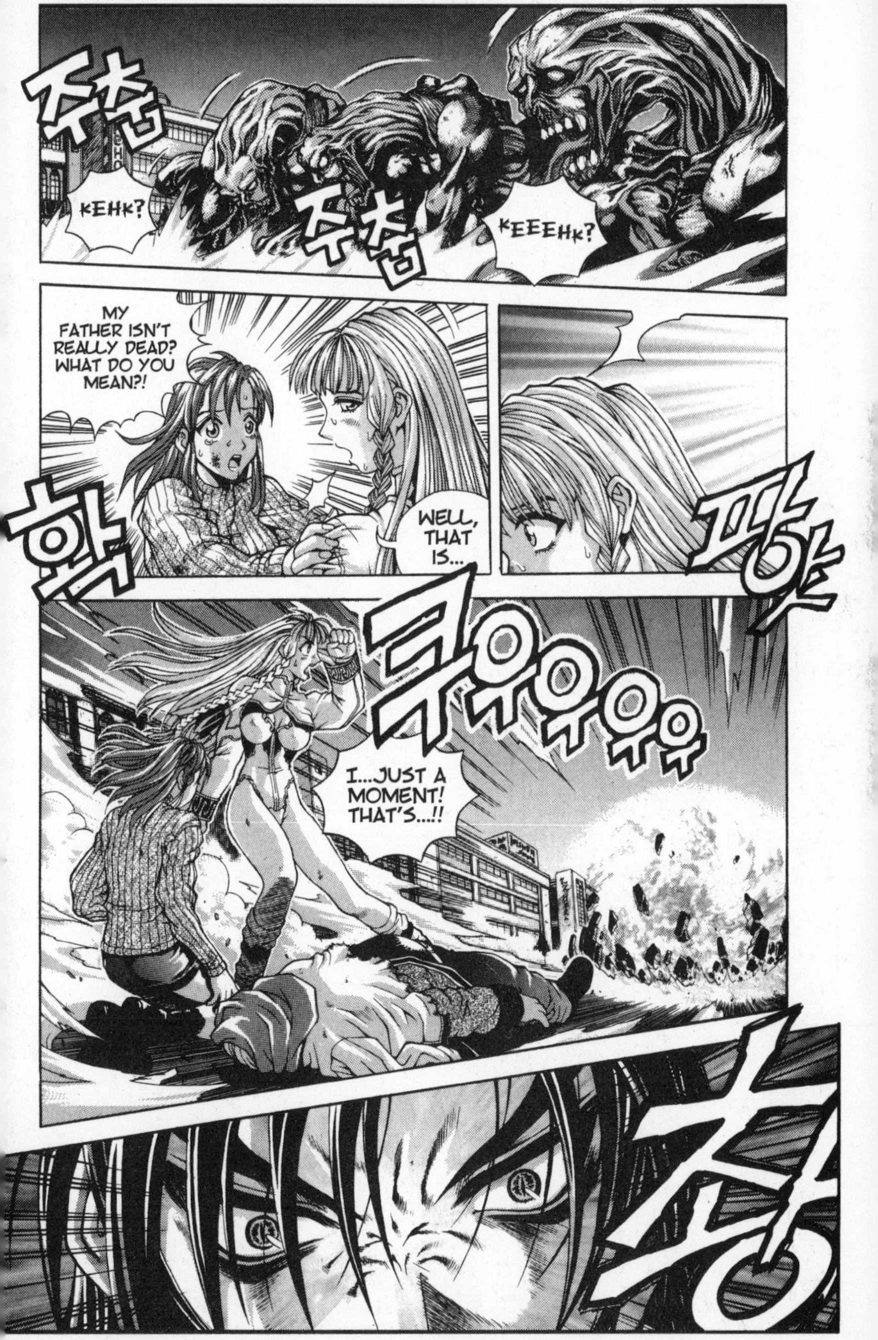
KEHK?
KEEEHK?
MY FATHER ISN'T REALLY DEAD? WHAT DO YOU MEAN?!
WELL, THAT IS...
I...JUST A MOMENT! THAT'S...!!

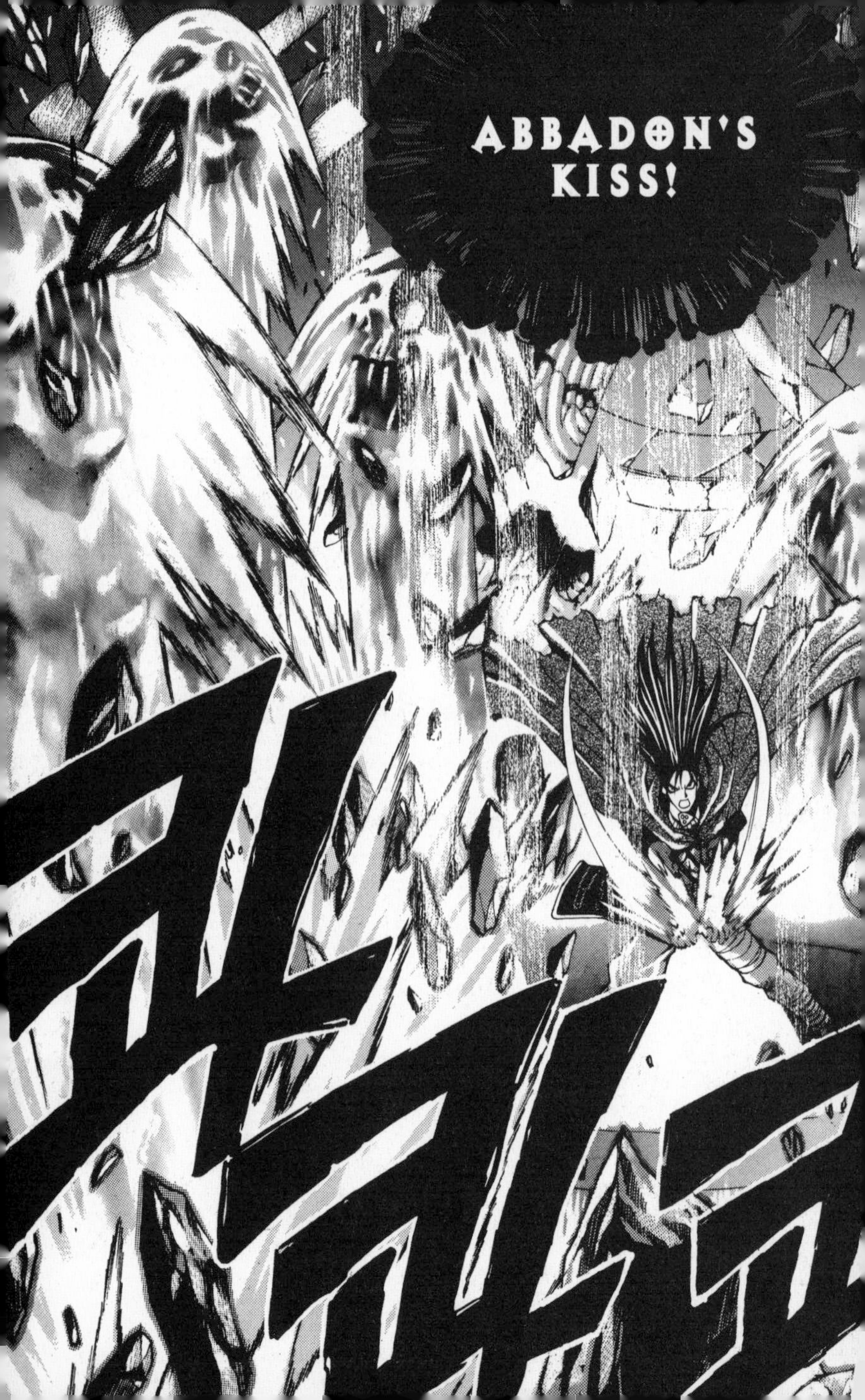
ABBADON'S KISS!

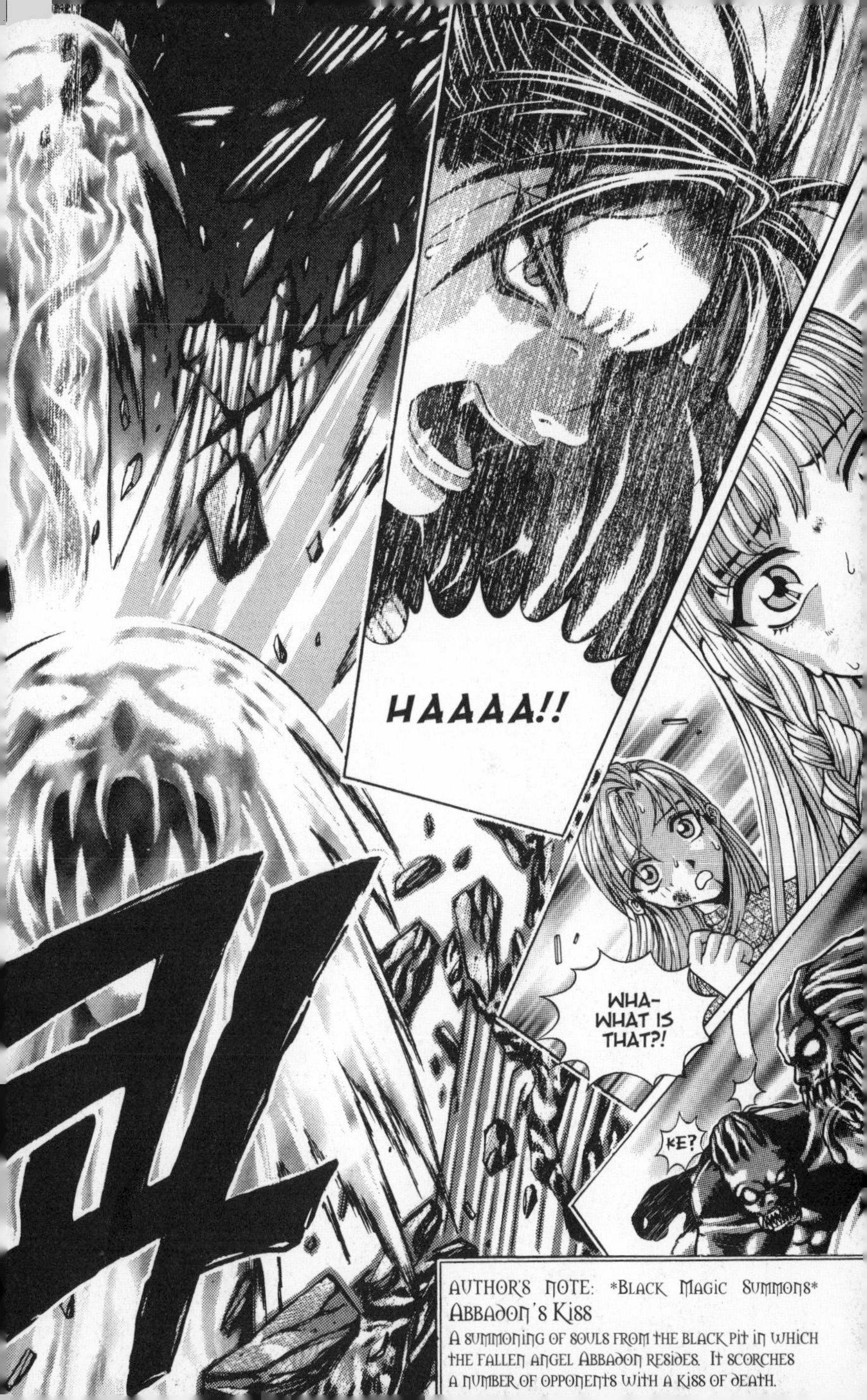
HAAAA!!
WHA-WHAT IS THAT?!
KE?
AUTHOR'S NOTE: *Black Magic Summons*
Abbadon's Kiss
A summoning of souls from the black pit in which the fallen angel Abbadon resides. It scorches a number of opponents with a kiss of death.

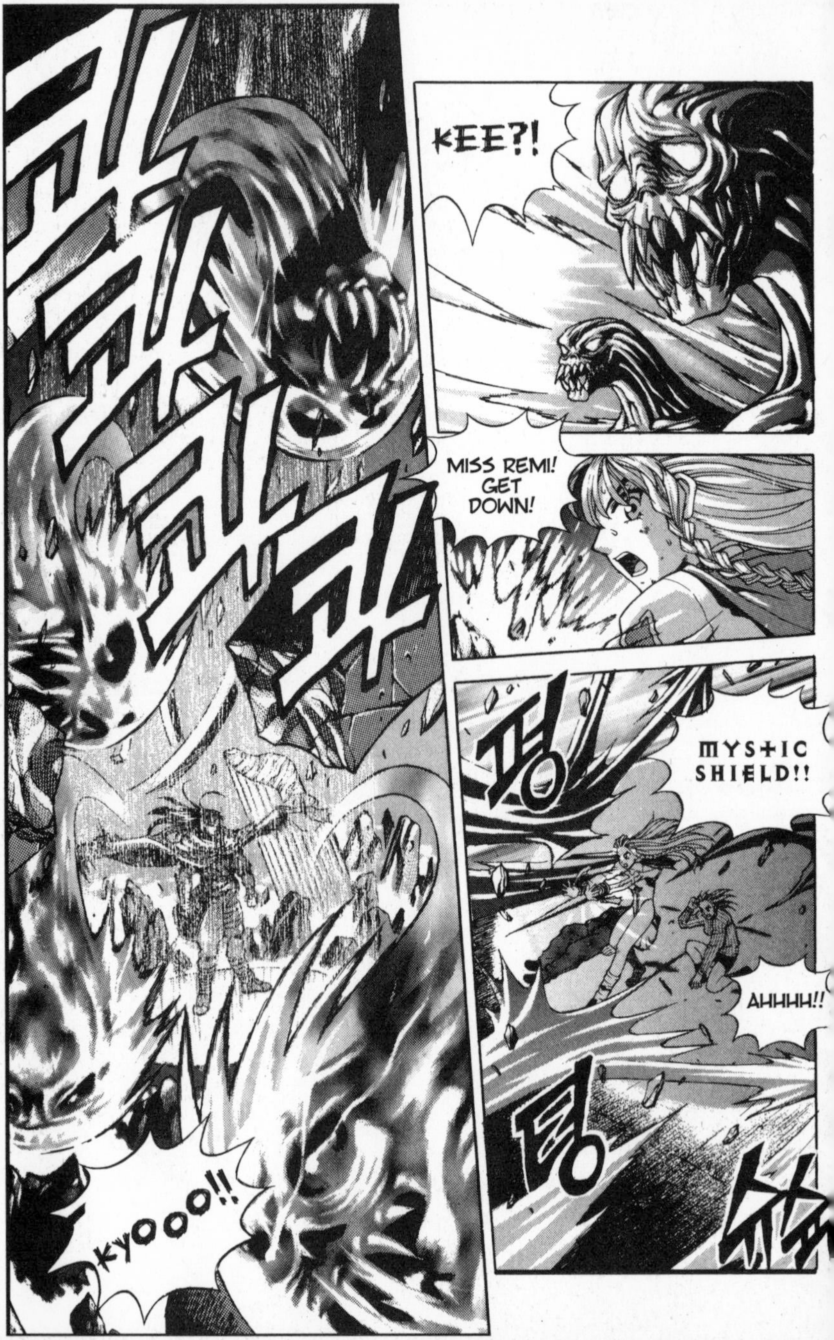
KYOOO!!
KEE?!
MISS REMI! GET DOWN!
MYSTIC SHIELD!!
AHHHH!!

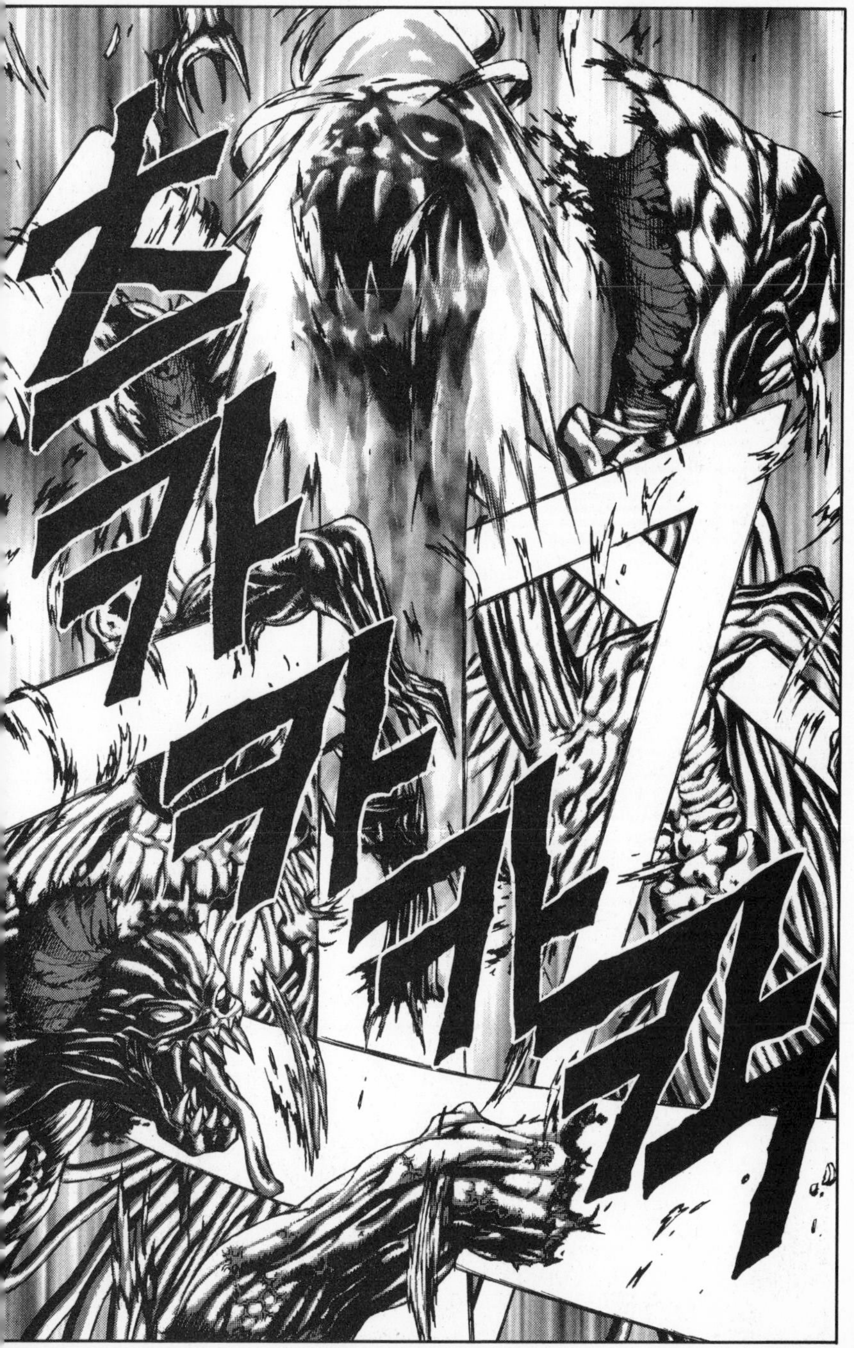

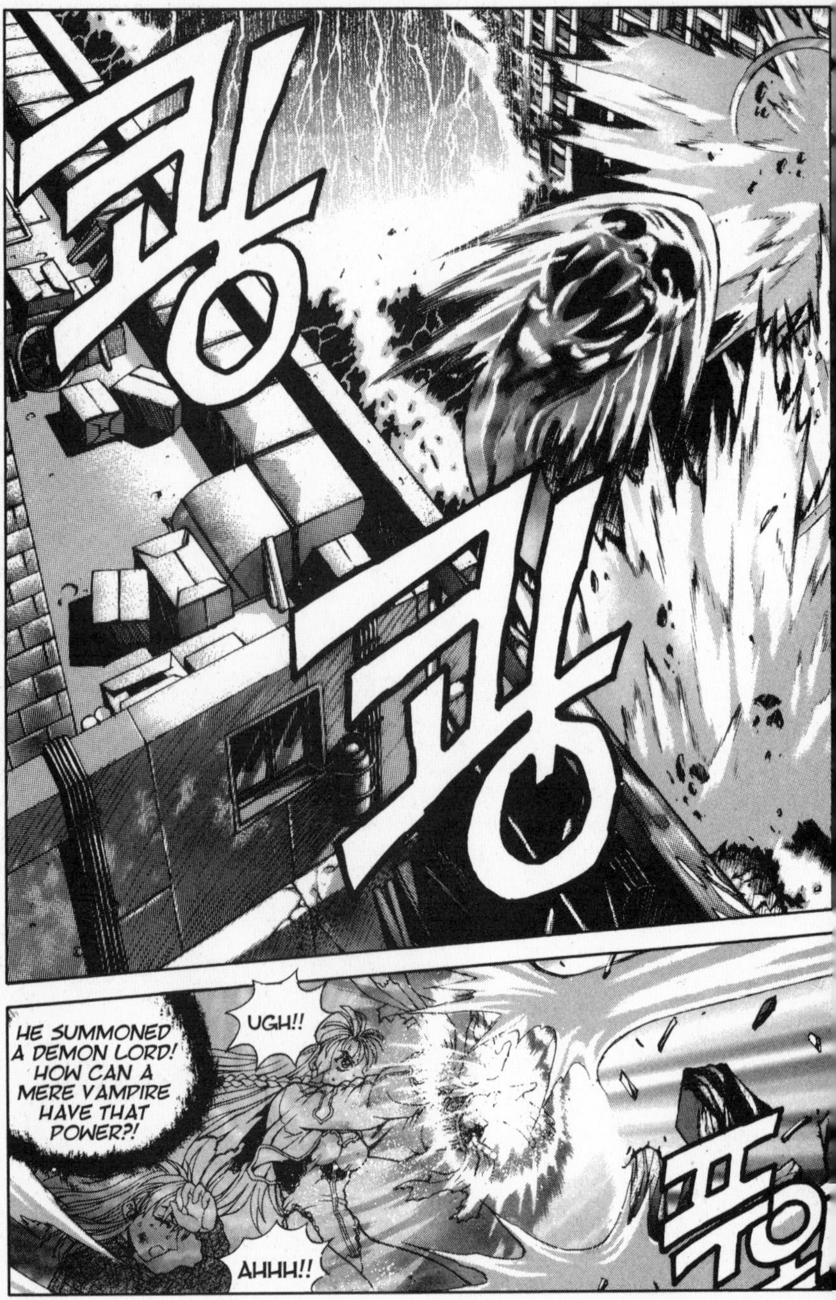
HE SUMMONED A DEMON LORD! HOW CAN A MERE VAMPIRE HAVE THAT POWER?!
UGH!!
AHHH!!

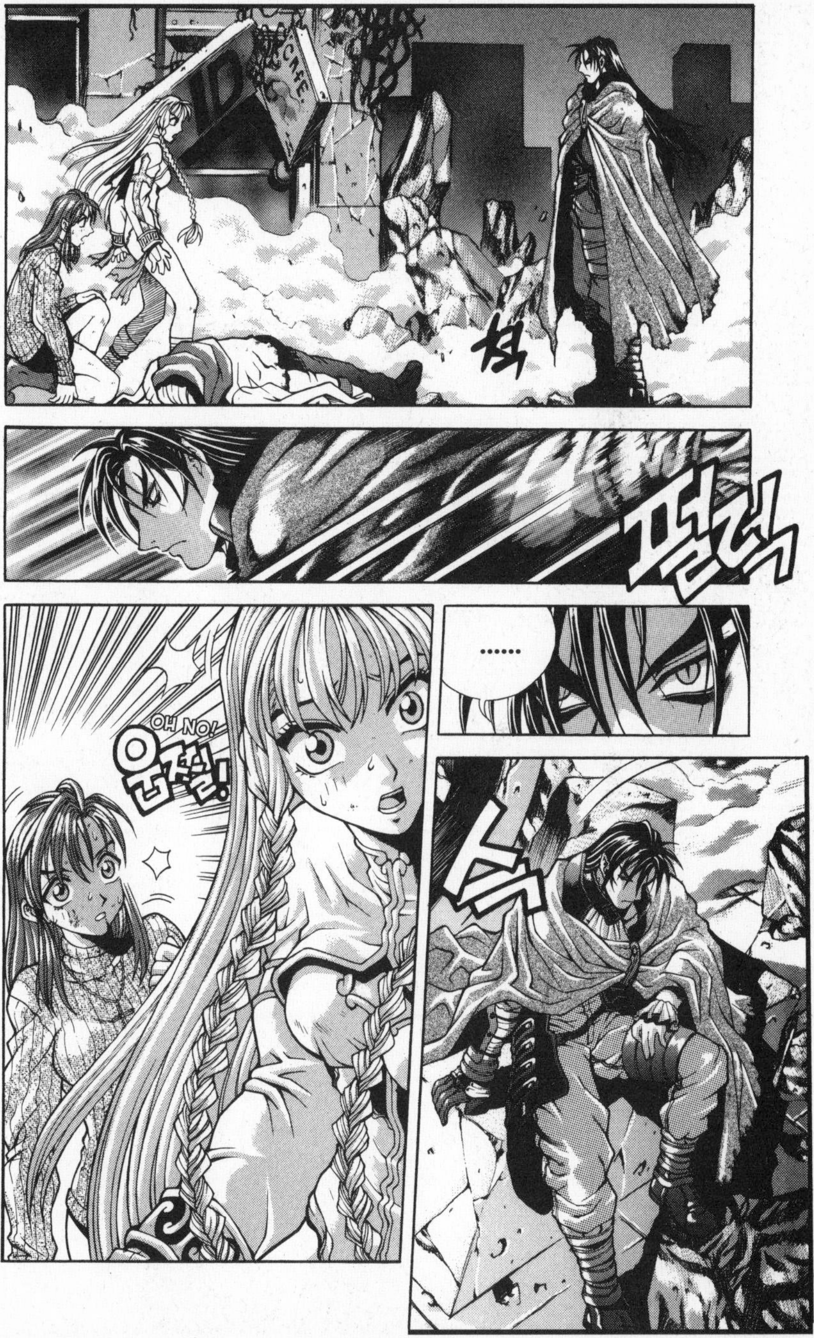
척
펄럭
OH NO!
움찔!
......

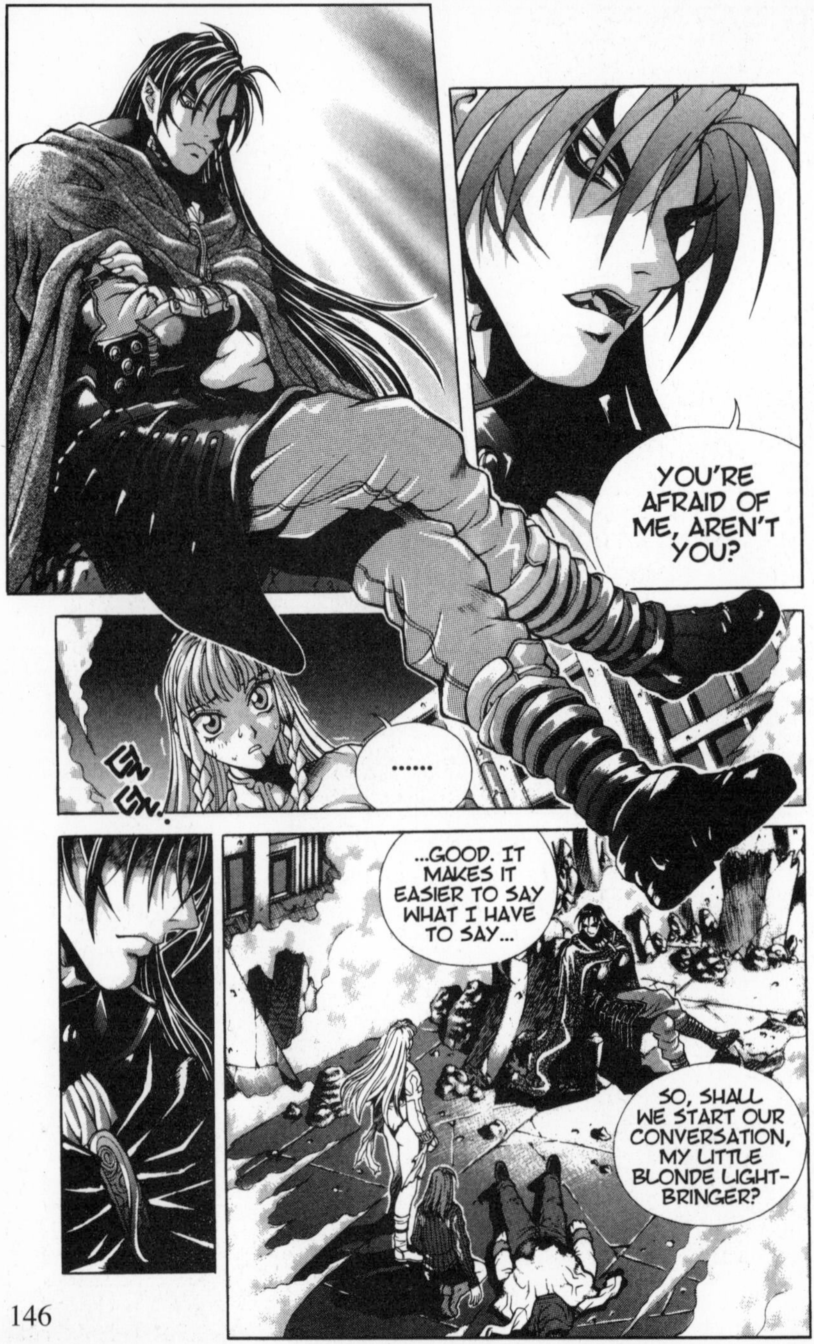
YOU'RE AFRAID OF ME, AREN'T YOU?
......
...GOOD. IT MAKES IT EASIER TO SAY WHAT I HAVE TO SAY...
SO, SHALL WE START OUR CONVERSATION, MY LITTLE BLONDE LIGHT-BRINGER?

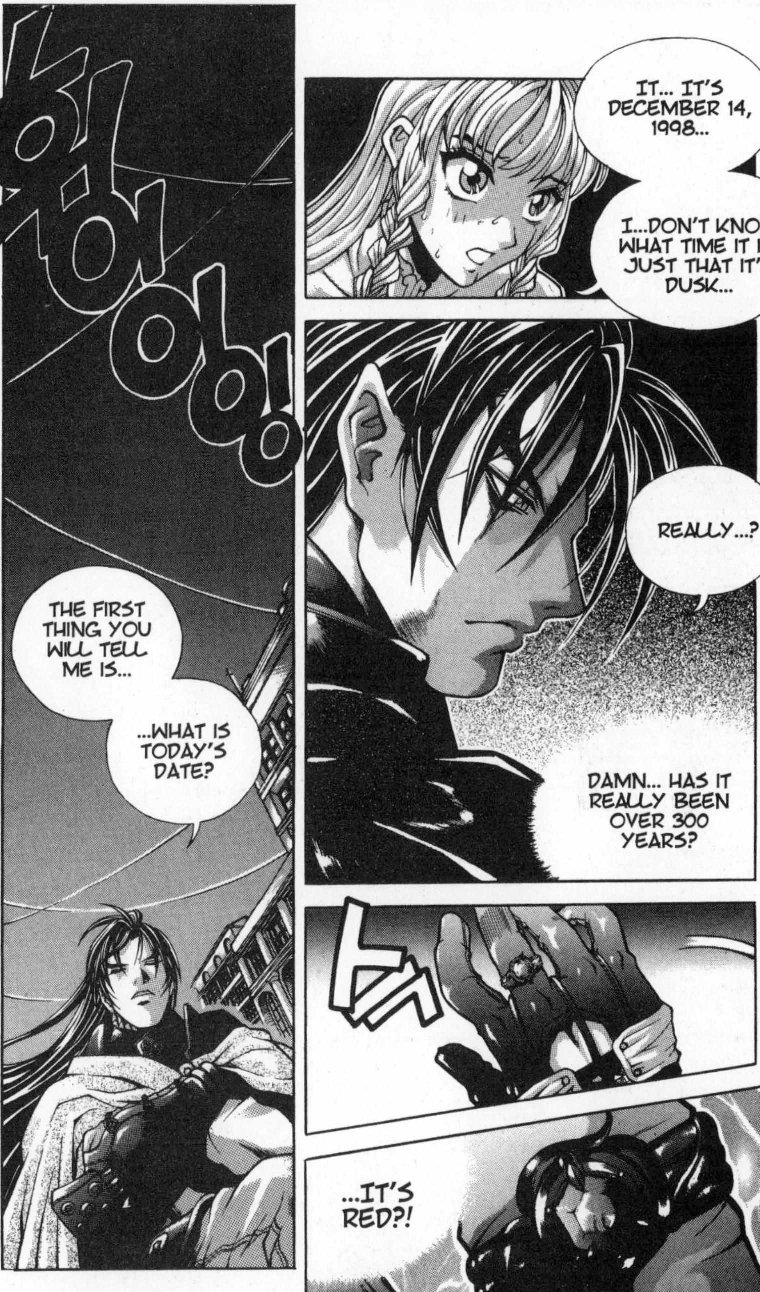
THE FIRST THING YOU WILL TELL ME IS...
...WHAT IS TODAY'S DATE?
IT... IT'S DECEMBER 14, 1998...
I...DON'T KNOW WHAT TIME IT IS. JUST THAT IT'S DUSK...
REALLY...?
DAMN... HAS IT REALLY BEEN OVER 300 YEARS?
...IT'S RED?!

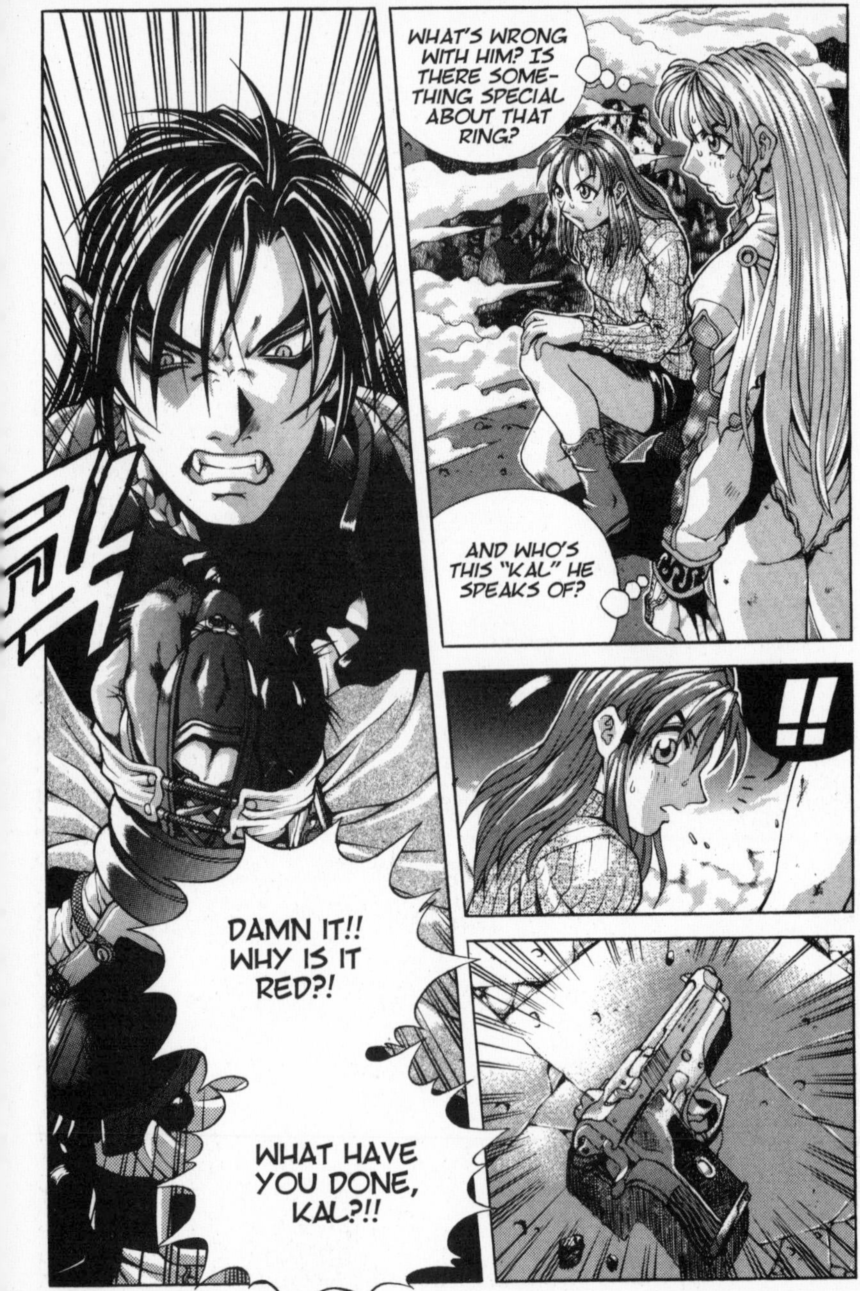
DAMN IT!! WHY IS IT RED?!
WHAT HAVE YOU DONE, KAL?!!
WHAT'S WRONG WITH HIM? IS THERE SOME-THING SPECIAL ABOUT THAT RING?
AND WHO'S THIS "KAL" HE SPEAKS OF?
!!

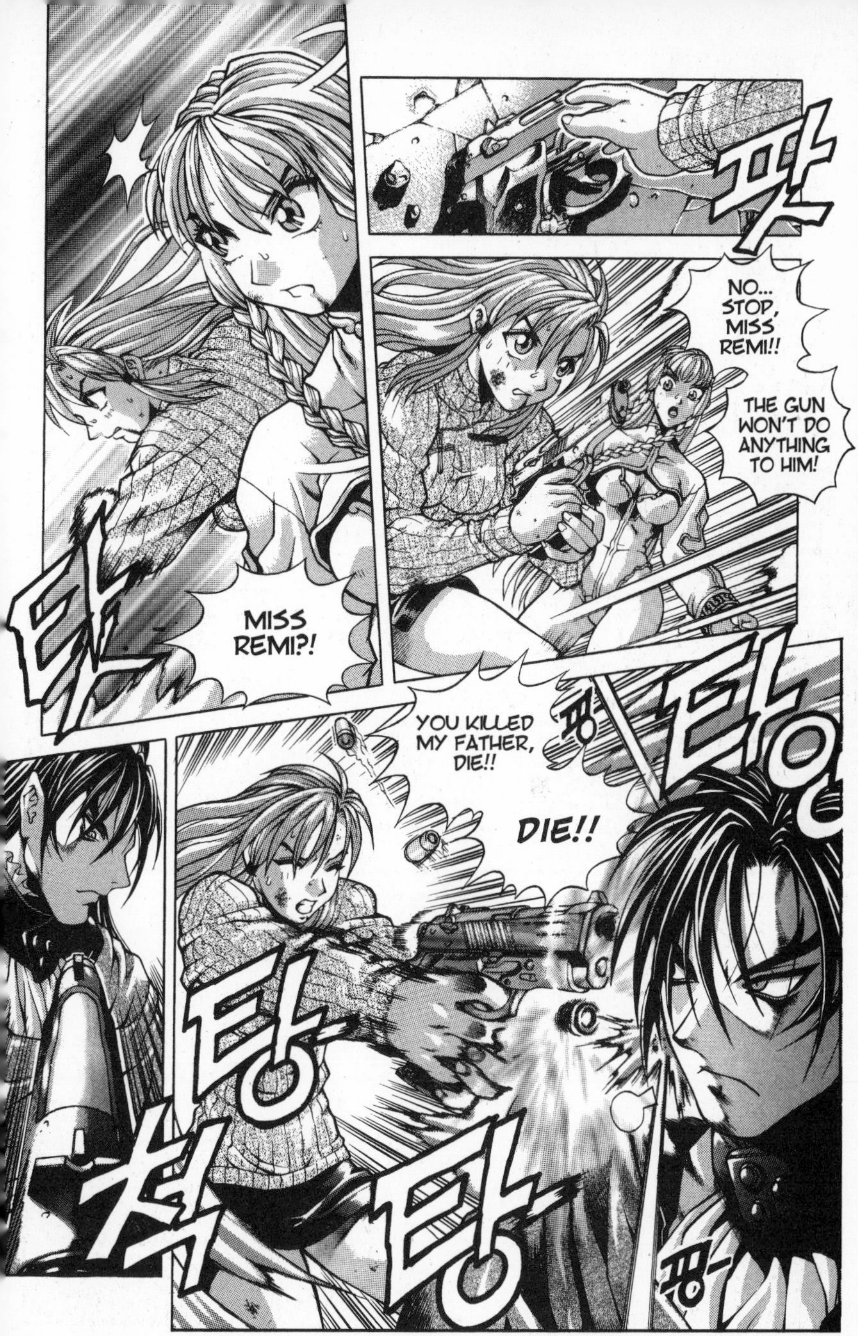
MISS REMI?!
NO... STOP, MISS REMI!!
THE GUN WON'T DO ANYTHING TO HIM!
YOU KILLED MY FATHER, DIE!!
DIE!!

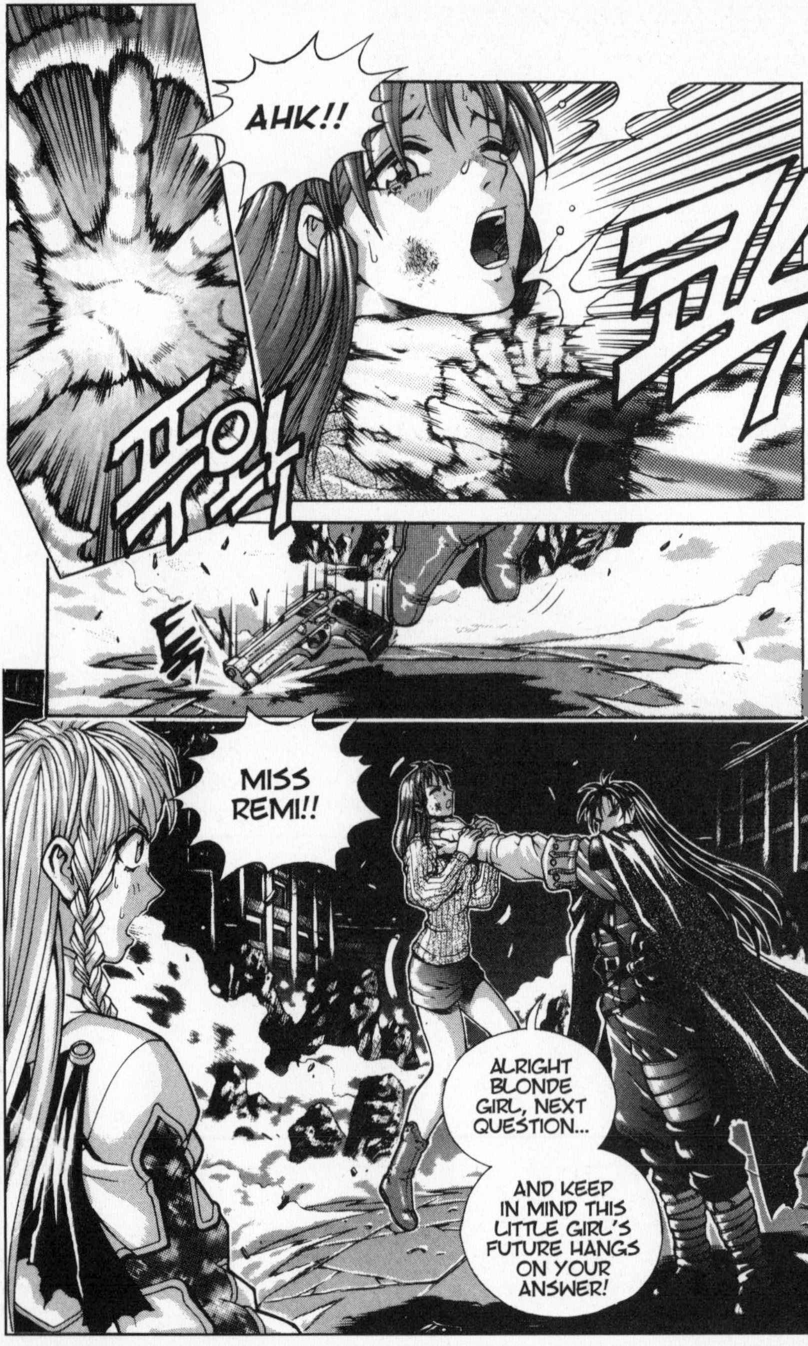
AHK!!
툭
MISS REMI!!
ALRIGHT BLONDE GIRL, NEXT QUESTION...
AND KEEP IN MIND THIS LITTLE GIRL'S FUTURE HANGS ON YOUR ANSWER!

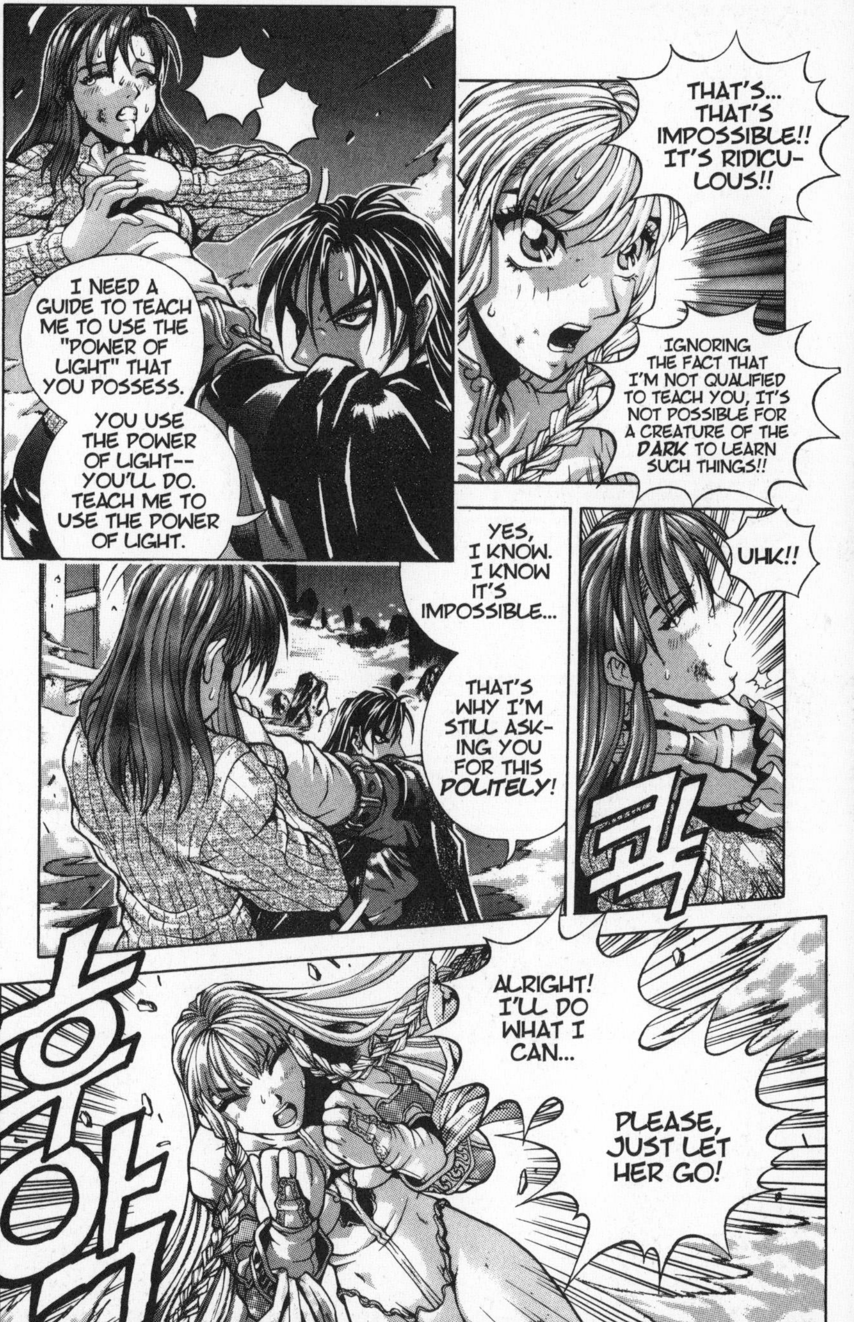
I NEED A GUIDE TO TEACH ME TO USE THE "POWER OF LIGHT" THAT YOU POSSESS.
YOU USE THE POWER OF LIGHT-- YOU'LL DO. TEACH ME TO USE THE POWER OF LIGHT.
THAT'S... THAT'S IMPOSSIBLE!! IT'S RIDICU-LOUS!!
IGNORING THE FACT THAT I'M NOT QUALIFIED TO TEACH YOU, IT'S NOT POSSIBLE FOR A CREATURE OF THE **DARK** TO LEARN SUCH THINGS!!
YES, I KNOW. I KNOW IT'S IMPOSSIBLE...
THAT'S WHY I'M STILL ASK-ING YOU FOR THIS *POLITELY*!
UHK!!
ALRIGHT! I'LL DO WHAT I CAN...
PLEASE, JUST LET HER GO!

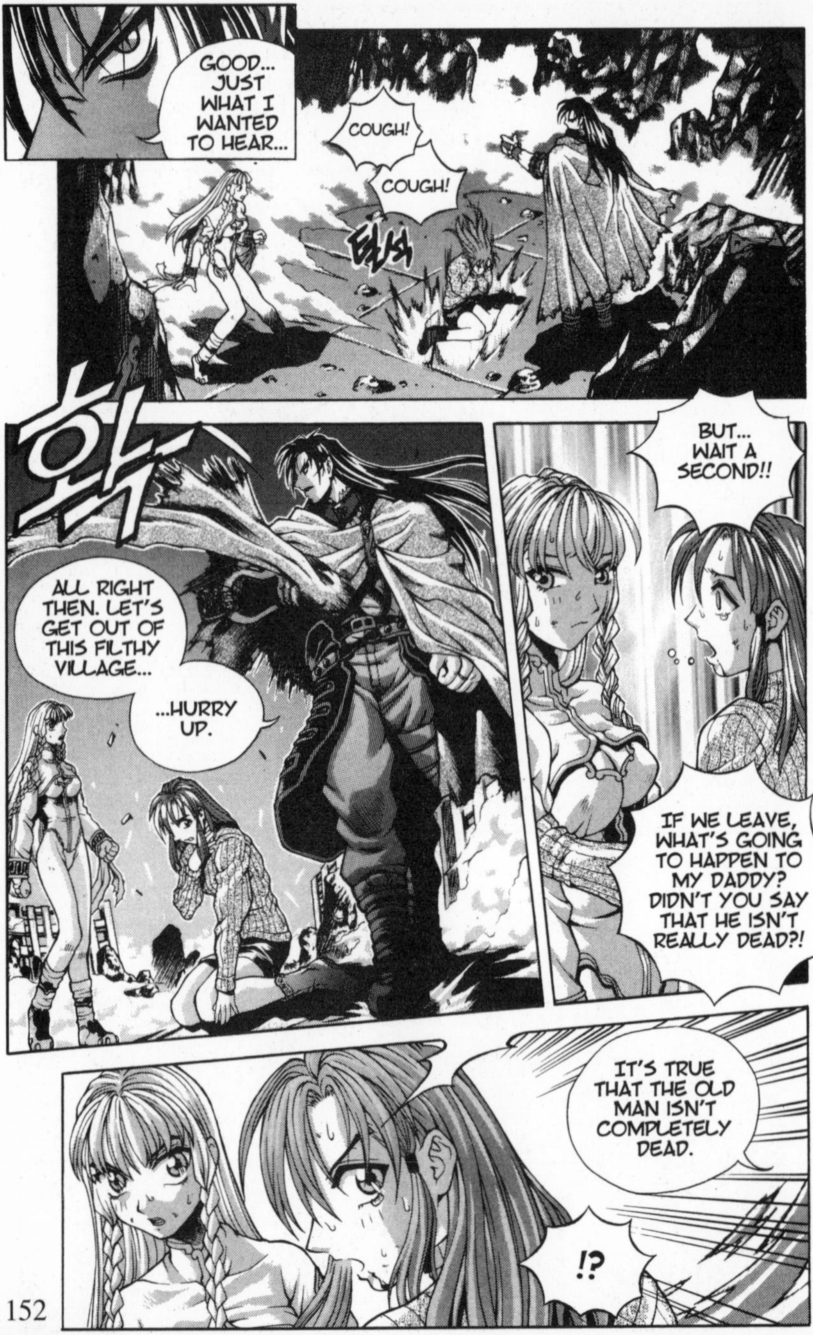
GOOD... JUST WHAT I WANTED TO HEAR...
COUGH!
COUGH!
확
ALL RIGHT THEN. LET'S GET OUT OF THIS FILTHY VILLAGE...
...HURRY UP.
BUT... WAIT A SECOND!!
IF WE LEAVE, WHAT'S GOING TO HAPPEN TO MY DADDY? DIDN'T YOU SAY THAT HE ISN'T REALLY DEAD?!
IT'S TRUE THAT THE OLD MAN ISN'T COMPLETELY DEAD.
!?

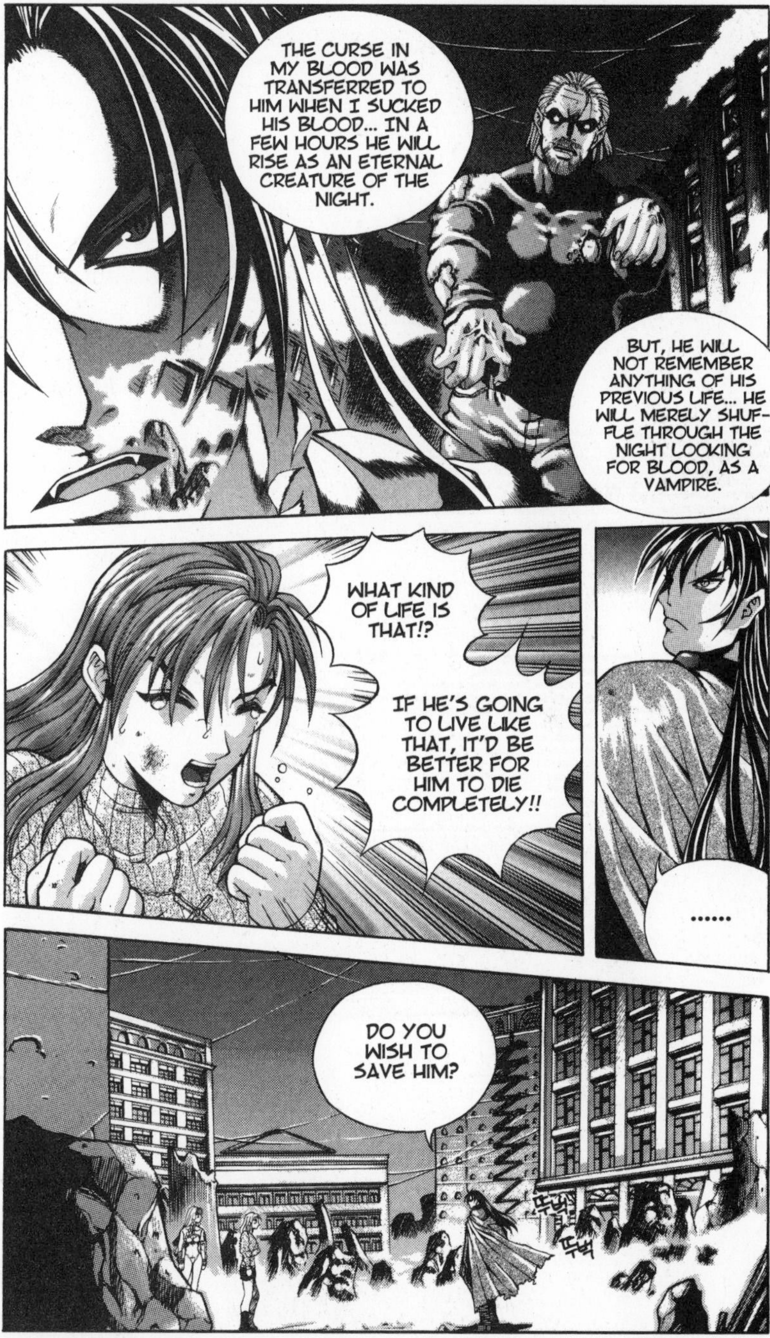
THE CURSE IN MY BLOOD WAS TRANSFERRED TO HIM WHEN I SUCKED HIS BLOOD... IN A FEW HOURS HE WILL RISE AS AN ETERNAL CREATURE OF THE NIGHT.
BUT, HE WILL NOT REMEMBER ANYTHING OF HIS PREVIOUS LIFE... HE WILL MERELY SHUFFLE THROUGH THE NIGHT LOOKING FOR BLOOD, AS A VAMPIRE.
WHAT KIND OF LIFE IS THAT!?
IF HE'S GOING TO LIVE LIKE THAT, IT'D BE BETTER FOR HIM TO DIE COMPLETELY!!
......
DO YOU WISH TO SAVE HIM?
뚜벅
뚜벅

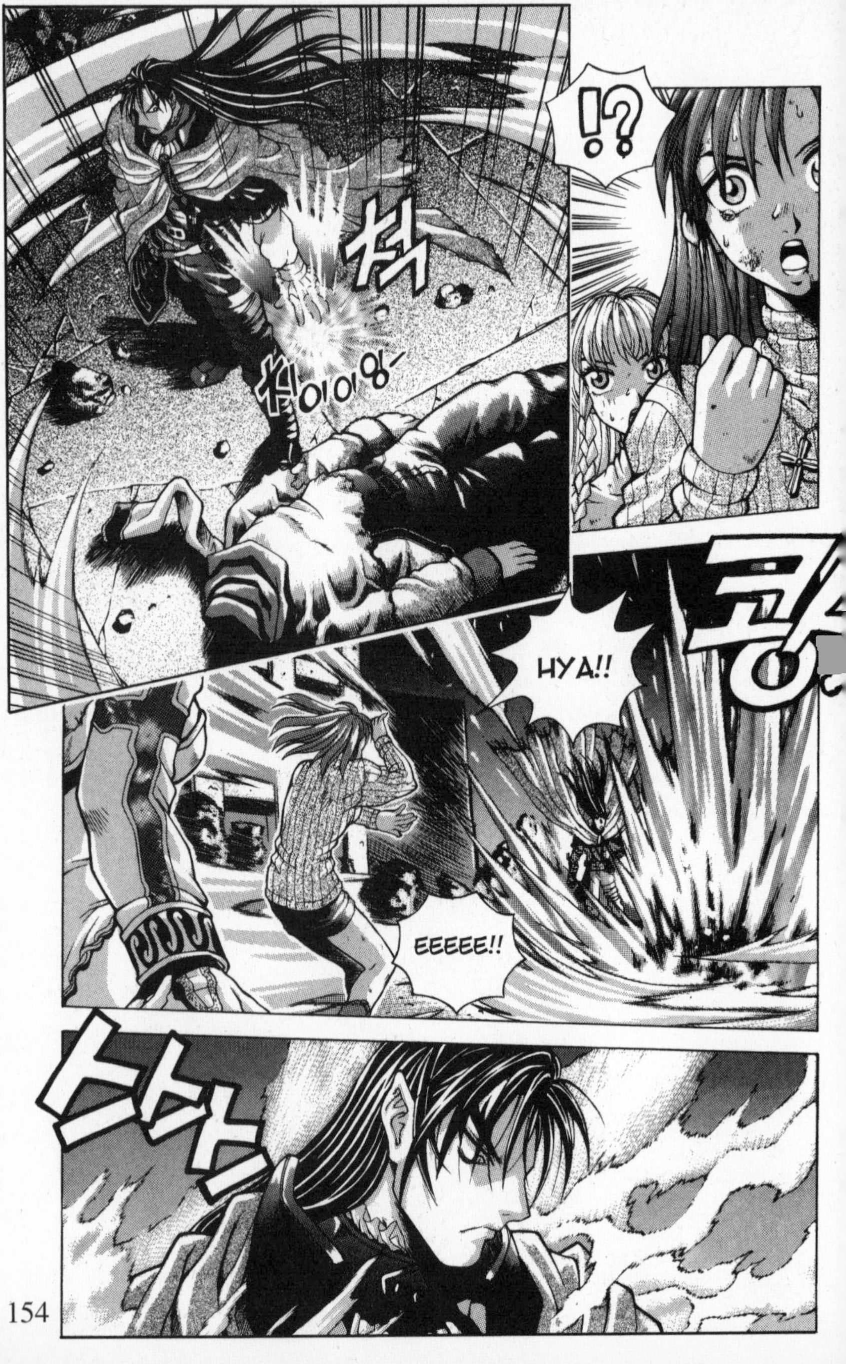

척
!?
치이이잉-
콰
HYA!!
EEEEE!!

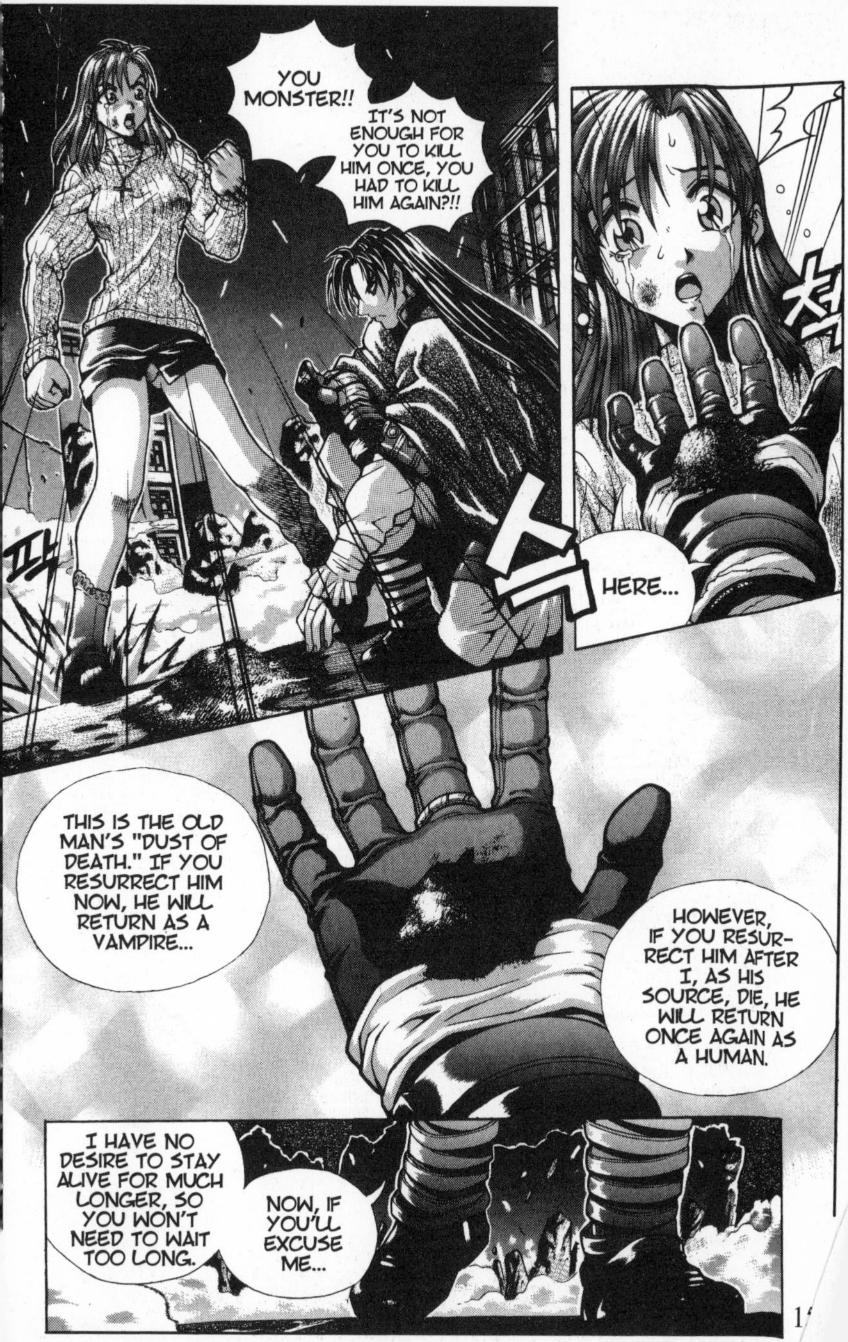

YOU MONSTER!!
IT'S NOT ENOUGH FOR YOU TO KILL HIM ONCE, YOU HAD TO KILL HIM AGAIN?!!
HERE...
THIS IS THE OLD MAN'S "DUST OF DEATH." IF YOU RESURRECT HIM NOW, HE WILL RETURN AS A VAMPIRE...
HOWEVER, IF YOU RESUR-RECT HIM AFTER I, AS HIS SOURCE, DIE, HE WILL RETURN ONCE AGAIN AS A HUMAN.
I HAVE NO DESIRE TO STAY ALIVE FOR MUCH LONGER, SO YOU WON'T NEED TO WAIT TOO LONG.
NOW, IF YOU'LL EXCUSE ME...

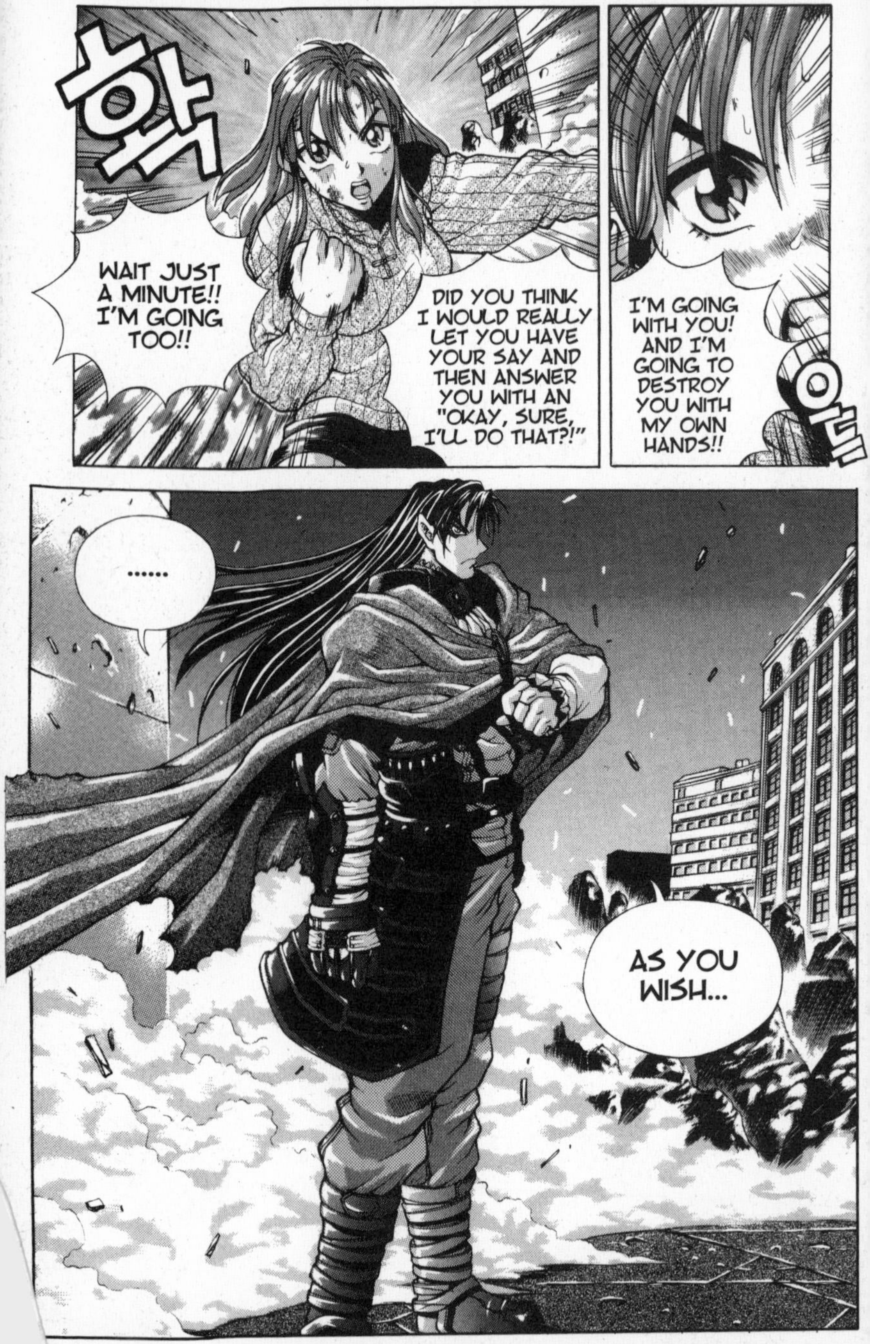
확
WAIT JUST A MINUTE!! I'M GOING TOO!!
DID YOU THINK I WOULD REALLY LET YOU HAVE YOUR SAY AND THEN ANSWER YOU WITH AN "OKAY, SURE, I'LL DO THAT?!"
I'M GOING WITH YOU! AND I'M GOING TO DESTROY YOU WITH MY OWN HANDS!!
......
AS YOU WISH...

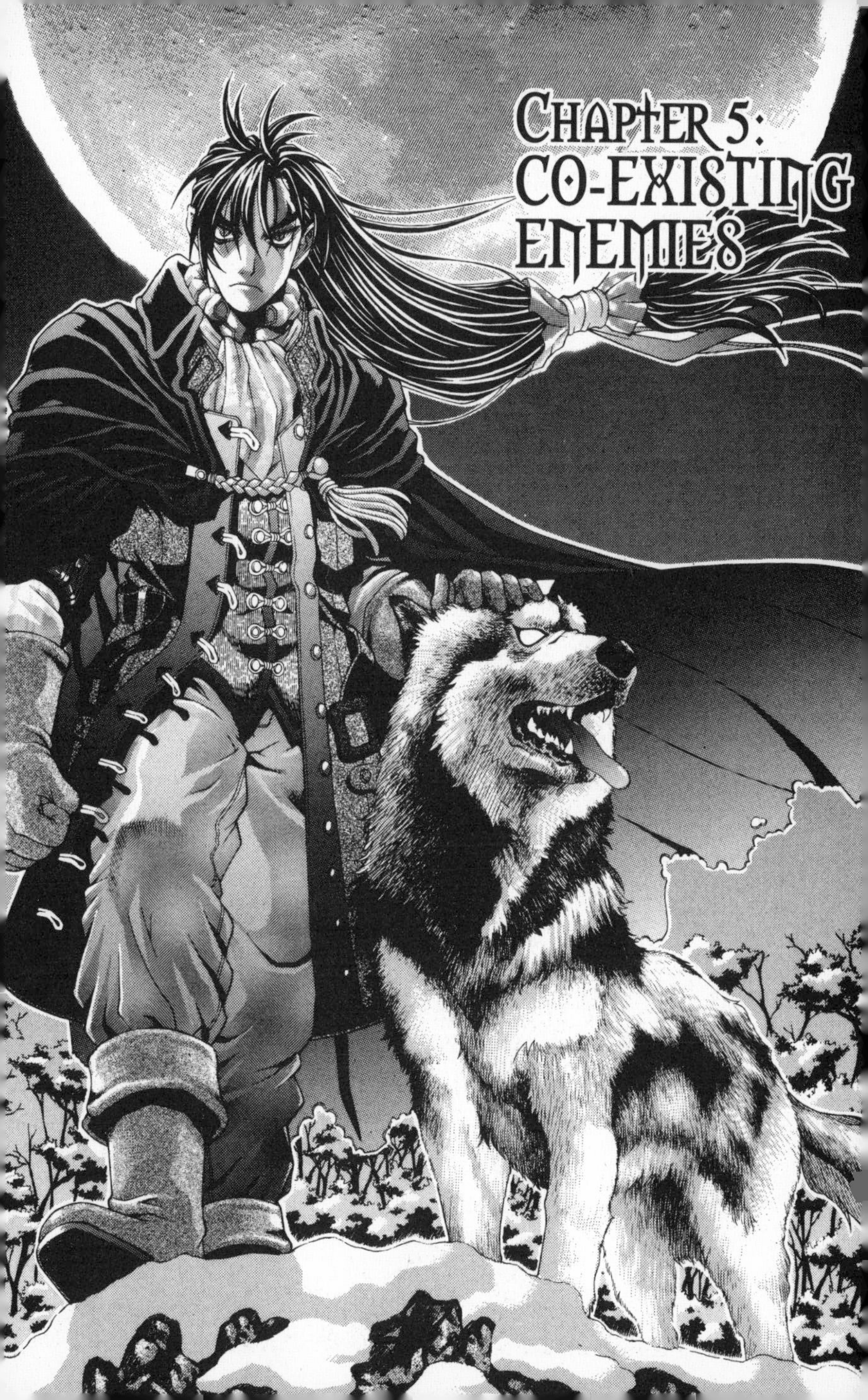
Chapter 5:
Co-Existing
Enemies

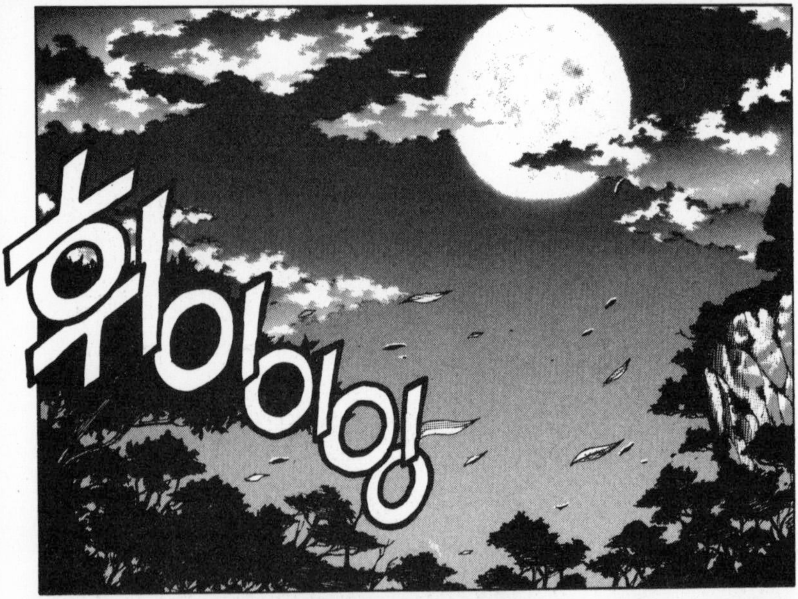
휘이이이잉

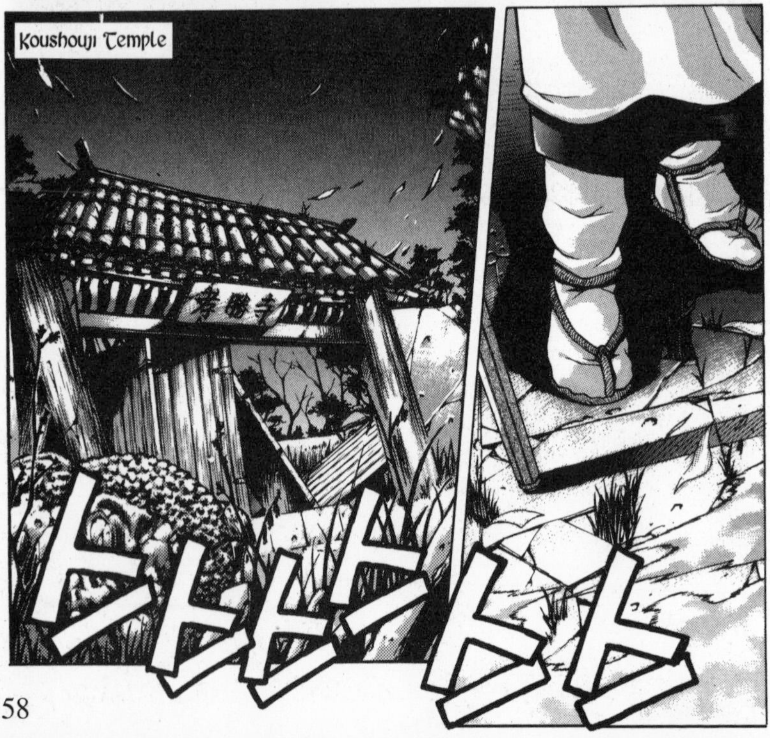
Koushouji Temple

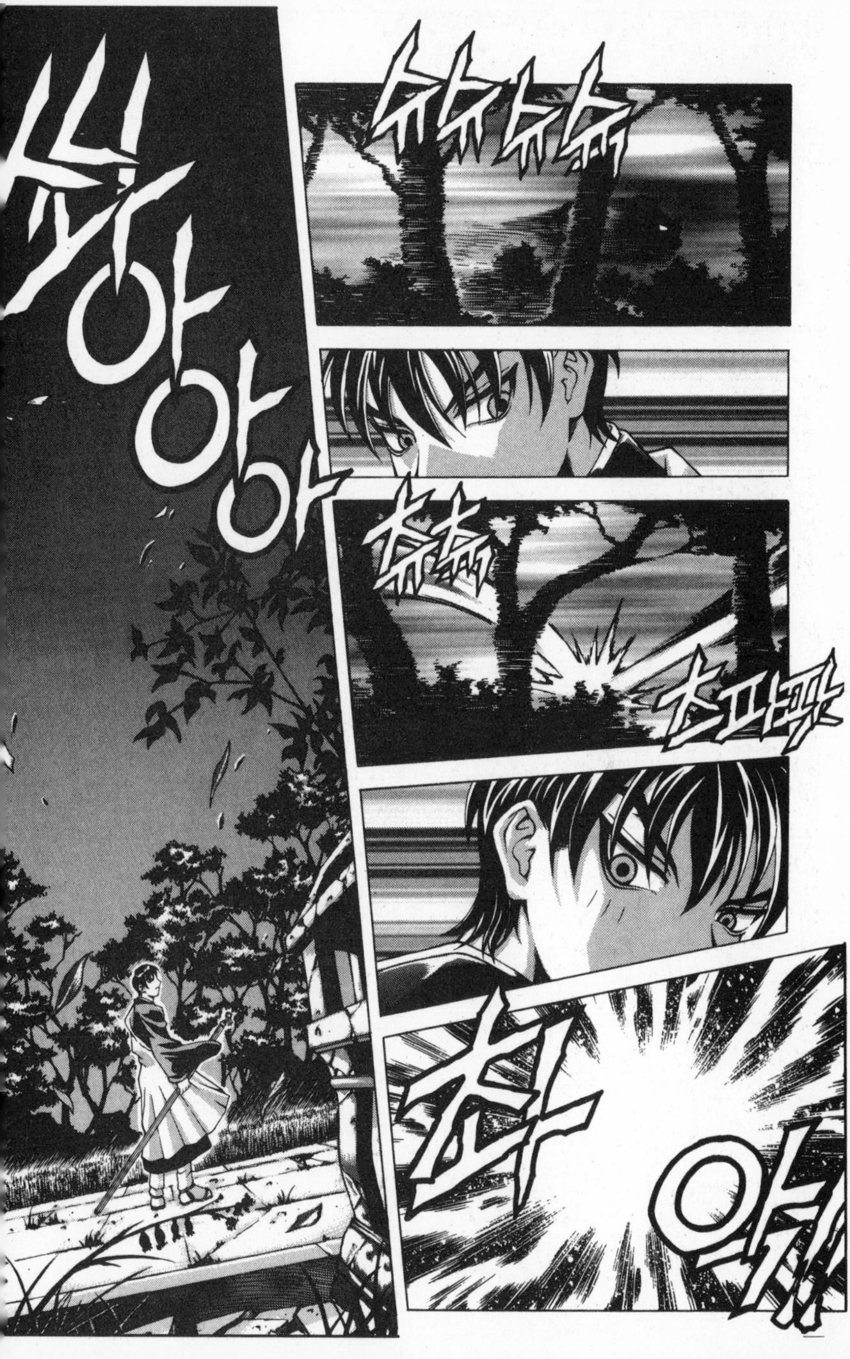

씨샤아아아
사사사삭
차착
츠팟
차아!!

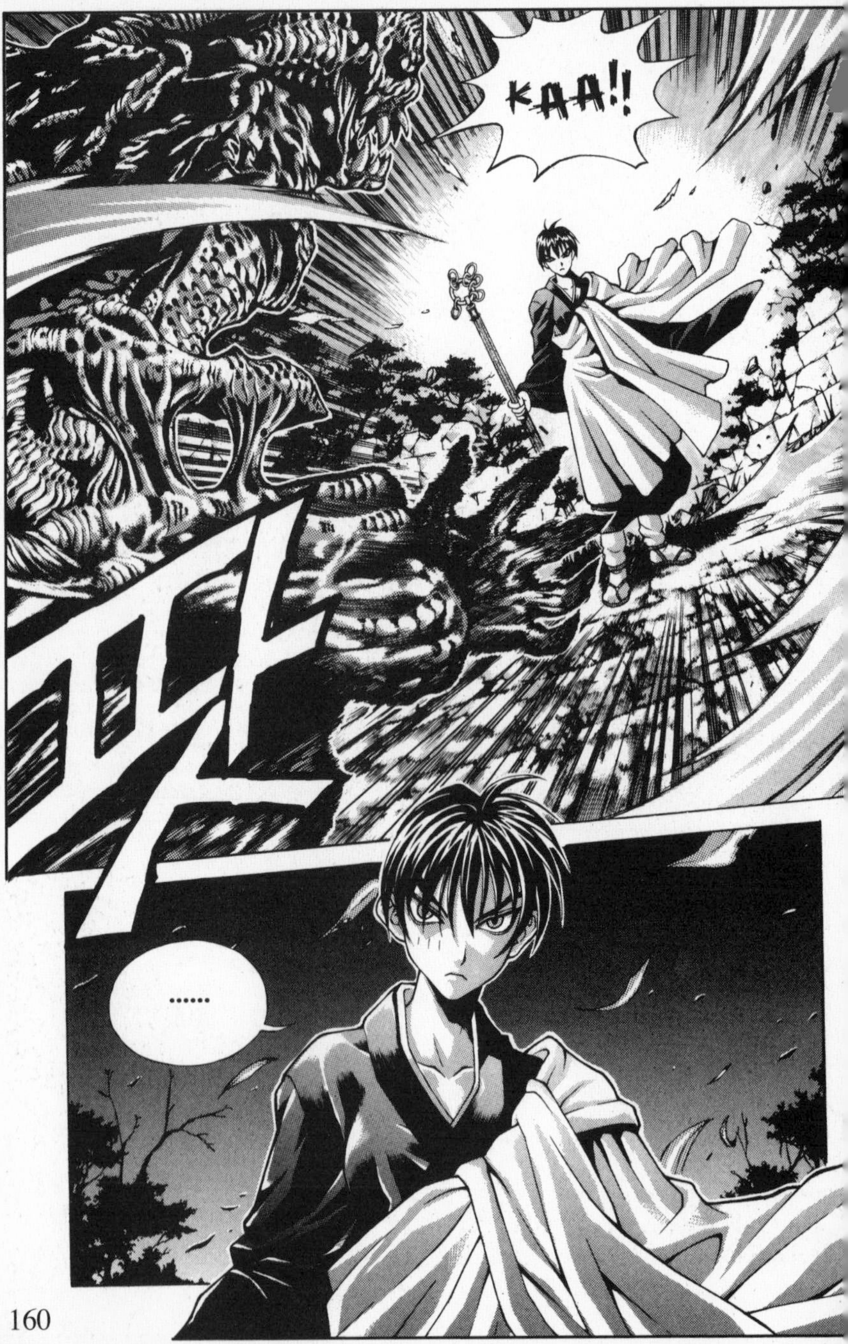
KAA!!
......

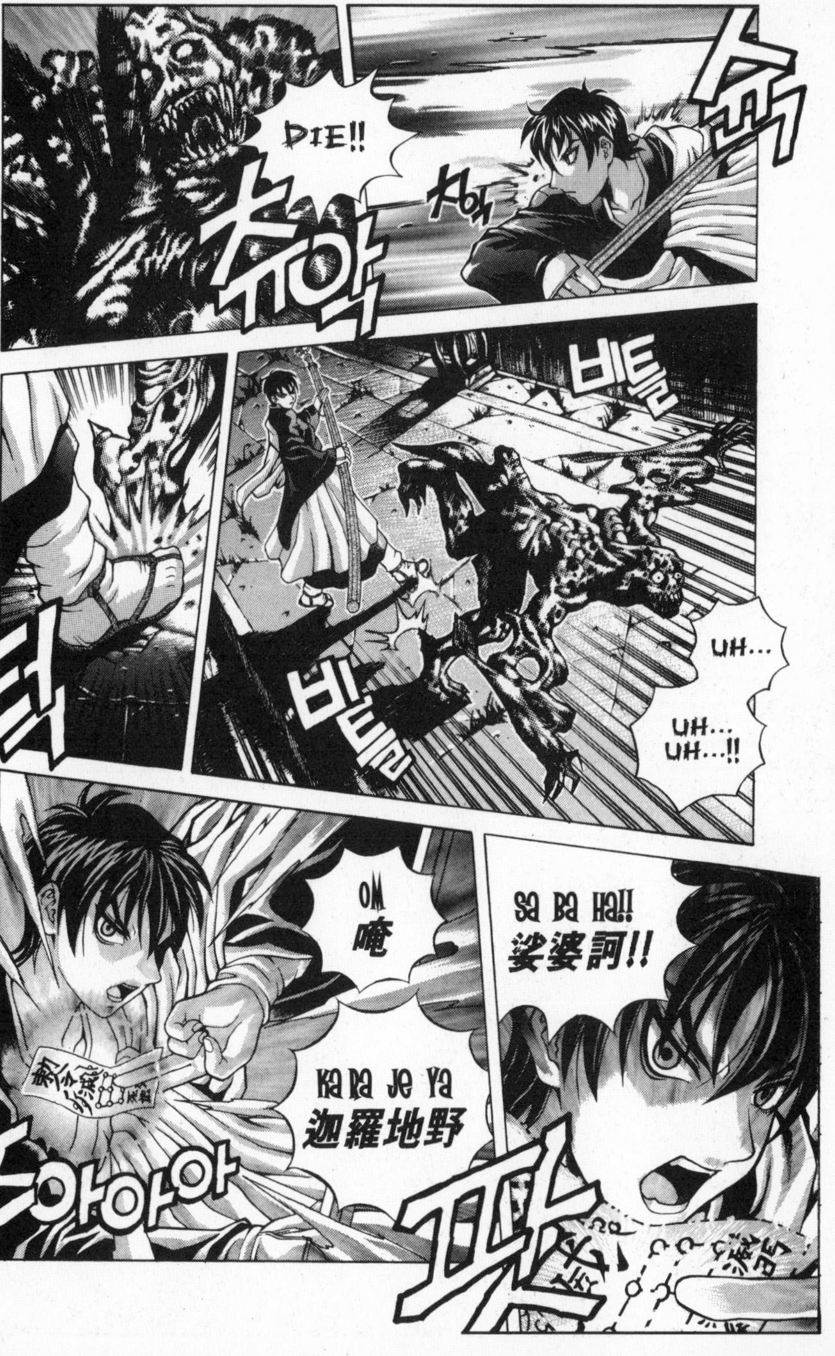
DIE!!
비틀
비틀
UH...
UH...
UH...!!
OM
唵
KA RA JE YA
迦羅地野
SA BA HA!!
娑婆訶!!

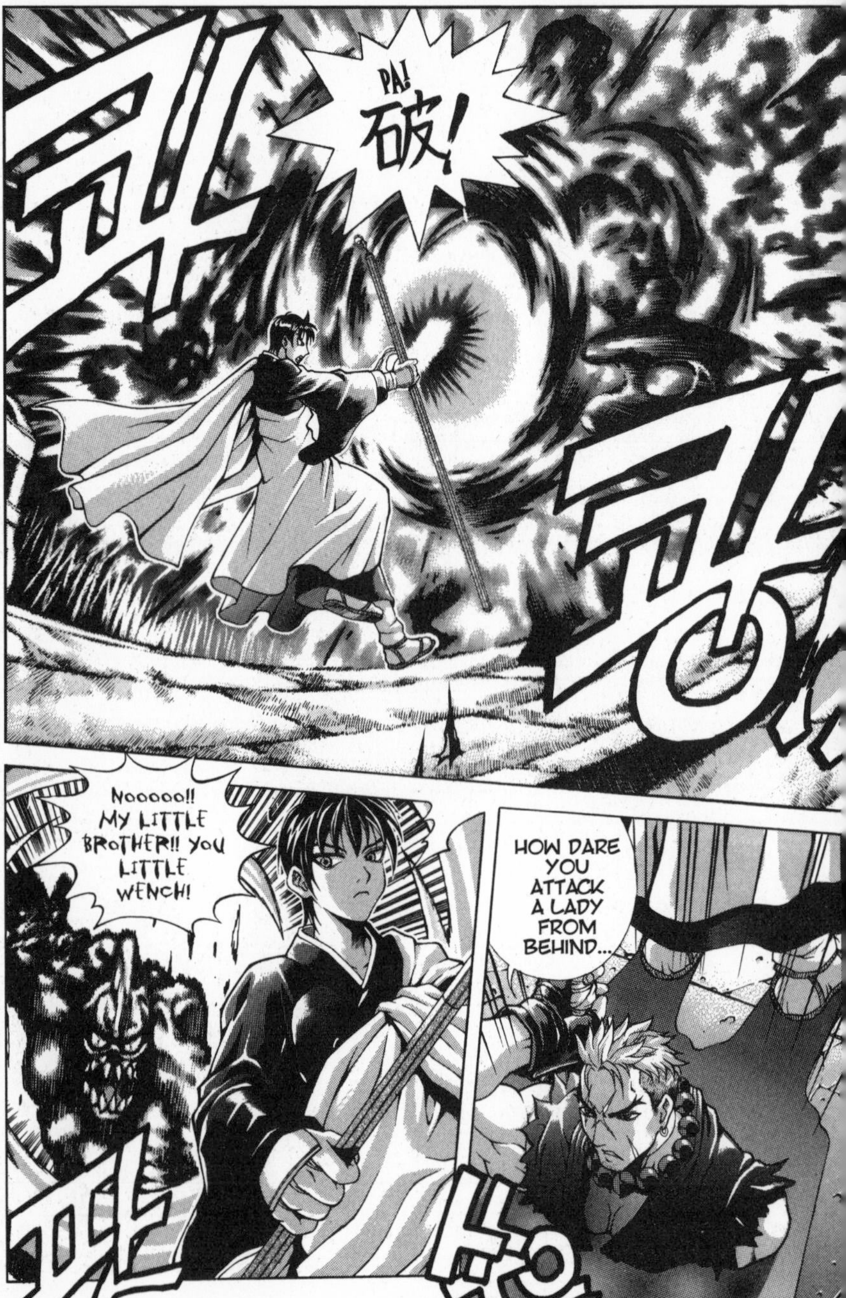
PA!
破!
NOOOOO!! MY LITTLE BROTHER!! YOU LITTLE WENCH!
HOW DARE YOU ATTACK A LADY FROM BEHIND...

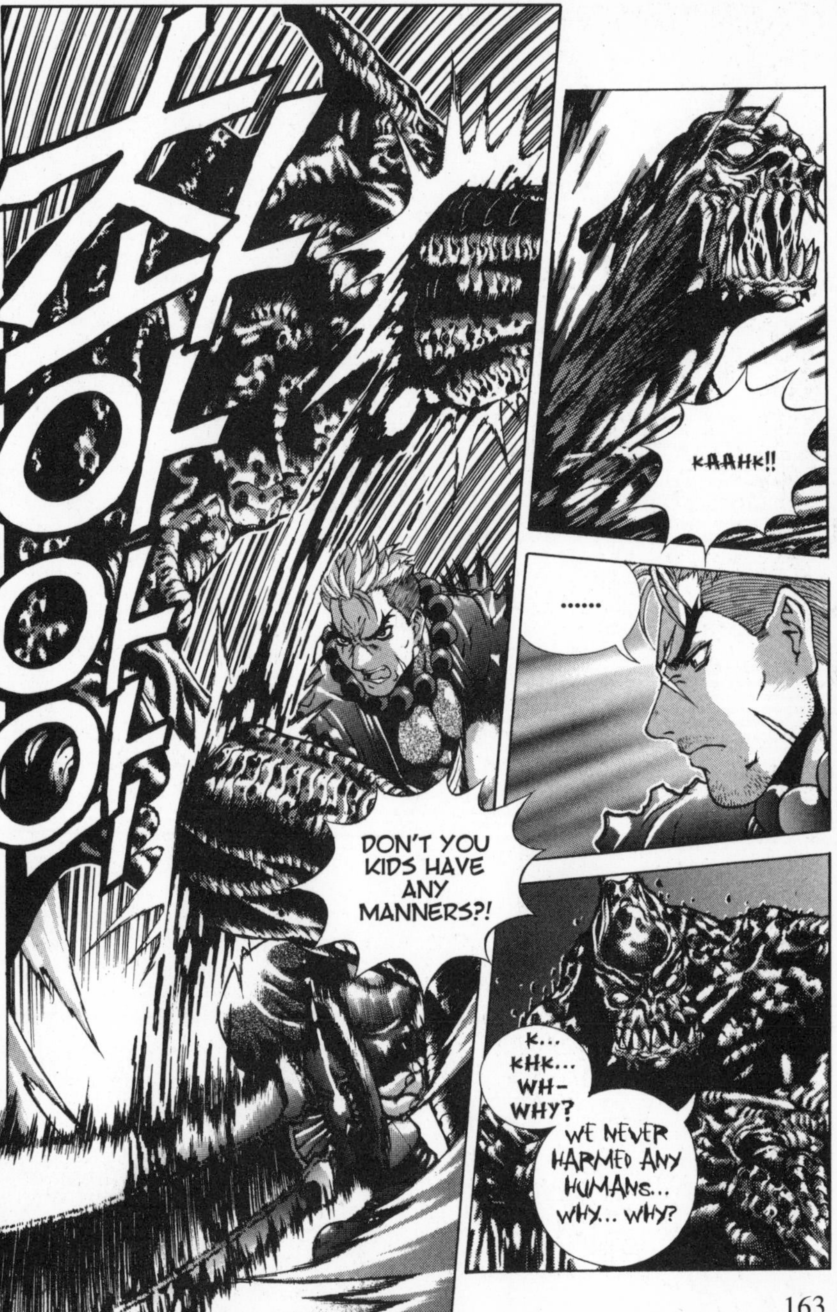
KAAHK!!
......
DON'T YOU KIDS HAVE ANY MANNERS?!
K... KHK... WH- WHY?
WE NEVER HARMED ANY HUMANS... WHY... WHY?

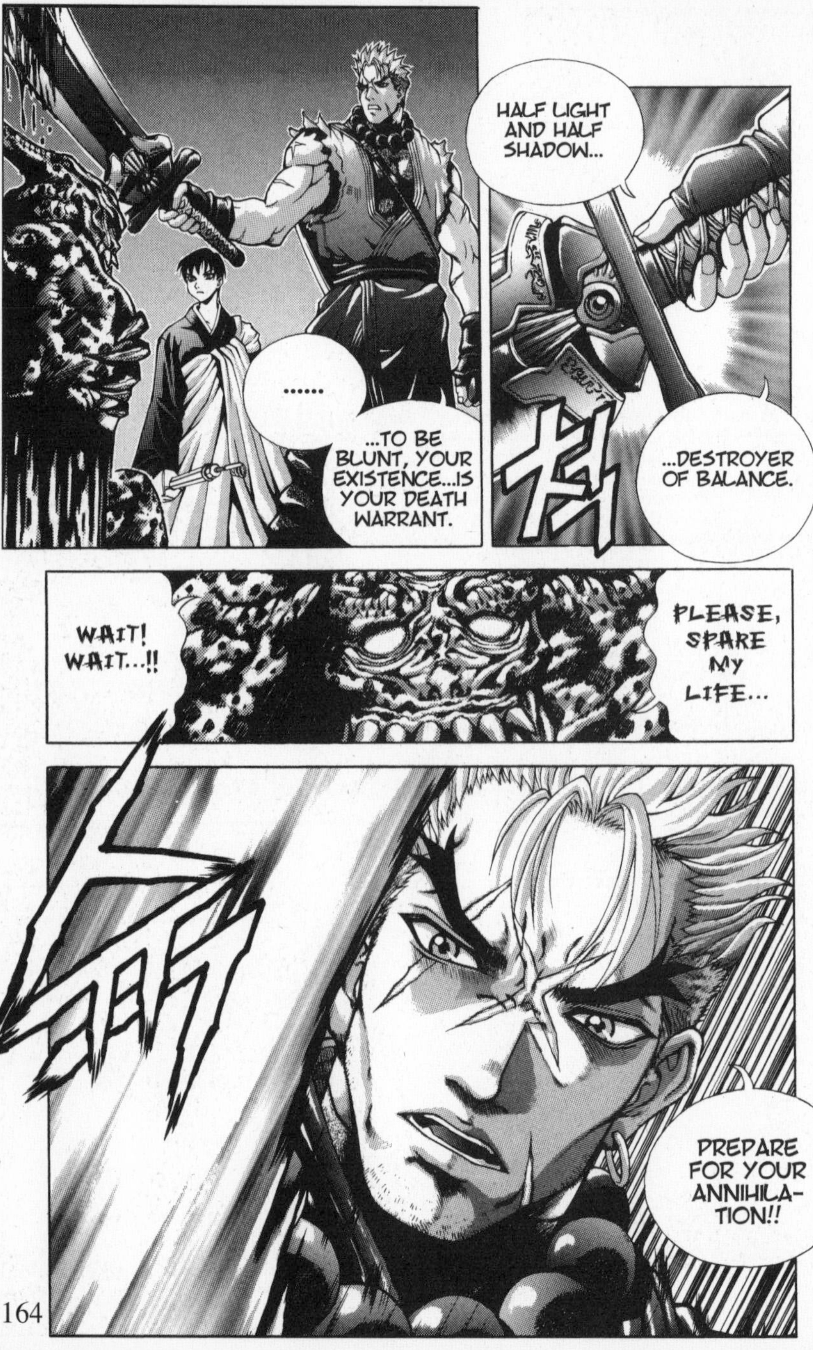
......
...TO BE BLUNT, YOUR EXISTENCE...IS YOUR DEATH WARRANT.
HALF LIGHT AND HALF SHADOW...
...DESTROYER OF BALANCE.
WAIT! WAIT...!!
PLEASE, SPARE MY LIFE...
PREPARE FOR YOUR ANNIHILA-TION!!

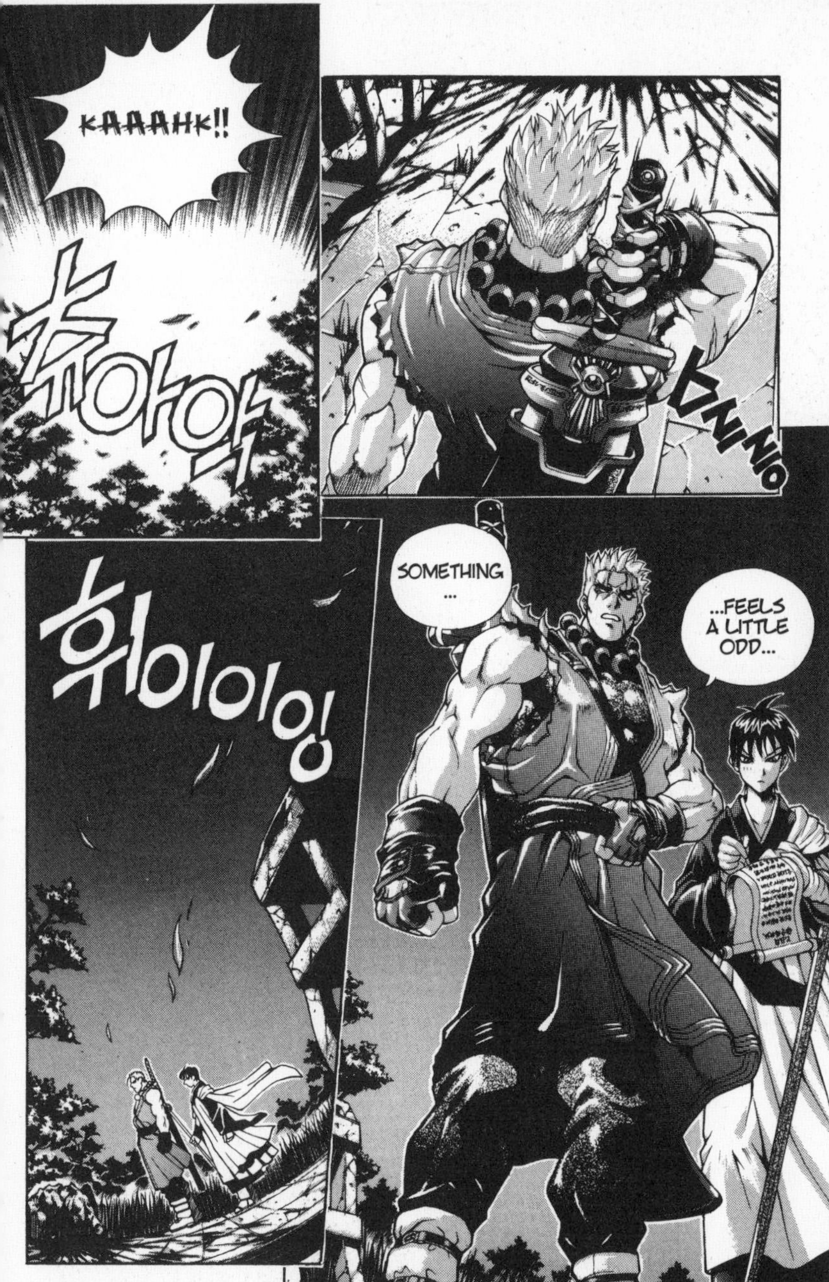
KAAAHK!!
촤아앙
휘이이이잉
SOMETHING ...
...FEELS A LITTLE ODD...

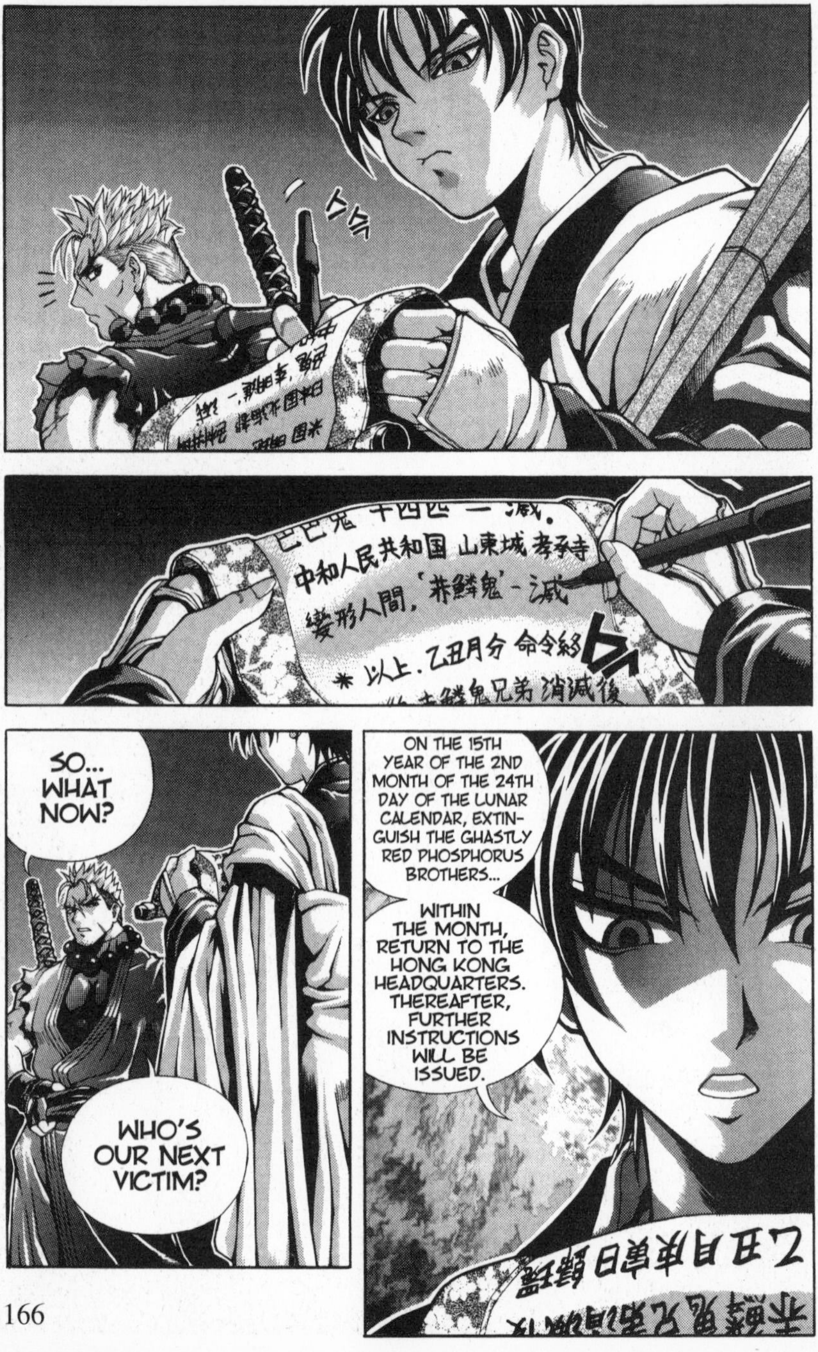
SO... WHAT NOW?
WHO'S OUR NEXT VICTIM?
ON THE 15TH YEAR OF THE 2ND MONTH OF THE 24TH DAY OF THE LUNAR CALENDAR, EXTIN-GUISH THE GHASTLY RED PHOSPHORUS BROTHERS...
WITHIN THE MONTH, RETURN TO THE HONG KONG HEADQUARTERS. THEREAFTER, FURTHER INSTRUCTIONS WILL BE ISSUED.

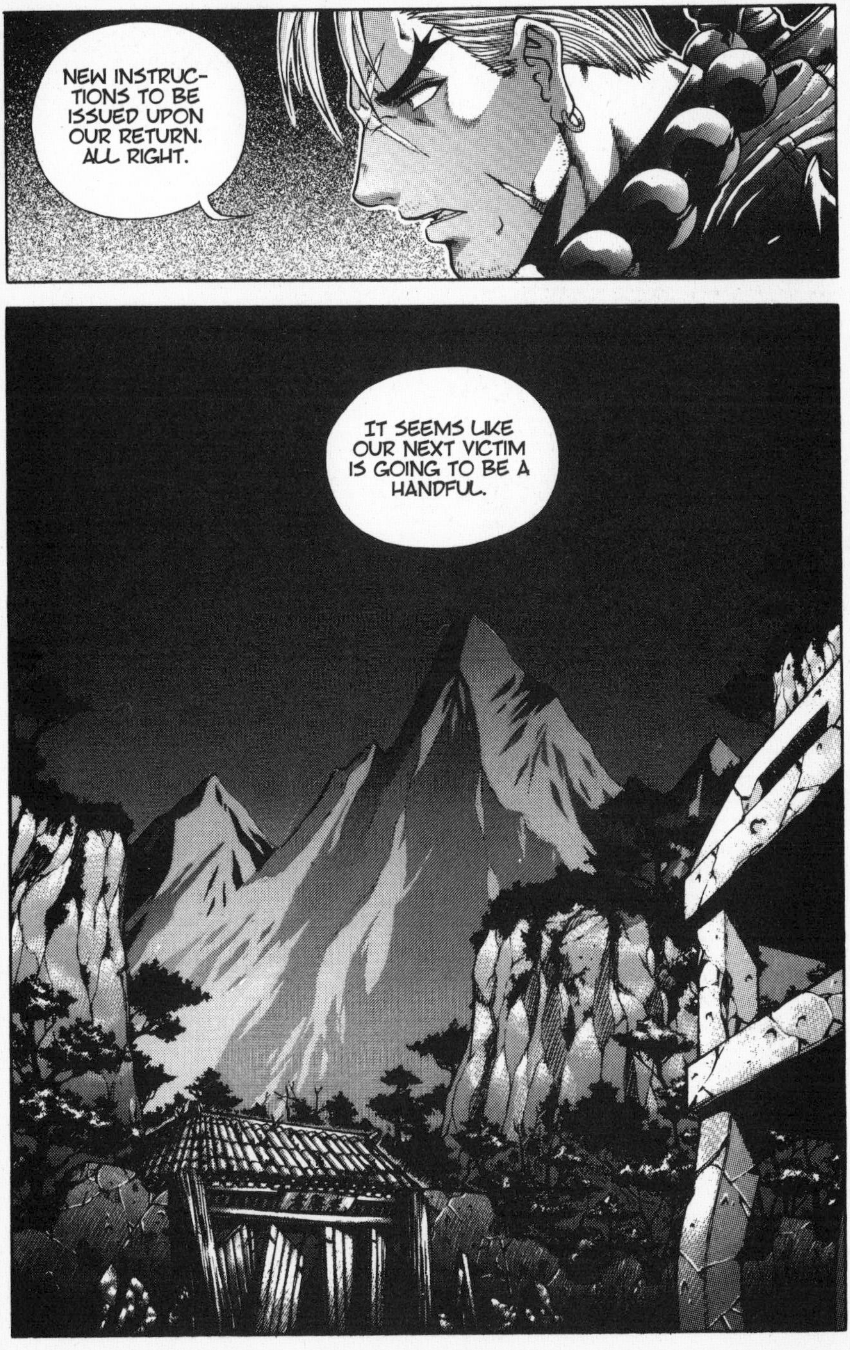
NEW INSTRUCTIONS TO BE ISSUED UPON OUR RETURN. ALL RIGHT.
IT SEEMS LIKE OUR NEXT VICTIM IS GOING TO BE A HANDFUL.

Special Section!! (-_-)

Rebirth Character creation proccess.

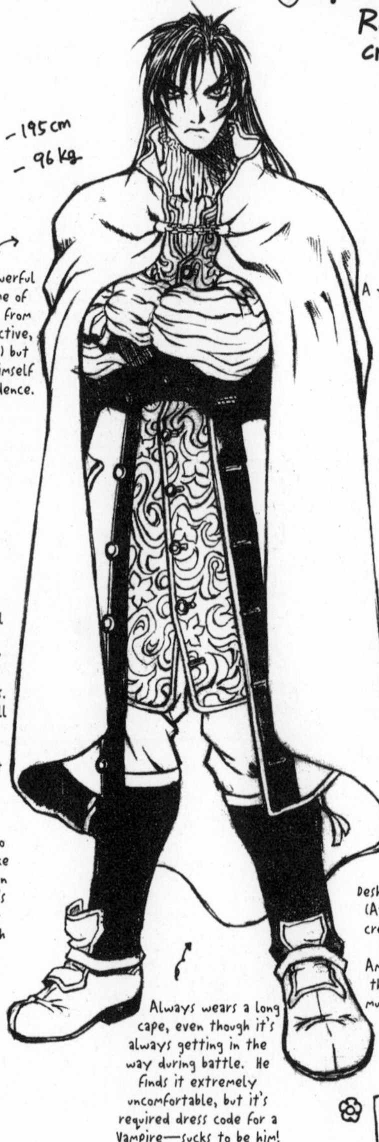

-195cm
-96kg

--Our protagonist--

Deshwitat · Lived · Rudbich

A young noble of the Netherworld-- (Barf~~!!)

385 years old -- Although since he was sealed in darkness for 357 years, he's really more like 28 years old. Why did I make him so much older than the usual Manhwa hero? Well, to be honest, I'm kinda sick of the 13-17 year old pretty boys that seem to populate every other manhwa title out there right now. I wanted more of a manly man as a lead—if that means he doesn't have a legion of female fans, so be it!

Although I want to draw him as a noble with a lordly presence, I'm afraid my drawing skills (or lack thereof) are a bit of a hindrance in pulling that off, and he seems to clash visually with his nemesis, "Kal." And because of other difficulties, his final persona comes off as more of a bully.

He's not very powerful in the big scheme of things (although, from a human's perspective, he's a monster...) but always carries himself with great confidence.

I hate the "righteous hero" type, so you will continue to see Deshwitat's nasty personality in subsequent volumes. I guess you can call him an antihero, but that sounds so cliché. It's not like he wants to be a hero—hero-dom was thrust upon him, so to speak. Kinda like Frodo. Only with an attitude. And he's a vampire. Actually, he's not much like Frodo at all. Bite me.

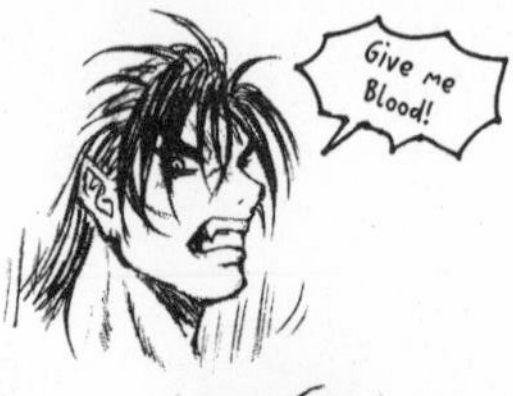

Give me Blood!

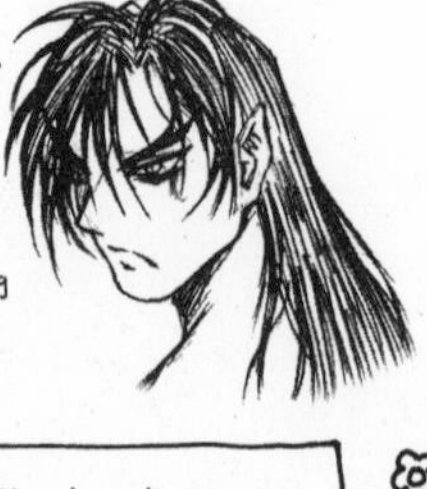

Deshwitat is European. (At least he's been created that way.) Millenear, the American and Remi, the Korean--What mutual understanding will these three reach?

Always wears a long cape, even though it's always getting in the way during battle. He finds it extremely uncomfortable, but it's required dress code for a Vampire—sucks to be him!

In the Champ Magazine evil character popularity poll, Deshwitat ranked seventh!
--Readers, thank you!!--

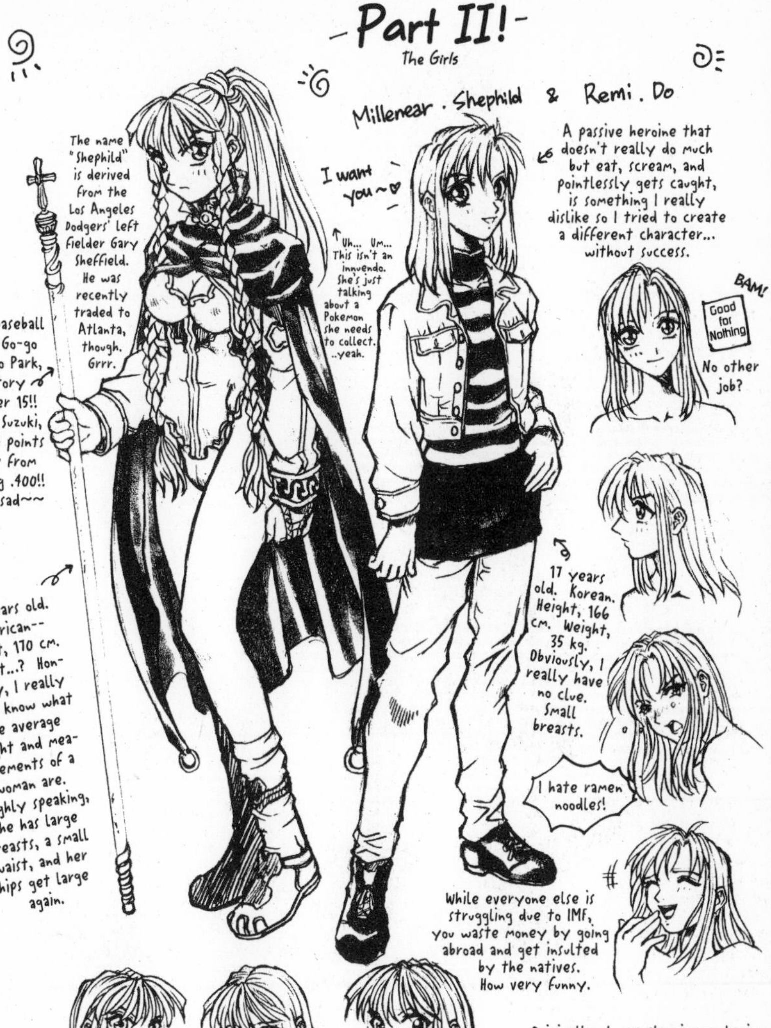

-Part II!-
The Girls
Millenear . Shephild & Remi . Do
The name "Shephild" is derived from the Los Angeles Dodgers' left fielder Gary Sheffield. He was recently traded to Atlanta, though. Grrr.
I'm a baseball fan. Go-go Chanho Park, victory number 15!! Ichiro Suzuki, only 4 points away from batting .400!! I'm so sad~~
21 years old. American-- Height, 170 cm. Weight...? Honestly, I really don't know what the average weight and measurements of a woman are. Roughly speaking, she has large breasts, a small waist, and her hips get large again.
I want you~♡
Uh... Um... This isn't an innuendo. She's just talking about a Pokemon she needs to collect. ..yeah.
A passive heroine that doesn't really do much but eat, scream, and pointlessly gets caught, is something I really dislike so I tried to create a different character... without success.
BAM!
Good for Nothing
No other job?
17 years old. Korean. Height, 166 cm. Weight, 35 kg. Obviously, I really have no clue. Small breasts.
I hate ramen noodles!
While everyone else is struggling due to IMF, you waste money by going abroad and get insulted by the natives. How very funny.
"I like your goatee."~
Originally, I was planning on having her as a useless sidekick hanging around the main character. However...drawing her was so much fun that her role was enlarged. She might possibly become the female heroine... (If she isn't already).

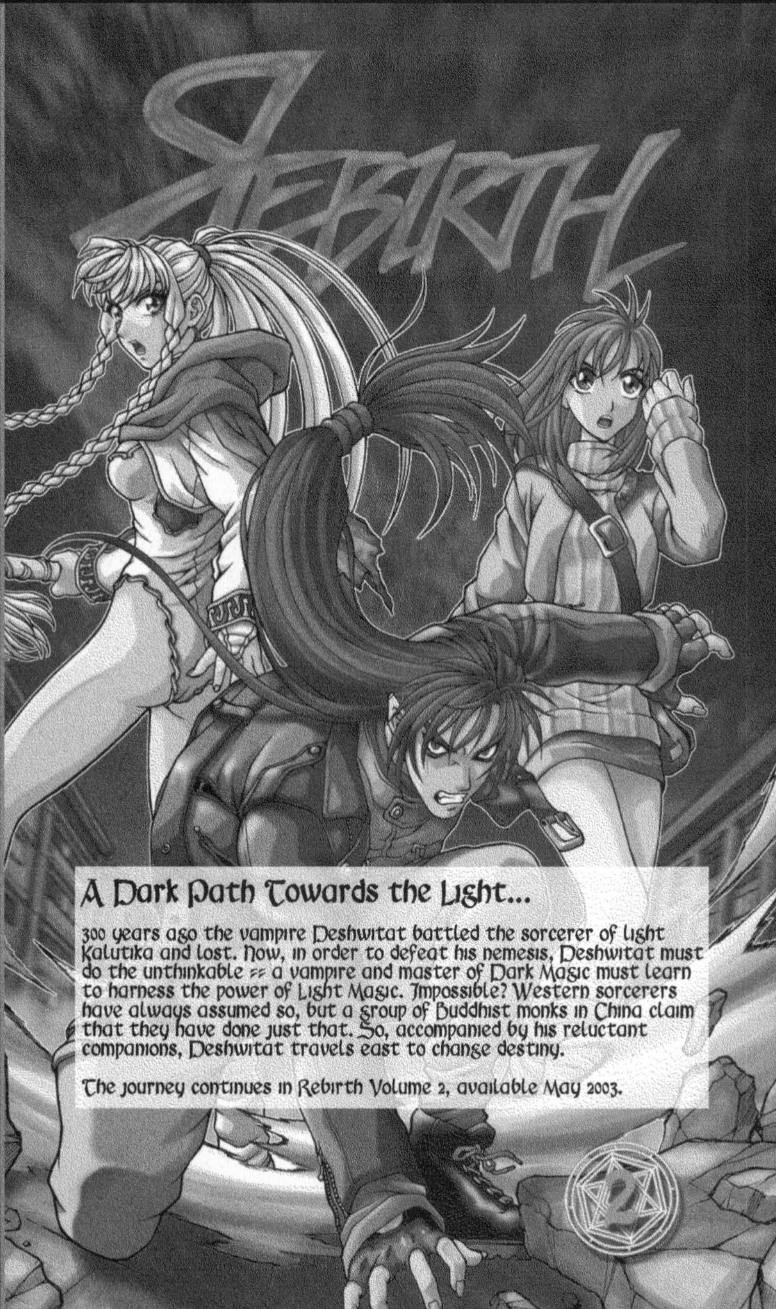
TOKYOPOP
REBIRTH
A Dark Path Towards the Light...
300 years ago the vampire Deshwitat battled the sorcerer of light Kalutika and lost. Now, in order to defeat his nemesis, Deshwitat must do the unthinkable -- a vampire and master of Dark Magic must learn to harness the power of Light Magic. Impossible? Western sorcerers have always assumed so, but a group of Buddhist monks in China claim that they have done just that. So, accompanied by his reluctant companions, Deshwitat travels east to change destiny.
The journey continues in Rebirth Volume 2, available May 2003.

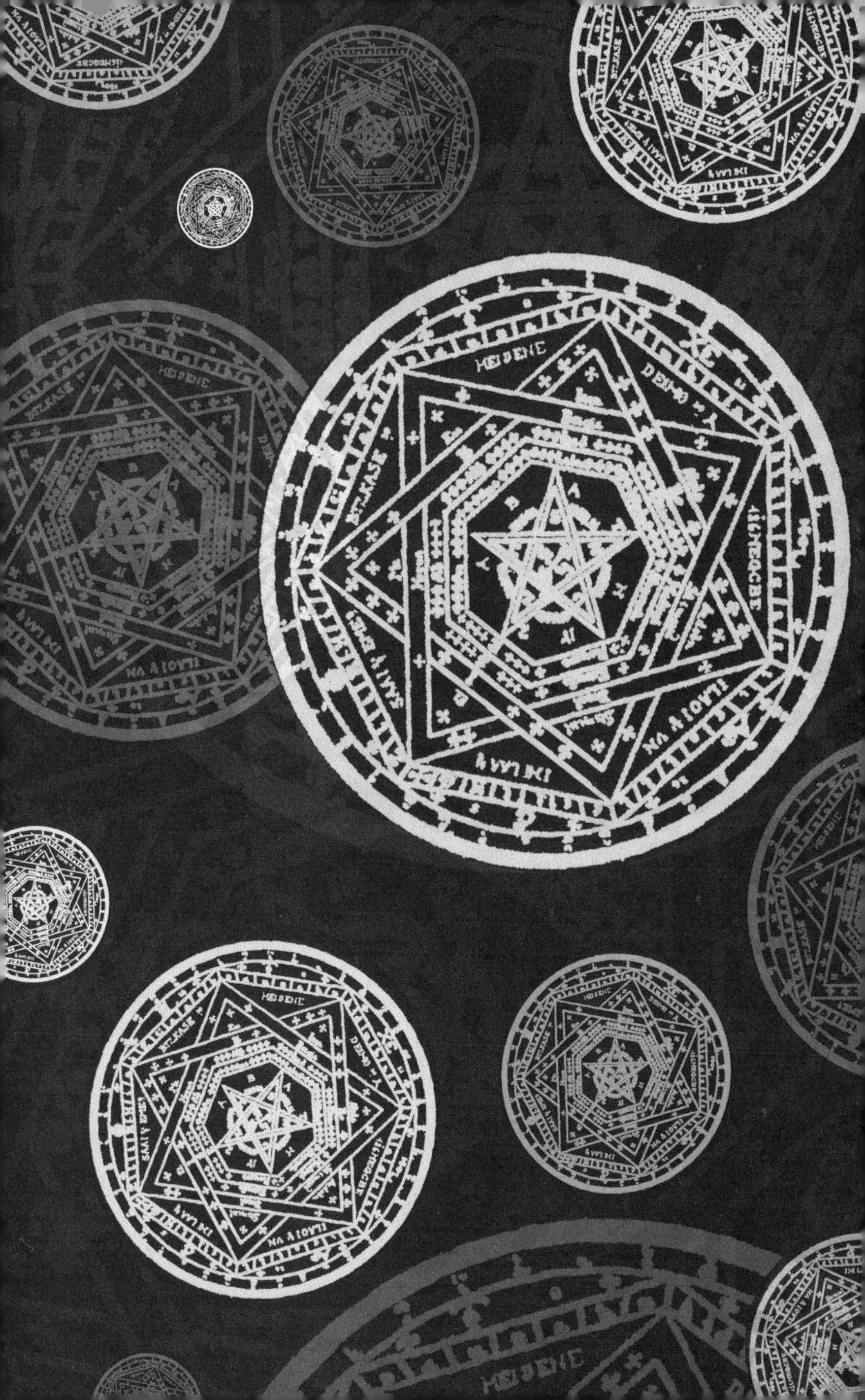

COMING SOON FROM TOKYOPOP®...

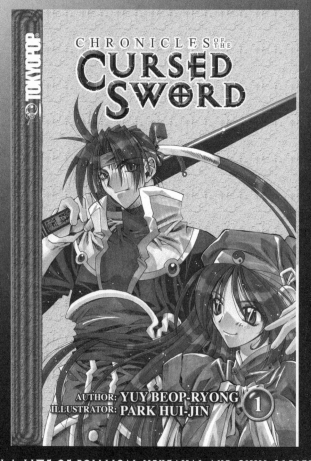

CHRONICLES OF THE

CURSED SWORD

AUTHOR: YUY BEOP-RYONG
ILLUSTRATOR: PARK HUI-JIN

1

IN A TIME OF POLITICAL UPHEAVAL AND CIVIL STRIFE, AN ORPHANED WARRIOR FINDS HIS DESTINY INTER- TWINED WITH THAT OF THE WORLD. YOUNG REYAN WAS ONCE HELD CAPTIVE BY THE EVIL VIZIER SHIYAN (WHO PLOTS TO OVERTHROW THE KINGDOM), BUT HE ESCAPED AND TOOK WITH HIM THE CURSED PASA SWORD, KEY TO SHIYAN'S PLANS. JOINED BY SHYAO LIN, A YOUNG SORCERESS, REYAN TRAVELS THE LAND IN SEARCH OF ANSWERS TO RID HIMSELF OF THE CURSE WHICH NOW FLOWS THROUGH HIS VEINS.

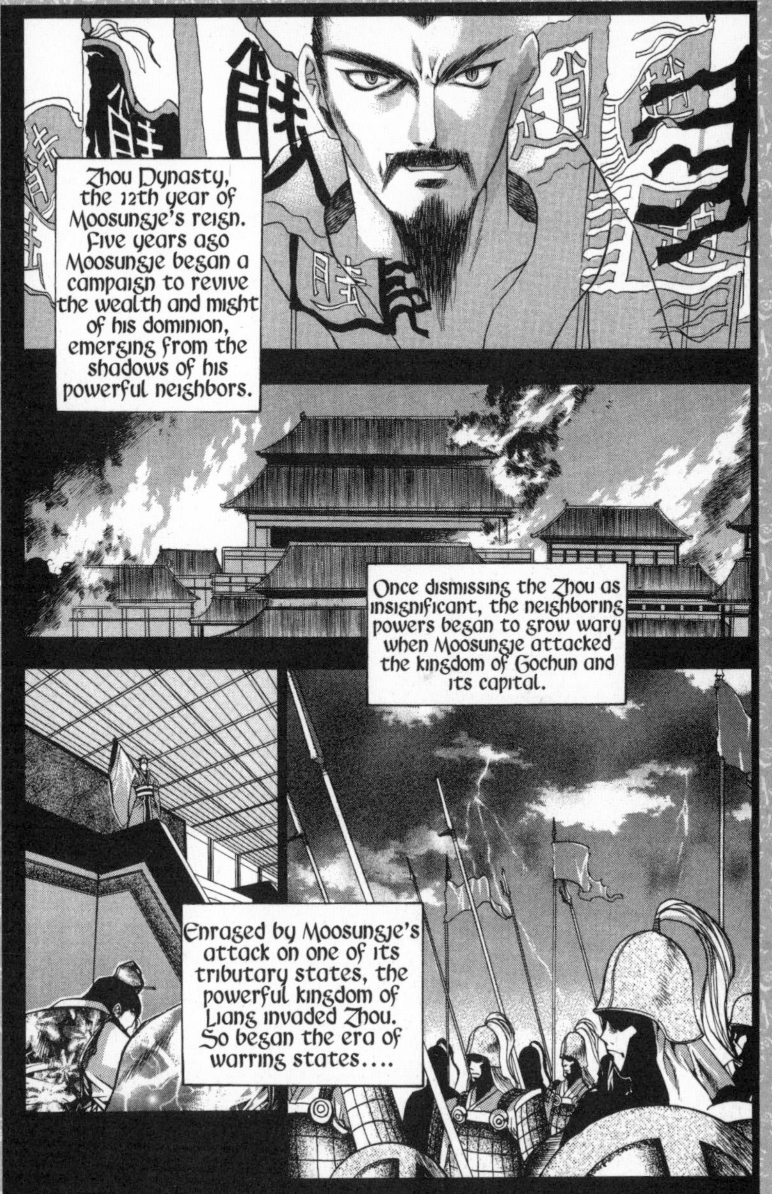
Zhou Dynasty, the 12th year of Moosungje's reign. Five years ago Moosungje began a campaign to revive the wealth and might of his dominion, emerging from the shadows of his powerful neighbors.
Once dismissing the Zhou as insignificant, the neighboring powers began to grow wary when Moosungje attacked the kingdom of Gochun and its capital.
Enraged by Moosungje's attack on one of its tributary states, the powerful kingdom of Liang invaded Zhou. So began the era of warring states....

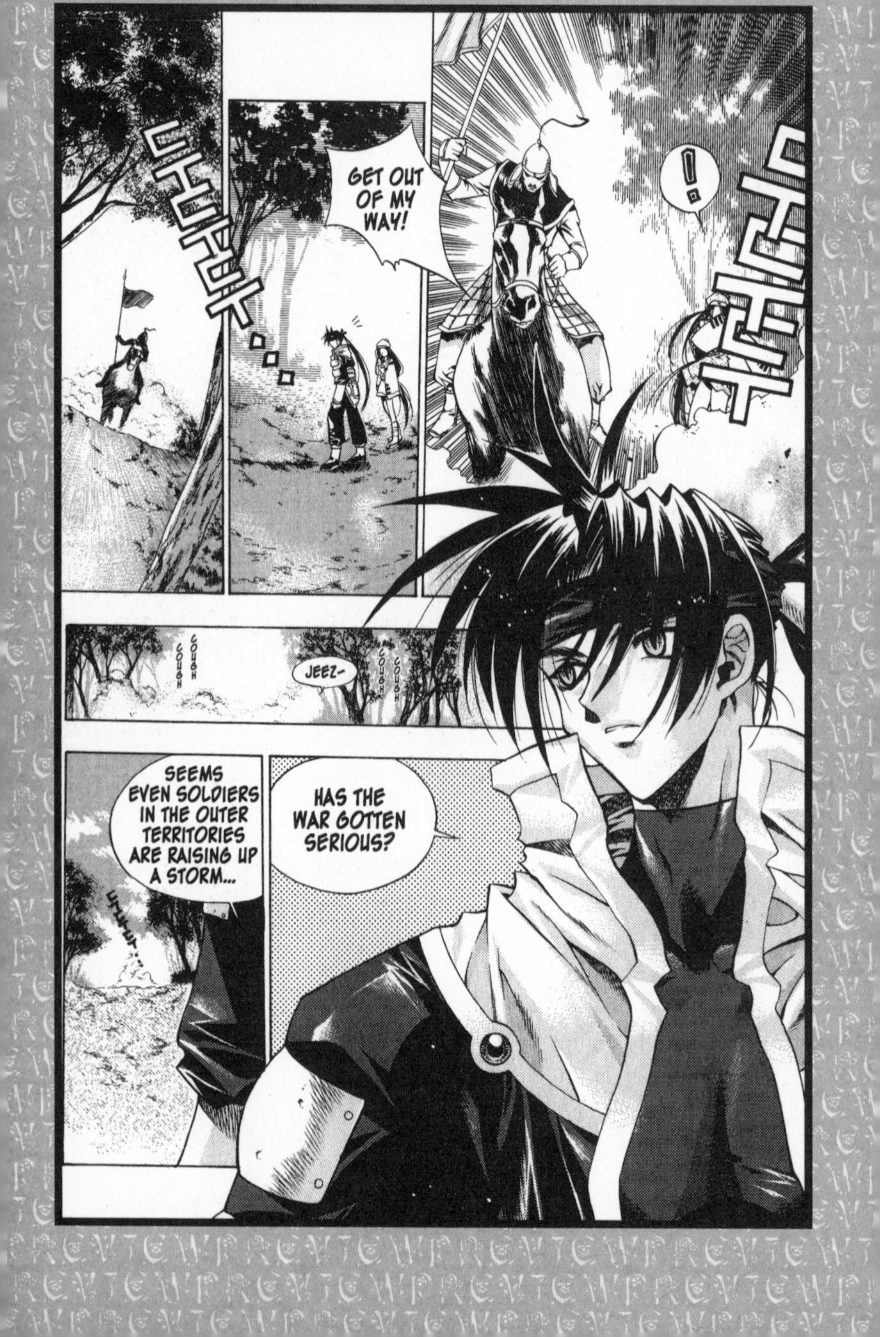
GET OUT OF MY WAY!
!
COUGH COUGH
JEEZ-
COUGH COUGH
SEEMS EVEN SOLDIERS IN THE OUTER TERRITORIES ARE RAISING UP A STORM...
HAS THE WAR GOTTEN SERIOUS?

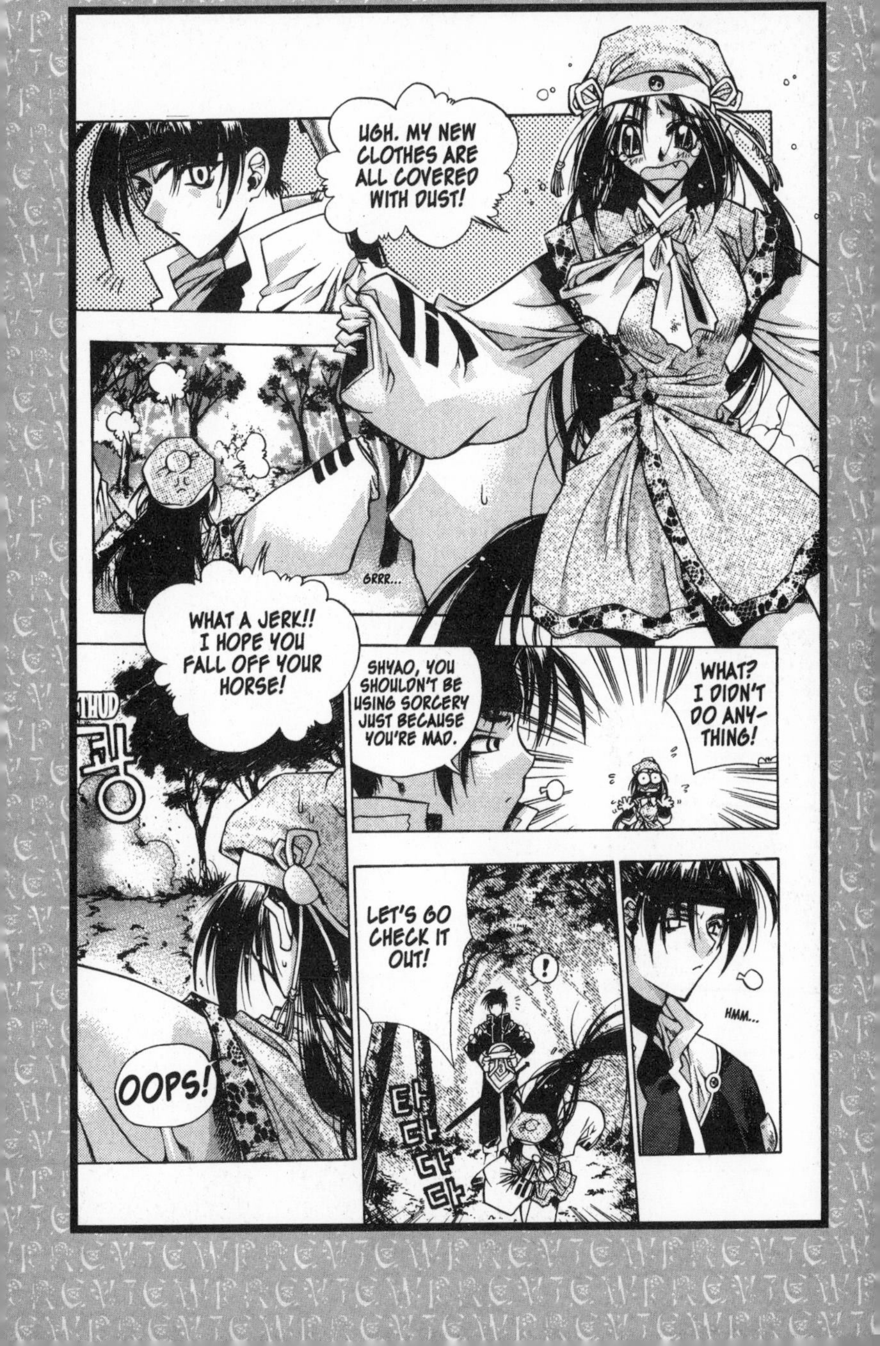
UGH. MY NEW CLOTHES ARE ALL COVERED WITH DUST!
GRRR...
WHAT A JERK!! I HOPE YOU FALL OFF YOUR HORSE!
THUD
OOPS!
SHYAO, YOU SHOULDN'T BE USING SORCERY JUST BECAUSE YOU'RE MAD.
WHAT? I DIDN'T DO ANY-THING!
LET'S GO CHECK IT OUT!
!
HMM...

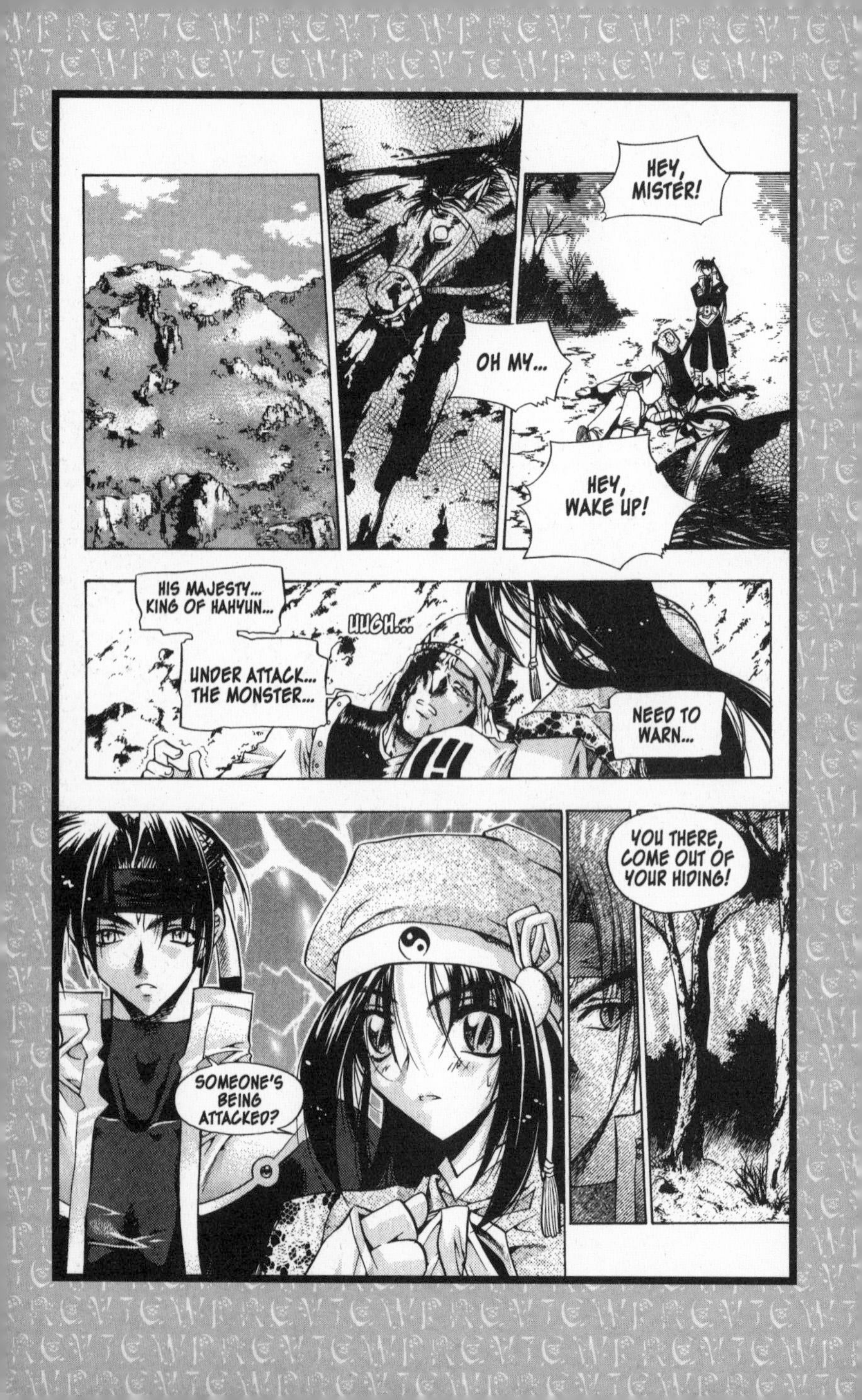
HEY, MISTER!
OH MY...
HEY, WAKE UP!
HIS MAJESTY... KING OF HAHYUN...
UUGH...
UNDER ATTACK... THE MONSTER...
NEED TO WARN...
SOMEONE'S BEING ATTACKED?
YOU THERE, COME OUT OF YOUR HIDING!

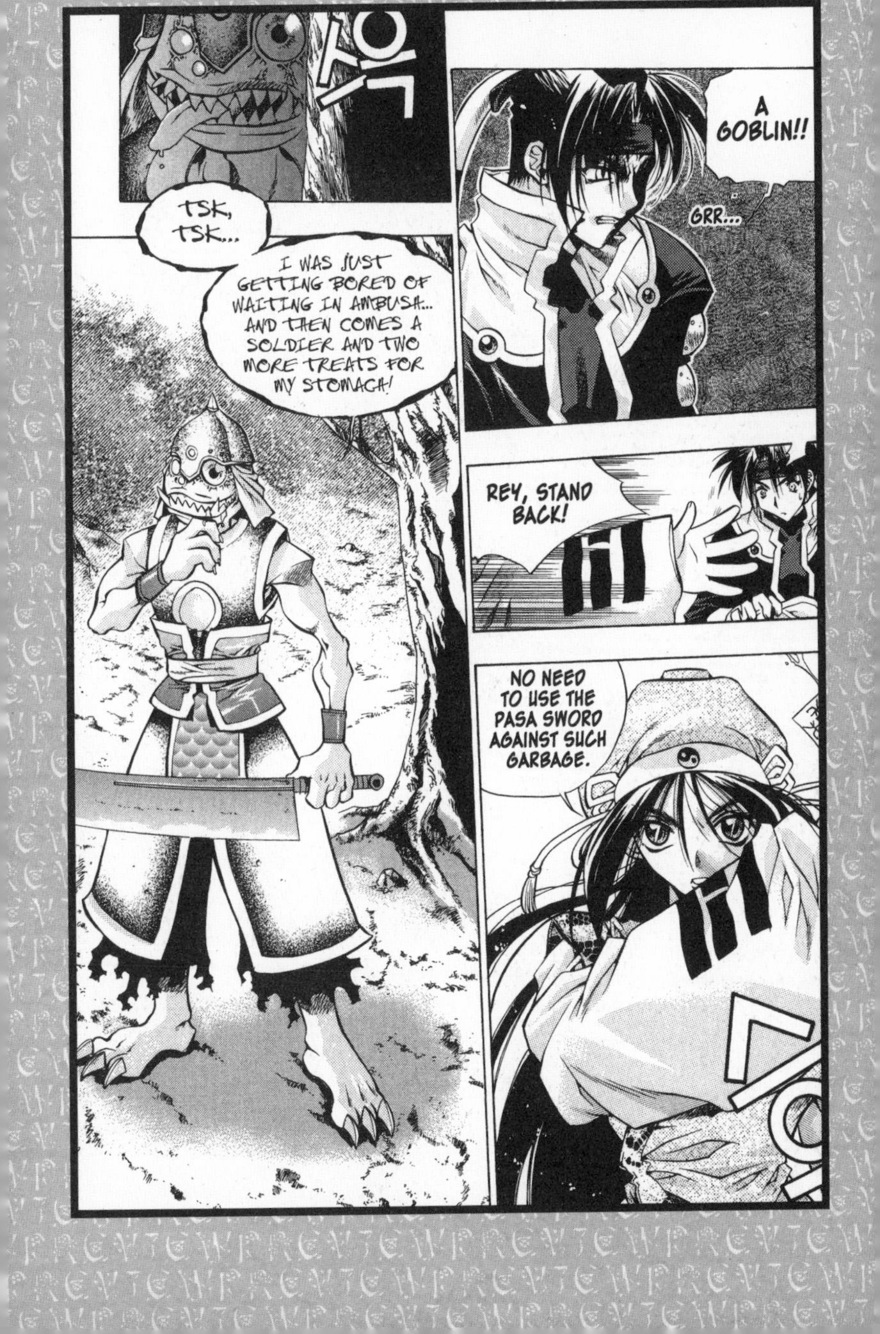
A GOBLIN!!
GRR...
TSK, TSK...
I WAS JUST GETTING BORED OF WAITING IN AMBUSH... AND THEN COMES A SOLDIER AND TWO MORE TREATS FOR MY STOMACH!
REY, STAND BACK!
NO NEED TO USE THE PASA SWORD AGAINST SUCH GARBAGE.

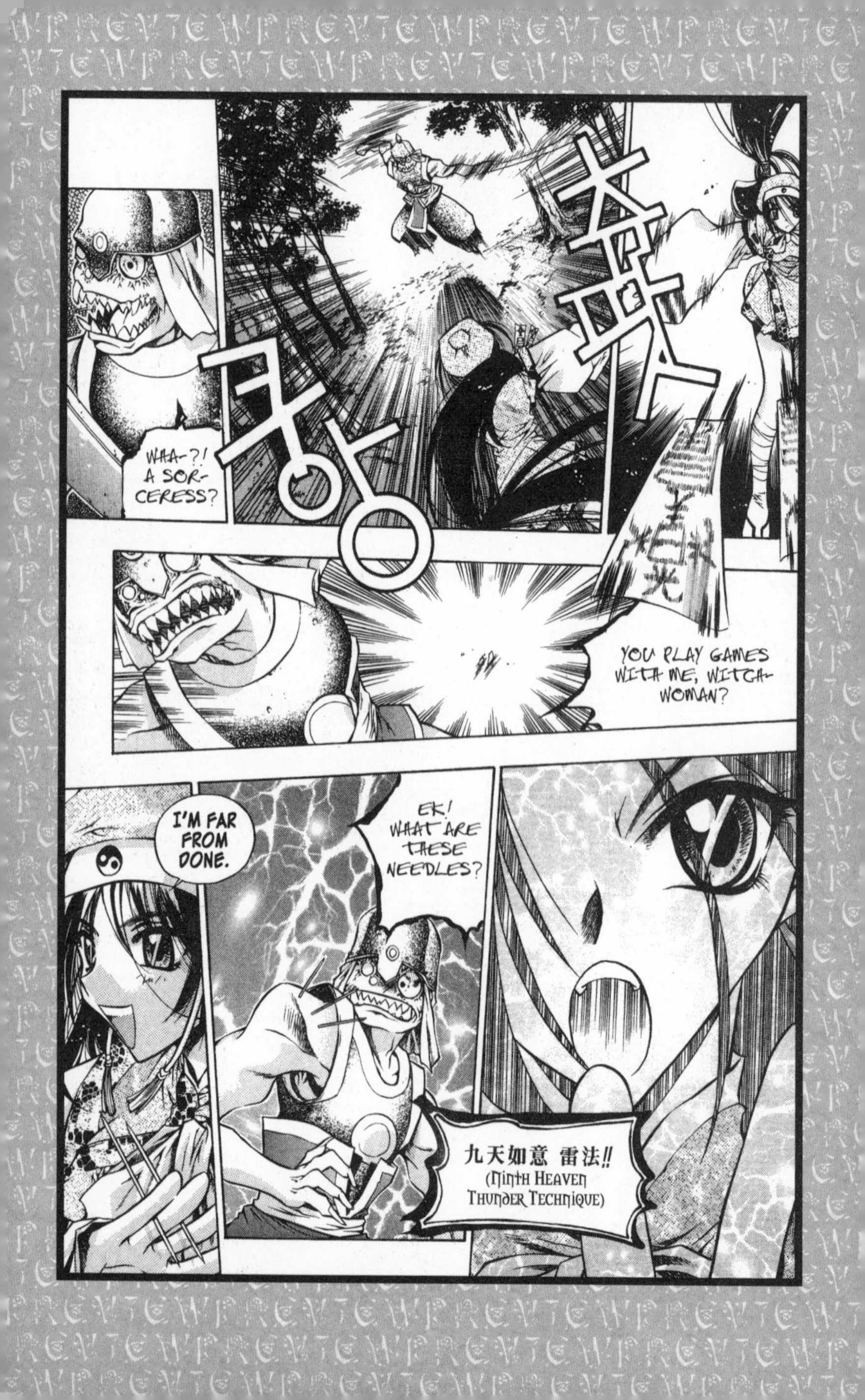
WHA-?! A SOR-CERESS?
YOU PLAY GAMES WITH ME, WITCH-WOMAN?
I'M FAR FROM DONE.
EK! WHAT ARE THESE NEEDLES?
九天如意 雷法!!
(NINTH HEAVEN THUNDER TECHNIQUE)

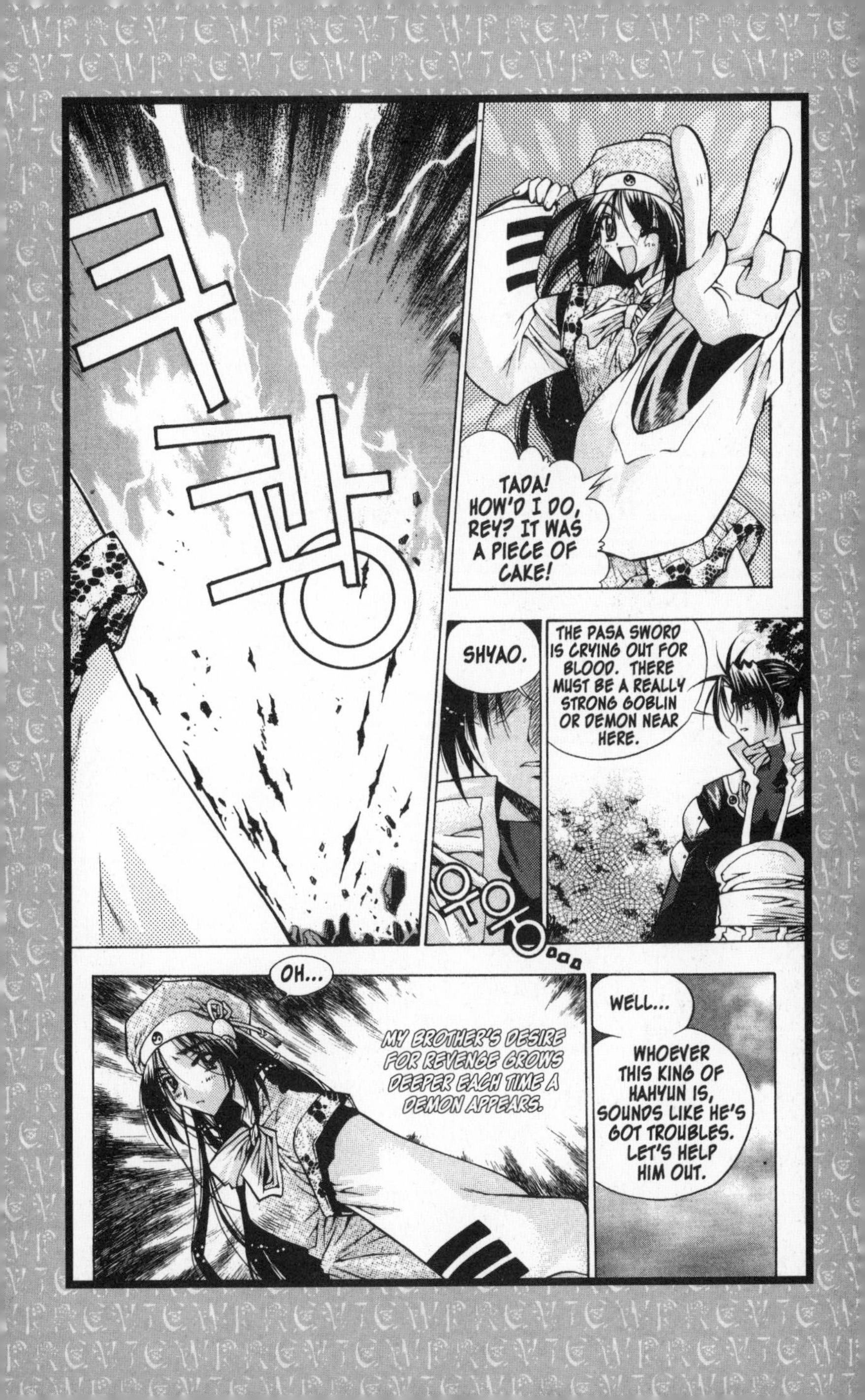

TADA! HOW'D I DO, REY? IT WAS A PIECE OF CAKE!
SHYAO.
THE PASA SWORD IS CRYING OUT FOR BLOOD. THERE MUST BE A REALLY STRONG GOBLIN OR DEMON NEAR HERE.
OH...
MY BROTHER'S DESIRE FOR REVENGE GROWS DEEPER EACH TIME A DEMON APPEARS.
WELL...
WHOEVER THIS KING OF HAHYUN IS, SOUNDS LIKE HE'S GOT TROUBLES. LET'S HELP HIM OUT.

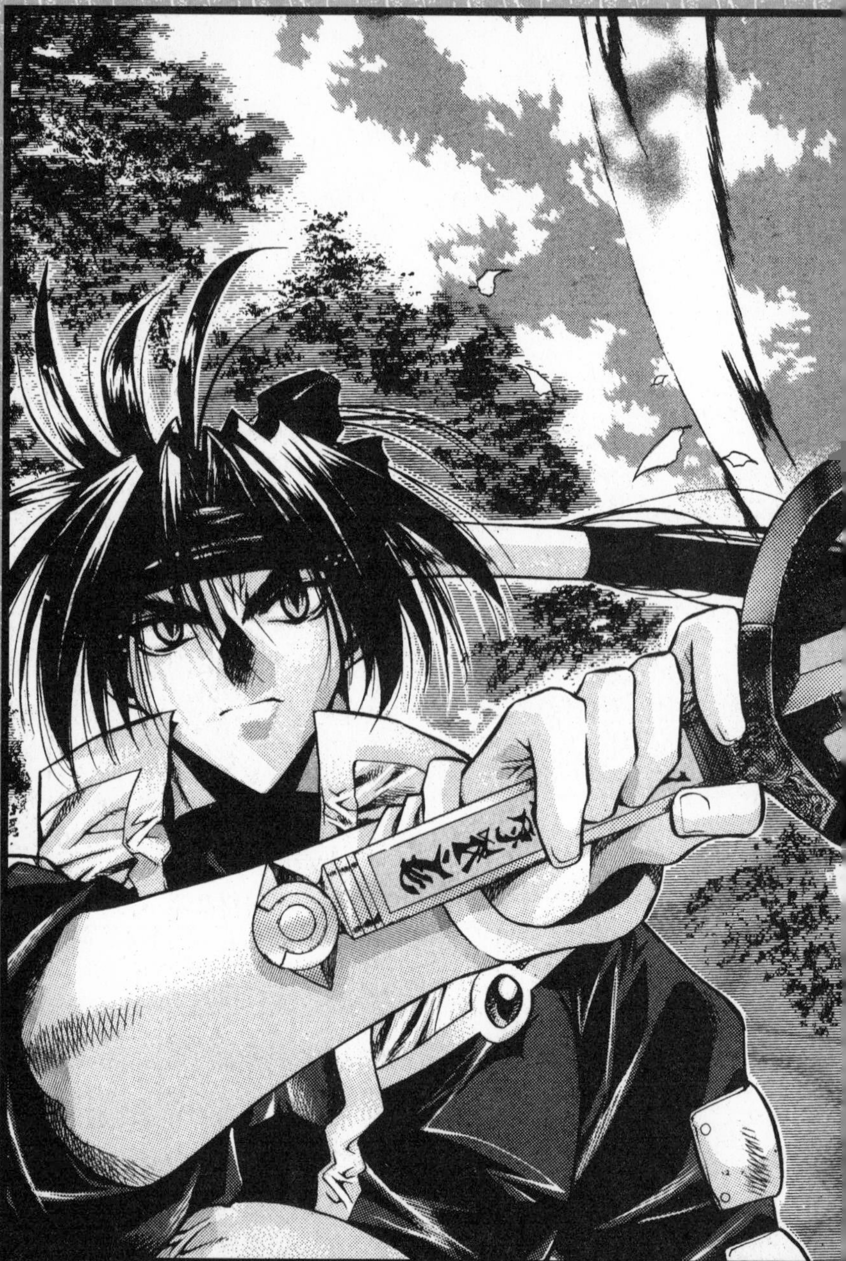

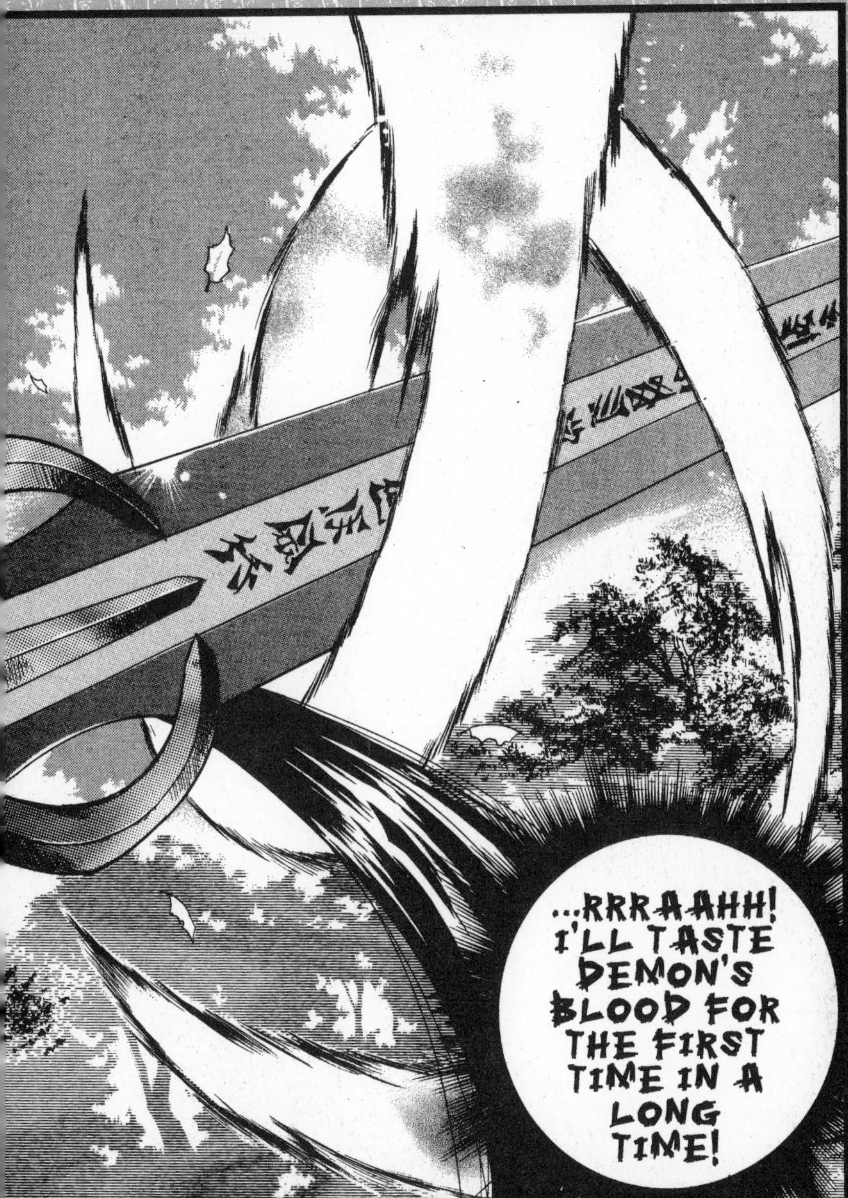
...RRRAAHH! I'LL TASTE DEMON'S BLOOD FOR THE FIRST TIME IN A LONG TIME!

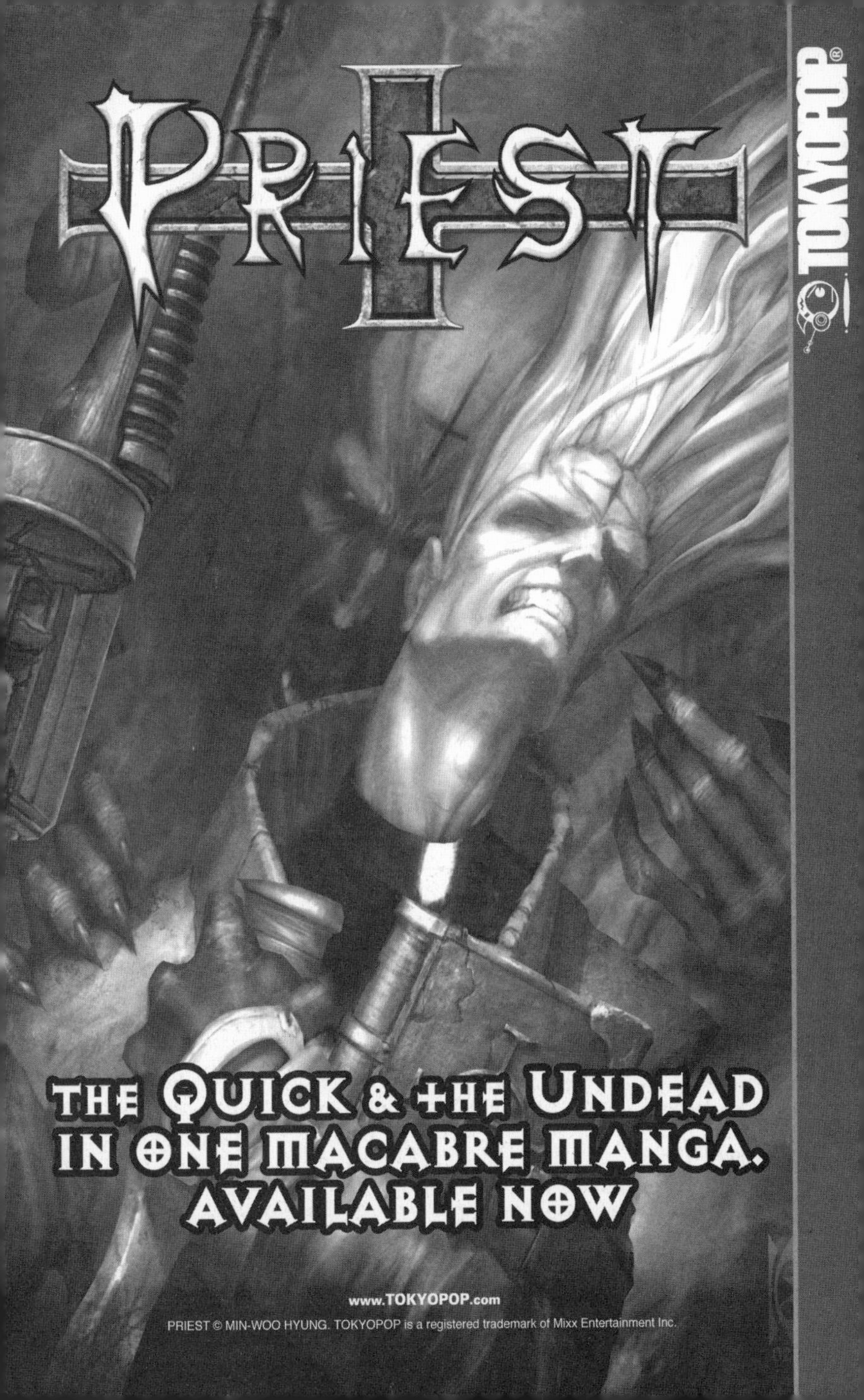
PRIEST
TOKYOPOP®
THE QUICK & THE UNDEAD
IN ONE MACABRE MANGA.
AVAILABLE NOW
www.TOKYOPOP.com
PRIEST © MIN-WOO HYUNG. TOKYOPOP is a registered trademark of Mixx Entertainment Inc.

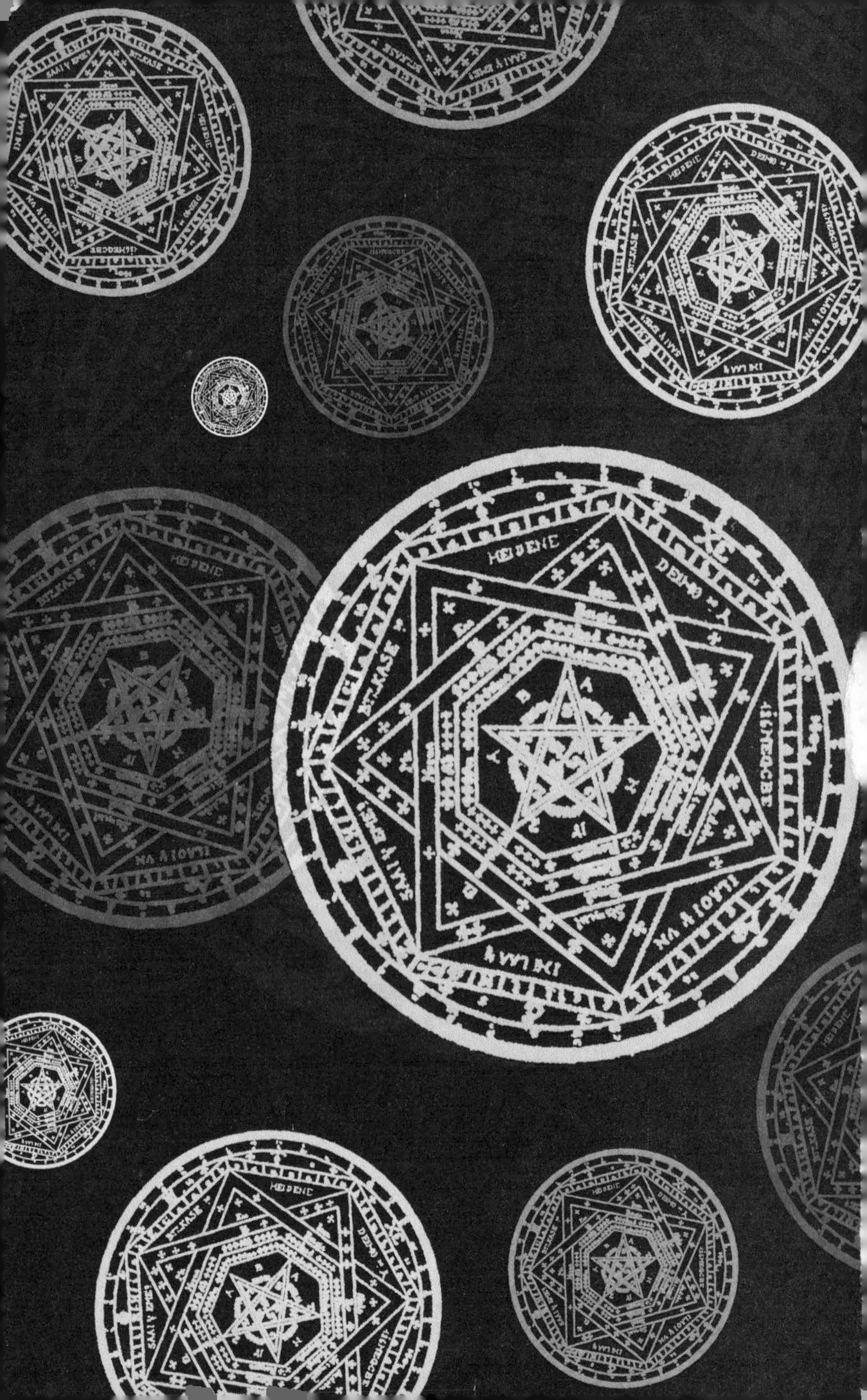